Also by Doug Richardson

Lucky Dey Thrillers
Blood Money
99 Percent Kill
Reaper
American Bang
The Night is Never Black

Other Fiction
The Safety Expert
Dark Horse
True Believers

Nonfiction
*The Smoking Gun: True Stories from Hollywood's
Screenwriting Trenches*

A LUCKY DEY THRILLER
DOUG RICHARDSON

HIP SLICK AND DEAD

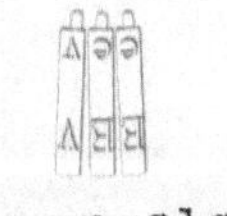

los angeles

Velvet Elvis Entertainment
6038 Tampa Avenue, Suite 366
Tarzana, California 91356

Copyright © 2019 by Doug Richardson
Cover photo by Neil Lockhart © 123RF.com
Cover design by Karen Richardson

More information at www.dougrichardson.com
ISBN: 978-0-9990366-8-6
Library of Congress Control Number: 2019909601

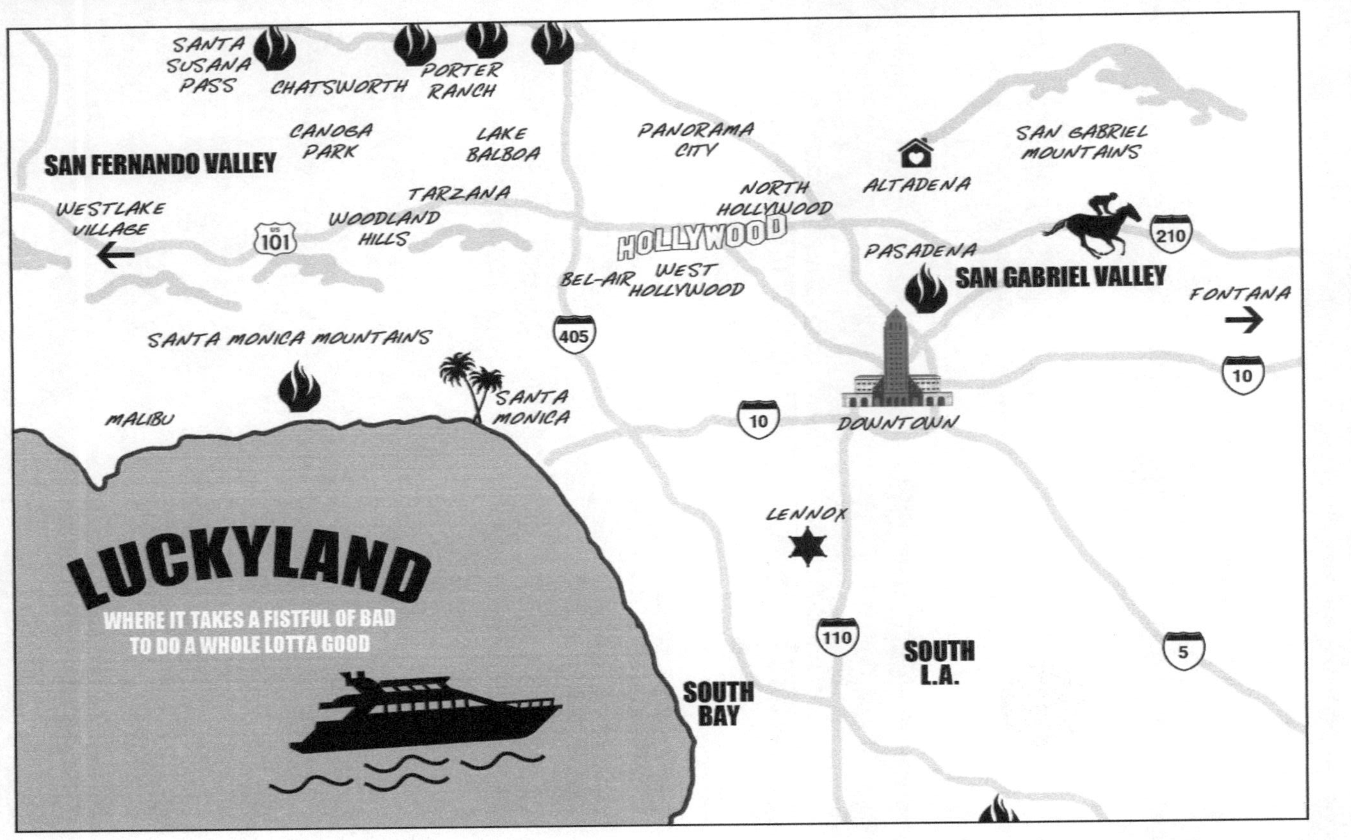

SANTA SUSANA PASS
CHATSWORTH
PORTER RANCH
CANOGA PARK
LAKE BALBOA
SAN FERNANDO VALLEY
WESTLAKE VILLAGE
101
TARZANA
WOODLAND HILLS
PANORAMA CITY
NORTH HOLLYWOOD
HOLLYWOOD
BEL-AIR
WEST HOLLYWOOD
405
ALTADENA
SAN GABRIEL MOUNTAINS
PASADENA
SAN GABRIEL VALLEY
210
FONTANA
10
SANTA MONICA MOUNTAINS
MALIBU
SANTA MONICA
10
DOWNTOWN
LENNOX
LUCKYLAND
WHERE IT TAKES A FISTFUL OF BAD
TO DO A WHOLE LOTTA GOOD
110
SOUTH BAY
SOUTH L.A.
5

Tuesday

1

Porter Ranch. Los Angeles, California. 7:32 p.m.

It began with a match strike, just one of a number of fire-starting options. He'd first imagined he would use something disposable. Something cheap and plastic, like what a chain-smoker would purchase for $1.99 at the corner convenience store. As arsons go, a lighter would leave barely a thimbleful of evidence. But Oren didn't know if the remnants, even if mostly melted in the planned conflagration, could provide some sort of identifying evidence against him. If trace human oil was able to survive a wildfire, a lighter would be expected to bear fingerprints or DNA. And were he to wear gloves, an unsullied lighter would appear too suspicious. Not that he was all that concerned about jail or prison. He pretty much figured that was where he'd end up. It was only a matter of when and how he would be caught and incarcerated for all his sins.

If Oren's life was an unwinding ball of twine, it was nearing its frayed end.

Because Oren's plan was for the blaze to appear as an accident, he settled on a saved book of matches he'd purloined from a recent day at the racetrack. A nonsmoker, Oren had laid in wait for one of the Santa Anita regulars, a greasy sad sack suffering from what Oren coined as MAD—or Multiple Addiction Disorder. The smoker Oren had marked was afflicted with not only nicotine abuse, but a gambling habit egged on by liver-killing alcoholism. When the sad sack reprobate had his eyeballs on the number-five horse in the eighth race, Oren nicked the book of matches from a spot perched atop a pack of Camels. Seconds later, Oren's own pick in the race, a two-year-old filly called Emperor's Price, claimed first place and put Oren back in the black for the day.

Kismet, he'd thought. *My fire was meant to be.*

Though the execution would take only minutes, he'd been planning the arson for months. He needed the fire to appear authentic—as if it had been accidentally set by one of the fifty-five thousand strong of hopeless human flotsam that had come to populate the dark corners and concrete riverbeds of Los Angeles County.

In the tinder-dry slopes and hills that both encompassed and divided the cities and neighborhoods—where eight months out of a year could be considered fire season—the local homeless population was often responsible for the threatening blazes to property and life. Encampments would crop up seemingly out of nowhere, hidden in the hills among the oaks, bushes, and chaparral, creating instant communities of needle-sharing addicts and comorbid schizophrenics. On cold desert nights they'd build campfires as a way to cook the bacteria out of their recycled meat or roadkill and to keep warm while they slept, many nodding off into a heroin coma after fixing with a few CCs of Mexican black tar sometimes salted with fentanyl. The untended fires would usually peter out. Yet, more often than local fire authorities would like, and when the weather assisted, a few wayward sparks would turn into a fiery hell.

Oren had gathered up his ingredients from a list he'd etched only in his mind:

1 book of matches
1 package of inexpensive hot dogs
1 discarded nonstick skillet
1 square foot of cyclone fencing
1 three-gallon paint can—empty
1 trash bag full of vagrant's clothing

Knowing he'd be able to find that last item in almost any alley or parking lot in L.A., he'd saved it for last. Discarded clothes, filthy and smothered in reeking DNA, were as much a part of the landscape as palm trees, nail salons, and luxury cars. Though no stranger to ugly smells—having breathed in chemicals for much of his career—the human stink in the urine-soaked concrete underpass had made Oren want to vomit. Yet he braved entry and picked up a pair of left-behind Nike sweats, socks, soiled underwear, and a ragged Baja blanket.

Now it was time.

Oren Elek Mankowski, all five-foot-six of him, twisted to face the breeze. Warm. Dry. It brushed his forty-four-year-old face like the soft bristles of a shoe brush. Forever undersized, his stout fireplug frame and jutting jaw more than made up for his stature and premature patterned baldness—or so he'd convinced himself as a teen and college wrestling All-American at Pennsylvania's Lehigh University. It was a Santa Ana wind, a Southwest phenomenon where the high-pressure system over the inland desert pushed down on the air, squeezing it across the sandy desert floors and through canyon bottoms until every last lick of moisture was removed.

Nature's blow-dryer, thought Oren.

When the Santa Anas came—technically a reverse wind from the usual sea-to-shore blow, much of the Southland would go on edge. Firefighting crews were doubled and put on alert as TV weathermen unanimously sounded the warning. It was winter in Southern California, barely a week into the new year, yet it was already fire weather. Conditions were ripe. Be aware, be vigilant.

Only days before, the Air Quality Management District board had sent out a countywide reminder that it was illegal to so much as burn a Pres-To-Log in an indoor fireplace or spark up a backyard charcoal-burning barbecue. Critics ruminated that this was an advertisement for firebugs, a sick, twisted subset who got their sexual kicks from setting fires and watching the ensuing destruction.

Oren knew as much, yet didn't blame the authorities for all the warnings. *As if firebugs couldn't lick their fingers to know that a foul wind was blowing from the east.*

Of course, *he* wasn't one of *those* miscreants. He had his own malignant perspective, especially in regard to Los Angeles. Yes, he loathed the city, the county, and perhaps even the entire Southwest region and nearly all who inhabited it. And yet that wasn't the rationale for him starting the wildfire. Oren had a scheme; a defined, for-profit motive. He'd been plotting since Labor Day. He'd even prayed that nary a drop of rain would leak from a cloudy sky before he could open that matchbook stolen from the racetrack sad sack, tear loose a single toothpick-sized cardboard stick, and scratch the match head until a flame appeared.

It wouldn't be the only fire Oren started that day. He'd already lit two others. One built to appear exactly what it was—an arson for arson's sake—and another to appear as if some thoughtless smoker had tossed his burning cigar butt out the window of his passing car. All for Oren's petty profit scheme. He'd saved the most complicated one—the one closest to his home—for last.

Petty, maybe. But, oh man. So damned satisfying.

With the coming darkness as cover, Oren crouched by the makeshift campfire, struck that single match, and lit the scrap paper and kindling he'd assembled inside the old paint bucket. A gust added some easy oxygen. The inside of the three-gallon can swirled hot with an apricot-colored flame. He placed the rusted square of cyclone fence atop the burning bucket, then the skillet and half the packet of Farmer John hot dogs.

Dodger Dogs, thought Oren. After his twenty-plus years in the

City of Angels, he'd even come to despise those blue-and-white togged boys of summer and the damned overpriced, low-quality franks the owners offered as genuine ballpark wieners.

With his collar popped high and bucket hat pulled low, Oren waited until the flames in the bucket looked as if they were going to overtake the fake meal. When the hot dogs had begun to sizzle, Oren kicked over the can and the burning coals inside. The dry grass around him ignited.

"It's finally time," said Oren to nobody but himself. He stood, dusted himself off, and turned down a sandy path. It was a mile-and-a-half hike he knew all too well, the trailhead emptying out at Via Medici, the sleepy Porter Ranch lane where Oren and his precious family of four had resided for the past eleven years. By Oren's calculation, if the winds kept their current pace, the wildfire he'd just unleashed would soon be bearing down upon his gated private neighborhood like an all-consuming beast.

It was one hell of a wager. The biggest bet of his gambling life. Win or lose, it was sure to be an adrenaline injection straight to his nucleus accumbens—the brain's pleasure center—or as Oren called it, "my fabulously untamed hypothalamus." *Now, that's a pony I'd bet on*, he laughed to himself. *Untamed Hypothalamus.*

He pictured such a horse, a black-on-black filly, dark as the nastiest feeling in his soul. Fiery eyes, jutting blinders, trussed in patent leather, and carrying a chimpanzee jockey silken in UCLA Bruins blue and gold. He pictured the muscled monster lunging at the starting gate, the painted metal clanging in battered restraint before the hydraulics pulled the chute wide. In his mind, Oren heard the distant sound of starting gate bells.

And they're off!

2

Downtown Los Angeles. 8:01 p.m.

For Lucky, if felt like being underwater for twelve straight hours, submarined in the concrete bunker called the Public Safety Division of the city's Personnel Department. The windowless basement floor was chock-full of retired cops engaged in second or third careers as background investigators whose sole job was to probe the lives of police academy applicants, wannabe firefighters, government employees, and nearly anybody else City Hall deemed deserving of more than a perfunctory perusal. With only five months on the job, Lucky had earned a reputation as having the division's lowest clearance rate. Where the average investigator had a monthly pass rate of three out of four candidates, Lucky's percentage had barely crested at 30 percent. This might have been reason for reprimand or dismissal if Lucky hadn't been able to back up his findings with airtight investigations and irrefutable, impossible-to-disregard evidence.

"Heading out right now," Lucky sighed over his mobile phone. He was hurrying across Temple Street, beelining for his black '99 Ford Crown Victoria.

"You already missed it," growled Gonzo, a.k.a. Lydia Gonzalez, his common-law-but-soon-to-be-legally-married missus.

"No. It's all good," promised Lucky by rote.

"You checked your watch? It's already after eight."

"And?"

"And he locks the door at eight."

"So I'll knock loudly."

"As far as you know, he's got plans tonight."

"I promise I'll come home with it."

"Wanna bet?"

"Said the woman with nothing to wager."

"I'm sure I can think of something." The tease in Gonzo's voice came across like a tinny purr.

Lucky could have informed Gonzo that he'd already phoned ahead, informing the neighborhood tailor he'd be late picking up his wedding suit. The clothier in question was a soft little grandfather of Lebanese extraction who lived with his wife above the same corner dry cleaner they'd owned since the late eighties. In Lucky's forty years on Earth, this was going to be the second suit he'd ever owned, the first being an off-the-rack black number he reserved for funerals. It always hung ready, alongside his pressed set of sheriff's dress greens reserved for formal cop burials.

Gonzo had long fancied the idea of Lucky in deep gray pin-stripes on the day of their nuptials. When Lucky mentioned he was attiring himself at a Pasadena Men's Wearhouse, a chain discount suit seller, Gonzo expressed a different desire. Her groom was going to be fitted into a fine ensemble that complimented his broad-shouldered surfer's frame. She'd strongly suggested Lucky ask their local dry cleaner for a recommendation. In reply, the aging tailor had practically insisted on personally constructing the former sheriff's deputy a suitable wedding suit.

On most days, Lucky's drive home was via the aging Pasadena Freeway. But a fresh grass fire near the base of Mount Washington had shut down the artery, leaving Lucky to consider a wider route. There was the GPS program that Travis, his soon-to-be stepson, had downloaded onto his phone—the ubiquitous Waze application that seemed a must for all Los Angeles drivers. The technology aggregated live traffic flow with its users' data to sort out the most efficient course of travel between points A and B. And though Lucky appreciated the tech, he preferred to rely on his rookie training and police officer's instinct to nose his way to a destination. Thus he chose to swing the '99 Crown Vic northwest and take the Hollywood Freeway, planning to hook his way back east through Burbank.

He'd already heard the weather reports. The fall and early winter had been suspiciously dry after a summer of record-breaking heat, and now January had arrived, sweeping in with a multi-day forecast of fierce Santa Ana winds. So it was of little surprise when Lucky spotted distant flames. As the grille of his car crested Hollywood's Cahuenga Pass, revealing the San Fernando Valley beyond, he was able to mark three separate brushfires already plaguing the northern hills. By his quick estimate, each conflagration was roughly two miles apart—practically equidistant and at elevations hovering near or just above the residential limits. Those Santa Ana gusts, charging down the sandy slopes like an invisible avalanche, would surely force the fire into populated edges of the Valley's legendary suburban sprawl.

Then, before Lucky could mutter an ominous "Shit," his mobile phone chimed in alert. It was a call to all Los Angeles deputy reservists—the 650-strong Los Angeles Sheriff's volunteers who signed to serve and protect at the snap of Sheriff Paul McGill's bony fingers.

Lucky, though no longer active as a sheriff, was officially listed as a reserve deputy. His position as a reservist was not so much voluntary but rather a negotiated settlement between himself and a department that had labeled him as a liability. Because Lucky hadn't been keen on handing over his badge, "hobby cop" status seemed the only viable salve to heal his very fresh wounds. He'd been a police officer since the age of twenty-two—fifteen years total as a Los Angeles sheriff's deputy plus a two-year sabbatical as a Kern County detective. Subtracting the thirteen months he'd spent rehabbing his back and waiting for his reinstatement to the Los Angeles police rolls, Lucky counted on that shiny six-pointed star as his primary identity. It was his reason for drawing breath, let alone a government-sanctioned license to chase bona fide bad guys.

Petty stuff, he'd later lament.

"Guess I'm not gonna make it," admitted Lucky, his first words after redialing Gonzo. "Woulda lost my bet with you."

"Moot," said Gonzo, an LAPD helicopter pilot for four years. "Just got called up myself. Gotta be up in the air in an hour. Fire crews already playing whack-a-mole out there."

"Jesus."

"Know where they're sending you?"

"Think I read Pacoima. Gotta dig out the uniform."

"How 'bout I leave it hanging where your wedding suit should be?"

"That's funny," Lucky conceded.

"Serious, Luck," she moaned. "This fire shit better not fuck up our Saturday."

"'Fire got a mind of its own,'" quoted Lucky, recalling the soot-messed face of an exhausted and defeated firefighter with whom he'd once shared a water break. "So I guess that means no promises."

"Ain't you a ray of sunshine?"

"Can't believe you're marrying me."

"Words outta my mouth," she joked. "Be safe tonight. Please?"

"You too," replied Lucky. "Hey. Wait. Where's the kids?"

"Trav's at Mark's," answered Gonzo. "Supposedly studying for his SATs, but I'll believe that when he scores a fourteen hundred. And Karrie's on the job."

Lucky released a chuckle. "On the job" was cop slang for a police officer at work. Nineteen-year-old Karrie wasn't close to being a cop. At least, not yet. But she held down a job that involved copious interfacing with walk-in customers.

"If I'm giving service to the public in general?" Karrie had amusingly argued somewhat recently. "And if I'm restraining myself from punching them in the face? Think I can call it 'on the job'?"

Lucky had pondered. Then agreed.

3

Westlake Village. 8:22 p.m.

It wasn't technically a smoking break.

Technically.

At ButterCrème bakery, the time cards referred to the ten-minute work break as "tens."

"My mom says the old-school term is 'coffee break,'" Karrie said to her uniformed coworker. "My dad calls it goin' 10-7. That's cop code for 'out of service.'"

Karrie took a deep hit from her vape pen.

"Should call this a weed break," joked her skin-and-bones associate, the pastel ButterCrème T-shirt and apron matching her eruption of pimples. "Bet he'd loooove to hear that."

"Oh, he knows I do the ganja," deadpanned Karrie. Her green eyes closed as she drew in the THC-infused vapor. Her strawberry-blonde hair ponytailed under a ButterCrème baseball cap, her constellation of freckles unimpeded by a single trace of makeup. "Even knows I got a medical marijuana card."

"Yeah, but he knows that's just 'cause you're not twenty-one, right?"

"He knows it's the only thing that puts a boot to my leg pain," returned Karrie, alluding to the leftover maladies from her car accident. Months of rehab, some speech therapy, and an unforgiving schedule of Muay Thai martial arts mixed with a return to sunset surf lessons with her adoptive father, Lucky Dey, had accelerated her recovery. "Ten's over, babe."

Karrie pivoted on her partially paralyzed left stem and cut her way back up through the stucco tunnel connecting the employee parking lot with the upscale shopping center's happy storefronts. As they emerged, Karrie smelled another kind of smoke wafting west from the San Fernando Valley.

"Getting nastier," said the coworker. "My boyfriend says there's fires popping up all over."

Karrie returned to her behind-the-counter post at Butter-Crème, a gourmet cupcake bakery that also served up fresh cookies and house-churned ice cream to the moneyed, sugar-addicted shoppers of Agoura Hills, Thousand Oaks, and Westlake Village. She was thinking about her commute home and how those burgeoning brushfires might turn her midnight drive back to Altadena into a traffic nightmare. Unfettered, the distance was nearly fifty miles, a massive hike by local standards, and hardly supported by her three-dollars-above-the-minimum wage. She'd initially interviewed for a job at the Pasadena bakery, the company's flagship store. Then opportunity knocked in the form of a promotion attached to a singular caveat—she'd have to work two shifts a week at the Westlake Village location.

Big mistake, she'd soon conclude. But it was too late. Karrie had made a commitment. She thought she owed it to the young chain's charismatic owner to toe the cupcake line, not to mention follow every the-customer-is-never-wrong rule, including the

ButterCrème corporate decree that bakery associates were to never ever utter the word no to a paying customer.

That even included those customers who, if their order didn't come out as nothing short of perfect, insisted that they should receive free cupcakes as recompense.

"Have you been helped?" asked Karrie just moments after returning to her position. The cupcake shop—modern, with splashes of bright geometric color—had a generous pink countertop, a cash register, and left of that, a glass case that displayed a variety of frosting-topped confections priced at almost $5 apiece.

"I'm still waiting," complained a stony-faced woman.

Karrie instantly clocked the thigh-heavy woman at pushing forty years old, casually dressed in Lululemon yoga togs, but with makeup so thickly troweled onto her scowling face, it could survive the most grueling of workouts.

Karrie guessed the woman's choice of exercise was spinning, the stationary bicycle classes favored by the more privileged.

"What was your order?" asked Karrie, forcing her friendliest smile.

"Dozen red velvet, dozen salty caramel, and one gluten-free blueberry," recited the woman.

"Was that a phone order?" wondered Karrie, searching the computer screen for the ticket.

"That was *me* ordering *here* over twenty minutes ago," seethed the woman.

"Right," nodded Karrie, quickly discovering the order on her screen. The time on the order was 8:18 p.m. Some quick math informed Karrie that the woman had placed the order only a mere eleven minutes earlier. Hardly the twenty-plus minutes she'd so sorely insisted she'd waited. "I'm assuming the associate did inform you that we were out of red velvet, but there was another batch coming out of the oven?"

"I ordered. I paid. How long should I be expected to wait?" griped the woman.

"I guess until the red velvets are done?"

"Miss," stepped the woman. "I don't like your tone."

"I'm sorry, ma'am. No offense intended," segued Karrie. "If you're in a rush, can I offer you something besides the red velvets? Have you tried our Colombian coffee cupcakes? Those are exclusive for January—"

"I ordered red velvet," angered the woman. "If I wanted Colombian coffee, I would've ordered a dozen of Colombian coffee, wouldn't you think?"

"My sincere apology," offered Karrie. "With orders as large as yours, most people phone ahead. Especially when we're ninety minutes from closing, our supply gets a little low. May I comp you with an extra gluten-free blue—"

"Do I look like I want to eat two cupcakes?"

"Excuse me?"

"The two dozen are for a kindergarten party tomorrow morning. The blueberry is for me. Now."

"Oh," smiled Karrie. "Would you like your gluten-free blueberry now?"

"Like I can't stand another minute without a sugar fix? Jesus! Can you believe this twat?" The easily annoyed woman was gesturing for agreement from a nearby family of five, either Pakistani or Indian by Karrie's guess, the three preteen children with their faces pressed to the glass as they surveyed the cupcake selection. The father shrugged. The mother barely shook her head, hoping to keep ignoring the woman.

"Ma'am," warned Karrie. "You really don't need to use that language—"

"Do I look like an old lady to you?" she interrupted. "And don't 'ma'am' me again. My name is Barbara Bianchi. It's on the goddamn order."

"And . . . let me check on that order, okay?"

Karrie had had enough. Checking on the woman's cupcake order was an excuse to step away from the counter, disengage, disappear into the rear of the store, and swallow her rising rage.

"I used to work retail, you know," barked the woman at Karrie. "This is not how you run a retail establishment."

Karrie paused her retreat and swerved on that stiff leg of hers.

"It's not retail, *ma'am*," ripped Karrie. "It's a bakery."

"That's it. You ma'am'd me again. And lemme tell you, I'm awful tired of that permanent smirk on your face."

My smirk, maddened Karrie, the worst lingering grievance from the car accident. Without reconstructive plastic surgery, she was most likely never to recover from the paralyzed levator anguli oris muscle above the right corner of her once perfectly pouty mouth. It left her face frozen with a smug little gleam. Lucky claimed to love every curve of it. In turn, Karrie had proclaimed that it matched her daddy's gnarled nose. Yet, as much as she'd become accustomed to her recently malformed face, for that awful customer to use it as another excuse for her bad manners . . .

"And you're pissing and moaning over fucking cupcakes?" spat Karrie in reply. "I mean, cupcakes, lady. Cake, butter, and sugar."

"Did you just curse at—"

"And here's a nutrition tip," Karrie couldn't help but add. "It's not goddamn gluten that makes your thighs fat."

"That's it," stomped the woman. "I'm leaving a Yelp review."

"Please do," pissed Karrie, leaning in, arms propped on the countertop as if ready to pounce across and pummel the woman into pulp. "And don't forget to say that the disabled bakery associate who tried so hard to help your sorry ass called you a *fucking cunt*. Can you spell cunt, *maaaa'aaaam?*"

"I wanna talk to your manager," screeched the woman. "Right now."

"Sorry. Not here," shrugged Karrie. "But if you like, I can show you exactly where you can lodge an official complaint."

"Oh, I will!"

"Easy to remember," relayed Karrie. "It's ButterCrème dot com, backslash, my thighs are thick and so am I."

Before the woman could inhale the insult, let alone command

even the most inept reply, Karrie had dropped her apron, ducked under the counter, and hit the door. It swung wide in front of her. She was instantly hit with the smell of smoke. In the minutes since she'd returned from her break, the air had been infected with the stench of distant fires. From her back pocket she withdrew her phone and speed-dialed a number. Two rings and he answered.

"I know," interrupted Karrie. "I'm hours early. But I think I just fired myself. Can you come get me now?"

4

Porter Ranch

Three years, thought Lucky. *Three years and how many days since I've been behind the wheel of a sheriff's black-and-white?* It was down in Compton, he recalled. He'd worn training officer stripes and for five months he'd sat beside his rookie charge, the impossibly beautiful Shia St. George.

And I thought that *radio car was a piece of shit?*

With the urgent need for deputies on the street, department policy was to open the doors of the county's fleet service garages to place volunteers in roll-worthy black-and-whites. The good news for Lucky was that the Sheriff's was fast following suit with the LAPD by replacing most of their radio cars with roomier Ford Explorer SUVs. This left a cornucopia of aging Crown Victorias that were either unsold or yet to be salvaged. The bad news was that the cars were bereft of equipment. In the vehicle he'd been issued, Lucky had no computer comms—the Box—and not even a backup shotgun locked upright in a rack. He'd been provided a black-and-white with just a light array, a radio, and a full tank of gas.

Unfamiliar with the neighborhood he'd been assigned—combined with the fires raging in the northern hills—Lucky chose that expedient navigation app to guide him west from Pacoima to Porter Ranch. LAPD had already performed their knock-knock drill twice, banging on doors and using their radio car bullhorns to strongly advise locals to calmly abandon their homes and belongings. It was a safety issue for both residents and first responders who needed to be unobstructed on neighborhood streets while fighting the fire. Yet, despite local news stations declaring the evacuations as mandatory, no locals not heeding the warning would be arrested. The most cops could do was urge, cajole, and strongly admonish citizens to steer clear of the danger and get the hell out of the way.

Porter Ranch bore a City of Los Angeles zip code. That made it LAPD turf. Though in matters of urgency, the County would often loan out its resources. As a volunteer deputy, Lucky was tasked with a neighborhood grid to patrol—in a last-ditch effort to convince evacuation-resistant homeowners to bug out, as well as a deterrent to would-be looters.

The Santa Ana winds were in full fan mode, urging the fire in the neighborhood's direction. The smoke from the encroaching fire had arrived in force but somehow hadn't dropped. It was more of a blanketing overhead. A geographic anomaly, figured Lucky. Somehow, due to the way the ground mass was formed, it left the streams of brown, choking air floating over the treetops like a dirty fog. From the protected inside of his black-and-white, the smoke appeared like a muddy, upside-down river. Defying gravity. Like a movie special effect.

Cul-de-Sac City.

Lucky had nicknamed the neighborhood the moment he'd viewed the map—this despite the gated locale's actual moniker,

Tuscany Estates. The planned community consisted of gentle rows of two-story homes—coined McMansions by architectural critics—on ample lots in a series of asphalt tentacles reaching up to the mountain's edges. Instead of streets that flowed on a grid, one drive intersecting with the next, the developer had designed wide vessels that all capped in safe, family-friendly cul-de-sacs. *Great for the kiddies*, thought Lucky. *Lousy for patrolling.* As he rolled past the usually manned security gate, Lucky guessed the residents had contracted with a private patrol service. Along with the gate guard, the armed security patrolman had long been sent home when Cal Fire orders to evacuate had come through.

The radio car shook as the vibrations of an unseen helicopter roared overhead. *A Firehawk*, guessed Lucky, a Sikorsky Black Hawk helicopter converted into an airborne firefighting machine. Gonzo had more than once expressed her wont for flying such a beast. In the dark and smoke, Firehawk pilots could fly in close proximity to the mountains' canyons and ridges, navigated entirely by sensors and a high-definition screen projected on their helmets' visors. A real feat, Lucky agreed. Though his own selfish desire preferred to imagine his soon-to-be missus hovering somewhere around five thousand feet, high and safe, well above the fiery fray.

The cable powering the radio car's steering had a bit of slip to it, sending an annoying, rubbery squeal into the night every time he performed a tight turn. He cranked the wheel, his headlights sweeping across the hopefully empty homes at the end of the cul-de-sac. Still, he keyed the mic on the external speaker.

"THIS NEIGHBORHOOD IS UNDER MANDATORY EVACUATION," spoke Lucky, his booming monotone echoing against the mountain beyond. "IF YOU CHOOSE TO STAY, CALLS TO 911 MAY NOT BE ANSWERED."

He checked his watch. It had been nearly two hours since he'd swallowed the Benadryl. Defense-wise, the allergy med seemed more necessary than his .45-caliber sidearm. On his last fire patrol, he'd encountered his share of dogs, terrified and somehow divided from their owners. And though Lucky loved dogs, their dander hated him. So some serious premedicating was key.

Each and every one of the surrounding homes appeared quiet and mostly dark—the only signs of life being the porch lamps or the occasional backyard glow from a swimming pool. Lucky counted fifteen McMansions from each cul-de-sac to the nearest cross street. Methodically covering his assigned territory, he made a right turn on his way to the next dead end, a cul-de-sac named Via Medici, to go along with the development's not-so-clever Renaissance theme. As he approached the oncoming lane, Lucky noted a pair of headlights fast closing in his rearview mirror. Bluish-white halogens, the kind of super bulbs usually found factory-installed on luxury sedans. *German model*, Lucky guessed. *An Audi S8*. The fast-approaching car braked sharply, falling in behind Lucky's black-and-white and preparing to make the very same turn up Via Medici.

Lucky gently applied his brakes, signaling a full stop. He switched on the emergency light array atop the unit. The red and blue lights spun in a universally urgent signal for the Audi to stop. Instead, the sedan cut to the left as if preparing to whip around and pass Lucky on his driver's side. Already anticipating, Lucky half-twisted the wheel counterclockwise, angling the black-and-white into a blocking move while making certain the Audi's headlights caught every pore of his disapproving grimace. The sole figure behind the Audi's windshield spanked the steering wheel in obvious frustration.

Like he'd performed dozens of times before, Lucky pushed his door open with his left foot as he stepped from the vehicle, one index finger pointing at the Audi's driver, the other glued against the release on the retention holster sheathing his SIG Sauer service pistol.

"STAY IN THE CAR! HANDS ON THE STEERING WHEEL!" shouted Lucky.

Ignoring the order, the Audi driver swung his door open. Out swept a thick man in a size-too-small polo shirt and basketball-style gym shorts. With an equanimity of speed, Lucky skinned his pistol and leveled the muzzle center mass on the V of the thick man's collar.

"HANDS!" Lucky shouted.

"Yeah, yeah," agreed the driver, shooting both arms at the sky, gesturing with one finger in the direction of the cul-de-sac. "This is my street. I live right up there at the end."

"Two steps forward, ninety degrees," ordered Lucky. "Hands on the hood of your vehicle."

"Dude. Seriously—"

"Believe me. You don't wanna get shot today," suggested Lucky. "Hands. Hood. Right now."

"You don't need to put your gun on me," bitched the man, reluctantly obeying, splaying his fingers, bending slightly at the waist, and bracing against the Audi's silver hood. "I'm complying, okay?"

"Musta missed the part where I said, 'Stay in your car.'" On approach, Lucky had already plugged the man's front license plate into his short-term memory: R8DXBRT

"But I fucking live here," griped the driver.

Reholstering his pistol, Lucky gave the man a cursory frisk, fishing a wallet out of the his gym shorts' front pocket. He took three steps back.

"Yo! My wallet, dude," said the annoyed man.

"Robert Bianchi," said Lucky. He read the man's driver's license with assistance from his tactical flashlight. "113 Via Medici."

"It's Bobby Bianchi," insisted the man, as if Lucky might somehow realize some greater meaning from his nickname. When Lucky showed little more than a flat "so what" expression, Bobby pointed again. "My street. Just going to my house—"

"You're temporarily evacuated," said Lucky. "You have family still in your house?"

"Fuck no," whined Bobby. "They're already safe at the Four Seasons. Just gotta get a change of clothes."

"Your missus didn't pack for you?"

"Dude. It's my house that I want to go to. My. House."

"Not a dude. I'm a deputy," reminded Lucky. "And like I said. You're evacuated until Cal Fire gives the all clear."

"All due respect, *deputy*," hissed Bobby. "I happen to know it's my God-given right that no matter what you say, I'm allowed to defend my property with a goddamn garden hose if I want."

"If you were *on* your property," agreed Lucky. "But you're not. You're on a public street in an area designated for evacuation. For your safety and that of emergency responders who might need to occupy this neighborhood in order to fight the fire, I need you to get back in your vehicle and about-face yourself outta here—"

Lucky pointed to the flames on the nearby ridge to punctuate the urgency of his message. "See that?"

"Five minutes," begged Bobby.

"Or I can put you in handcuffs and you can grab ass in the back seat of my black-and-white until I'm relieved."

"Jesus!"

"Sir," annoyed Lucky. "Get in your damn car. And please go."

Lucky clocked Bobby's eyes, a wide pair that appeared closer to the bridge of his nose than average, set inside a bulbous head that was shaved despite the appearance of a full compliment of thirty-five-year-old hair. There were no signs of dilation—of drug use or inebriation—nor chemical panic. Though when Lucky had Bianchi over the hood of the Audi, he'd noted a blossom of back acne climbing out from underneath the musclehead's shirt, crawling half-way up his thick neck—a sometimes sign of anabolic steroid abuse. Other than that, Lucky had pegged the man as spoiled and unaccustomed to being denied. Bobby Bianchi's eyes yearned to cross the near three hundred yards to his house at the end of the cul-de-sac.

"This is unfair," complained Bobby, lips pressed together until they'd formed a thin, hardened crease. "Not right at all. No way. No how."

"Is what it is," sighed Lucky, his patience wearing thin. It had been a few years since he'd been in uniform and the stoicism required to swallow the bile that came out of so many citizens hadn't always been his foremost asset.

"Here's what's gonna happen," relented Bobby, attempting to sound friendly. "If I don't get to drive my car up and into my house—right now—then the minute I get back to the Four Seasons, I'm gonna pour shots from a two-hundred-dollar bottle of tequila while I dial up every councilman, county supervisor, and boss who can make the rest of your life a goddamn misery. Just because you're not gonna let me enter my own property. How's about that, *deputy?*"

"I say knock yourself out," replied Lucky. "My name is Lucas Dey. My immediate supervisor is David Kavanaugh. He's in charge of all volunteer deputies—"

"Volunteer?" shot Bobby. "You're not even a full-time cop? Just a goddamn wannabe?"

"Complaints are still welcome."

"You got no authority!" spat Bobby. "Fuckin' hobby cop."

"I'm a deputy on duty with full authority—"

"Fake cop keeping me from my own front door!"

"Return to your vehicle, Mr. Bianchi."

"Move your fuckin' cop car!" pointed Bobby, rage rising in him.

Steroid rage? wondered Lucky.

"I'm going to my goddamn house right fucking now!"

Lucky sighed deeply, fresh out of words to cajole the entitled lunkhead back into his luxury car. Then it happened. Frustration got the better of Bianchi, who found himself launching forward, arms extended and popping Lucky in his Kevlar vest with both palms. It wasn't a full-on strike. Bianchi's move was more of a schoolyard shove, a thoughtless expression of force—a wordless command—directing Lucky back into his radio unit. At the start of the slow-motion moment, Lucky's hands were neutrally poised, relaxed, hanging to his sides at the end of his arms. But the millisecond Bianchi had lurched, Lucky had automatically rotated his right shoulder, diffusing both blows while trapping Bianchi's left arm. As Lucky continued turning, Bianchi was already on his heels and off balance. All Lucky had to do was let go and the dumbass would have probably spun onto the pavement like a top losing centrifugal force. Only Lucky wasn't quite the kind of cop to let an out-of-line citizen wonder just why he or she had been introduced to the pavement. So, Lucky leveled a sharp left elbow at head height. It connected squarely and with significant blunt force against the shaved hair behind Bianchi's ear.

Bianchi went down. Not in a stumble because his knees had given way. Nor because he had been struck unconscious. It was more from the speed and impact of Lucky's move. Lucky's full weight on the back of his knee pinned him to the road's surface.

"Time for a reality check," said Lucky. "Nod if I have your full attention."

"You motherFUCKER—"

"Pay attention," hissed Lucky. "I politely asked you to move along. You did not. You reached out to strike me and that's how you ended up eating asphalt. Now, because I'm just a hobby cop, as you put it, I don't rate a body cam to prove my point or disprove yours. You wanna press some kind of complaint against me? Well, that's your call. Strongly suggest you think otherwise. Now, you can do that calculus while cuffed and riding around for the next few hours in the back of my black-and-white. Or you can do it in your cushy hotel room. Giving you to a count of three to choose. One, two—"

". . . Hotel," Bianchi finally wheezed, his scraped and bloody lips muffled by the blacktop.

"Can you get up on your own?" asked Lucky, unweighting himself off the big mouth.

"Yeah," said Bianchi, pushing up onto his knees, swilling in a lungful of foul air, and using the Audi's hood as a handhold to hoist himself to his feet. Bianchi didn't dare look back at Lucky. He stumbled back around to his driver's side door and plunked into the stitched premium-leather seat.

Lucky, in turn, slid back behind the wheel of the black-and-white, shut his door, and waited for Bianchi to maneuver his luxury sedan in the opposite direction. If the radio unit had come with a computer, Lucky might have felt inclined to make notations on the annoying encounter. That would have been consistent with Sheriff's policy. But his present assignment wasn't about making paper trails. It was about public safety.

Lucky listened. The retreating sound of the Audi's engine was eventually swallowed by a distant siren. Resuming his patrol, he pointed the black-and-white up Via Medici while manipulating the manual spotlight from side to side with his left hand, igniting each driveway. The beam pierced the ever-thickening air. And for one briefest second, at the light's penetrating peak, Lucky thought he'd seen a figure. Walking quickly, crossing the far end of the cul-de-sac. Though it might have been a shadow, a trick of refraction when the manual spotlight swung across the radio car's headlamps.

"YOU THERE!" Lucky called out over the car's loudspeaker. "THIS NEIGHBORHOOD IS UNDER MANDATORY EVACUATION. HOLD IN PLACE WHILE I APPROACH."

As far as Lucky knew, he was giving warning to nobody whatsoever. Still, he gassed the worn Crown Victoria and surged up the gentle slope with only the slightest expectation that he'd encounter either a stubborn resident or looter.

He found neither. Only smoke and porch lights.

5

Oren had seen the headlamps. One set was from a cop car. The other, a piercing blue tint from a civilian's vehicle, meaning it might even have been Bobby Bianchi's. And wouldn't that have been an ugly happenstance if the police officer had allowed Bianchi to proceed up the lane to the cul-de-sac's end? Partially guarded by a chest-high, manicured hedge of Italian cypress, Oren stood statue still, arms extended, both hands gripped around the wooden handles of a crusty wheelbarrow. In all his plotting, he'd somehow forgotten to figure out precisely how he'd move his bounty. He knew the path was clean, free and clear of video surveillance, as only a few of his fellow Tuscany Estates residents had installed cameras. It came off as redundant, especially considering they'd purchased homes behind a guard booth manning an imposing private gate and were part of a homeowners association that employed a full-time roving security patrol.

He'd been so obsessed with the route he'd take, he'd blanked on the means until he'd seen the wheelbarrow.

Inside the double layer of disposable latex gloves, Oren's hands were swimming in perspiration. For a moment, he realized that by waiting for his chance he might just squander it. So while the two distant figures by the cars appeared to tussle, Oren pushed off, the front tire of the wheelbarrow hopping off the curb as he beelined for his own driveway. He chose not to glance right, keeping a bead on his destination. 144 Via Medici, otherwise known to him as Mankowski Manor, where he was sole owner, proprietor, and resident of his own spacious Tuscany Estates McMansion.

Spacious living, laughed Oren to himself, his grimace turning into the slightest smile. *More like cavernous.*

In no time whatsoever, Oren was thumping the wheelbarrow down the path of gravel and concrete pavers along the side of his house, guarded by both a pine plank fence and the smooth stucco exterior of his garage. Once through the back gate, he kicked away the plaster gnome holding the spring-loaded hinge at bay. The gate swung closed with an unnerving *kuh-clang*. From there he hairpin-turned and eased the wheelbarrow down through a pair of open storm doors, revealing an easy slope of steps down into an unlikely basement. It was too dark to see, but once he felt the floor level, he lowered the load and scrambled back up to the storm doors. As he leaned across to pull the first door shut, he heard the echoing sound blare from the cop car.

"THIS NEIGHBORHOOD IS UNDER MANDATORY EVACUATION. HOLD IN PLACE WHILE I APPROACH."

"Oh, I'll hold in place, all right," muttered Oren to himself. "In my own goddamn tornado cellar."

Oren loved referring to the basement as his tornado cellar. The substructure wasn't part of the original model plan. Because the vast majority of Southern California homes were not in danger of either tornados or floods, nearly all post–World War II homes were constructed without basements or pillar foundations and were built atop reinforced concrete slabs. When the Mankowski family chose to build in Porter Ranch's Tuscany Estates, Oren had insisted on the subterranean space, planning to use the extra square footage for a man cave and a wine cellar—this despite the fact that he was more of a bottled beer drinker than a tilter of fine cabernets and pinot noirs. His wife at the time, Beth, hadn't protested in the least. Oren's guess was that she'd already begun planning her big escape. Divorce style. All the way back then. Three and a half long years ago.

Eons ago.

Only after the build was complete did she serve him with the papers. Her evil expectation was that to fully split their assets, they'd have to liquidate the dream house. With that, she'd under-estimated the resolve of a man to keep what he had built. His very own castle. In the end, Oren was willing to part with practically everything to keep his name on the title of the Via Medici address. Even the shared custody of his three children.

For that, she'd called Oren evil.

Ever since, the accusation had eaten at him like a slow-growing cancer. During a nasty split it was so easy to assign mal-intent to the other's words or actions. But unlike Beth's pro forma complaint for the divorce—his failures at the racetrack—Oren's behavior seemed almost obsessive, as if his entire self-worth was tied to the house.

I'm not evil. I'm just morally messed up.

He sometimes wondered if he was mentally ill. After all, what kind of father wouldn't fight for his children if not for some kind of cranial impairment? Mental health was in the news. Mental health was all around. *So why not me?* excused Oren.

With the storm doors bolted from the inside, Oren worked by the dim glow of a single floor lamp plugged into an electrical outlet. The man cave had never materialized beyond the big-screen television mounted on the wall. The floor was unfinished concrete. Against the opposite side was a couch so fatigued, the leather was cracking. A humming mini fridge served as an end table. An old door laid across cinderblocks served as a coffee table.

Exposed wooden two-by-fours ran from floor to ceiling, giving an illusion of rooms, along with the unfinished plumbing for a bathroom. In the temperature-controlled wine cellar, polished oak racks held enough space for a thousand bottles of wine. Not a solitary slot was occupied. Rolling the wheelbarrow between the shelving to the far wall, Oren pressed at the center pillar. It clicked inward, unlocking a secret latch. Oren reached inside a wine slot and pulled. Half the wall-side wine case opened on a silent hinged door, aided by tiny rubber wheels hidden under the baseboard. On the other side was the makings of a panic room, equally unfurnished as the rest of the basement—the remnant of just another one of Oren's never-ending list of unfinished ideas.

Returning to the wheelbarrow, Oren rolled it and its precious cargo into the hiding space, next to the rest of his emptied loads. It had taken eight trips across the street and back to cart the entire haul. He then carefully walked the wine case door shut until he felt the lock catch and click. He ran his fingertips along the smoothness of the joint. Perfect. Unless anybody was clued to it, there'd be no way to guess that behind the empty wine case there was a vault of sorts. And inside of it, collectibles worth something close to $1 million.

Oren heard the front door chime, the sound a melodic, resonant trickle down the basement stairs. Ears tuned, he captured the low rapping of a heavy fist and perhaps even a voice. *Probably that cop*, he reckoned. Another sweep. Oren had missed the first evacuation call, as he was still hiking down the mountain trail after having set the third and last blaze. Soon after his return and a shower, he'd spied an LAPD officer on his security camera. She was thin with a pixie cut, looked five-foot-nothing and balanced only by all the equipment slung onto her duty belt. She had rung and knocked and rung again. The protocol was to assume nobody was home. Which was what Oren would do now that he was home. Play possum. And watch the home across the cul-de-sac, doing just as he'd been asked by his friend and neighbor so many times before. Why?

Because I may be mentally ill, but I'm a good goddamn neighbor.

Oren laughed, cracking himself up so hard, it almost ached. He was such an awesome neighbor, he was willing to brave the oncoming brushfire to keep his end of the cul-de-sac safe from predators. If things worked out as plotted, firefighters would soon invade the neighborhood and beat back the blazing mountainside, saving the property of all those good taxpayers who provided their training, equipment, and salaries.

And if things didn't work out—if the fire Oren had kindled somehow jumped from the hillside to the McMansions of Tuscany Estates? Oren was resolved to burn to death, his empty castle serving as his private crematorium.

6

Castaic. 9:18 p.m.

The interior of the Cal Fire crew truck was a sweltering eighty-six degrees. According to the driver, the air conditioning had reached its cooling limits somewhere south of Buttonwillow, the condenser fan motor making its last turn with the familiar stink of an electric burnout. It filled the entire cabin, tickling the already annoyed nostrils of inmate firefighter Dave Bustamante.

Since that air conditioner burnout, Dave and his fellow convict firefighters had stripped their orange Department of Corrections custom fire suits to their hardened waists. In an effort to stay hydrated, the team had already torn into the cases of bottled water stored by the pallet on every crew truck. To a man, each had learned that proper water consumption was key to surviving the heat from the flames they'd sworn to battle, not to mention the perspiration-inducing thirty-five pounds of heavy-duty fire protection.

That's if we survive the friggin' drive, joked Dave to nobody but himself. Winter wasn't supposed to come with hot breath.

He took a slow, cleansing breath. Then another. More calming inhales and exhales would follow the more they neared Los Angeles County. He hadn't wanted to return. At least not yet—not until he was ready.

No. Not until I've got a firm grip on my inner idiot.

It had been a year and a half since Dave had completed the inmate firefighter program, allowing him to transfer from the concrete and razor-wire confines of Mule Creek State Prison to one of the forty-four separate conservation camps operated by the Department of Corrections and Rehabilitation. Each fire camp was based in one of California's most remote and "matchworthy" regions. For the past year and a half, Dave Bustamante's prison bunk was in the Cuesta Fire Camp, located in the countryside just three miles west of the Central Coast's San Luis Obispo. From there, he and his fellow inmate firefighters trained with the same rigor as other wildfire specialists. The only true difference between skill sets and equipment were the colors of their fire suits. Whereas the inmates wore bright orange Kevlar fiber, the Cal Fire regulars were defended in reflective yellow.

Dave had felt at relative peace serving out the remainder of his sentence fighting fires for the state. The routine reminded him of his time in the Marines and later as a private soldier for a defense contractor. The camaraderie. The hard men, most whom had been lucky enough to plead their cases down to nonviolent crimes, the foremost prerequisite for service on convict fire crews. Dave's only request had been to serve in the northern regions of the state. His excuse was his allergies—something about the pollen in and around sunny Southern Cal—from Los Angeles all the way down to the even more temperate San Diego. Though convict firefighters weren't usually granted such provisos, Dave was lucky that his had been heard and heeded. Sure, the allergy scam was bullshit. He just knew that the nearer he was to Southern California—to Los

Angeles in particular—the harder it would be to keep his head clear from an obsession of his, a singular fixation of his inner idiot's. If not managed wisely, it might prove unhealthy to his own physical health, as well as that of any number of people who might get in the way of his petty fantasy game of revenge.

Ah, the mere idea of it. Revenge.

To Dave, the word held more than just a primal quality. Revenge defined the most primeval of human acts—something emanating from a necessity more akin to a need than an actual choice. Like sex. Or love. The more his feelings were involved, the greater the possibility for errors. Mortal mistakes . . .

Those dangerous *aw, fuck* moments that could bury a man up to his neck in fire ants.

"Hey, Beemer," shouted a firefighter in the second row, a barrel-chested Hispanic O.G. they all called Jefe. "How's them allergies?"

"Let you know when I blow my snot downwind!" Dave replied.

Beemer was Dave's nickname. At least that's how he'd explained the BMW tattoo that had long ago been inked between the spikes of his shoulder blades. The story was only partially true. Dave's name wasn't Dave at all. Nor was the surname of Bustamante. It was an alias with enough veracity behind it to fool a few police agencies and, so far, the California State Department of Corrections.

The crew cracked up over Beemer's snot joke. For seconds, it broke the tension and the heat.

Beemer, fully committed to not allowing a molecule of his body to become dehydrated, snapped the cap off the top of yet another water bottle and sucked back a few gulps before dripping a spare few ounces onto his hands. He rubbed his hands like applying moisturizer, forcing the liquid to mix with the sweat from his pores. With his thumb he massaged an itchy tattoo on his left wrist, the lone remnant from his time in Iraq. Nearly all his jarhead pals had gotten ink to commemorate their overseas tour. Lance

Corporal Greg Beem—a.k.a. Beemer—had chosen a design he felt was apropos to that particular time and place. It was a simple red A contained within a perfect circle.

The international sign for anarchy.

As it worked out, one of the Cuesta camp guards moonlighted as a tattoo artist. In exchange for five minutes of oral sex with Beemer, he'd reciprocated by freshening up that anarchy tattoo. The vermillion ink the guard used had left Beemer's wrist itching for nearly a week.

"About twenty-five minutes from touchdown," shouted the crew chief from the cab. Cappy, as he was known, was neither an inmate nor a prison guard. He was a bona fide yellow-uniformed Cal Fire crew runner, equal parts drill instructor and father figure. A pure civilian who imparted so much Christian love and attention toward his convict fire crews that each and every one would have gladly trailed him into the mouth of Hades. Under his fire-retardant layers, Cappy wore a necklace his father had made while in captivity in Vietnam. It was constructed from bamboo beads and strung with sandal thread. Hanging from the black leather was a holy cross fixed from pieces of sun-bleached monkey bone.

"If Jesus got my ol' man through three years in the Hanoi Hilton," Cappy liked to bellow, "then he sure as shit can give you the strength required to beat back the fires of hell."

Cappy's most ardent follower was Dave Bustamante. Only believing in Cappy's God meant believing in Satan, the power of evil, and all that heaven versus hell jazz. Strangely, the devil was easier for Beemer to comprehend, having felt Lucifer's fingers working under his skin more times than he could remember. But did that mean there was a benevolent, all-knowing, and loving God? Beemer didn't bother answering, certain that if Jesus died on the cross, it sure as hell wasn't for him, especially when considering all the violence he'd unleashed upon Mother Earth so far.

After assembling his crew, Cappy informed them that Southern California was so tinder-dry that they were to decamp and post up somewhere south of Bakersfield. The conditions in and around

Los Angeles were so dire that extra hand crews were needed. They'd barely geared up for the road trip when Cappy announced that brushfires had already cropped up at the northern end of L.A.'s San Fernando Valley. There would be no rest. No chow at the camp where they were to bunk. It was going to be, as Cappy coined, "straight into the jaws."

"Hydrate, you assholes!" barked Jefe. "And Beemer, don't forget your Claritin!"

Beemer sucked back the rest of his twenty-four-ounce water bottle, crushing the plastic before returning the screw cap. He sucked in another deep breath and held it for seven seconds. Then he exhaled, hoping that along with the expressed air, he would expel the name that had come to haunt him with every yard the truck propelled them to Los Angeles.

Lucky Dey.

Beemer replaced the name on his mind with images of fire—flames the size of skyscrapers. If controlled breathing exercises wouldn't make the demon disappear, fighting a merciless conflagration with little more than a shovel and a McLeod hoe should do the trick.

Wednesday

7

Porter Ranch

Near 6:00 a.m., Lucky was able to call it a night. He was plenty grateful when the radio call came for him to clock out. Unfortunately, the respite came with a caveat. *Keep the vehicle and prepare to be called back to duty at 1800 hours.* The weather reports predicted only the slightest daytime lull in the Santa Ana winds. For the oncoming evening, foothill breezes were expected to kick up to nearly forty miles per hour with mountain top gusts reaching sixty-five, twice that of the night before. Any fire containment gained during the day would surely be lost again come nightfall.

Lucky's low back ached from a night glued to the black-and-white's butt-worn, velour-covered seats. He badly needed to stretch and sweat and shower off the acrid stink of smoke that had permeated his pores. So, instead of returning to the Altadena bungalow he shared with Gonzo, he pointed the radio unit toward a boxing gym on South Hill near his downtown office. There he'd see the trainer he'd occasionally lean on for core strengthening and building elasticity in his forty-year-old frame. The erector set Lucky had for lower lumbar joints needed daily attention if he hoped to avoid a return to painkillers stronger than a fistful of ibuprofen. He still had the Vicodin cravings, but those had been relegated mostly to his non-waking dreams and mental tune-ups provided by occasional Alcoholics Anonymous meetings.

He took a brief shower after his workout, pulled on some spare workout togs, and with his uniform neatly rolled up under his arm, strolled the two blocks from the gym to his basement personnel office. Since his call to duty, brushfires had kicked up at the north end of the San Gabriel Valley, blowing snowflakes of fine ash and the smell of burning mountainsides to the skyscrapers of downtown. It almost amused him that so many businessmen and women, upon showing up to work that early morning in their sharp suits, would start their day appearing as if they'd suffered an avalanche of embarrassing dandruff.

Lucky could have worked out and showered at home. But when he could be recalled to duty at any moment, he didn't want to risk stumbling into some family drama that might interfere with his much-needed slumber. That's why the old cowhide sofa in his office beckoned. He'd owned it since before his stint in Kern County. Gonzo said it was too discolored and tattered to fit the tight confines of their bungalow. That, and the cushions had been so permanently imprinted with Lucky's perspiration that she claimed she'd be able to identify it as his couch simply by the body pattern worn into leather.

He locked the office door, unplugged both the phone and his computer screen, and switched off the overhead fluorescents. *God bless the windowless basement space*, he thought once his body landed on the cushions. The room was blacked out but for the faint stripe of light from the corridor bleeding underneath his door. He rolled left to face a burgundy and kelly green checkered throw pillow—a moving-in gift from Gonzo, claiming to want to liven up the gray-on-gray government office. The pillow still smelled of either Pier 1 Imports or Cost Plus—wherever the hell she'd purchased it. Breathing in the scent, Lucky unconsciously played a game of anagram on the inside of his eyelids.

R8DXBRT

The license tag on the Audi.

What was that asshat's name? Oh, yeah. Bianchi.

During his shift, that had been the only negative encounter with a civilian. To a man, woman, and dander-laced dog, all appeared compliant and polite, including the significant few who had decided not to heed the evacuation warnings. Lucky's well-worn gambit was to kindly ask they provide him with their full name, social security number, and name and address of their family dentist.

"Dentist?" a stubborn homeowner would inevitably reply.

"Makes it way easier to identify the corpse," Lucky would deadpan.

One such intractable citizen, a skin-and-bones septuagenarian whose idea of fire defense was to wet his house with a garden hose, delivered the memorable quip of the night.

"Oh, I don't mind," said the old man. "Think of what my grandkids'll save on incineration fees."

Despite his crushing fatigue and weary eyes, that sequence in his head wouldn't fade.

R8DXBRT

Lucky had easily deciphered the first part of the vanity plate. Rated X. Perhaps to signal to the world that Mr. Bianchi was some kind of proud player in the pornography game. That would make sense, considering the history of the adult film business. Decades earlier, the masters and mistresses of the porn game had settled in the north end of the San Fernando Valley, making the sloping hoods of Chatsworth and Granada Hills their own exclusive Hollywood-esque enclave. Well depicted, Lucky recollected in his half-sleepy state, in the movie *Boogie Nights*. It starred that Marky Mark and the Funky Bunch kid wearing a prosthetic penis in the shocking final frame of the film. Lucky wasn't a big movie fan unless the motion picture provided a bucket of belly laughs. Otherwise, why buy a ticket? But that film had stuck with him simply because the characters seemed both pathetic and painfully close to his own experiences. Lucky found himself trying to cast Bobby Bianchi and his $100,000 Audi in the movie as if it would help him make sense of why that annoying five-minute encounter had crept under his skullcap.

Just the niggling thought of Bobby Bianchi felt as if it had become a barrier between Lucky and sleep. Half of him wanted to rise, flick on his computer, and run that license plate to see where it might lead. But in doing so, he'd be succumbing to personal curiosity alone. This when his body demanded rest. So, instead of putting himself at a deficit, he lay there, allowing himself to sink deeper into the old, comfy sofa. His mind returned to the anagram game. In the dreamy place between fully firing synapses and unconsciousness, Lucky's brain tried to untwist the license plate like it was a Scrabble problem, as if behind it were some kind of answer.

But an answer to what exactly?

Sleep toyed with Lucky, pretending to overcome him only to kick him back to consciousness over and over again for what seemed like an hour—only it was barely eight minutes.

"Fuck it," Lucky mouthed, choosing to give Bobby Bianchi a ten-minute digital exam. He flung himself from the sofa and sat at his desk, rubbing his eyes as the computer screen returned to life. He felt a give in the chair's retention spring, so he rotated the tension wheel until the back was at ninety degrees, forcing him to sit up straight and awake. He next logged into the city system under his personal ID and password. Then he began a simple query. Four simple search terms:

ROBERT.
BIANCHI.
VIA MEDICI.
PORTER RANCH.

8

Westlake Village. 8:19 a.m.

"Valet's already bringin' up the cars. C'mon. Let's get movin'."
Bobby Bianchi was at the foot of the king-size bed, haphazardly stuffing and then zipping his overnight duffel. This while his wife, Barbara, was happy in her lovely Neverland, blissfully snoozing between cotton sheets with a thread count north of five hundred.

"You friggin' kidding me?" Barbara mumbled, face stuck in her pillow.

"News says the neighborhood's safe. The fire's moving west so we're out of danger. Nothing left to burn in the hills above the house. I wanna get back home."

"Bobby," grunted Barbara, her body motionless but for her barely moving lips. "Where are we?"

"The Four Seasons."

"Exactly."

"I wanna get back to the house."

"And I want strawberries 'n' cream, a long massage, and a late checkout."

"Barbie. Let's go."

"It's the Four fucking Seasons."

"We were just here for New Years."

"Maybe if you woulda booked a suite for dinner."

"And what about the kids 'n' school?"

"Closed cuzza the fires."

Bobby performed a frustrated half turn on the rug. Any further and he would feel as if he screwed himself deeper into the lush suite, a mix of hardwood and rich floral fabrics. Warm yellows and periwinkle blues throughout, down to the precisely set ceramic bathroom tiles. The Bianchis's three children were either sleeping in the other bedroom of the suite or propped up on pillows playing games on their smartphones. In other words, precisely what they'd be doing if they were in their own rooms in their Tuscany Estates home.

"C'mon," pleaded Bobby. "We got our own Four Seasons for a house."

"Then run along home," she softly harrumphed before rolling over, arms wrapped around a feather-stuffed pillow.

That's all Bobby needed to break loose. Without even a kiss or a goodbye, he spun on a sneakered heel and left the suite behind. Once in front of the Four Seasons entrance, he crumpled a $5 bill into the valet's mitt, climbed into his luxury Audi, and sped back to Porter Ranch.

The fires had left the morning sky a mix of soot and gray-blue. As he traveled east on the Ronald Reagan Freeway—also known as the 118—Bobby could see how the fires had progressed along the mountain slopes, helped by the northeast wind that bent the occasional stands of palm trees lining the roadway. Black smoke billowed from the mountainside where the flames were expanding through the high grass and chaparral, white steamy clouds in the places where water-dropping aircraft were on the attack. All along, the usual commuters packed the highway, sending a message that Wednesday's work and commerce wouldn't be delayed by anything. Five fires in all, reported News Radio 1070. And that was within the boundaries of Los Angeles County. South of the city in Riverside and San Diego Counties, there were even more blazes, stressing fire crews and support resources from as far as Phoenix and Las Vegas.

The fire teams charged with defending Bobby's Porter Ranch neighborhood had succeeded in spades. As he pulled through the community's private gates, he couldn't help but marvel at how the scorched hillside appeared like a black carpet that stretched all the way to the development's edge. Yet every stucco McMansion and its rust-tiled roof, along with the mature palms and leafy elms and sycamores, appeared in bright relief, practically as shiny and fresh as the day they were finished.

A modern friggin' miracle, he thought in a rare moment of appreciation.

Bobby's sunny disposition changed the moment he turned up Via Medici. He found himself remembering that prick of a sheriff's deputy—a hobby cop at that—who wouldn't so much as allow him to venture up the cul-de-sac to check on his own damn property. That badge-heavy wannabe had dropped Bobby to the asphalt and threatened him with a humiliating arrest. His face heated up at the memory. Embarrassed. Bullied.

Me? Bullied? A victim?

Beefy Bobby Bianchi couldn't extract from his memory the last time—if ever—he'd been bullied by anybody other than his father, Joey. It was Bobby who'd borne the brunt of bullying accusations in school. And oh, how he'd loved his rep. Being the campus oppressor made him friends, alliances. While in attendance, he felt like the student capo of his own high school mafia.

As it should've been. After all . . .

The Audi rolled into the Bianchis's driveway, a sun-filled

landscape of Southwestern brick and fully grown succulents. Home at last. Instead of parking in the garage, Bobby set the brake in the driveway and chose to enter his palace through the front door, an arched plank of solid polished oak hung with the balanced precision of a pendulum clock. His key turned the Baldwin lock. The bolt slid and the door glided inward. To the right of the door was an alarm keypad. By habit, Bobby swiveled to the keypad, index finger poised to punch in the security code. Only the alarm pad hadn't sounded with the usual beeping delay, warning whoever was entering to key in the six correctly ordered digits to disarm it.

The electricity was on, yet the security system appeared to be turned off. *Odd*, thought Bobby. He tested the unit to see if it was functioning. He touched every button, each designed to give off a specific tone, but heard no sound whatsoever. Somewhere, somehow, his security system was down. Dead. Lifeless. Yet, as he glanced about, nothing in the foyer appeared to have been disturbed.

Ever so quickly, he began to move, poking his head into various rooms, checking for signs of theft. None of his high-priced paintings from California's plein air movement appeared the least bit askew. The obvious electronics, the TVs, the kids' computers, all appeared in place. With an irrational fear, Bobby launched himself up the sweeping staircase, two steps a leap, rushing into the master bedroom and then into each humongous walk-in closet— a pair of his and hers—each complete with a built-in safe. Both lockboxes were just as he'd left them—sealed, tumblers untouched.

Just when panic began to empty from his lungs, a nagging, cold sweat formed at the base of his skull. It was about to trace down his spine when he rushed from the master. He steadied his ever-weakening legs with the arcing handrail as he reversed back down to the main floor.

Fuck, no. Please, please, no . . .

In the rear center of the house was a small library, designed to be the owner's office or study, a kind of windowless sanctuary.

Barbara had even suggested that she should claim the space as her own—a personal meditation room. "No!" Bobby had barked hard at her. The roughly 250-square-foot room would serve him to a tee.

A temporary tee until I build my special bunker.

In the windowless room, he kept and displayed his prized collection. Each precious item had its own perfectly angled UV-filtered lighting, displayed for Bobby and whichever guest he'd deem worthy enough to witness the greatness of his hard-won acquisitions.

It was, for the time being, Bobby's personal trophy room.

The door to Bobby's room, so rarely left open, was eight inches ajar, a neon glow bleeding from the interior. Custom-built pieces of xenon, argon, and krypton mixed in a hue resembling a dirty blue cocktail. Bobby eased inside, all breath leaving him. But for those four custom-crafted pieces of neon script he'd installed on the top shelf of each wall, the room had been emptied of every single treasure. Disappeared. Vanished from Bobby's stopgap sanctuary and into another's possession.

"FUCK!" Bobby stomped. "FUCK, FUCK, FUCK, FUCK!"

Tears streaked his face and the neon stung his corneas. Anger swirled into his gullet and choked him until he was bent over in a coughing fit. It was between the spasms that he thought of that hobby cop. That fucking reserve deputy who wouldn't allow him to rightfully return to his house. That had to have been when it all went down. The robbery. And the goddamned sheriff's deputy was obviously part of it. He had to be. Some kind of lookout. Parked as a sentry to guarantee the robbers enough time to disable the house alarm and load up their bounty. Bobby's bounty. His most precious and prized assemblage of music rarities. In his general estimation, the total cache was valued at just over $1 million. At least that's what Bobby had paid over the years at auctions and dickering with private sellers.

All of it ripped from his possession.

Adding further insult was that the thieves had left four pieces of custom plugged-in neon. Each mounted and angled downward at forty-five degrees, having embraced the absent collection in a rainbow of heavenly glow. Four neon arrays. Four names written in perfect script.

John. Paul. George. Ringo.

9

San Fernando

Deciding to get it over with, Karrie sat on the toilet seat in nothing but her underwear and dialed Lucky. While her beautiful crush remained asleep, she'd crept from the bed—an old box spring and mattress pushed into a corner of the studio apartment's floor—started a pot of coffee in the kitchenette, and slowly closed the bathroom door until the latch caught with a delicate click.

"Hey," said Karrie once Lucky answered. "I wake you up?"

"Time is it?" asked Lucky.

"Dunno. Eleven-thirty or somethin'," she semi whispered. "Where are you?"

"Office couch."

"Gonzo know?"

"Texted her. Probably gonna be twelve on, twelve off until they get the fires under control."

She could hear Lucky righting himself, the rusty couch springs creaking over the phone as she pictured him sitting up. "Had some stuff to do here, so . . ."

"You gonna screw up the wedding?"

"So, you think I lit all those fires to get out of it?"

"Busting balls," smiled Karrie. "Now comes the bad news."

"Bring it," croaked Lucky.

"Got fired from my job."

"Cupcake job?"

"Not really fired. Kinda quit and walked off before they could fire me."

"Quitting cupcakes," quipped Lucky. "Not exactly a resume builder."

"Seriously hated being between all those entitled white bitches and their sugar fix."

"Who say what about white bitches?" called her crush from the other side of the bathroom door.

Karrie covered the receiver, kicked the door, and made a hushing sound. Though she was all about admitting to Lucky that she'd quit her cupcake job, she wasn't yet ready to muster up the truth about her boyfriend.

"Do me a favor?" asked Lucky.

"Yeah?"

"Pick up my wedding suit at the cleaners," he continued. "Bring it downtown so I can try it on, make sure it fits. The tailor? Ghasif? He isn't gonna wanna let you have it. Either that or he's gonna wanna come down here with you to make sure it fits the way he wants. Tell him if there's anything wrong, I promise to bring it back to him. Blame the fires—"

"Stop," she interrupted. "I got this. No problemo."

"Hey. Gonzo around?"

"Uh . . . I'm not at home."

Whoops, thought Karrie. She knew that briefest of pauses was a dead giveaway. At eleven thirty in the morning, she could've been anywhere. It was just that sliding even the smallest lie past Lucky was harder than cheating a Google algorithm.

"He got a name?" pressed Lucky, skipping directly to the meat of the matter. "Or she? Don't wanna be politically incorrect."

"I'm bringing your suit," redirected Karrie.

"You know I can find out things," teased Lucky.

"But you won't. Because you love me and respect that I'm eighteen."

"How'd you get to know me so well?"

"I can hear you smiling," she played.

"See ya soon," said Lucky. "And thanks. Love you."

"Love you too," replied Karrie before hanging up.

"Love you too!" whined the crush from the other side of the door.

"Ha ha," feigned Karrie, kicking the hollow door once again.

"But what if I'm not lyin'," said the crush.

Karrie chose not to answer. The thought was a tangle she didn't want to even begin to unravel. An unfathomable problem. Since physical rehab, she'd learned to keep her problems like her goals—small and achievable. Like picking up Lucky's wedding suit.

"Need me to drive you?" called the crush.

"Don't you gotta work?"

"I'll take me a personal day."

Appreciating the gesture, yet with an internal insistence to decline, Karrie stood and opened the bathroom door to a bedroom paneled in images of greenery—a veritable forest of photographed flora. Karrie didn't know yet if she truly loved Frosty—at least not in a forever kind of way. The young man with alien eyes, skin like black licorice, and a murderous history had committed himself to Jesus Christ and the forgiveness of sins. Twice already he'd confessed to her that he would never ever take another life as long as he drew breath. Even in the defense of his mother, his precious Gra'nana, or Karrie. God had saved Frosty from the gangster life for his purpose. Therefore he owed God and Karrie and Lucky to spend the remainder of his days on Earth preserving life. Plant life. And hell if that wasn't what Karrie loved about him—Frosty's dedication to all things growing and green.

10

Downtown

The call from Karrie was Lucky's second surprise awakening. Some ninety minutes earlier—before sleep had completely overtaken him or he could recall even where he'd fallen asleep—a warm hand was gently rubbing his shoulder. *Gonzo*, he thought. That was how she would wake him. A light touch, the slightest of squeezes, working along his trapezius muscle. Then he'd hear her softly say, "Luck?"

But the voice wasn't familiar. It was a mix of smoke and velvet with the scent of a Tic-Tac. Lucky turned and squinted. In the half dark, the first thing he noticed was the blonde highlights.

"I said you were snoring," informed Angie, apparently repeating herself.

Lucky attempted to focus, his eyes barely adjusting. The first feature he recognized was her crooked teeth framed between two distinct dimples. *Angie Greenwalt*, he summoned. Retired LAPD officer and his investigator neighbor from across the corridor. Besides her very obviously surgically enhanced breasts, every other piece of her appeared close to perfection, especially for a woman pushing fifty. Or so was the consensus of Lucky's fellow personnel department detectives.

But those teeth, Lucky wondered. *Why?*

"How'd you get in here?" croaked Lucky, trying to recollect if he'd locked the door before he'd begun turning off every source of light.

"C'mon," grinned Angie. "A woman don't give up her secrets. Then again, you're Lucky damn Dey. Bet you could beat a basic privacy lock just by lookin' at it."

Lucky remained prone. He rubbed his head.

"Why?" he asked.

"Snoring so loud that everybody could hear it all the way down to the water cooler," she said. "You ever been tested for apnea?"

"My girlfriend snores bigger than me."

"Maybe you both should get yourself a sleep study. Sleep apnea can take years off a life."

"Good advice." Lucky checked his watch. It was barely past 9:00 a.m. He'd planned to sleep for hours longer. "Mind shuttin' the door behind you on your way out? Got a couple more hours of noisemaking to do."

His eyes, somewhat accustomed to the light, could read the understanding smirk beneath eyes so faint he could barely call them blue. She stood, her dazzling figure in silhouette. Her uniform never changed. Sprayed-on blue jeans, tight T-shirt, and a rodeo-style belt buckle that glinted as she turned. When she touched the same doorknob she'd somehow managed to defeat, she gave it a gentle twist.

"My secret technique?" she teased. "Is a good, old-fashioned hand job. Beats most locks *and* cops."

As she pulled the door shut, Lucky was certain he saw her wink at him.

"Right," Lucky mumbled before slinking back into a semi-fetal ball. While hoping slumber would return quickly, he caught a whiff of her perfume. A reminder that she'd been there. Familiar. Angie never went a day without her trademark scent. He slept until Karrie called and woke him again. After that, he chose not to add up his hours of sleep for fear the sum would be a number too depressing to count. Lucky stretched in place, signaling his body in a "ready or not, I'm getting' up."

Where was I? he asked himself. *Oh, yeah. That asshat in the Audi. Bobby Bianchi.*

The screws in Lucky's lower lumbar were quick reminders of his usual range of motion—or lack thereof. He rose slowly, remaining in his stocking feet as he eased himself around the tanker desk the city had most likely purchased long before he was born. At least the chair wasn't so ancient. But as Lucky lowered himself into the mesh seat, the back panel gave with the least bit of his weight, leaving him surprised and in a partial, uncomfortable recline. His distinct memory was that he'd last locked the chair at a stiff, tiltless ninety degrees.

Angie Greenwald.

Until that second, he hadn't so much as remembered that the bottled blonde had beaten his door lock to let herself in and warn him of his offensive noise. Had his snoring masked her entry? How long had she sat in his desk chair watching him sleep before squeezing his shoulder and giving up that throaty, "You were snoring"?

Lucky's right hand slipped down to the plastic wheel, rotating it once to reintroduce the spring's tension. He imagined Angie sitting in the same chair she was accustomed to, feeling uncomfortable at Lucky's upright angle and unconsciously twisting the knob counterclockwise until the tensioner allowed her a more comfortable angle.

But if so, what exactly had Angie done? Had she placed her feet up on his desk and gazed across at her sleeping associate? Overtly flirtatious as she was, Lucky couldn't imagine her possessing that measure of curiosity in him.

Not a chance.

Had he left his computer screen on? Or his password-protected account open and available for Angie's perusal while he was rattling the walls with his incessant snores? And if so, what would she have been seeking? Where Lucky was concerned, he couldn't have given a red hot damn if anybody knew his personnel bureau business. His record of calling balls versus strikes on city nominees was hardly a secret.

Shit, breathed Lucky. *I'm overthinking my shit.*

He needed caffeine in the tank. He stepped back into his workout shoes, swung open his office door, and instantly considered Angie in her own office, phone stuck to her ear. Upon seeing Lucky, she finger-waved with her acrylic nails and quickly returned her attention to her work. Three sharp turns later, Lucky was in the kitchen seeking a clean mug and popping a pod into the coffee maker. While waiting that minute for his morning joe to brew, he made the very instinctive decision that this was the day and time to make better acquaintances with Angie.

Cup of hot coffee in hand, Lucky stopped at Angie's door, leaning into the doorframe.

"How're you on giving tutorials?" he began.

"There's about a million ways a girl can answer that," she smiled. "And near most of 'em can get me laid or hung on harassment charges."

Lucky's ploy was his confusion in trying to cross-reference the department's new data system with the previous arcane paper archives. Angie happily agreed to walk him through it. So, Lucky rolled his desk chair across the corridor, slid it in behind Angie's, and settled in for some private education.

"Wait, wait. Show that to me again," Lucky asked, sneaking a pointed finger past Angie's shoulder, directing her eyes to the corner of the computer screen.

"Okay," Angie explained. "And why they didn't make this shit simpler is beyond me. There's the new archive here where we upload our work. Then there's the old archive—which has been uploaded into this secondary database. We can search one or the other, but never at the same time. At least not until they're done."

"Done with what?" asked Lucky.

"Done with the merge. Big brick shithouse they got on East Third. All the paper personnel files are still in there. Every investigation ever. Like, fifty years' worth. Least, what I was told."

"They done with the brick shithouse?"

"And everything that's in it. Got some no-dick one-man minion scanning one page at a time and uploading to digital. When it's all done, then we merge the old with the new." Angie turned to Lucky, interlocking all her fingers until they bumped, bumped, and bumped again in a blunt tease. "And then all this will finally come together."

Lucky ignored her obvious come-on. "So, until then," he attempted to conclude, "I'm gonna get two answers for every result. One from the new archive, one from the old, and the last one might not even be complete."

"Why they pay us to hate the light. We're all moles lookin' for our second coming." When Lucky feigned to miss the innuendo, she twisted her neck and whispered, "Meaning no penalty for a second dip of your wick."

"Right," relented Lucky. "You win."

"And what would that be?" she cooed.

"The most come-on lines inside two minutes."

"From me?" she pretended. "I may have to name you Butterfingers for all the dropped balls—"

"Lucky?" sounded a voice from behind.

Lucky spun his chair at the first syllable. Gonzo stood in the corridor, framed by both his and Angie's open office doors, his pinstriped wedding suit slung over her shoulder.

"Hey," said Lucky. "Was expecting—"

"Karrie," finished Gonzo, looking less at Lucky and more at Angie's flushed cheeks. "I was already at the tailor's. Plus, they got me on an extra shift."

"Oh," realized Lucky. "Angie Greenwald. This is Lydia Gonzalez."

"Fiancée," added Gonzo, pressing her lips into a toothless smile. "At least until Saturday."

Lucky didn't have to guess how Gonzo had made it past the basement's security. She was six feet and imposing. Add to that a slick LAPD aviator's jumpsuit topped by her wild spray of kinky black hair and Gonzo walked through most doors as if she already owned the room. The four-hundred-pound security guard stationed at the elevator hadn't a chance in hell once Gonzo added a gleaming smile to her Amazonian presentation.

"Givin' a tutorial," piped Angie. "And he forgot to introduce me as former PD."

"Sisterhood," joked Lucky.

"Pleasure to meet you," lied Gonzo. "Luck, I got, like, five minutes to see if this fits before I'm due at Hooper, so . . ."

Hooper was the heliport where the LAPD runs its Air Support Division. As the crow flies, it was less than a mile away. But downtown was generally an ugly snarl of vehicles, foot traffic, and construction delays. Lucky stood, saluted Angie for her assistance, then dutifully rolled his chair back across the corridor and into his office.

After giving one final smirk in Angie's direction, Gonzo made certain to shut Lucky's door a little more abruptly than necessary.

"Nice meeting you too," finished Angie.

11

Santa Susana Pass. 12:12 p.m.

The heat was almost unbearable. And that was despite the modern protective gear. Beemer had trained and fought fires while garbed in Kevlar from foot to the top of his skull. Yet even with all the pre-hydration, he'd never felt so baked. The midday sun was straight overhead and the constant rising hot air from the San Fernando Valley and Simi Valley met at the Santa Susana Pass in something akin to an earthen convection oven. The conditions not only fed the flames the crew was tasked to hold at bay, but made Beemer feel as if he were a piece of meat wrapped in foil cooking slowly until tender enough to consume. He continued to fight the desiccation, guzzling water at every chance.

The crew had been diverted to the Santa Susana Pass while en route to the fire in Porter Ranch. Just seven miles to the west, this latest blaze had started when a fatigued O-ring on a transmission tower built during Woodrow Wilson's presidency failed in the fifty-miles-per-hour winds that had screamed up the granite range during the night. Suddenly unrestrained, the high-voltage lines had whipped around in a frenzy, lashing against the metal tower and spraying molten aluminum across the dormant vegetation. The inferno was instantaneous.

Since dawn, the entire crew had been advancing up the same steep rocky ridgeline, gouging the earth with pickaxes and wood-handled McLeods. The McLeod tool was like a stiff tined rake on one side, a heavy hoe on the other. Cappy had even given them a history of the tool, which was invented in 1905 by Malcolm McLeod, a forest ranger based in the high Sierras. During training, Cappy had held his McLeod up over his head as if it were Excalibur itself, proclaiming that for over a hundred years firefighters had embraced that exact same tool to cut trail, rip firebreaks, and clear fuel from a fire's hungry mouth. Beemer recalled how heavy the tool felt upon his first handling. And so very rudimentary. As if the inventor was a mad dirt farmer. Yet, after hundreds of hours of practice, he'd come to marvel at its utility. So simple and efficient. He'd learned to clear three to four feet of firebreak in a single stroke. The repeated practice had hardened his core and upper body like nothing the Marine Corps had ever imagined.

Only now, that fearsome body was aching for relief and water.

The crew was trying urgently to cut off the advancing flames that, were Beemer to look up, appeared to be wholly consuming the mountain above him. The helicopter heroes—the yellow-suited regulars from Malibu's famed Fire Station 8—had flown in on Black Hawks and dropped onto the ridge nearly a half mile above them. Though theirs was an easier downhill trek, the mission was the same: build a break wide enough to keep the advancing fire from crossing the Ronald Reagan Freeway and endangering the suburban sprawl below.

Fucking suburbia.

Beemer didn't dare give it a look. Not once. Since daybreak when the sun had cleared the hills above Burbank, Beemer hadn't given in to the temptation to gaze across the San Fernando Valley behind him. It was suburban horizontalism at its evolutionary extreme. As he hacked and ripped at the earth, battling fatigue and heat, he knew that behind his back and below were almost two million people in their cozy air-conditioned homes—nearly a quarter of them with a backyard swimming pool filled with blue liquid cool. He tried not to fantasize. After all, that was something he couldn't have in a long list of couldn't haves. Like a frosty beer. Or money beyond the pennies paid by the state. Or weapons. Or the carnal love a woman.

Lucky Dey. He has all of those couldn't haves.

Beemer had been trying to purge all thoughts of Lucky. Yet his mind was flooded with everything he knew, most of which was courtesy of the thirty minutes of evening internet access he was allowed—a privilege allotted prisoners living in a fire camp. The entitlement was available as long as firefighting inmates weren't seeking pornography or interactions with other criminals. The trifecta of accessible camp computers had filters installed to prevent as much. With little effort, though, Beemer found free software to bypass the digital sanitizer with a program that even covered the tracks of his browsing history. Were the Department of Corrections to assign a computer forensic team to divine Beemer's internet footprints, they'd have come up with an almost singular, obsessive search.

Sheriff's Deputy Lucky Dey.

From what Beemer could gather, Lucky had earned a lot to lose, the most precious of which was his life, his liberty, and his family. While Beemer allowed his mind to wander from his immediate dirt-scraping task, he recalled one thing for sure that Lucky didn't have. And that was a cool, sweat-killing swimming pool.

"KEEP SKINNIN' IT!" sounded the inmate next to Beemer, passing along Cappy's orders from the top of the line.

Beemer knew the instruction well. Automatically, he widened his stance to get better leverage with his McLeod tool. He dug with the blade side, pulled the dirt loose, and flipped the tool over to the toothy rake, clearing away the wild flammable grass before hitting the repeat button in his brain. Cappy had often described making a firebreak as akin to skinning the world's most gargantuan elephant with a paring knife. Only the animal wasn't dead. It was merely asleep. One man in a race versus a slumbering beast.

The sound of his and the other convicts' tools laced with the scream of dueling chain saws and the kinetic scrapes of his fellow firefighters' boots underneath, had a musical rhythm to Beemer's ears. Calming, even. And his mind would, once again, wander.

Oh, the magic of the World Wide Web.

With a little know-how, Beemer had been able to follow Lucky Dey's dubious career and life trajectory. In the span of five years, he'd discovered Lucky's rejoining and subsequent retirement from the Los Angeles Sheriff's Department. The number of documented and suspected violent altercations that Deputy Dey had been a part of appeared almost legendary—at least, once Beemer had found ways to access the private bulletin boards populated by gossiping cops. Lucky's name had even shown up in a police-hating site run by Antifa SoCal, the local link to the supposedly anti-fascist group that, in Beemer's opinion, talked and behaved more like anarchists.

The internet had disclosed that Lucky had purchased a small house in Altadena with an LAPD aviator by the name of Lydia Gonzalez. Beemer couldn't count the number of times he'd wondered if she'd been with Lucky that fateful night. For sure there'd been a second cop. A woman. Tall. Imposing. But Beemer couldn't place the face he'd eventually dug up through the licensed aviator database.

Could it actually have been her?

When Beemer exercised the fantasy, there had been moments of fancy during fire training when he'd imagined burning them both alive inside their little antique bungalow.

"COMIN' ACROSS!" shouted Cappy from the top of the line.

"ACROSS THE LINE" was passed along from firefighter to firefighter until the warning landed on Beemer's ears. He held his

McLeod tool still, directing his perspective up and past the line. Perspiration steamed up his goggles. Yet the blur of an encroaching wall of flame roaring down the ridgeline was unmistakable.

A sudden wind gust of wind practically knocked Beemer off balance, followed by a wave of burning embers that surged and crashed overhead, jumping the carefully scraped firebreak and igniting the grasses on the southwestern side of the slope.

"LINE JUMP!" Beemer heard a fellow inmate squeal.

An over-the-top voice sounded. It was Cappy, barking like a throaty NFL quarterback who invoked just the correct frequency to cut through the roar of the crowd.

"HEAD FOR THE BLACK!" shouted Cappy. "TWO O'CLOCK! TWO O'CLOCK!"

Like a rogue wave, the wind-driven fire had curled over the top, setting the trees and brush behind the team aflame. Using the dial of an imaginary clock, with Cappy as the hour hand, Beemer and every orange-clad convict moved their view to the right and pictured what Cappy had ordered. Across eighty yards of gulch was a blackened hillside the fire had already consumed. There was safety where the flames couldn't reach. And the fire couldn't return to what had already been scorched to the dirt. Safety lay on the other side the chasm, a rocky-sided slash in the earth, thirty-five feet down in an artery of uncooked scrub oak and sagebrush and an unstable climb out.

But once across, there was certain safety in the black.

Beemer saw his convict brothers pitching themselves over the ridge and either sliding or foot-skating into the gulch. His instinct was to shuck his fire suit, just for speed's sake. Minus those forty pounds of safety Kevlar, Beemer imagined he could cover the distance in half the time. It was the training, though: *Never ever shake your suit.* One never knew when or what kind of flames a firefighter would have to battle next. No. The order was to head for the black and that's exactly what Beemer was going to do. No distractions.

No second-guessing.

Cappy says. And I do.

Using the McLeod tool as a crutch, Beemer pulled the handle into himself before pushing off with the toe of his boot. He could feel the small boulder beneath him holding his weight . . .

. . . until it didn't.

The heavy rock, he later guessed at eighty to one hundred pounds, had been lodged in the earth for how many millennia? In the moment, it was perhaps the strangest thought he'd ever had.

That rock underneath me had been jammed into that part of the mountain for ten thousand years before what? Moses and the burning bush?

The physics came to him instantaneously. Probably every single one of his fellow inmate firefighters working the line above him had been gouging the mountain. Each had passed the same boulder and stood upon it, compressing the nearby dirt and sand. Shifting matter. It all made such perfect sense in that frozen nanosecond before it happened.

The boulder gave way. Beemer tried to lunge ahead in hope of using his McLeod as a brake—like a mountaineer burying his ice ax into a glacier to stop himself from plummeting into a deadly crevasse. But the loosened rock acted like a wheel. As gravity pulled the rock downward, Beemer slid across the top and then underneath it. He caught a flash of dirty spinning granite as it brushed the bill of his helmet. It was gone in an eyeblink. His own tumble, though, had developed an energy unto itself, carried by his 190 pounds plus the weight of his fire suit. He flipped and hurtled backward, bouncing off sand and rock and patches of freshly burning grass.

He could only recall the rest of the fall in patches. There was sky. Smoke. Flame. Branches. Shale rock. In the end, he felt as if he were being vacuumed into the earth, propelled by gravity as thousands of sharp pebbles dragged him downward, boots first. When he finally stopped, his body felt like a cork sucked into a bottle. The mouth was twenty feet above with traces of dirt and rubble caving in, a slice for an opening that revealed shades of blue sky above and smoke beyond.

Beemer squinted, the pain of his fall staved off by the adrenaline still coursing through his veins. He was just beginning to assess himself when it was as if an invisible straw had been lowered into the gulch and Mother Nature was sucking all the oxygen from it. For the briefest moment, he thought he must be dead and mid-deliverance on his own journey into hell. Above, the wildfire was in a rage, inhaling everything in its path, including all of the oxygen. Beemer imagined he was about to be sucked into the yawning maw of Satan himself—to be burned alive for his life of sin.

12

Porter Ranch

"You mind showing me where your alarm box is?" asked the uniformed LAPD officer, a man with an affect so flat he appeared not to have a pulse.

"Forgive my attitude," elevated Bobby Bianchi, trying like hell—and miserably failing—to keep from sounding curt and entitled, "but I get robbed of my million-dollar collection and all I get is one cop?"

"It's the fires, sir," replied the uniform, a police officer so classically attractive Hollywood could have cast him as Superman's stunt double. "Usually, we answer burglary calls in pairs. It's a manpower thing—"

"I called more than six hours ago," complained Bobby, standing in his marble-floored foyer, chest out, gesturing broadly.

Nearly filling the front doorway was Bobby's brother, Peter.

Two years older, Peter Bianchi was half again heavier than his sibling, mostly in his unexercised middle. He was permanently bespectacled under a weak crop of curly black hair.

"Bobby," lamented Peter. "How 'bout you let the police officer do his job?"

"The alarm box?" reminded the uniform.

"Yeah, yeah," complied Bobby, leading a path to the closet under the stairwell.

Seconds after Peter had vacated the McMansion's threshold, Oren appeared on the doormat, energized with an odd kind of self-ebullience, the clear sky behind him showing no trace of the previous day's pyre. The Santa Anas had ushered his fire to the west and heroic first responders had saved the highly taxed homes of Tuscany Estates. Most importantly, Oren's gamble had worked.

"Helloooo?" called Oren. "Yo, Bob? It's Oren from across the street!"

"This way," Bobby called back from the deep center of the house.

Hands in the pockets of his cargo pants and swimming inside a severely faded UCLA football sweatshirt, Oren sauntered into the palace. He thought of whistling as a way of sounding nonchalant. At ease in Casa Bianchi.

And not the least bit guilty.

Oren knew that the alarm system's brain was located in a cupboardlike space hidden behind the paneling underneath the stairs. He'd already seen the LAPD patrol car parked outside and suspected that Bobby was showing the cop to his jimmied alarm system. Yet Oren attempted to behave as if he were somewhat lost in the home, looking in and out of every room off the primary corridor until Peter stuck his head around a corner.

"Back here," beckoned Peter.

"Pete!" Oren's face broadened in a surprised smile. "Where's the Super Pig?"

Super Pig was the name Peter had given his car, a vintage 1973 Lincoln Continental Mark IV. It was candy-apple red with a recently restored bone leather interior. "A big-assed car for a big-assed man," Peter would joke. What wasn't funny were California gasoline prices. The Lincoln's mammoth V8 engine sucked back one gallon of fuel for every seven city miles, a true air-polluting gas-guzzler. It had been in the Bianchi family since Bobby and Peter's grandfather had paid in cash and driven it off a Long Island car lot. Peter loved the car for that as well as its look and its road-hogging scale—not to mention that it was his middle finger to all the environmentalists.

"Super Pig's at the car doctor. As usual. I had to fit my wide ass into an Uber," replied Peter, switching back to the problem at hand. "Bobby had a break-in."

"You're shittin' me!" lied Oren, scurrying to join the impromptu grouping behind the stairwell. "Hey, Bobby. Everybody okay?"

"Everybody but me. Babs and the kids gettin' massages and shit at the Four Seasons. Meanwhile, it's all gone except for the neon."

"What's gone?" asked Oren in a fake, blithe repose.

"My Beatles collection," growled Bobby. "Every last piece."

Oren noted the uniformed cop directing his flashlight beam into the custom-built closet, carefully examining the exposed alarm system. He sincerely doubted the police officer had a clue as to what he was looking at, how the system operated, or how Oren had easily defeated it by simply disconnecting the phone line at the outdoor telecom box. By cutting the two tiny wires, the system was unable to send a signal to the security office. As for the external siren that rang when the alarm was tripped, Oren had already discreetly disconnected the speaker cable when Bobby had begged him for a free top-to-bottom insect inspection. The Bianchi house, as it turned out, was suffering an infestation of Argentinian ants.

"Pesky buggers. Hard as hell to eradicate," Oren had told Bobby more than a month before the actual burglary. "See. That genus of ant has more than one queen. So it's not like setting a coupla bait traps will kill the one colony."

Asking for free favors was Bobby's style. And he was fully

aware that his good neighbor Oren had once run a significant pest-control operation. Fifteen trucks. Sixty employees. That was, of course, before Oren began his downhill slide. It was because of a pony—a racehorse—an unlucky filly that had cursed poor Oren. Something he'd confessed to Bobby.

Yeah. It all came unraveled after that one evil bitch broke my back, along with everything else I thought I loved.

"What's important to me is the time of the alarm trip," insisted Bobby to the uniform cop, his finger indicating the time on the system's LCD screen. "And that was almost exactly the same time that hobby cop deputy prevented me from accessing my own goddamn house."

"Yessir. You already mentioned him," deadpanned the uniform as he used a cell phone to photograph the alarm system from various angles. "I'll put it in my report. But if he's L.A. Sheriff's, you need to direct your complaint to them."

"A fuckin' hobby cop!" repeated Bobby.

"You mean a reserve deputy," corrected the uniform as he re-holstered his phone. "Think that's just about it for now."

"You're not gonna dust for fingerprints?" complained Bobby. "And what about my trophy room? You haven't even looked at that!"

"Or the hole in his backyard," teased Peter.

"It's not a hole," corrected Bobby. "It's gonna be a sound bunker. Acoustically perfect. With room for my collection."

If the uniform cop appeared lost, Oren was happy to clarify.

"He's building a place to play his music, store his shit," Oren translated.

"There will be a case number," said the uniform, careful to keep his voice flat and unaffected. "It will get assigned to a detective team. They will contact you soon enough."

"So until then . . . what?" asked Bobby. "My house is some kinda crime scene? Don't touch a thing?"

"Your house is your house, sir," replied the uniform, ever so calm. "If the detectives think there's need to bring in a forensic team, then that's what will happen. I'm just your first contact, writing down what is pertinent to your burglary. Such as what is the estimated value of what was stolen?"

"No less than a million dollars," said Bobby. "Million and a half?"

"For your sake, sir, I hope it was insured." The uniform's body language was meant to inform Bobby that he was finished and would like to be walked out.

"You know, I been watching what you write," declared Bobby. "And how many times have I mentioned that sheriff's deputy? Three, four times now? Have you written that down? I even told you his name. L. Dey. It was on his goddamn name tag." Bobby was using an angry index finger, jabbing the place on his own chest where Lucky's sheriff's ID was pinned.

Peter had retreated to the open door of Bobby's trophy room. He was examining the empty shelves, hoping his thin smile was well disguised. How many times had he warned his brother about insuring his collectibles? Bobby, in turn, would always imply Peter had an ulterior motive. Peter just so happened to be a financial services manager. But Bobby insisted on calling his brother what he really was: a fancy-titled insurance salesman.

Sure, mused Peter. *Bobby mighta been right about that. But he still shoulda took my advice.*

"Bobby," interrupted Oren. "The good police officer clearly has other calls. Walk him out and let the detectives do their job."

"My house is a crime scene!" bellowed Bobby. "What am I supposed to do? Leave my family at the fuckin' Four Seasons at a thousand bucks a night?"

"Here's an idea," offered Oren, already certain of the answer. "You all can stay across the street with me. Big empty house. Plenty of room."

A sour look crossed Bobby's face. Oren knew that the idea of Bobby and his family staying over at the unfurnished McMansion across the cul-de-sac would never fly. *My family? In your shithole?* At least, that's how Oren read the look on Bobby's mug. He was impressed that Bobby, an adult man known for his lack of impulse control, had so far restraint enough to keep that opinion to himself.

"Nice of you to offer," resigned Bobby, almost winded. He let out a significant sigh.

"Hey," said Oren. "If you need a brief distraction, I'm dusting my crown molding. I got beer. Maybe you hold the ladder?"

"Like I don't have enough to worry about right here?" replied Bobby, showing his annoyance.

"I could use a beer," announced Peter, who remained at the threshold of the trophy room. "If all it costs me is holding a ladder, I'm your man."

"My brother," moaned Bobby. "The ultimate cheap date."

Oren and Peter strolled across the cul-de-sac. To the casual observer, the pair looked like a present-day Lennie and George from *Of Mice and Men*—the over-bloated beast of a man befriended by the human runt. When the uniformed police officer rolled out in his black-and-white and they heard the sound of the Bianchis's solid oak front door slamming closed behind them, Peter's shoulders automatically lowered. The big man released a long exhale, as if the greater the separation from his brother, the lower his blood pressure's systolic and diastolic numbers dropped.

It was always between 97 and 102 paces from the Bianchis's front door to Oren's. Oren knew because he always counted. Compared to the Bianchis's impressive polished oak door, Oren's was painted in a white semi-gloss, the factory bake job already beginning to chip and crack. Oren saw it as punishment for going Home Depot cheap on the home's finishing touches. All the windows were framed in extruded plastic instead of wood; the front door handle manufactured by Kwikset instead of Baldwin.

As Oren pushed inside, Peter followed and was instantly struck by the smell. Musty. Stale.

"Jesus," remarked Peter. "Open a damn window or something."

The house was dark, every drape and shutter closed. It left the downstairs in the dull navigable shadows of day. What furniture there was—sparsely dispersed throughout the open design—appeared suited for a vagrant. Each piece looked as if it had been left out on the side of the road or parked near a set of garbage cans in hope that somebody might want to rescue the item and save the discarder the cost of hauling it away.

"See you still haven't hired decorator," joked Peter.

"Why the hell would I?" grinned Oren, eyes igniting with some kind of crazed internal excitement. "The shit people leave behind. It's beyond amazing. It's a goddamn miracle."

"Leave-behinds," remembered Peter, or so he thought that was Oren's phrase.

"Called a come-across," corrected Oren. "Least that's what Beth named it whenever I'd stop the car. Shit I'd leave behind we called roadkill."

"Hard to believe your ex was into it."

"Oh, she hated it," confessed Oren. "Kids 'n' me came up with the roadkill part. They loved it like it was a game. Sweatshirt I'm wearin'? It's a come-across." Oren turned a proud 360, modeling the garment.

"That?" Peter's asked with disgust. "Found that on the side of a road?"

"Middle of the road. Route 150 'tween Ojai and Santa Paula. Family day trip. Saw it laying right on the stripe. So I slowed down, opened my door, and scooped it." Oren mimed the act, the memory leaving him with an impish grin. "Beth freaked. Like I'd picked up a dead skunk. But, hell. It was free. Stuffed it under my seat and washed it soon as we got home."

"No wonder why she left you," joked Peter.

Joke or otherwise, Peter was closer to the mark than he imagined. Oren's come-across game was a telling sign. The risky behavior Oren had picked up betting on horses had begun to infect his home life. The couple's therapist had put it quite simply: gambling addicts were hooked on their own adrenaline. Mixed with Oren's diagnosed OCD, it made for a dangerous cocktail. The come-across game was only a tiny piece of the ever-complicated puzzle. Not only did Oren have to stop the car to examine every discarded roadside item, but he'd even started a wager-of-the-day game with the kids. Winnings and losses were how he doled out their chores.

Oren was remarkably self-aware of his risky behaviors. He'd even signed up for a twelve-step program to help curb his impulses. At the first meeting, when it came his turn to share, he rattled off such a laundry list—from purposefully running red traffic lights to shoplifting from Best Buy to picking random fights with bikers—that the moderator suggested that if Oren wanted to die so badly, why not start having unprotected sex with IV-abusing hookers.

"You never know," Oren had quipped in reply.

As long as Oren's pest-control business was thriving and the family lived comfortably, his wife forgave his horse-racing addiction. But the fistfights were her last straw. Then came that one Friday when Oren returned home to an empty house. His wife had taken the kids and left without so much as leaving a note. Instead, she'd texted him after arriving at her destination. Phoenix. Her parents' home. After a night without sleep, Oren returned to the racetrack and wagered the entirety of the family's available savings on a single horse race.

The divorce was brutal. In the split, he was forced to sell his business. Including child support, Beth got everything but the house and the cash Oren needed to pay the property taxes for five years.

That was six years ago.

Peter swiveled, pointing at a faux Tiffany torch lamp.

"You got that on the side of the road?" asked Peter.

"Come-across," answered Oren proudly.

"What about the rug?" swiveled Peter, referring to a Persian-style rug centered in the living room.

"Come-across."

"The big screen?" pointed Peter.

"Come-across," grinned Oren. "Fell off the back of a truck,

cartwheeled into a dry ditch. Still in the box. Talk about being in the right place at the right time."

"Now, that stuffed Homer," nodded Peter at the life-sized Homer Simpson propped up in a corner chair. "That's gotta be a come-across."

"Thought the kids might dig it. Right? Had it double dry-cleaned and Beth still wouldn't let the kids get ten feet from it."

"You're one weird dude," expressed Peter, nearly impressed with the collection. He noted a wicker basket piled with worn baseball gloves dating back to the 1930s, plus two Louisville Slug-gers stuck into the leather pile like chopsticks in a bowl of sticky rice. "Come-across?"

"Naw. That all me. I collected for a bit. Legit. Like, Ebay."

"Like my brother."

"Different league."

"Speaking of Bobby . . ."

"You asking if I came across anything related to, say, the Beatles?" With one the baseball bats, Oren feigned a Charlie Chaplin–style jig.

"And by the looks of my brother's trophy room, you got *all* of it?"

"Every last lick of the lollipop," returned Oren. "Took me just under an hour and eight wheelbarrows. Prolly lost three pounds in sweat."

"And the cop?"

"Which one?"

"The one Bobby kept harping over. L. Dey or D. Dey . . ."

"No clue. But whoever he is, think maybe we owe him a piece for saving my ass?"

"Not a chance," chuckled Peter. "Well, maybe what comes from that fucking John Lennon record. Gave me the willies every time he stuck it in my face. He ever do that to you? With the Len-non album?"

"Yup."

"So?"

"So?" shrugged Oren.

"Can I see it?" clipped Peter.

"It's gone. I got it. All you need to know." Oren crossed his arms confidently over his chest. "Your turn."

"My turn what?"

"Bring the money, I give you the collection."

"The money . . ."

"Five hundred K. That's what you said. Half the value—"

"Of the collection," finished Peter. "Yeah, yeah. But I gotta line up the buyers first."

"Buyers?" Oren's face screwed into a question mark. "Our agreement was simple. I steal Bobby's collection. You pay me half a million—"

"Like I've got that in available cash? Jesus, we're partners on this—"

"Partners, my ass. This is transactional," spat Oren, gesturing with the bat in the direction of the Bianchi house. "And so far I've done all the work. The plotting. The timing. The goddamn *doing*. And you don't have the money?"

"Partners like this." Peter held up both his hands. "One piece at a time. I make contact with the buyer. We do the deal. I split the money with you. Over time—"

"Over time? Like, how much time?"

"Year. Maybe two."

"This is bullshit!"

"Hey!" angered Peter. "This started with me. Remember? Groundbreaking party? You were playing the 'Oh, poor me' card and we got to talkin' about Bobby's shit."

It had indeed started at a party. Bobby had thrown a big blowout complete with a huge backyard tent and a 1980s-themed cover band. It was all in celebration of breaking ground on the construction of his underground sound bunker. He even had the plans for his acoustically perfect listening space blown up and displayed for friends and family to ogle. Bobby had spent much of the night singling out neighbors to impress with private tours of his Beatles memorabilia. Oren's drunken lament had dovetailed nicely with Peter's loathing for his older brother—the gross wealth on display and a lifetime of never measuring up in the eyes of their aging father. The liquor flowed and a plot between the two men had begun to unfold.

"Shit's not even insured," Peter had laughed. "And *I'm* the family idiot?"

"Your little brother's a top-shelf a-hole," Oren had slurred. "Deserves what he gets."

Now that half the job was complete, Oren demanded his reward.

"All you've done?" complained Oren. "So far? Is talk, talk, and more talk. And *the talk* was that you would pay me five hundred thousand dollars if I were to steal—"

"I didn't say I had the money."

"You implied it!"

"Dude. The money will come! I promise!" glowered Peter. "But the only way we get paid is if I privately peddle the stuff."

"Yeaaaaah," moaned Oren. "But no."

"No what?"

"You find the half mil. Then I turn over the collection."

"Did you hear me? I don't have the money."

"Then find it."

"Where?" Peter offered an overwrought shrug.

"Get it from your daddy?"

"You *don't* wanna go there. Believe me—"

"Impasse," interrupted Oren. "We're not getting anywhere. So, you need to leave."

"Leave? Now?"

"Go figure out how to get me paid. I don't give a shit how."

The big man froze, his girth finding an odd balance. There came a shift in the air.

"I walk out that door?" pointed Peter. "Without first seeing the stuff and picking out a piece which I can use to tease a buyer?"

"Yeah?" goaded the much smaller Oren.

"Swear to Jesus," insisted Peter. "I will walk right back across the street and tell my brother that you just bragged to me about stealing his shit."

"Sure you will," dripped Oren, his sarcasm hardening like fresh-poured cement.

"Don't fuck with me," warned Peter. "And don't fuck with my family."

"Really?" pitched Oren. "Because that's what I thought I just did. WITH YOU!"

Peter Bianchi, fresh out of dialogue, let alone some kind of witty reply, pivoted. His bulk seemed to move a fraction behind his intention. The sound of his trousers made a rubbing hiss.

"Come back with half a million dollars," shot Oren.

"Comin' back with my little brother," called Peter. "He'll probably pay me a finder's fee—"

Peter never finished the sentence. His words ceased the millisecond Oren's vintage Louisville Slugger connected with the soft spot in the skull above his right ear. It was a perfect strike. The unleashed foot pounds of energy hidden beneath Oren's come-across sweatshirt transferred fivefold to the business end of the baseball bat. Peter's head caved, his neck muscles wrenched in reverse spasm, all while his legs lost their motor. The room shook as Peter's body slapped the floorboards before releasing a slow wheeze of air.

Oren rotated around the nearly dead carcass, prepared to deliver a finishing blow. Peter had to be brain-dead, or nearly so, figured Oren. His eyes were half open and fixed, blood bubbling from his mouth after every slowing breath, arms limp to his sides, his unmarried ring finger involuntarily twitching.

Lowering himself into a cross-legged sitting position, baseball bat across his lap, Oren gazed for a bit as Peter's life was leaving him. He checked his watch, then made a bet with himself.

Six minutes. That's the over/under on when this asshole stops breathing. But which side should I bet? The over? The under?

Or the exacta?

The exacta would have been a bet that Peter's last release of air would come at six minutes. Exactly. If it were a horse race, the odds would have been astronomical. And hitting the mark would be an adrenaline boost worth more than any payout.

"Let's go for it," agreed Oren with himself as he began to count down those six minutes. "C'mon. Hang in there, you prick. Need you to die right on my number."

Meanwhile, the second hand on Oren's watch swept in tiny clicks. *5:43 . . . 5:42 . . . 5:41 . . .*

13

Canoga Park. 3:31 p.m.

The nearer the sun came to dipping below the horizon that was Agoura Hills—the San Fernando Valley's westernmost perimeter—the greater the velocity of those hell-breathing gusts known as the Santa Ana winds. The fires across the north side of the Valley hadn't yet come close to even partial containment and turned the sky into a dirty blanket of smoke filtering the slowly setting sun. The color spectrum bled from red to a glowing burnt orange— spectacular, in an almost end-of-days omen.

And Lucky was heading dead into it.

It was his preference, if given the extra time, to drive at gutter level. If he could afford to leave early for a destination, he'd travel via surface streets. In a decade that seemed all about peoples' safe spaces, Lucky found his when cruising the asphalt in a Ford Crown Victoria sedan, be it his old '99 or even the rickety, stripped-down black-and-white currently supplied by the sheriff's motor pool. Lucky found navigating the streets and boulevards that intersected the seemingly endless city sprawl—instead of traveling the mostly elevated freeways—somehow grounding. In doing so, he felt connected to the city. He could feel the comfort of it slow his heart rate to under sixty beats per minute.

The eighty-foot-tall palm trees that lined Sherman Way looked perfect in their silhouetted imperfection. Too tall to safely trim, their beards shimmied and their trunks bent at differing angles with each gust.

Sherman Way, man. Did I pick this strip on purpose? wondered Lucky.

The afternoon had been a sketchy blur. The short morning sleep. The discovery that his coworker Angie Greenwald had for some unknown reason been spying on him, followed by his effort to shift gears into office flirting mode in an attempt to discover why she'd skulked through his recent database searches. Then getting caught at it by his soon-to-be wife, who'd come to deliver his wedding suit. Once behind his office door, no argument had ensued between Lucky and Gonzo. But the chill in the air was unmistakable. Gonzo wasn't known to show her jealous bones. Over the on-again/off-again relationship, she'd always been blunt, something Lucky adored about her. There had been a few indiscretions. And those that had surfaced had been dealt with in relative calm. But that morning had been different. Lucky could tell the pretend closeness she had witnessed between him and Angie had left Gonzo shaken. She had parted with a single perfunctory question.

"You still wanna do this?" she'd asked.

"The wedding?" he'd replied. "Hell yeah."

Then she was gone, headed back to her helicopter as Lucky returned to an hour or two more at his desk job investigating city personnel. Only the personnel he was checking out was that musclehead he'd had a run-in with up in Porter Ranch. Bianchi. Bobby Bianchi. Or, as his driver's license read, Robert Salvatore

Bianchi. The city database had given up little on the Audi driver. The best Lucky could surmise from further searches on the internet and social media was that Bobby Bianchi was independently wealthy or some kind of trust funder—a member of the check-of-the-month club.

Or Lucky Sperm Society, Lucky had quipped to himself.

Bobby Bianchi was a married father of two. He had an older brother named Peter, who, according to public records, worked as an insurance salesman and lived in a Valley neighborhood called Lake Balboa in a modest-sized condo, the deed of which had been a direct transfer from Peter and Bobby's father, Joseph Bianchi.

And that's where it turned into interesting reading. The city's private database had vomited up a bounty of valuable information on the thrice-married patriarch. Joseph Bianchi was a Brooklyn-born suspected member of the Gambino crime family. He'd moved to Los Angeles in the late 1970s to oversee the books on the mob's various interests in the pornographic business. In the go-go seventies, the golden era of "porno chic," the adult film industry had settled into the sleepy San Fernando Valley for some simple obvious reasons: the weather; the abundance of motion picture equipment, muscle, and filmmaking know-how; and the constant influx of beautiful actresses prepared to lower the bar of their cinematic ambitions.

And that east-west stripe called Sherman Way?

As the porn business—along with all the cash that came after it—metastasized into the Valley's north end, Sherman Way became the Sunset Strip of the XXX world with restaurants, discotheques, and adult film and fetish shops.

Swinging a tight right onto Winnetka Boulevard, Lucky added things up. Bobby Bianchi and his bad attitude bore all the symptoms of an entitled child used to getting things his way. Fires were raging. Bobby Bianchi's hearth and home were threatened. And their brief tussle during the neighborhood evacuation should have been long forgotten. Lucky had to ask himself why he even cared.

Instinct, he answered. *Hairs on the back of my neck.*

The residual gnawing in Lucky's gut, informed by his inner tuning fork, had set off his bad-guy alarm. Over his career, Lucky's trust in that tuning fork had served him well and saved his and others' lives.

Yet the tuning fork wasn't *always* correct.

With the brushfires in the Santa Susana Mountains still unchecked, Lucky chose to backburner Bobby Bianchi and get his mind back on the job. The cop job.

Okay, asshole, Lucky corrected. *The reserved deputy job.*

His assigned neighborhood for the night was Chatsworth, where the suburbs abutted the hills and rock formations familiar to fans of old Hollywood westerns. One of the brushfires, now officially named the Indian Springs Fire by the powers that be at Cal Fire, had jumped the Ronald Reagan Freeway at the Santa Susana Pass, the two-mile-long link between the San Fernando and Simi Valleys. For Lucky, what lay ahead was the same as the previous evening: offering last warning to citizens and perhaps rescuing terrified dogs. And what were the odds that he'd run into another putty-brained ox like Bobby B.?

Likely as hell.

Too bad for Lucky those prophylactic tabs of Benadryl didn't offer protection from asshats.

14

The air had equalized. The flames had passed. But for just how long Beemer had held his breath, he didn't know. During MARSOC, the Marines Special Forces training, a group of Beemer's pals had wanted to see if they could beat the Navy SEALs' test of holding their breath underwater. They made a competition pool for a few dollars—just a single $20 bill per jarhead. But mostly it was, as one Marine put it, "for shits and giggles." After a few weeks of practice, Beemer had been able to dip his head underwater and survive without oxygen for just over two minutes, well within the SEALs' requirement. He'd pocketed $160 and left that game behind.

When the rush of fire had passed over the crack in the earth into which Beemer had slipped, he had automatically inhaled what last breath he could manage and put a cork in his lungs. He held his air, feeling as if the heat from the fire overhead might burn his hair and melt the skin on his skullcap all the way to the bone. By the time the fire passed, Beemer had begun to breathe without any memory as to just when he'd released the air trapped in his chest. He tugged off a glove and touched the top of his head. His scalp was dry and only the tips of his russet brown hairs felt singed.

Now the mouth overhead revealed only wisps of smoke, beyond which was perhaps the bluest sky Beemer had ever witnessed. Clean. The lighter side of azure. And with that view, hope returned. He was alive. In a brief check of his limbs, nothing felt broken. There was a tenderness in his left thorax. Bruising, for sure. Possibly a cracked rib or two. Only with an X-ray, and perhaps in the hours ahead, would he know for sure.

After examining the fissures in the surrounding sand and rock walls, Beemer saw his escape as somewhere between extremely difficult and impossible. Tripping back through his mental training files, he recalled the protocol if a firefighter got lost from his group. First, there'd be a count, meaning someone must know he was missing. That would mean a search and Beemer could assist his own rescue by calling out. So he did just that.

"HEYYYY!" he screamed. "HELLLLPPPP!"

His side ached with every bellow. Yet he carried on. Ticking down to the minute, then repeating his volumed plea for rescue until he was hoarse. Nobody came. And the sky was fading into streaks of red smoke against denim blue. The sun was setting. Darkness neared.

They have to be looking for me, he hoped over and over again. For both civilian fire teams and convict teams, the head count was paramount. Time after time, he'd heard Cappy shout out a loud "Count it off" and in order, crew members would bark back their assigned numbers. A missing digit meant a man was down, injured, or left behind. This was when the crew would instantly swivel from a firefighting stand to a rescue effort. It was ingrained. So, what was it about him that they had left him behind?

By Beemer's estimate, he'd been in that earth crack for three-plus hours without even a peep from his crew of inmates. That, and nobody but nobody had responded to his minute-on-the-minute shouts for help.

A thought flashed. It was the very recent memory of Cappy ordering the team across the brushy ravine and into the black beyond. They'd all been ordered to the safety of the freshly scorched slope on the other side after the fire had jumped the line and was in danger of reversing on them from behind. All of them had begun a mad rush down into the ravine. But Beemer had erred. Pushing off and slipping backwards, he had tumbled backward into the hidden fissure. Beemer pictured what might have happened. Could it be that his convict fire team, led by their faithful, Jesus-loving Cappy, crashed into a ravine choked with brush oak and manzanita? Prevailing gusts of air were known to join forces with a massive brushfire and create their own winds, about-facing in direction and sometimes creating vortexes known as fire tornados. YouTube was chock-full of such videos and Beemer and his team had been strongly encouraged to watch as many as possible to better educate themselves on fire behavior.

Had there been a vortex? If a fire tornado had formed in that ravine, Cappy and the rest of the fire team would have been consumed in a flash. Some would be dead. Perhaps all. Beemer might have been left behind because he was the only one able or even alive.

Aw, fuck.

Another life moment in the miles of life moments Beemer had long ago named his *"aw, fuck* moments." Most of these had been performed by the alter ego he called his inner idiot. Adding up all those *aw, fuck* moments, each had proved to be a stupid error that generally served as a trajectory-altering pivot on Beemer's learning curve of existence.

I lost my cool.

I lost my footing.

And it may have saved my life?

The mouth of the fissure had lost all color, leaving only a black lens where there had once been sky. Beemer began plotting a way out that didn't involve a rescue rope with a pair of fellow firefighters pulling the opposite end. Dehydrated and weak, yet resolved to overcome the obstacle in front of him, he wriggled until each foot could feel a toehold. Next, he used his leg muscles to press his back against the opposite side of the fissure. Beemer spread his elbows wide, dug them into the cool dirt wall, and flexed himself an inch or two upward in a crab-like motion. He put one foot above the next and repeated the sequence. The pain in his left side turned into a searing pinch, like a knife sliding between his ribs.

Beemer somehow swallowed the howl he wanted to release and, with it, any conscious remnant of his inner idiot.

Push, crab, slide, repeat.

"And breathe, you pussy-ass motherfucker!" Beemer growled to himself.

15

Porter Ranch

It wasn't that Oren didn't have a single idea what to do with Peter's body. His problem was choosing one of his myriad options. Since the divorce, he'd added another addiction: true crime television. *Discovery ID. Dateline. 48 Hours.* His mind had become quickly flooded with variations, successful and otherwise, on the disposal of a human cadaver. From sinking it in the ocean to running it through a wood chipper to dissolving it in various acids: sulfuric, hydrofluoric, hydrochloric. Over the hours, he made a mental checklist and began crossing off schemes one by one in the same way he'd peruse a racing form, redlining the horses that didn't excite him.

Whatever he decided, he concluded he should begin in the basement. The first matter was to get Peter's 310-pound carcass rolled into that come-across faux-Persian rug. Oren maneuvered the rug next to the dead man and, using a cinderblock as a fulcrum, shoveled Peter one flip at a time until he was fully rolled up. The slickness of the wooden floors proved useful for phase two, which was dragging the body the forty-five feet to the basement stairwell. After that, the rest was about letting gravity do the work as the body thump, thump, thumped until it came to rest on the basement's concrete floor at last.

Oren's upper body ached from fatigue, lack of sleep, and fast-rolling those wheelbarrow loads of Bobby's Beatles collection, something he kept training his mind away from. *First things first*, he reminded himself. *Get rid of the body before figuring out what the hell to do with a panic room full of memorabilia.*

He quantified one thing for sure. He'd been lucky, a subject he was more than acquainted with. In winning a bet—and that was any sort of wager where chance was a factor—luck always played a part. And when luck happened, it swept in like a surfer riding a perfect wave. Peter's car, the vintage Lincoln he called Super Pig, was in the shop getting repaired. He'd taken a rideshare service to his brother's house that day, leaving Oren without a car problem. As in: *Once I figure out what to do with the body, at least I don't need to figure out what the hell to do about Peter's car.*

"The Baby-Raper," Oren said aloud with a heavy exhale, as Peter's body just came to rest at his feet. He fist-pumped with a resounding, echoing, "Yes!"

Peter and Oren had something else besides larceny in common: vintage vehicles. When Oren was forced to shutter his pest-control business, he'd kept the original 1990 Chevy panel van he'd first started with. It was white and rusted, his triple A AAAlpha Pest Control logo nearly faded from view. Every so often, when he'd park the van on the street outside their home, Beth would complain that it looked like the kind of vehicle a baby rapist would own. Thus came the name the Baby-Raper. The marriage was already crumbling, so his ex-wife's annoyance tickled

Oren. He'd even stretched the gag further by supergluing his collection of come-across action figures to the heap's dashboard.

Beth proclaimed that he was sick.

No shit, Sherlock.

Oren unrolled the body from the rug with the same shovel and cinderblock he'd used upstairs and fished through Peter's pockets until he came up with the dead man's cell phone. The battery was at 63 percent—long enough for Oren to execute his next move. With that life-sized stuffed Homer Simpson underarm, he scooped up the keys to the Baby-Raper, entered the garage through the kitchen, seat-belted Homer into the passenger seat, and fired up the engine. The time on the dash read 7:46 p.m. The sun had long set. It was Oren's bet that any surveillance or traffic cameras recording his route would reveal little more than a large heavy-set passenger to the driver's right. Paired with any recovered GPS tracking or cell tower data, it was going to appear that neighborly Oren had kindly driven the hapless Peter Bianchi back to his Lake Balboa condo.

And that's precisely what Oren did.

The drive itself took sixteen minutes. Concerned there might be some form of surveillance system at the condo complex, Oren picked a drop-off spot in a nearby alley under the cover of trees. After making sure the sight lines were empty, he set the brake on the van and unbuckled and tossed Homer Simpson into the darkened rear. Then, after wiping Peter's mobile phone of fingerprints and, he hoped, DNA, he tossed it out the window before accelerating and turning up the next side street.

Moments later, while idling at a Sherman Way stoplight, he attempted to refocus his thoughts back to the actual dead body in his basement and how he should dispose of it. That's when his scalp began to itch. His pores were opening, releasing an urgent, unconscious cascade of sweat. His body shook. His eyes filled with nervous moisture. With that, he found himself no longer focused on the red light, impatiently waiting for it to turn green. Instead he fixed on the three action figures glued to his dash. Batman. Yoda. Malibu Barbie.

His eyes settled on the lightsaber-wielding Yoda. The little green Star Wars character's voice sounded inside Oren's head:

"Powerful you have become. The dark side I sense in you."

"That's right, Master Yoda," claimed Oren. "I murdered a man today. So powerful I am."

16

*D*ownhill. That's what Beemer kept reminding himself. *Just keep it moving downhill.* He knew that eventually all trails would lead to a populated area. Subdivisions. Homes. Refuge. Inside one of those houses he hoped to find a change of clothes so he could jettison his neon orange inmate togs. Until then, he had to keep to the darkest ravines and steepest pitches. With the skies choked with smoke, there was no moonlight, just the increased electric gray ambience from the San Fernando Valley below. It made for nearly impossible footing as he relied on gravity and feel rather than actually recognizing what was sometimes directly in front of his face. Bloodied and scraped from trips and rock-eating stumbles, he could only hope to escape discovery. Twice he'd crossed dirt roads, slipping behind—and even once, between—fire trucks and yellow-jacketed crews. He kept his profile low to the ground, sometimes even snaking on his belly.

Eventually, the roads he met were covered in the asphalt of civilization. Beemer stuck to the ditches and brush where he could find cover until he came upon fifty-plus feet of steep sandy slope. Below was a tiny stucco house with a red-tiled roof. In the rear yard was an aboveground pool, circa 1958, empty, having long ago leaked its final chlorinated drop.

Patience, reminded Beemer. *Don't pick the first stupid house.* But the longer he crouched and watched, the more convinced he grew that whoever lived in the dwelling either had been evacuated or simply wasn't home. He looked past the rooftop and spied other houses. Equally empty? The neighborhood's streetlamps appeared void of electricity, a certain signal of a forced power outage, most likely caused by someone at the local utility flipping a switch as a safety precaution. A mile above, the brushfire raged unabated.

Sore and with particles of dirt congealing in every coagulating cut, Beemer slid feet first down the slant, his body and boots ripping open a hillside scar in the recently planted ground cover. At the bottom, he trained his ears for audible signs of life. He heard only the Santa Ana winds gusting above and the faint wail of a single siren.

This is the house, he decided.

He chose to gently try the lock on the sliding door to a bedroom. After a couple of vertical jiggles, the tiny latch released and the door eased left as if the channel had been greased recently. In the utterly opaque dark, the convict wandered forward, arms outstretched, and bumped into an empty bed. Neatly made. It informed Beemer that the owner—or tenant—was no slob.

Beemer sat on the bed and listened again.

He waited for his heart rate to slow and his hands to stop their constant quivering. Then, in the top nightstand drawer he fished for a flashlight, lighter, or box of matches, only coming up with what felt like papers, pens, and a heavy, soft-covered Bible.

His fingertips traced the embossed cross on the cover. *Greek?* he wondered. With one last sweep of the drawer, he came up with something plastic and oddly bendable, like a snake with two heads. That's when it hit him. He waved an arm over the nightstand and along the wall above the headboard. There was no lamp. No light source for reading. Fiddling with the plastic two-headed snake, Beemer discovered a tiny switch. He hoped and flicked. And snap, an LED bulb ignited, revealing the device to be a book light with a flexible neck.

Bingo.

He stood and turned in place so he could examine his surroundings. The room was smaller than he imagined, plain, undecorated but for a single framed praying Jesus near the bedroom entry. He moved to the louvered closet, folded the doors wide, and sighed in relief. He saw an equally neat array of clothing. Man-sized. Large. Flannel shirts. Denim. Worn, but clean. Everything hung on wire hangers. The wardrobe of an older working man.

I need a shower. Clean this shit off.

In the cramped bathroom, Beemer stripped and examined himself in the mirror. His face was red, dirt-stained, and so awfully scraped that his features were nearly beyond his own recognition. The mirror began to steam, so he carefully stepped into the tub, pulled the shower curtain closed, and placed his head under the stream, all the while thanking fate—or whatever divine presence had delivered him—as he let the hot water scour every pore, scratch, gash, and laceration. What didn't sting under the scrub of soap and water simply ached. His entire body was bruised. That, and he more than suspected a few of his ribs were cracked. He decided his next chore must be to rummage for painkillers. Ibuprofen, Tylenol, or . . .

. . . prescription painkillers. Even better.

Then he heard it. A vibration. Staccato. He twisted the double valves until the water was only a drip.

Thump, thump, thump.

The surprise sound of knocking cut through the uninsulated

walls of Sheetrock and studding until it echoed inside the curtained shower. For a split second, Beemer thought it was the bathroom door, then he remembered that he'd purposefully propped it wide open with that Greek Bible.

Thump, thump, thump.

It was the front door because it had to be. Somebody was pounding a fist onto it. Dull. Powerful. *Of course*, Beemer reasoned. *There was no juice to power a doorbell. If this stupid shack even has a doorbell!*

"SHERIFF'S DEPARTMENT!" shouted a muffled voice. The deputy at the door was clearly male. There followed a brief pause, then even more pounding, and the deputy's affectless voice, "LOS ANGELES SHERIFF'S. C'MON. MANDATORY EVACUATION. SAW YOUR FLASHLIGHT MOVIN' 'ROUND SO I KNOW YOU'RE IN THERE."

THUMP, THUMP, THUMP, THUMP!

Beemer's eyes slammed shut. He mouthed a numb "Fuck me" before pushing the shower curtain wide.

"I'M IN THE SHOWER!" Beemer bellowed back—the expansion of air into his lungs and its expulsion in loud words created an unexpected pain. His sore ribs screamed. He found himself unconsciously gathering the shower curtain in his grip until some of the plastic grommets snapped at the pole. Beemer gathered himself and inhaled slowly before releasing another agonizing missive, "BE RIGHT THERE."

Damning the pain in his rib cage, Beemer breathed and reasoned to himself.

He's not here for me.

He's here because I live here.

He only wants me to evacuate.

Beemer plucked a fresh towel from the single shelf above the toilet, wrapped it around his waist, and thanked the stars that the house was so small, otherwise he might not have been able to find a path to the front door. He picked his dirtied, convict-orange fire suit off the floor and packed it into as tight a ball as he could.

The living room was equally as small and austere as the bedroom and curtained with flimsy fabric that filtered the headlamps from the sheriff's radio car. The fireplace was open. No screen or glass door. So he crouched and shoved his bundled clothes up the flue as far as he could reach.

Thump, thump . . .

"Yeah. Coming!" announced Beemer, mere feet from the door, scouring for a weapon . . . anything. "Did you hear I was in the shower?"

"Did you hear this neighborhood is under mandatory evacuation?" sounded the deputy.

"Hang on. I'm naked!"

Left of a brick-faced fireplace was a wrought-iron set of fireplace tools. Beemer crept over, carefully withdrew the heavy poker from the stand, and bootlegged it to his thigh. He had no plan to use it. He had zero compulsion to kill a police officer. Yet, if it came down to a "him or me?" circumstance, Beemer had every intent to make it the cop's *aw, fuck* moment instead of his own.

Beemer twisted the deadbolt latch slowly until he felt it release. He turned the knob and cracked the door inward about fifteen inches. Standing before Beemer was the silhouette of a man, six feet and athletic, a rim of light edging a tightly buzzed head of hair.

Then he heard a simple click-clack.

Beemer was instantly blinded by the deputy's tactical flashlight. It was aimed head high and directed to penetrate the convict's corneas. But in the same nanosecond he squinted and brought his left arm up to shield his eyes, Beemer experienced a flash of recognition. Something about the cop at the door. His posture. Height. The curve of the dome of his buzzed scalp.

Couldn't be him, flashed Beemer.

The odds would have been astronomical, like drawing all six Powerball numbers with a $2 lottery ticket. Then again, winners happen. *So why not me?*

In that micro moment, Beemer's survival mechanism flicked into full alarm.

Fight or flight? his adrenalized amygdala screamed.

In his life as a Special Forces Marine, Beemer had learned that his primal response was the former. *Fight, not flight.* Kill over not be killed.

"You okay, sir?" asked the deputy. "What happened to your face?"

"My face?" asked Beemer, if only for an extra beat of his heart.

"You have an accident?"

"Mountain biking," lied Beemer. "Wanted to get a closer look at the fires."

"Well, it's cuzza the fires that I strongly suggest you evacuate until—"

Beemer didn't wait for the cop's sentence to conclude. As he pushed the door wide and began to cock the poker, the towel around his hips lost its grip, dropping to the threshold and leaving Beemer fully naked and exposed. Though it was entirely unplanned, the accidental act proved quite a fortuitous distraction and caught the deputy by complete and shocking surprise.

17

“Suspected prowler in backyard. Residents locked themselves in the bathroom . . .”

In Los Angeles, the second-by-second dispatch of urgent radio calls floated across a variety of channels. There were different frequencies for different jurisdictions, territories, and law enforcement agencies. Police helicopter pilots, be they LAPD Air Support or Sheriff's Air Ops, had the option to either micro- or macro-monitor their calls—ergo they could switch to a local channel while assisting just a few units on the ground or choose to funnel all emergency calls through a single port.

Gonzo called it the Fat Band.

“All units, gunshots reported. Alameda and East Compton . . .”

Tuning into the Fat Band was Gonzo's preference when not backing up cops on the ground with her cornucopia of surveillance equipment, the toys afforded her and her newest helo-mate, Tactical Flight Observer Eric Golder. The Fat Band, pumped into Gonzo's rotor noise–cancelling crash helmet, allowed her to comb through the calls, picking and choosing where she could best supply that special brand of aviator aid.

"Woman reports husband breaking restraining order. Standing in driveway with a butcher knife . . ."

The Fat Band was a nonstop, never-ending cacophony of pleas for help. Such a wall-to-wall assault on Gonzo's ears might have driven her crazy if she weren't hovering above it all. The cushion of air between the chopper's skids and the Earth's surface acted as a buffer between the pain below and the serenity above.

"Pursuit in progress. Blue-green Dodge Caravan, northbound 110 at Imperial . . ."

From her five-thousand-foot altitude, Gonzo noted that the greater Los Angeles region took on a number of different appearances at night. On some evenings and early morns, L.A. appeared as an endless blanket of Christmas lights. Ceaseless. Aglow. Plugged in as if to blithely abuse the power grid from dusk to dawn. And then there were other nights when a gauzy marine layer of clouds pushed in from the ocean, reversing the perspective to something more akin to peering at some distant galaxy through the light-gathering lens of an astronomical telescope. But mostly, at least of late, Gonzo had come to see the city as Lucky described it: like a living, breathing beast. The freeways, for example, with the headlights and taillights always moving in organized opposite directions, acted like arteries and veins delivering blood cells to and from a heart. The neighborhoods and small incorporated cities were the vital organs. The millions of miles of concrete were the bones and the hilly ground formations and surrounding mountains were some kind of hard worn scar tissue. The rest of it was gift wrapping, call it skin or clothing or stylish fashion, all there to disguise the city from the darkness boiling up from the inside.

And tonight, the beast was aflame. Gonzo counted seven fires. Five to the north, one to the southeast wicking along the low hills of Orange County's Yorba Linda, and now a new blaze eastward in Chino Hills. All evening long, she'd unconsciously kept her eye to the distant San Fernando Valley, where Lucky had been deployed to evacuate the homes in Chatsworth threatened by the Indian Springs Fire, the largest and most unpredictable of the bunch.

"Code 3! Deputy needs assistance!"

Gonzo's ears were piqued, as were those of probably every officer within radio range. An emergency call from a police officer in trouble was a straight gunshot to the nervous system of any cop who bled the color blue.

"1944 Crestview, Chats—"

"Chatsworth!" Gonzo finished without thinking. Before her thought was even complete, she had banked the aircraft to the right, feathering the pedals into a practiced but very hard turn. The whole cabin bucked on a pocket of warm rising air.

"What the hell you doing?" piped Golder.

"You heard it," replied Gonzo. "Lucky's working Chatsworth!"

"And we're working the lower forty!" reminded Golder. "Let the Valley boys handle it."

"It's Lucky!"

"He's not the only deputy up there! We can't just abandon our patrol sector!"

Gonzo's eyes briefly rolled backward, revealing the quick glaze of tears she was holding back. Golder was not only correct, but smart to use a semi-hardened tone to snap her out of whatever worry she'd been chewing over. Reversing the helo's trajectory, Gonzo maneuvered left, this time in a slow, calm about-face until her windshield was filled with the terminals and container cranes of the Los Angeles Harbor.

"You wanna talk about it?" suggested Golder.

"No," snapped Gonzo.

Like hell I wanna talk to anybody about it.

It had been weeks of grinding. Since they'd set the wedding date, Gonzo's generally stoic pose had been imperceptibly crumbling to nearly everybody but herself. She felt as if her insides were slowly caving in with worry. She'd been through so much with Lucky. *Correction*, she thought. *They* had been through so much. The breakups. The violence, both on the job and the kind of danger that sometimes followed Lucky home. The inquiries and injuries. It had been a roller coaster of in love and out of love, with a guarantee that nearly every upswing would be followed by a nerve-jangling twist.

Gonzo shook out her right arm, guiding the stick with her left until the soreness in her reconstructed elbow eased. She breathed in counts of four.

Inhale, one, two, three, four.

Exhale, one, two, three, four.

If asked, Gonzo would have generally called herself an optimist, a cup half-full kinda gal. But she was cautious as well. *Maybe a bit too cautious*, she'd often wonder. Now, her fear was akin to the other shoe dropping. As she closed on the wedding day, casual though the plan was, her scraping gut was telling her that someway, somehow, the shit would hit the fan. That's what it was like living in Luckyland. With him, the shit *always* seemed to hit the fan.

It was the first Wednesday night of the new year. Saturday was beckoning. And beyond the smoke and ash, something ominous was in the air. It haunted her. Chilled her. She one-handed the stick and reached into her breast pocket for her cell phone with the other. She speed-dialed Lucky and hoped to Christ he would answer.

18

Chatsworth

Lucky had been weighing his contrasting assignments. The night before, he'd been playing cleanup for the LAPD, knocking on the doors of those million-dollar-plus McMansions in Porter Ranch's Tuscany Estates, urging those who'd chosen to ignore the evacuation order to heed the warnings.

That was Tuesday.

Wednesday's orders for the Sheriff's reservist and his junkyard black-and-white Crown Vic were to perform the exact same community service—this time at the northwestern edges of Chatsworth. And what a difference a night made. The hodgepodge of pre–World War II *ranchitos* and 1970 remodels were a far cry from the private gated community of Tuscany Estates. The asphalt on the streets was terribly cracked and potholed. Nary a civic thought had been given to installing sidewalks. It was a corner zip code of depressed property values. And though equally in danger of becoming engulfed by the nearing brushfires, Lucky knew the truth behind Cal Fire's prioritizing algorithm. In cases of stressed or thinned-out equipment and fire crews, attention would be diverted to the higher-value neighborhoods. Tax rolls set the pecking order. Wealthier suburban tracts before trailer parks, McMansions in lieu of the Chatsworth shantytown.

Lucky had once again chosen to patrol the grid by placing his efforts on the streets and dwellings nearest the knolls and rocky faces chock-full of fresh dry fuel for the oncoming fire. Block after block, he'd turn his wheels uphill and start at the homes with backyards bordering the brushland. Thusly, he'd arrived at an aging stucco cottage. What had probably once been an adorable bungalow for a blue-collar migrant family had been left to such disrepair that long horizontal and vertical cracks appeared like jagged ruptures through the faded façade. The posts supporting the modest front portico hadn't seen new paint in decades. Yet the yard boasted that the owner or tenant possessed some measure of residential pride. The weeds that were once a front lawn had been mown down to a manicured length and the short grove of succulents that fronted the domicile were tended in a chalky base of painted lava rock.

According to the Department of Water and Power, the neighborhood had only lost power within the last hour. Lucky lit up the house with the Crown Vic's high beams. Before making his approach, he recorded the address on a yellow scratch pad. He regarded the house. For a cop, the immediate danger of knocking on strange front doors was second only to that of traffic stops. Experience had taught Lucky well enough. *Wait. Observe. Plot your approach.*

He shouldered the car door open, but before his foot touched the pavement, his radio sizzled, "Code 3, Code 3! In a . . . fight!"

Lucky stalled. Code 3 meant an immediate and urgent emergency. Over the open mic he heard the sounds of a scuffle, the unidentified officer's voice in a panic.

"1944 Crestview, Chats—!"

Flashing to an address on the adjacent street grid, Lucky fell back behind the wheel. He'd jacked the transmission into reverse before his door had even closed.

"Naked . . . Male . . . White . . ."

The sounds of a beating spat through the thin radio speaker. It was furious, the officer squealing for assistance. And then as fast as it had begun, there was only that familiar hiss of an empty radio signal, interrupted every few seconds by a wordless, deathly cough or gurgle.

The grille of Lucky's derelict black-and-white ate up the road. Grateful that at least the lights and siren worked, he damned the potholes and hoped to hell the chassis and over-tired shock absorbers could withstand the punishment. The speedometer ticked past seventy. And at a rise separating neighborhoods, that past-its-prime radio unit became briefly airborne, bottoming out with a spray of sparks. It continued its surge downhill while Lucky ticked off the street names like some kind of countdown.

Wadsley.

McKinley.

Hopper.

Peach Tree.

Gladice.

Crestview . . .

Lucky braked the black-and-white, charted a left-turn sweep that threatened to separate the rubber from the wheels, then hammered the engine up a rising slope until he saw a human figure heaped at the turn in the road. The headlamps closed on three distinct colors: the L.A. Sheriff's forest green and khaki— and the glistening red of blood. Beyond was a decrepit hovel bearing the emergency address.

He keyed his shoulder mic.

"Deputy down, deputy down!" called Lucky, his voice calm enough for clear communication. It felt like he was braking, parking, and vaulting from his radio car in a single motion. "1944

Crestview! Deputy's radio car nowhere in sight! Assume vehicle stolen by armed suspect! Naked white male."

The unconscious deputy was almost fetal on his left side, his head and neck gouged beyond recognition. A sickly burble issued as his mouth foamed with a cocktail of pink fluid and saliva.

"Help's comin'," calmed Lucky, crouched over the downed deputy.

The victim's breathing was sporadic and labored. Blood was pooling, the thick spread widening toward the steel toes of Lucky's boots.

"Hang in there," begged Lucky.

The deputy's left arm, pinned under his head, was outstretched, forearm to open palm. As Lucky shifted on the balls of his feet, he reached for the deputy's right wrist in hope of finding a pulse. Only Lucky froze, unconsciously grabbed for his tac light, and thumb-clicked a close-up blast of hot white lumens. There was something odd painted on the deputy's wrist. Messy, but clearly distinct, having been drawn by the downed man's blood-covered left index finger, presently twitching in a death spasm.

Yet there it was, scribbled by the dying man in his own coagulating gore, his exposed left wrist as a canvas: the capital letter A contained in a crude but definitive circle.

Anarchy.

A chill cut through Lucky like a pair of cold invisible hands were closing deathly fingers around his neck. He's seen the artwork once before on the left wrist of man he'd long hoped was dead. That man's name was Greg Beem.

19

"**M**om's gonna be pissed. Just sayin'." Sixteen-year-old Travis was lazing in the BarcaLounger he'd recently rescued from a neighbor's garage. Gonzo had let him keep it with the caveat that he keep the musty chair in their own garage, a detached, single-car shed that Lucky and Karrie had recently converted into a home rehab gym.

"Don't you have a porn site to troll?" queried Karrie, her tone cutting between her heavy breaths.

"Five more," deadpanned Frosty, flicking a sideways glance at Karrie's adopted brother. Frosty stood over the weight bench, spotting Karrie as she pressed two twenty-pound dumbbells over her chest in an imaginary triangle.

"Don't get mad," said Travis. "I like Frosty—"

"Don't talk at him like he's not here," angered Karrie.

"I like you, Frosty," corrected Travis. "I really do."

"And I like you," smiled Frosty.

From Karrie's perspective, Frosty's ivory teeth and crooked smile were upside down with his deeply dark skin practically fading away in the garage space illuminated only by the streetlamp at the end of a hundred-plus-foot driveway. She loved his three-quarter grin. To her it revealed Frosty's character along with a hint of all the ugly history he'd overcome.

"Your funky smile matches mine now," Frosty had teased when he'd first visited her in physical rehab. Through her pain, through her struggle to relearn how to form certain words, as well as his dedication to physical therapy, she had come to love him.

"Just sayin'," repeated Travis.

"You already said that," moaned Karrie. "And when you say 'just sayin',' it's super redundant."

"No, it's not," argued Travis.

"Yes, it is," said Karrie, finishing her set and handing the weights off to Frosty. "You say something. Then you follow it by saying 'Just sayin',' like nobody was listening in the first place."

"Maybe you—"

"I heard you the first time!" Karrie sat up, toweling her face and arms. "And what Mom don't know is what Mom don't know."

"Said she didn't want Frosty in her house."

"And we're not *in* the house," gestured Karrie. "We're *in* the garage."

"Detached," added Frosty.

"Technicality," argued Travis.

"True," added Frosty before pointing his index finger down the driveway. "And your moms, she's got a point. Right over there's where it happened."

"Where my sis kicked your ass," laughed Travis.

"Best day of my life," grinned Frosty. "Was saved by Karrie, then Lucky, then Jesus that very day."

"Seriously, Travis," annoyed Karrie. "Go do your homework or something."

"All done," shrugged Travis.

"Take a hint!" Karrie swiveled on the bench, eyes burrowing Travis like any teenage sister aggravated by a younger brother's inflexibility.

Karrie's phone buzzed. Frosty snatched it off a shelf then waggled the screen.

"Ears was burnin'?" said Frosty.

"Shhh," said Karrie, aiming the message at Travis. She accepted the phone and answered. "Mom."

"Don't want you to be worried," began Gonzo, the heavy thumping of the helicopter rotors giving her voice a warbling effect. "Called your dad. He's working the fire above Chatsworth and he's not picking up. All I know is there's a cop down and—"

"It's not him," insisted Karrie.

"How do you know? He call you?"

"No. I just gotta believe it's not."

"I know, I know. But I'm working. And can't be dialing every deputy and his brother from five thousand feet. You mind checking in on him?"

"Yeah, yeah. We got this."

"We? Travis with you? He's got a history paper to finish."

"Not we. I will," Karrie corrected. "I got this. No worries. Call you soonest?"

"Thanks, sweetie."

"Saturday's gonna happen," assured Karrie. "We're gonna play 'Here Comes the Bride' and all that."

"Better not," Gonzo warned. "Call me."

The wah-wahing sound of Gonzo and her lofted helicopter cut off in Karrie's ear. Surrounded by silence, Karrie lowered the phone, feeling the tension from both Frosty and Travis, who'd unconsciously pulled his long legs up until his arms were wrapped insecurely around them.

"Wha's that about?" asked Frosty, noting the chill that had somehow been passed from Gonzo through countless cell towers, and through the speaker of Karrie's mobile phone. Karrie took a cleansing breath, exhaled, and nodded.

"Lucky," she said. "He's not calling her back so she's more worried than she should be."

"He's not answering his—"

Karrie cut off Travis with a stalling palm.

"Lucky's good. Just out of pocket," assured Karrie. "Wants me to pester him 'til he answers his stupid phone."

"I'll call Temple Street," Travis announced, as if he knew that by phoning up the Los Angeles Sheriff's downtown headquarters they'd have for him an instant, salient answer.

"You got a history paper." Karrie pointed at the house. "Her orders. Not mine."

"So, what you gonna do?" asked Frosty.

"You and me," repeated Karrie. "Mom's big day is Saturday. Our job is to ease her nerves. If we can't get him to answer his phone, we'll just have to get in his face."

Karrie slapped her thighs as if to cue her legs to straighten underneath her.

"Wanna stay home, babysit Travis?" offered Frosty. "I'll dig him up. Get Lucky found."

"It's like I caught her virus." Karrie shivered and shook her head no. "I wanna go. Shit, he'll call her back in five minutes and this'll all be just stinkin' thinkin'."

"Let's pray on it," said Frosty, gripping her hand and closing his eyes.

20

Chatsworth

There wasn't time to squeeze a thrill out of it. Beemer could see how some felons, given a split second, would have loved to have sat behind the wheel of a sheriff's black-and-white. The eight-cylinder beast roared in response to the simplest touch of the accelerator. But the truth was that, in the moment, it wasn't the least bit fun. Not even slightly amusing as Beemer ticked off the pertinent facts regarding the situation:

I'm an escaped convict.

I've assaulted a cop.

I've stolen a cop car.

I've left fingerprints and DNA in the house.

I have only minutes to make a move.

And I'm buck-assed naked.

He aimed the supercharged SUV downhill, knowing all the

while that his time behind the wheel of the showroom-polished black-and-white Ford Interceptor—equipped with a complete array of the latest crime-fighting hardware—had to be severely limited.

One minute? Two minutes?

At the first major boulevard, Beemer banged a hard right, his eyes scouring the landscape before locking on the first strip mall that came into view. Sandwiched between a Yum Yum Donuts and Ernie's Discount Liquor Mart was a neon-scripted sign reading *Laundromat*. Beemer swerved right, set the brake, and hopped out.

Cool, he told himself. *Walk like you belong. Like you were born to live naked and free.*

The laundromat was bright with happy hues of pink and blue pastels, shocking the night with a high-powered fluorescence that made the vented space appear as if it were vibrating. Once through the door, Beemer was assaulted by the hum of machines. The air smelled dry and choked with static. He kept on the move, never once stalling, aimed in the direction of a bank of double-stacked dryers. He chose a load that was spinning across from a soft, dark-skinned, middle-aged Hispanic man in secondhand clothes. The man was comfortably seated on a stackable green plastic garden chair and was reading *La Opinión*, the daily Spanish language newspaper favored by south-of-the-border immigrants, legal or otherwise.

"You!" Beemer snapped his fingers between the Hispanic man's reading glasses and the newsprint. "This yours?" With his opposite hand, Beemer rapped his knuckles on the spinning dryer.

The man looked over his lenses, first at Beemer's bare chest and hardened face, then his gaze lowered until the shock of Beemer's nakedness sent him stumbling to his feet. The plastic chair tipped.

"Yours?" pointed Beemer again at the dryer, chin aggressively jut forward.

"*¡Aléjate! ¡Estas desnuda!*" spat the old man.

"*¡Sé que estoy desnudo, viejo pedo!*" returned Beemer, no longer waiting for an answer. He spun, yanked open the upper dryer, and gathered up an armful of clothes before the barrel had finished turning.

"*¡Tus zapatos!*" demanded Beemer. "*¡Ahora! ¡O tal vez llama ICE!*"

At the shock of the word ICE—the acronym for the federal government's Immigration and Customs Enforcement—the man kicked off his sneakers and, after an uncomfortable pause, gently placed them atop the pile of almost-dry clothes in Beemer's arms.

Beemer damned the few other can't-believe-their-eyes customers and released a madman's howl—as if to cement in their brains that he was nothing more than another crazed homeless meth head. He followed by making haste for the fire exit door at the back of the laundromat.

The second Beemer busted into the alley, he heard the oncoming sirens. Multiple wails from multiple directions. He dropped the stack of clothes and chose a pair of dungarees and a blue and red soccer jersey from Mexico's most popular *futbol* team, silkscreened with the Chivas logo. He forced his wide feet into the sneakers, an uncomfortable size too small. Then, ignoring his pain, sore ribs, and aching and unnourished muscles, he dared a vault onto the six-foot cinderblock wall that separated the alley from a residential tract. He tumbled into a tree-covered backyard, hoped to hell for no run-ins with vicious or barking dogs, and listened for the telltale sounds of the practically inescapable police helicopter overhead. Beemer needed cover and he needed wheels. Quick, like. As he launched over one neighborly boundary after another, his mind was keen on what he could recall about stealing and hotwiring a car. Eighties- and early nineties-model Japanese cars. Hondas. Toyotas. Nissans. They were the most easily beaten. All he needed was a screwdriver.

Need to get me one of them. And fast.

21

Lucky's primary impulse was to cut the officious debrief short by excusing himself, retreat to his junkyard black-and-white, and begin his own one-man hunt for the cop killer. The poor deputy who'd knocked on the shack's door, only to be bum-rushed by God knows who wielding a fireplace poker, was a West Valley burglary detective who hadn't worn a uniform, let alone seen the inside of a sheriff's black-and-white for nearly eight years. Yet, in his final moments of consciousness, he'd had faculties enough to draw the distinguishing tattoo on his own left wrist.

An A for anarchy.

The good deputy had bled out as a cop to his very last breath.

As for the symbol, Lucky was familiar enough with it. In his policing career—especially at the start when all sheriff's trainees spend their first years of duty working the L.A. County Jail—

scrutinizing tattoos had come with the job. More often than not, it was body ink that identified a suspect and his affiliation with either a gang or race group. Lucky knew the mapping all too well, having gang-affiliated ink on his own left calf—a grim reaper wielding a pistol—identifying him as a Lennox Reaper.

But an anarchy tattoo was an outlier as an actual identifier. It was an expression used by fringe dwellers—popular with punks, gay groups, neo-Nazis, and leftists hanging over the political edge who foresaw a rise of the minority over the tyrannical majority.

Only one anarchy tattoo had ever truly stuck with Lucky. It was in red, thickly drawn, on the inside of a man's left wrist.

Greg Beem's wrist.

Lucky knew it was a leap. The chances that the cop killer was Greg Beem were from long to nil. After all, Greg Beem was assumed dead in the annals of the federales at the FBI. Gonzo's last lick at the bad guy had put a bullet in him before he'd pitched into a raging river, in which it was suspected he'd drowned.

Now a deputy was dead, bludgeoned and left to die under Lucky's watchful eye. And over the intervening two and half hours, as the fires whipped into a rage on the nearby mountains and Lucky chomped at the bit to go after the cop killer, he was remanded to the crime scene, answering every and all questions in regard to his involvement. Again and again, he replayed his second-by-second personal account, from the moment he first heard the radio call for help to when the first LAPD radio car arrived as backup. Complicating matters were the competing jurisdictions. The territory was LAPD's. The murdered deputy was with Sheriff's. That meant Lucky had to recite the same answers to three sets of police officers—the arriving uniformed team plus duos of homicide investigators from both county and city departments. Making matters more frustrating was the extra lot of queries aimed at his reservist status. A hobby cop. It was a clear signal that he'd never again be afforded the trust given a deputy who was still on the job.

Not once during the exhaustive interrogations had he been

able to check for missed calls on his cell phone. Only upon his return to that old black-and-white did he discover that he'd left his mobile device wedged between the seat cushions. There were three hours-old calls from Gonzo, voicemail messages, plus copious texts from Karrie.

"You've been calling?" Lucky asked, phoning Karrie first. Instead of reading her messages or listening to the voicemails, he thought it simpler to just ring her back.

"Where've you been?" she piped.

"Underwater," replied Lucky. "Phone was in the unit. I wasn't. Sorry. Everything all right?"

"That's what we all wanna know."

"You. Gonzo. And Travis?" guessed Lucky.

"And Frosty. He's been helping me."

"Helping you with what?"

"Looking for you. We've been driving Chatsworth street by street."

"You're near here?" In the moment it was an out-of-context head-scratcher. "Look. I know I've been out of pocket, but—"

"But mama-san says check on Lucky and I say, 'Why the hell not?'" explained Karrie. "Anyway, she's somewhere over South Central worrying her ass off, so . . ."

"Oh," was all Lucky could manage in reply.

"Oh, yeah."

"Hey, Lucky," called Frosty, chiming in loudly from a short distance.

"Tell Frost-man 'Hi,'" returned Lucky. "I'm fine. Still on shift, though. So you guys should turn around and get back to—"

"Just call her back, will ya?"

"Yeah, yeah."

"You coming home after?"

"With all these fires? Can't say yet."

"It's soooo crazy, isn't it? At our house, not a trace of smoke in the sky and then comin' across the North Valley, it was like we're driving through a version of hell—"

Lucky was jolted by a shriek. It was Karrie's. As if she'd interrupted herself with an involuntary Halloween scream. The sound alone, coming through Lucky's cell phone, was enough to raise goose bumps on his scalp.

"Karrie!" he shot back into his phone. "KARRIE!"

22

The fires were simply mesmerizing through the wide screen of a vehicle's windshield. While Frosty piloted Karrie's Toyota Prius, she'd begun the first leg of the westbound drive phoning Lucky between dialing the other numbers she'd saved on her device—namely his Reaper pals Bledsoe and Lopes, as well as the various sheriff's stations and substations she could pull up in a web search. Her concerns for reservist Deputy Lucky Dey were politely accepted with a consistent response such as, "Sorry, ma'am. Because of the fires we're spread pretty thin tonight."

Karrie had crabbily dropped the phone in her lap at roughly the same moment the Prius crested the freeway at Lake View Terrace. As they'd begun the descent into the San Fernando Valley, the trifecta of fires that continued to storm along the shelves and ridges of the Santa Susana Mountains appeared in a stacked three-dimensional relief. The Valley below, shaped in a shallow oblong bowl, appeared as if sealed by a cling-wrapped ceiling of smoke. The reflected atmospheric light from millions of suburban bulbs was like a surreal, suspended, feather-filled blanket stained in shades of umber and gray.

"It's beautiful," Karrie had remarked. "God. Is that wrong of me to say?"

"Not even close," salved Frosty. "God made fire. And God don't make nothin' that's not beautiful."

"Scary somethin' so mesmerizing can kill you," said Karrie.

"You're mesmerizing," he charmed. "And you nearly killed me that first time."

"Asked you not to bring that up."

"Sorry," replied Frosty. "Instead of killin' me, you kicked the sense of Jesus into me. How's that?"

"Same subject. Tired of it."

"How about I just drive?"

"How about it?" she finished.

So Frosty drove, the nose of the Prius aimed toward the West Valley and Chatsworth. Karrie did her level best to bury her annoyance. She'd said everything but demand that Frosty never mention it again—the *it* being the moment they'd met. Not the night. Not the hour. But the very instant the two had first been in physical proximity when she'd dropped him with a Muay Thai down round kick, otherwise known as a Tae Kod. As Frosty went down, so had Karrie in a practiced maneuver, hyper-extending his wrist, trapping his arm underneath her while using his body as leverage to strike his head with the heel of her jogging sneaker, over and over and over . . .

If Lucky hadn't pulled me off . . . she often wondered.

Frosty had nicknamed that fateful meeting as his moment of conversion. He didn't recall if he'd dropped the gun before or after he'd slapped the concrete, but ever since he'd dedicated his heart to Jesus, Lucky, and Karrie—in that precise order.

As for Chatsworth, beyond the rough boundaries found on Google Maps, Frosty only knew it was the home of the infamous Spahn Ranch—a.k.a. the Spahn Movie Ranch. In Hollywood's halcyon days, the five-hundred-acre spread served as a backdrop for movie and television Westerns. Then in the 1960s, while aging, decrepit, and no longer in use, the Spahn Ranch became the temporary home of the killer cult better known as the Charles Manson family. Frosty had read about it all in the true crime book *Helter Skelter* by former L.A. prosecutor Vincent Bugliosi. He made the book the subject of a high school English paper, recording it as his only A before dropping out. While scouring the Chatsworth boulevards for Lucky, Frosty made conversation by recounting what he knew about the ranch, its history, and the Manson murders.

"Kinda not in the mood," Karrie said. "Considering, you know?"

"Yeahhhh," realized Frosty. "Sorry. Just spinnin' out what's in my head. Wasn't really thinkin'. Sorry."

Frosty admitting he was sorry didn't come close to cutting it. The young man he once was still ate at him. He'd spilled enough blood that he was certain the sin of it all would forever reside inside him on a molecular level. A burden he'd have to carry for the rest of his life on Earth.

Mine own cross to bear.

"Really, really sorry," said Frosty, heartfelt.

"You already said you're sorry."

"Then sorry I doubled down on the sorry."

"That supposed to be funny?"

"'Bout I answer your question with another question?" switched up Frosty. "Is this our first argument?"

"I dunno," she said sharply, her frustration wearing thin. "Is it?"

"Think maybe I should shut my gums. Keep drivin'."

Frosty dropped the temperature of the car's air conditioner to sixty-six degrees. Hard as the compressor and filter were working, the internal cabin smelled of the fires. Outside, a near blizzard of ash was falling from the sky, collecting on the blades of the windshield wipers.

"Ever seen snow?" asked Karrie.

"Once," answered Frosty. "When I was a kid, my Gra'nana drove us up to Crestline or some such mountain. She had a lesson in it. Wanted us to see somethin' that was 'whiter than white folks.'"

"And the lesson was?"

Before Frosty could reply, Karrie's phone trilled. Lucky's name and picture had appeared on her mobile's screen. Karrie breathed a sigh of relief before answering.

"You've been calling?" Frosty could hear over her phone.

"Where've you been?" Karrie had asked, as much an exclamation as a question.

"Underwater. Phone was in the unit. I wasn't. Sorry. Everything all right?"

"That's what we all wanna know."

Frosty began reorienting the Prius in the direction of the nearest freeway back to Altadena, beginning with a legal U-turn at the first intersection he reached. The turn was tight, so he spun the steering wheel and put some gas to the hybrid's engine. Underfoot, he felt the tiny four cylinders kick, assisting with the power turn. That's when he reflexively switched to the brake, stomping on it like a bug, shifting g-forces, and forcing a shriek out of Karrie that sonically matched the squeal from the car's tires.

At the end of the skid stood a sweaty man in baggy jeans and a Chivas soccer jersey. Red and blue. He had a forearm up and shielding his freshly scraped face from the headlight glare, the other hand bootlegging something behind his right leg.

"Jesus!" said Karrie.

"'S all good," calmed Frosty. He held both his hands up to the windshield as if to apologize for what was really not his fault.

The man stood frozen, mere feet from the bumper. Staring through the windshield. Then gingerly he pivoted, continuing to cross the boulevard. As quickly as he'd appeared, he was gone. Out of sight. Vanished behind a manicured buckthorn hedge.

"Jus' some homeless dude," dismissed Frosty.

"Homeless dude we almost killed," exhaled Karrie.

"Yeah," was all Frosty could muster. His face was creased, eyes still fixed on the spot where the man had stood, briefly glaring back at them.

'Member how I say I'd never kill again? Frosty thought before answering his own cryptic question. *Never figured it might be from some idiot accident.*

"Shit," whispered Frosty, not keen on contemplating a new complication to his mantra.

Beemer had waited a good minute before he attempted to cross the five-lane boulevard. He'd picked a dim stretch between streetlamps. Zero cover, but dark enough. Up until the little Toyota Prius trundled past, there'd been a consistent flow of police and fire vehicles. So he'd waited, crouched in the shadow of a US Mail box. Then came that compact hybrid. As the Prius braked for what appeared to be a right-hand turn, Beemer thought he'd timed it perfectly, beginning his quick sprint the moment the headlights scraped by.

His mistake was in assuming the Prius was turning right rather than beginning a wide U-turn to the left. There'd been no blinking turn indicator. So, Beemer had picked his spot, aimed for the opposite curb, and launched himself off across the asphalt divide. His side panel hurt with every other stride, like a punch in the ribs with every left-footed landing. Then came the headlights again, sweeping into his periphery as the hybrid's engine broke through the silence. Beemer's trajectory was off. If the driver didn't brake hard, there'd be a certain collision. Man versus car. And in nearly 100 percent of such cases, man comes out the loser.

Beemer slowed and spun himself to face the grille of his attacker, his right hand reaching for his back pocket, where he'd stowed the stolen tool. Finding a screwdriver had proved far more difficult than he'd first imagined. Home garages had been locked. The advent of so many inexpensive closed-circuit security cameras was a second unexpected obstacle. The tree-covered neighborhood he'd stalked appeared rife with wireless lenses aimed every which way. An hour had passed in a heartbeat. He'd even begun to revise his plan to something more aggressive—say, a carjacking—when he'd come across a contractor's long-bed pickup truck hanging ass end out of a short driveway. The tailgate was lowered like a drunken afterthought, a rusted red toolbox lay within easy reach.

Time was slipping, though. His ears were permanently keyed to the constant *thwap-thwap-thwap* of the LAPD helicopter, perhaps only a half mile away, as it moved in concentric circles in search of the cop-killing villain. He was abandoning one subdivision for another—a hopeful greener pasture where he might find a stealable escape vehicle—when he came knees to bumper with that Prius. And once the car stopped mere feet from crippling him forever, Beemer found himself reimagining the car-jacking scenario.

He marked only a driver and a passenger. Male and female. A black man and a white woman.

How adorable, thought Beemer's inner idiot in the most random of notions.

Millennials in love.

Beemer stared the pair down. He considered that flathead screwdriver, a veritable foot-long dagger of heavy-gauge steel with a rubberized grip. He pictured himself covering the distance to the driver's side door, shattering the glass with a single sideways strike. The sheer speed of it. The girl would surely scream as Beemer dragged her male friend to the asphalt. How long would it take her to unbuckle and get out of the car in time for him to gas the little hybrid into a clean escape?

Nothing clean about it, idiot.

Beemer was still anonymous. Under the radar. The manhunt for the cop killer had to still be somewhat generic.

Unless they'd already put together the murder with the naked homeless man in the laundromat.

A carjacking would be a spotlight moment. More witnesses. More mistakes. With that he cast his eyes downward, disconnecting and signaling defeat. He even threw in a pair of off-kilter shoulder twitches, selling a drugged-up game of pretend vagrant. With that he swiveled his hips and finished crossing the street before turning up the sidewalk. In a matter of seconds, he'd disappeared from the wash of headlights by scooting behind a hedge. He never glanced back. Not once. He'd already spent far too much time in . . .

What the hell is this shithole suburb called?

Beemer's inner idiot was in sudden conversation mode—that voice of unreason that caused so much trouble, always infecting his forward progress. The idiot was a worrier. The idiot was always afraid. The idiot was responsible for the majority of pain and suffering in his life. And for a moment there, the idiot was in charge. That meant anything could happen.

Anything at all.

Thursday

23

Runyon Canyon Park. 6:34 a.m.

The hiking trail was called Inspiration Point. At the dirt path's highest point, a ridge flanked by the kind of shrubs and chaparral currently fueling the fires in the North and West Valley, the vista was rather spectacular. It was nearly 180 degrees of landscape and horizon, a spot where Angie Greenwalt could breathe in views of downtown, the Hollywood Sign, and Griffith Observatory. She squinted into an unfiltered sunrise, a sign that no wildfires had kindled to the east, a sharp contrast to the clouds of black smoke choking the western horizon.

Red sky at night, sailor's delight, she recalled from a sunfish sailing class of her Martha's Vineyard youth. *Red sky in the morning, sailor's warning.*

Considering the lousy air quality, Angie had worried about exposing her lungs, especially during a hike. As a precaution, she'd packed a disposable filtered mask plus a pair of goggles to protect her eyes. But during the climb up, she was pleasantly surprised to find herself in an air channel that was clean. On either side of the ridge, she could watch the smoke move and gauge its speed, pushed along from the lips of Santa Ana's ghost. Yet somehow she was in a tributary of unpolluted air. A safety zone. Her emergency provisions remained in a fanny pack that matched her camouflage trail leggings.

Angie checked her heart rate. It was barely below one hundred beats per minute, even after nearly ten minutes of rest. It had to be nerves, she reckoned. *He* made her anxious. That was, after all, *his* way—enigmatic, charming to a fault, but always so distant. His way was to keep everybody within his orbit, both friends and enemies, just off balance enough to leave him with a tactical advantage. It was the polar opposite of how he worked his constituency. To the citizens of Los Angeles, Mayor Ramon Avila played the part of the city's stalwart defender of populist values. Through the greater grapevine that stretched from City Hall to seemingly every political outpost, Angie had heard that Mayor Ram—what everybody called him, including local radio talk show hosts as well the *L.A. Times*—had employed twice-weekly polling as justification for keeping his finger on the public pulse.

Sirens broke the silence, thin and distant. Arcing into the Cahuenga Pass on a half-mile stretch of the 101 was a phalanx of police black-and-whites, perhaps twenty long, sedans and SUVs, emergency lights in full spin. *Reinforcements*, she reckoned. Speeding toward the fires, convoying into the fire zone.

The sirens faded, giving way to the sound of approaching footfalls. It was like a shuffling of troops, jogging, running soles scratching at the dirt. What followed were the first two bobbing heads of the mayor's LAPD security detail, both decked in blue-black athletic sweats. The pair was followed by the mayor himself. Clad in Los Angeles Lakers running shorts and a Cal State Los Angeles hoodie, he appeared at his most attractive. Beneath a black tussle of perfectly cropped hair was a fifty-two-year-old Hispanic

Adonis. Fit. Muscled. His golden-brown skin shined with just enough sweat to catch the morning light. Two rows of perfect white teeth acted as a bull's-eye on his telegenic face.

"Angie!" he called out, slowing his pace to a walk. Behind the mayor, taking up the rear, were two more police officers, radio-wired for any emergency.

"I'm so impressed," she swiveled, shoulders back, her buxomness straining at her purple zip top.

"That I ran it?" he asked, hands on his hips, sucking back the fresh stream of air. "I jog this trail twice a week at least."

"No, no," said Angie. "With all the fires. You been able to sleep?"

"I have a competent staff. And I manage my time accordingly." Mayor Ram twisted in place, not so much taking in the view as sniffing the air. "Wow. Looks like we caught a pocket of fresh stuff."

"I brought a face mask and goggles," admitted Angie, slapping her fanny pack.

"So, whatcha got for me?" he segued.

"Cut right to the chase, huh?"

"You said it. There are fires to put out. Figuratively and literally."

"Right. You wanna walk?"

"Let's."

Off the mayor's gesture, the point pair of cops hustled ahead. As Mayor Ram and Angie chatted, they strolled in what's known in protective services as a security cradle.

"It's Lucky Dey," started Angie.

"Oh, him," moaned the mayor, as if reminded of a hidden hemorrhoid. "He behaving down there in the personnel basement?"

"Well, you asked me to spy—"

"I remember quite well what I asked."

"Well, this sounds pretty petty and small. But I caught him using the city's secure data system to investigate someone outside his assigned purview."

"Personal biz?" queried the mayor.

"Don't know. But you said anything out of the ordinary—"

"It all adds up. First infraction. Start a list. Eventually, I'll be able to flush the son of a bitch."

"You're the mayor. If he's such an enemy, why haven't you flushed him already?"

"He's one of those guys. Knack for getting out of jams. Understands leverage and how to apply it." Mayor Ram revealed an almost admiring smile. "Seriously. You should read his jacket. Career shit magnet."

"Permission to access it?"

"Surprised you haven't already."

"I'm a good girl," she pretended. "Digging up shit on our fellow personnel folks is a serious infraction."

"I'm your protection," he suggested. "The more you know about him, the better."

"So, what's he have on you?" Angie braved.

The mayor stopped their stroll. Angie was looking down, uncertain she should meet his eyes. Instead, she stared at his red New Balance trail shoes. They were perfectly dusted with a fine coating of sand and decomposed granite.

"My business, Angie," whispered the mayor. "Hey. Look at me."

"Sorry," she said, meeting a pair of brown eyes that could play it warm—or rock hard—depending on the man's mood.

"My. Business," he repeated. "Wanna ride my wake to whatever's next? Head down. Do as I say. Just like this morning. Right here. Out of sight, out of earshot. You tell me what I need to know."

Whatever's next, repeated Angie to herself. By her guess, as well an overwrought measure of rumors, Mayor Ram was aiming for either California Governor or United States Senator. Some insiders had even floated the mayor's name as a Democrat candidate for president. A long shot, she figured, though she didn't consider herself adept at those kind of politics. It was above her pay grade. But even Angie knew that in the history of the United States, a city mayor had never been elected president, let alone earned the party's nomination.

"Robert Bianchi of Porter Ranch," she added.

"That's who he was looking up?"

"Yeah. Looks like some trust funder. Rich daddy, you know?"

"That all?"

"Bianchi's father was some kind of porno gangster. Businessman now. Suspected mob ties, but . . ."

"But?"

"But nothin'. Just know I'm your bitch," she teased, uncertain if that's how she'd answered the first time he'd asked her to be his eyes and ears inside the personnel department.

"As mayor, I can't abide you referring to yourself in such a disparaging manner." Mayor Ram revealed a grin. "But as a dog with a few shots left in my arsenal, I can still appreciate the reference."

"Not into blondes?" she sassed, arms akimbo, breasts first.

"Are they real?" he asked, though it was as if he already knew.

"Don't matter," she quipped. "What they are is magnificent."

"I'll bet," he teased back.

He snapped his fingers three times before resuming his jog. The security foursome moved along in perfect formation.

"Thanks, Angela!" he called back.

"You got it," she feigned, feeling more rejected than accomplished.

He's so above your pay grade, she exhaled to herself. *Wayyyy above.*

24

Encino. 7:17 a.m.

The Bruckmann Aquatic Therapy Center was built around two large indoor swimming pools heated to a comfortable eighty-eight degrees Fahrenheit. Open six days a week at 5:30 a.m., the steamy water would quickly fill with Valley elderly in search of relief from the aches and ailments that came with old age. On the half hour, the shallow pool was repopulated with bathing-suited women in their seventies, eighties, and nineties, damning their own wrinkled vanity in exchange for classes in water aerobics accompanied by beat-pounding hits from the 1980s.

The deepwater pool, separated by a ten-foot-tall brick façade, was reserved for patients undergoing FCSD treatments—otherwise known as Flotation Controlled Spinal Decompression.

Joey Bianchi had a better name for the therapy: a lifesaver. His youngest boy, Bobby, had come to refer to it as something altogether different. He called it sitting duck therapy. Bobby couldn't count how many times he'd imagined his father as a victim of a mafia hit. He'd both feared and fantasized about it. Dad's history and his mob connections had often fueled Bobby's romanticized ideas of life as a gangster—this despite his old man's insistence that any affiliation he might have once had with organized crime had long ago dissolved. Joey Bianchi had never sold himself as more than a highly compensated bean counter. His legitimate enterprise as a financial wealth manager was nearly a generation old, easily looked after by a more than competent executive staff, allowing the seventy-year-old to spend much of his aging days playing golf at his beloved El Caballero Country Club.

Without the floating traction therapy, Joey surmised he would hardly be able to swing a nine iron.

"If I was a hit man?" leveled Bobby for the umpteenth time. "This is where I'd do it."

"If you were a hit man," groaned his father, "you'd be dead or in prison."

"I beg to differ," quipped Bobby, legs dangling over the pool coping, calves and feet getting a free soak, the smell of bubbling chlorine exciting his nostrils. "I'm not as stupid as you think I am."

"Never said you were stupid," righted Joey, readjusting his weight belt, causing his rail-thin arms to be inactive long enough for him a dip down to his Adam's apple before the flotation vest counteracted with increased buoyancy. "Reckless doesn't mean stupid. Careless doesn't mean stupid either."

"You look like one of them bobbers. You know?" shifted Bobby. "For fishing. Remember when you took me and Pete fishing?"

"So I'm no longer a sitting duck?" quipped Joey, elevating his voice above the eighties electronica bouncing off all the surrounding concrete and glass. The noise was convenient enough, often acting as a sonic blanket to mask any covert conversations.

"Maybe you're safe . . ." played Bobby. "Safe from everybody but Peter. He could fall into the pool and swamp you to death."

"You talked to your brother?"

"Yesterday. During the thing."

"Called him last night. No answer."

"Maybe he dropped dead of a heart attack. All those steps up to his condo. No elevator."

"He's not healthy, your brother. You should be helping him with that."

"How's this?" shifted Bobby. "You help me with my thing? And I'll get Pete to the gym."

"You should've insured that shit," bobbed old Joey. "Now *that* was stupid."

"Wouldn't change what I know," snapped Bobby, good humor fading at the thought. "That fuckin' sheriff's deputy—"

"You don't know what you don't know."

"I KNOW!" shouted Bobby before recognizing his loss of composure. Then he withered under his father's glare. "Sorry for shouting. But remember how when me or Pete would do somethin' wrong? You didn't know what we did, but you sure knew we'd done it? You *knew*. Well, that's how I know. It's here. In my solar plexus." Bobby slapped his overly hardened abdominals.

"So what if you do know?" argued Joey. "If a cop stole your stupid collection, then there's even less to do. Cons get away with it most of the time. Cops get away with it *all* the time."

"You know people."

"I'm not a boss. Never was a boss—"

"Pops!"

"No!"

"All I ask is you talk to Meltzer."

"No."

"During one of your golf games. C'mon. How hard can that be?"

"When we play golf, we talk golf. We don't talk business. Especially not my son's business, which isn't even a business," reminded Joey. "When I play golf with Bruce, I'm way too busy keeping him from taking my money."

"You're worried about a five-dollar bet when I'm worried about my million-dollar collection?"

"Insurance. You shoulda bought it."

"And if I decide to handle it myself?"

"What's that supposed to mean?"

"It means what it means." Bobby's mouth was pursed, his jaw set. "It means whatever I do, you won't get your nose outta joint."

"You keep it between the lines," warned the father. "Stick to what you know how to do."

"Which, thanks to you, is a lotta nothin'," clenched Bobby.

It wasn't the first time Bobby had revealed such resentment. That trust fund Joey had set up for both sons had become so *infantilizing*. Not that Bobby knew the word infantilize. That notion had been planted by a therapist. On Barbara's insistence, Bobby had begun weekly visits to a shrink in hope of taming his anger issues. He hadn't considered disclosing to the doctor his steroid abuse because, in Bobby's warped perspective, he wasn't abusing. He was building a positive body image through increased muscle mass.

"No good deed goes unpunished," retorted the old man. "Did I mention that you shoulda used your goddamn trust money to buy insurance for your goddamn collection?" Joey punctuated his repeated insult with a rare smirk.

Bobby knew well enough when his protests had fallen on deaf ears simply by the look on his father's face. The eyes would swerve, the old man's lower lip would eventually pull up under the upper resulting in a wafer-thin, downturned mouth. At least Bobby knew not to leave on a sour note. He even bid his father goodbye with a hearty "I love you" before slipping back into a pair of flip-flops and aiming for the exit.

A timer sounded and a trained practitioner hopped into the pool, removing both forty-pound weights from Joey's ankles and then the belt around his waist. As he climbed out, Joey dropped the flotation vest and left a trail of wet footprints all the way to the locker room. After a shower and towel dry, he dressed into a tailored suit. Italian, of course. Then, before pocketing his wallet and tying the laces of a pair of freshly shined oxfords, he sat on the bench and scrolled through the contacts on his mobile phone. He chose a familiar number and listened to the phone ring.

"This is Bruce," answered the voice.

"Meltz. It's Joey."

"Saw it was you. Why I answered," said the attorney.

"Need you to look up a skirt."

"Dirty work. Nice."

"You know what I mean."

"Yeah, yeah."

"Sheriff's deputy. Name is L. Dey."

"Elle Day? This a woman cop?"

"L as in Larry. But don't have the first name. Last name Dey as in D-E-Y."

"Got it. What's this in reference to?"

"Somethin' with one of my boys. Regret the day I ever set up that trust fund. Entitled little shits."

"I hear ya. One of 'em in trouble again?"

"It's a Bobby thing. Think this deputy had something to do with his house during the fires."

"His house survive? Fam okay?"

"They're all fine. Bobby's just in one of his hissy twists over a burglary. Last thing I'd do is let him know I'm doing him a favor by asking you—"

"Not doing him a favor," reminded Meltzer. "Doing yourself a favor. Shit your kids get into sometimes gets on you. That's what I'm here for. To clean up the shit."

25

The block surrounding El Mirasol looked as if the Mexican restaurant was ground zero after an act of modern terrorism. The streets were choked with emergency vehicles, fire trucks, EMT vans, and police and sheriff's black-and-whites. But rather than a confluence of first responders charging into imminent danger, the men and women tasked with fighting the North and West Valley fires had been invited to El Mirasol for much-needed sustenance. The restaurant's owner, a big-hearted migrant from Oaxaca, felt he owed a forever debt to America for taking him in. So he sent out the word that first responders desiring fuel for their bodies and souls were welcome for a day of free meals. The response by firefighters and cops was so resounding, the restaurateur had to set up beyond his restaurant doors and take over the parking lot. From his catering locker he broke out banquet tables, folding chairs, and pop-up tents for shade. The night before, his staff and family had stayed from closing until dawn to prep and cook stuffed tamales by the bushel.

"Dunno if this isn't the best tamale ever," said the soot-smeared firefighter seated across from Lucky, "or I'm so drag-ass tired I'd eat Styrofoam and call it a Kevin-quality cook."

The firefighter's last pair of syllables were drowned by the roar of a Bombardier 415 Turboprop, otherwise known as a Super Scooper. The amphibious aircraft with the yellow-painted hull tipped its wings at the first responders below after having completed a drop. Lucky guessed the pilot was pointed toward the Pacific on the way to scoop up yet another 1,600 gallons of seawater.

"Sorry. You said 'Kevin Cook'?" asked Lucky, worried he was ear-fatigued and not quite catching the reference. It was of minor consequence. Polite conversation wasn't Lucky's forte. After his rough night, he was grateful to talk about anything non-fire or murdered cop–related while plowing his plastic fork into the pile of steaming sweet corn masa piled on his paper plate. Mexican rice and refried beans framed the tamales with a rib-sticking promise.

"Kevin J.," clarified the firefighter. "He's our firehouse chef. Dude should open his own place. Seriously. My station eats, like, gourmet almost every night."

"Where you in from?" asked Lucky, keeping the small talk moving by asking questions to answers he was barely listening to.

"Tehachapi."

"Kern," Lucky nodded, referring to the county where he'd taken a sabbatical. It was during that two-year hiatus that he'd lost his little brother Tony. Gunned down. Then torched by the evil Greg Beem.

"Know your way around up there?"

"Spent my share of time up thataway." Lucky stood, thirsty. "Gettin' somethin' cold. What you want? Think there's Kool-Aid and sodas and—"

"Water, water, and more water," said the firefighter.

"I hear that. On my way—"

"IS THAT LUCKY GODDAMN DEY?" bellowed a man from across the room.

Lucky wheeled, scanning across the tops of all the firefighters and police officers, hoping his tired eyes would land on a friendly face. He was in no mood for confrontation. After a night of verbally prying sticky homeowners and tenants out of their shelters and into safe evacuation zones, Lucky worried he might just bust the nose of the next ass clown with a load of lip. Instead, he discovered a familiar cowboy swagger on a serpentine path toward him. It was his Reaper compadre Jorge Lopes. The former Lennox detective had since climbed the career ladder all the way up to the number-two spot in the Sheriff's Professional Standards and Training Division. His crown of thinning curls had nearly turned baby-powder white and gone forever was the ubiquitous seventies porno mustache for which Lopes had received piles of good-natured derision. But his smile was the same, wide as all outdoors. Intact, along with the irreversible Reaper tattoo hidden underneath the shoulder of his gold-on-green sheriff's windbreaker.

"Lord *haaave* mercy. Didn't think I'd ever see you in a uniform," declared Lopes. His outstretched hand pulled Lucky into a warm brotherly hug.

"Ya think?" answered Lucky. "But shit happens."

"Got you on knock-knock duty?" asked Lopes.

"Just finished a full fourteen. Then five minutes ago they extended my shift to a twenty-four."

"Sucks to be you. Especially after the night you had," remarked Lopes. "Saw your name on more than one report. I was like, 'Shit-balls and jingle bells, Lucky found himself another couple messes. How does he do it?'"

"Sure it was all me? Got just the murdered cop thing. Spent half my shift answering to detectives."

"Deputy thing is bad. I didn't know him. Had four kids and a hefty chunk of child support."

"Anything on the suspect?"

"Nothin'. Fire's got everybody in cars and moving warm bodies."

"Copy that."

Lucky considered bringing up his earlier suspicions regarding the suspect. How he'd found the victim had swirled a red anarchy A onto his left wrist. But the further removed from the murder scene, the more Lucky felt that Greg Beem as his suspect was a big stretch.

"Somethin' else," said Lopes. "Came across my phone as an IAB alert."

IAB was the acronym for Internal Affairs Bureau, a division directly under Lopes's purview. On its own, Lopes being boss over a team of detectives in charge of investigating dirty cops was almost laughable. Did the department even know the man, called Mighty Mouse by many of his Lennox brethren, was a tattooed Reaper?

"Think this was yesterday?" guessed Lopes. "Some evacuated guy up in Porter Ranch claims you were working as lookout for a B and E crew that robbed his house."

B and E. More cop code. Breaking and Entering.

A burglary.

And that asshat musclehead named Bianchi.

Lucky's eyes shut with a side-to-side shake of his chin. The day just got that much better.

"Think I know a little about you're talking about," fibbed Lucky. "Came off as a real clown. Entitled. Wanted back in his house because, I dunno. He'd already been evaced. Stopped him maybe a hundred yards from his property. Wasn't happy."

"Says that was the exact hour he got robbed. House alarm has a time stamp to prove it."

"C'mon, Jorge." All Lucky could offer was a shrug. "You know me."

"That I do. Just thought I'd give you a heads-up. Guys under me still want to give you a cavity search. Just make sure your whistle is clean, knowwhatImean?"

"For them?" joked Lucky. "I'll go full commando just to see the look on their faces."

"And I'll be first in line to buy that ticket."

The men shared a lingering veterans' laugh.

"So, Saturday," asked Lopes. "It still gonna happen?"

"You know Gonzo," smirked Lucky. "She sets her mind on something. House could be on fire by then and she'd still insist on walking that dress."

"You seen it already? That's supposed to be bad luck."

"Like either of us believe in that."

Lopes chuckled. At Lennox Station they'd seen far more than the average neighborhood cop—including LAPD and Sheriff's—of humanity's unfairness. Bad luck or good luck, life in South Los Angeles was a matter of playing the breaks, positive or otherwise, keeping peace, and delving out justice—one minute at a time.

26

Porter Ranch

B*ing-bong.*
   The door chime was a verified antique. Long before the acrimonious divorce, Oren's eldest boy had shown a brief interest in tinkering. So, father and eight-year-old boy set off to refurbish a mid-century doorbell, purchased parts on eBay, and after a weekend of rewiring the electric motor and polishing up a pair of brass long bells, Mankowski Manor had a 1960s-style announcement whenever a visitor landed on the doormat.

"BE RIGHT THERE!" Oren shouted out from the basement, launching up the steps and closing the door behind him before making a hard S-turn into the kitchen and to the apron sink to rinse the dried blood off his hands. "JUST A SEC!"

Oren wished he had one of those chimes with the attached fish-eye camera that wirelessly delivered a picture of the front door visitor to the screen of his mobile phone. With the curtains drawn, any peek through the gap might reveal that Oren was home and not answering the door. Thus, he called out, played for time, and faked a twelfth-race winner's smile before pulling on the door handle.

Bobby Bianchi stood at the threshold in his ubiquitous work-out gear—tank top and Adidas shorts. Flexing biceps and a fresh coat of spray tan completed the image.

"Jesus, brother," remarked Bobby. "You look like shit."

"Good morning to you," Oren volleyed before changing the subject of his sweaty pallor and the bags under his eyes. "What's going on?"

"Got a minute?"

"Yeah," Oren turned, leaving the door wide open before drawing up a new lie. "Was just making a second pot of coffee. You want?"

"Don't drink it since I found out it screws with insulin sensitivity," followed Bobby. "Makes the body less efficient at handling glucose."

"What's glucose?" called back Oren, knowing perfectly well that the answer was sugar. It was part defensive wordplay, part curiosity to see if Bobby actually knew the difference between glucose and sucrose.

"It's like that sugar shit in your body that diabetics gotta worry so much about."

"But you're not a diabetic. At least as far as I know."

"It's 'cause I take supplements," revealed Bobby. "What I put in my body is like a recipe for muscle-building. Gotta be really precise, ya know?"

Especially with the steroid injections, thought Oren, who knew too much about Bobby's abuse. Peter had served as Bobby's supplier, accessing the illegal androgenic and anabolic compounds from a wholesale pharma distributor he wrote policies for. Oren also knew that Peter charged Bobby a 20 percent markup without telling his younger brother. Oren had wondered if that's how it had started—Peter's jealousy regarding Bobby's inherited wealth. At one time in their lives, both brothers had equally funded trust accounts. But whereas Bobby had placed his trust fund in the hands of a money manager, Peter had squandered his on dubious investments, mainly a chain of fast-food restaurants with an Italian theme. Peter had oh so cleverly named the enterprise Parma Go Go. The citywide rollout of five drive-thru footprints was a cash burn that had resulted in colossal failure and inevitable bankruptcy. Neither Peter's brother nor father had missed an opportunity to tease him about it. He climbed out of the hole by taking a job shucking insurance. He drank and ate and his weight ballooned. Big brother Peter became big, fat Peter.

And now he's big, fat, dead Peter.

"What's that smell?" asked Bobby.

"I look like shit, you don't want coffee, and now my house smells?" defended Oren.

"Seriously, dude. There's a stink."

"Think it's a cracked sewer line. Think our little cul-de-sac ain't rated to handle the weight of fire trucks."

It was a bald-faced lie. The foul scent was leaking from the cellar. Peter's body had already begun to rot. Oren's delay in discarding the body had resulted in his house—or at least the downstairs and basement—taking on the sickly sweet scent of decomposition. After waking up with a hangover and an emptied vodka bottle next to the mattress, his nostrils had flared at the stink. Within minutes, he'd cursed the pounding in his skull and quickly assembled tools for dismemberment—a hacksaw and a semi-serrated camp knife he'd come across during one of the research sorties he'd made into the hills behind his house. It was on one of those hikes that he'd identified the perfect spot to kindle his third and final fire. The rusted camp knife had been a bonus.

The disgusting job was nearly half complete, the dead brother's legs and arms disarticulated and bound in layers of butcher's wrap and stacked neatly in an upright freezer. Oren's plan was to follow with the head, rib cage, and lastly, the spine, leaving only the innards and entrails that he'd distribute in the nearby wilderness to be devoured by the local coyotes that preyed on his neighbors' cats and small dogs. He planned to dissolve the frozen body parts later in an acid bath in a fifty-five-gallon drum.

Then came the bells of that *Brady Bunch* door chime.

"Your water worth drinking?" asked Bobby.

"Glasses in the corner cabinet," answered Oren, rinsing out the coffee pot before preparing to measure fresh grinds into the filter.

"You seen my brother?" The question from Bobby wasn't coy. Or at least it didn't appear so as he searched the kitchen cabinet for a suitable tumbler.

"Yesterday," answered Oren. "You were there. And by the way, what's going on with that burglary thing?"

"Gonna get the fucker who did it. That's for sure. Starting with that bullshit deputy."

"Think you'll get your stuff back?"

"So pissed, I'm gonna break somethin'. Coulda been hawked to a million pawn shops by now."

"Sorry to hear—"

"Pete. He came over here to hold a ladder for your short fuckin' legs."

"He didn't wanna drink my coffee either. Why you ask?"

"'Cause he ain't answering his phone. Not from me or my old man."

"After I dropped him off—"

"You did what?"

"He Ubered, remember? Super Pig's in the shop?"

"Okay. Yeah?"

"I game him a lift back to his condo. Lake Balboa."

"You drove him?"

"Dropped him off," continued Oren.

Bobby paused at the sink, ready to fill his chosen glass with tap water.

"Fat ass," angered Bobby, shaking his head. "Probably in his condo, dead from a heart attack."

"He's your brother," warned Oren. "Don't wanna talk that way."

"He's a candidate for heart failure," argued Bobby. "Wouldn't surprise me or anybody else."

"All I can hope is that you're wrong," continued Oren, filling the coffee maker's water reservoir from the cleaned pot.

"Was he weird with you yesterday?" asked Bobby.

"Weird how?"

"Weird," repeated Bobby.

"No weirder than he usually is," shrugged Oren.

"Kept harping on the insurance thing. 'I told ya so. Shoulda had you some coverage. Blah, blah, blah.'"

"And that's weird?"

"Probably just sticking the robbery up my ass for all the times I gave him shit about Parma Go Go going belly up."

"Switzerland."

"What about it?"

"I'm Switzerland," clarified Oren.

"You're a fuckin' Pollack from Pittsburgh."

And you're a bigger idiot than your dead brother, shitforbrains.

"Switzerland," explained Oren, trying his best not to condescend. Bobby still liked him—or so Oren thought. And this particular string of horse manure needed to be played out for as long as humanly possible. "The Swiss were famously neutral in World Wars One and Two."

"Oh. So, you don't wanna get between us brothers. Smart." Bobby tapped an index finger to his freshly shaved temple, then downed his glass of water in a series of animalistic gulps. "Guess I should ask the cops to do a check on my brother."

"A welfare check?"

"He was almost poor. His own stupid fault. But not on welfare."

"Welfare check is—"

"I know what it is," grinned Bobby before feigning a punch to Oren's shoulder. "Just fuckin' with ya. Gotta go. Want me to shut the front door behind me? Or leave it open so you can air out whatever this smelly shit is?"

"Outside smells like burnt toast."

"Inside smells like burnt shit."

The two men shared a friendly laugh, Oren's side of it being entirely counterfeit.

"Barbie still at the Four Seasons?" asked Oren, holding the front door.

"Don't get me started!" waved off Bobby.

Oren posed at the threshold, confident Bobby hadn't a glimmer as to his depravity, all the while gamely surveying the landscape while his eyes continued to flick back to Bobby on the retreat. Backed into Bobby's driveway was a standard U-Haul box truck. Two taller but comparably muscled men climbed from the cab. Bodybuilder types. Not the usual south-of-the-border construction crew that had been prepping Bobby's sound bunker for the concrete foundation pour before the fires.

Oren watched Bobby shake hands with the U-Haul duo, hardly wondering what or why they'd backed a truck up to the garage. He momentarily basked in a satisfaction unlike any other—not even that of his one and only superfecta win, which was exponentially more difficult to land than a trifecta. Oren's only immediate worry was the lack of his own human remorse. He'd stolen what wasn't his. He'd murdered his co-conspirator. And still he'd felt little to no regret. If there was any guilt, it was buried deep beneath an unhealthy sense of accomplishment. After losing his business, his family, his self-respect, and maybe even his will to live, Oren was back on the rise, moving up on his own warped ladder of success.

I'm back.

27

Porter Ranch

Lucky banged on the front door with the meat of his fist, surprised by how quickly the action had turned into a habit. Ring the bell, pound on the door. Over the past couple of days, he'd repeated the same act over and over again. *How many doors to how many evacuees?* Lucky couldn't count, nor even estimate. But when he landed at the Via Medici address, as much as he'd reminded himself to be polite to a fault, the newly found habit of urgently rousing occupants inside a house had somehow slipped past his behavioral filter.

The sun was low and casting sideways shadows, the sky streaked in terracotta and persimmon. Lucky had been relieved of his twenty-four hours of reservist duty and granted a twelve-hour rest. He was expected to return to the job at 4:00 a.m. the next morning. Despite his need for sleep, he was making a single side trip before heading east to his home in Altadena, or maybe he'd crash at his downtown office again.

He didn't remember the particular house. It had been smoky and dark and he'd been in a hurry to clear the property as unoccupied and move on to the next. He'd rapped on so many doors that his knuckles had become as sore as they were calloused.

"Yeah, yeah," said the oncoming voice from the other side. The latch sounded and the heavy door swung inward.

Divided only by the strip of weather-protected threshold stood Lucky and Bobby Bianchi. The dumbstruck shock on Bobby's mug quickly dissolved into a mash-up of annoyance and pent-up anger. Just seeing the uniformed hobby cop squared on his own doormat was enough to make him want to lash out. Only the last time Bobby tried to get physical with the cop, he'd found himself kissing the pavement before he could mentally utter "Whoops."

Sensing Bobby's discomfort—not unexpected—Lucky broke the awkward silence with a friendly smile.

"Mr. Bianchi," he began in a rehearsed but short speech. "Forgive my stopping by unannounced. But I thought speaking to you in person was the most efficient way to straighten this out."

"Straighten what out?" Bobby said reflexively, especially considering he knew precisely what the issue was. He was taken aback.

"I think you and I have a misunderstanding."

"No . . ." replied Bobby, stiffening. "No misunderstanding. I know what's what. And so do you."

"I take it your family is home and safe?" segued Lucky, keeping his tone flat but cordial.

"Still at the Four Seasons. What's it to you?"

"My job. It's all about concern for human safety. Which brings me to the other night."

"The other night," repeated Bobby.

"I understand you were robbed?"

"You would know," bit Bobby.

"In fact, I didn't. Not until this morning. And I understand you lodged a complaint in regard to my actions."

"You kept me from going to my house."

"I had cause, sir."

"Hell yeah, you had *cause*. That's when my house was getting robbed."

"I had nothing whatsoever to do with your loss of property," leveled Lucky firmly, as if it were the end of the argument. Not that he expected assent. If anything, and in Lucky's general estimation, men like Bobby Bianchi sometimes didn't know how to deescalate conflict. Lucky merely wanted a record that he'd personally made the effort to address the aggrieved party in hope of assuaging the accusation.

"I got the evidence," pressed Bobby. "My house alarm was disabled at almost the exact same time you were using your badge to push me around on my own street."

"You pushed, sir. That's assault on a deputy. I could've had you arrested. Instead, I—"

"Instead nothin'! It couldn't have been by accident. You stoppin' me."

"Coincidences happen. I'm sorry you lost your property—"

"I didn't lose shit," cut Bobby. "You and whoever you're workin' with up and ripped my collection. So, why don't you back the fuck off my stoop, talk it up to your partners, return my stuff, and maybe—and I mean maybe—I'll go easy."

"Easy . . ." Lucky nodded slowly. It wasn't so much a question, nor was it rhetorical. It was as if by repeating the word he might divine what Bobby Bianchi meant by it. Would there be a civil complaint? Followed by an internal investigation? For a second or two, Lucky wondered if his acceptance of reserve deputy status was worth the indignity.

Or was that spoiled spawn of a retired porn gangster looking to take matters into his own hands?

"Sir, I came by to apologize for any misunderstanding," said Lucky, cementing that an effort had been made to make amends.

"Hey, hobby cop," spat Bobby in a rude reply. "Go fuck yourself."

"I hear ya," said Lucky, fishing into his pocket for a card. "Think I already gave you one of these. But just in case you lost it, this is how you can find me."

Lucky held forth the business card, not caring if Bobby took it. It was the last olive branch he would offer. Perhaps the final card he'd ever pull from a uniform shirt pocket. No. Lucky wasn't tired of the job. Even as a volunteer reservist. He was just full up on the bullshit. Open wide and swallow. Yes, it was part of the gig. But some days it felt as if he were swimming in a sewer with his mouth ajar.

"Have a good day, sir." Lucky stuck the card in the crack between the stucco and the doorjamb and about-faced himself back to his black-and-white junker.

"Oh, I'm gonna have a good day," called Bobby. "It's gonna be ten thousand kinds of awesome!"

<h1 style="text-align:center">28</h1>

The microsecond the door latch kuh-lunked into the brass strike plate, Bobby performed a basketball pivot and began what felt like a full-court sprint to the kitchen.

"THAT WAS HIM!" he hollered. "GET YOUR ASSES ON THE HOP! NOW!"

In Bobby's showpiece kitchen, a cooking paradise of stainless steel and granite, sat a pair of bodybuilder pals comfortably parked on barstools fashioned to look like baseball gloves.

"Where does a dude get a chair like this?" queried Buggie, the thicker of the two, trimmed beard and unfortunate bulging eyes dominating his broad face.

"That was him!" pointed Bobby toward the front of the house.

"Your brother?" wondered Dakota, the blue-eyed Aryan

throwback with hair so blond he appeared trimmed in butter-scotch when backlit by the sun.

"The fuckin' cop!" barked Bobby.

Buggie was barely a half step ahead of Dakota.

"The one you wanted us to—"

"At my goddamn front door!"

"But why could he be?" asked Dakota, revealing an Oklahoma drawl.

"Are you guys doing this or not?" asked Bobby.

"Like, now?" asked Buggie.

"The job just got easier, dipstick!" spoon-fed Bobby. "Now all you gotta do is follow his ass!"

It was as if they'd been poked with a cattle prod. Both brawn-jockeys levitated out of those comfy stools and scrambled to their feet on the tiled floor.

Bobby found himself wrestling with a momentary measure of regret.

"Yo!" cautioned Bobby. "You guys can do this, right?"

"We got this," chilled Buggie, stalling in the doorway with an "All's good" gesture. "We just sat down for Diet Pepsis, dude. Caught us a little off guard. Never said he'd just knock on your door."

"Just don't leave me with buyer's remorse. Get it done, 'kay?" urged Bobby. "And get my shit back before it gets sold off!"

Bobby thought of that *Step Brothers* movie—the one with Will Ferrell and that other curly-haired funny man whose name he could never remember. They played moronic siblings by marriage, barely able to function at a fifth-grade maturity.

They better not fuck this up, worried Bobby.

Buggie and Dakota had long been Bobby's unofficial sidekicks since meeting at the Northridge Crunch Fitness. Once aware of Bobby's father's connection to the classic porn days and possibly even the Cleveland mob, they'd stuck themselves to Bobby like he was a mafia prince whose shine might someday rub off. It was classic Los Angeles cachet. If you *weren't* a somebody, then second best was to *know* somebody, to be in their circle of limelight. And Bobby wasn't one to deny the attention.

Bobby had complained about the robbery during a furious workout. Afterward, the trio retired to a post-exercise steam. Like the Romans of old, a plot for recompense unfolded. And to prove their loyalty and worthiness to Bobby Bianchi, Buggie and Dakota had schemed up a plan to turn the dirty hobby cop into an asset. With the correct turn of a screw, the reservist deputy would surely cough up info on his co-conspirators. The happy ending would include the return of Bobby's collection with the perpetrators arrested and incarcerated. All for a price cheaper than whatever deductible he'd have paid for one of Peter's insurance policies.

Bobby climbed the grand, curving staircase befitting a prince. With each step he replayed the plot as if from an instruction man-ual. Tab A into slot B. Yet he couldn't help but skip ahead to the satisfying result. The look on that asshole cop's face was going to be priceless, a feeling nearly as powerful as when he gazed upon his Beatles collection. The possession of it—be it the collection or revenge—would be his and his alone.

29

North Hollywood

Los Angeles. The City of Angels.

More like the City of Vagrants.

Beemer found the prospect of a city government that refused to manage its homeless population—of which the vast majority suffered a cocktail of drug addiction and untreated mental illness—a repugnant disgrace. Not that he cared an ice-cream lick about human welfare. Beemer was, if anything, a devout Darwinist. The philosophy of survival of the fittest made primal sense to him. The nation's forefathers were uniquely qualified to establish the freest form of governance—a pure meritocracy disguised as democracy.

Genius.

During the hour of bunk time before lights out, he'd been consuming random history books. Incarceration had tapped Beemer's inner reader—opposed to his inner idiot, the side of him that pre-ferred television and video games over more cerebral endeavors.

Only that inner reader had been entirely missing in the hours since he'd escaped Chatsworth. The idiot had not only been loos-ened, it had been dominating Beemer's mental motor since that sheriff's deputy had interrupted his soul-centering shower. The search for a simple household screwdriver had taken way too long. It was the idiot's game plan. And it was only a matter of time before the homeless-looking man in the Chivas shirt trolling back alleys and driveways was pictured on someone's doorbell camera—or worse, rung up by police officers on the hunt for a cop killer.

And then he'd stumbled upon a way out.

Braving the brightly lit intersection of Devonshire Street and De Soto Avenue, Beemer caught a glimmer of it in the gutter—a TAP card. Blue and white. A reloadable plastic Metro Pass. Lost or emptied of credit and discarded? Beemer had stepped from the curb, bent over, and snatched it into his scabbing fingers. What better way to escape Chatsworth than on a bus? Eastbound. But were the buses running that late? Smoke hung in the air, leav-ing the intersection and all its lights—red, green, and yellow, walk and don't walk—aglow in the haze. Beemer scoured. On the concrete post supporting the traffic signals' crossbeam were direc-tional placards to bus stops and various lines. They were in code: Line 244-245. Route 158. Orange Line East/West.

The idiot might've flicked the card into the street and carried on with plan A—stealing a car. But Beemer's calmer self had at last pushed through and prevailed in the moment. He swiveled south, jogged his aching frame across the boulevard, and kept to the dark edges of the sidewalk. Within minutes he came upon a lit bus stop. Awaiting the next ride was a cotton-topped pair. *Hus-band and wife*, reasoned Beemer. Huddled on the bench, each was a teacup-sized reflection of the other with a rich, umber face. To filter the smoke, they had kerchiefs held to their noses and mouths.

The waiting couple was a sure sign that the buses were still running. Beemer hung back in the shadows under the awning of a nail salon. Aware of his presence, the couple merely glanced rearward, clearly designating Beemer as someone destitute and, like them, waiting for the next transport.

"How long do you think?" Beemer had asked from the dark. "The next bus?"

"Five," the man had said, his accent something resembling East Indian or Pakistani. "Maybe ten."

"Thanks," muffled Beemer, who found a partial seat on the nail salon's windowsill.

"Oh, already!" exclaimed the woman.

Breaking through the smoky air, pinwheels of turbulence behind it, appeared an orange bus, its natural gas–powered engine thrumming as the hydraulic brakes were applied. Beemer, with his hands in his baggy pockets, eased in behind the couple, covered his face as if defending himself from the smoke, and slowly climbed the steps. He flashed the TAP card to the driver.

"Tap it and sit," the heavy-lidded driver had nodded, his flicking pupils drawing Beemer's attention to the smudged screen that read *TAP HERE*.

"My little sister's," lied Beemer, his nerves intact, but girding against the card being rejected. "Dunno if it's got anything left."

"Never know 'til you give it a go," returned the driver.

As Beemer neared the card to the sensor, the TAP screen lit up surprisingly green.

"It's your lucky day," muttered the driver, levering the automated door shut while releasing the brake. The coach rumbled as it moved forward.

Beemer balanced his way to a seat towards the back, shading his still-guarded face toward the window. He heard sirens. Seconds later, he watched a pair of LAPD radio cars scream past, charging in the opposite direction. Inside, both Beemer and the inner idiot sighed a breath of momentary relief.

"It's your lucky day," recalled Beemer, the driver's baritone

still repeating in his ears. *If he only knew. Lucky day or Lucky Dey?* Something was guiding him, delivering him from out of the fires and into the civilian world. Los Angeles. The land of Lucky Dey.

Luckyland.

The Metro TAP card had turned out to be a game changer. The same stupid taxpayers who paid the mortgages for police officers and firefighters were also on the hook to subsidize Los Angeles's under-utilized transit system. The irony of it amused Beemer. Joe and Jane Citizen had subsidized his escape via the Metro Orange Line while all available cops scoured the West Valley for the unidentified cop killer.

Along the thirty-four minute leg to North Hollywood, Beemer couldn't count the number of homeless. But he did count the average number of tent cities or encampments between Metro stops. One point four, he calculated. That was per mile on a single horizontal plot line. It repulsed him. Part of him wanted to bolt, run away, escape the Los Angeles underbelly, climb back into those blackened hills, and plot to be found wandering aimlessly, concussed, and separated from his convict fire crew.

Don't forget forgiven.

Something else was pulling at him. It was either from his bones or an unknowable external and otherworldly force. This betrayed his evolutionary belief and made for a hard pill to swallow. Yet there it was. Serendipity or something darker, pulling him back to Lucky. Revenge, he argued, was satisfaction for his inner idiot. But that other force felt far more ominous—more dangerous—than anything his inner idiot could conjure.

During those intervening daylight hours, Beemer kept his profile on the down low, staying to the shadowed alleys off the NoHo arts district. He quelled his hunger by palming peanut butter nutrition bars from a corner convenience store. He hydrated from a dirty garden hose behind Lankershim Boulevard's Mr. Eggroll Chinese Wok. When darkness at last returned, he used that Metro TAP card to catch a subway ride south and east.

Upon his arrival at downtown's historic Union Station and while searching for information on his next transfer east, Beemer happened upon one of the many television screens permanently installed to pacify bored passengers. The monitors were glowing rectangles of modernity, neatly inset into restored marble- and oak-paneled walls and always tuned to a local news station. This was how Beemer heard the sad finality that his entire strike team had been consumed in the fire.

"Cal Fire announced tonight the first casualties of the Fern Falls fire, one of the three uncontained blazes currently plaguing the north and west San Fernando Valley," said the local news anchor. "Twelve convict firefighters out of San Luis Obispo's Cuesta Station lost their lives when the fire jumped the line they were cutting and caught them in a ravine filled with scrub and oak . . ."

Beemer carefully watched and listened until the ninety-second story concluded. There was no mention of the thirteenth convict crew member. No alarm had been sounded that a surviving inmate had escaped. Then came the dark space between the news broadcast and a commercial. In the TV's reflection, Beemer caught a first look at himself. Scraped. Bedraggled. Ill-fitted clothes. By all appearances, he looked as indigent as the vagrants he'd so denigrated. He questioned his current status. Indeed, he *was* homeless. All he possessed was on his back and in his pocket—a screwdriver and a Metro TAP card. He surmised it as a brilliant disguise, allowing him to walk unmolested, almost unseen. Ignored by most citizenry and authorities. Beemer was now part of a legion of the designated invisibles.

How perfect.

He walked over to an enlarged map of bus and rail lines behind an equal-sized pane of Plexiglas in Union Station's vaulted plaster and beam main terminal. He found the city of Altadena, his index finger drawing a quick route back to the YOU ARE HERE icon.

The Metro Rail gold line was his next late-night leg. Pasadena's

Lake Street platform was the nearest stop to the Alta Vista address he'd branded onto his brain along with a bucketful of other useless information he'd dug up on the dark web.

Cohabitant with Lucky Dey is Lydia Gonzalez, an LAPD heli-copter pilot.

The mortgage on the Alta Vista bungalow was $500,000 on a sale of $721,000, the debt financed by the couple's respective police officer credit unions.

4387 Alta Vista Drive was built in the year 1917 and was a slight 1,678 square feet.

Also residing at the address was Lucky's eighteen-year-old adopted daughter, Karrie, and Lydia's sixteen-year-old son, Travis.

The address had survived break-ins. The most recent, a mysterious entry resulting in a dead dog. That very same night a man had been discovered shot to death in the middle of the same sleepy street, only four doors to the west. No direct link was ever proved.

There were four registered vehicles sharing the same address. A 2014 Toyota Prius. A 2012 Ford Explorer. A 1999 Ford Crown Victoria and . . .

"For you," a woman's voice whispered in Beemer's ear.

Beemer snapped awake. The interruption left him disoriented and trying to shake off the onset of dopiness. He was in the same window seat he'd chosen on the sparsely populated train car. Somehow, he'd been sucked into slumber with his head propped against the window. Outside were the lights of Pasadena and beyond—confusing because when he was last awake the light-rail vehicle had been motoring ahead on underground tracks.

"You look like you need it more than I," said the woman in a dirty-blonde nest of a wig.

He reckoned she was no younger than seventy. Into his fist she'd folded a single note of currency. As she receded, Beemer opened his hand, revealing a crumpled $20 bill. Surreal as the moment was, Beemer feared he'd missed his stop.

"What station?" he called out.

"Lake!" she called back.

Jesus!

He bolted from his seat and chased up the aisle to the nearly closed automated door. In a lunge onto the platform he first felt the cold. It must have been forty-five to fifty degrees. At last, a winter temperature for the overpopulated desert. Only the air hit him like it was subzero, biting at his cheeks like a walk-in freezer. The chill pulled him back six years in his mind to a time when he'd worried his face and fingers were frostbitten, all because he'd forgotten to equip himself. Suddenly, warmth was what he craved more than revenge. And perhaps some food and water.

Maybe even a beer.

Hands in his pockets, he caught the last glimpse of the kind woman's dirty-blonde wig as she hurried along a platform decorated in cheery advertisements for Pasadena's annual Rose Parade before disappearing down the escalator. He walked after her, keeping his distance while debating whether or not to abuse her of more generosity. Where there was a $20 bill, perhaps there was a car ride. Or how about a cozy cot in her garage? *No*, his smarter self reasoned. His sleep might have been why she was brave enough to apply her charity. Running after the old woman—or even appearing as if he were—might lead her to call out. He needed to keep to his plan. Stay invisible and camouflaged amongst the mostly forgotten. He'd keep the vagrant act going as a means to get as close to that Alta Vista address as humanly possible.

30

Downtown

Lucky couldn't remember the last time he'd felt so depleted. He'd pulled plenty of double and triple shifts, surviving the sleepless stints on mostly caffeine, adrenaline, and will. Yet, after he'd departed Porter Ranch and the intentionally awkward tête-à-tête with Bobby Bianchi, he'd pointed east and set a timer for his head to hit the nearest pillow. In order to mitigate the happy-to-be-home chitchat, he hoped to get head start on his mobile phone, but the conversation with Gonzo was sadly short.

"You're not the only dude stacking shifts," returned Gonzo. "I'm not in the air but I'm stuck at Hooper workin' a flight desk."

"Sucks for both of us," Lucky said.

"Watchin' the TV," she added. "Doesn't look good for us on Saturday."

"What's Saturday again?" jibed Lucky.

"Hardee har, har, har," she mocked.

"Oh, it's so on," he insisted. "Otherwise, you're gonna have to find another groom."

"Don't tempt me."

"Paid for the suit. You back out, I'm gonna burn that lacy dress of yours."

"You're not supposed to have seen my dress. Bad luck, remember?"

"Or bad Lucky," he yukked before an unconscious but very audible yawn.

"You sound exhausted."

"Nothin' bed can't fix," he said, trying like hell to sound glib. But he was so drained, his words spilled over his lips in near grunts.

The soon-to-be bride and groom exchanged a few short shares of their harrowing day. When Gonzo repeated her concern that the fires and emergency schedules would swamp their Saturday wedding, Lucky offered a snippet he'd heard in the news. The weather had begun a slow return to the January norm. An ocean-cooled breeze was expected to lower temperatures in the region while adding some double-digit humidity. He figured the firefighters would have the conflagrations under a modicum of control by Saturday.

"You hear about the inmate fire team?" she asked, thinking if by keeping the conversation moving Lucky would make it home safe and awake.

"Dead in a ravine. That them?" Lucky had heard some grapevine talk, but nothing confirmed.

"Really sad."

"Yeah. Not my choice . . ."

"Not your choice?" she asked. "What the hell?"

"Choice of ways to die," he clarified. "Sorry, babe. I'm fried to my brain cells."

Talking for Lucky had become a chore. He found it hard to summon words, let alone order them into cogent strings of thought. Making things worse was the ache in his lower back. The getting in and out of the car and hours upon hours of driving—

all without his usual cocktail of stretches, exercise, and physical therapy—were taking their toll. The architecture of metal screws and fused bone radiated with a familiar and distracting hurt.

Then he hung up.

Aw, shit, he realized.

Perhaps it was the subtle power of suggestion when he pictured Gonzo at her post inside downtown's Hooper Heliport. Or maybe there was no reason whatsoever other than he was following his last path to slumber. But somehow, while talking with his fiancée, he'd wandered off his eastward course to his bed in their cozy Altadena bungalow. Instead, Lucky had accidentally cut south, unconsciously heading downtown via the 170 freeway to the 101. When he realized his error, the thought of home versus the much closer office sofa turned into an easy decision. He needed serious rest. And the sooner the better.

"Christ, what a moron," Lucky said, aloud and chastising himself.

He rolled down his window in hope that the cooler air would put a waking spank to his face. Next he hit the 3rd Street off-ramp at an ambitious speed. He was counting down the distance to when he could lower his eyelids. Eleven blocks east, five blocks north. Park, cover Temple Street in twelve smooth strides, four stairs up, thirteen down, corridor, office, collapse, sleep.

Then came the roadblock. Lucky braked and found himself staring at flashing yellow lights attached to the tops of blue and white sawhorses. A Water and Power project, he reasoned. They were forever replacing the aging water mains, laid out some one hundred years earlier by William Mulholland. The wannabe engineer and human force of nature had delivered water to the desert, without which Los Angeles would never have flourished into an iconic horizontal megalopolis. Lucky once read that Mulholland had used a variety of crews to bury the pipe, keeping the actual map of the underground infrastructure only in his head. The rationale was for nothing more than job security.

What random-ass thoughts, mused Lucky. *Shit you think of when you're dog damned tired.*

To his left, Lucky noticed a three-story brick building. *Brick shithouse,* he recalled Angie saying during her digital tutorial. *That's it,* he thought, *the repository where all the city's personnel records are kept—every investigation going back how many years?* Lucky's unfocused brain imagined the bodies buried within those files.

And all the secrets . . .

Lucky was jolted back to the present by the noise of knuckles rapping against the passenger window. Had he fallen asleep at the wheel, right foot fortuitously still resting on the brake pedal? He twisted his head right, noting only the shadow of man, thick in the neck, neat hairline.

His muscles tensed. Not from fear or concern, but autonomously. Starting at his neck and like a lightning bolt, through his arms into his thorax and legs. For a fraction of a split second, he actually worried that one of the screws in his back had come loose and penetrated his spinal cord. Then he recalled his training. All police officers were required to voluntarily take both a face full of pepper spray and be on the receiving end of the fifty thousand volts delivered through a Taser gun.

Fuck me. I just got tased.

31

Altadena

"Nice tent."

"Who's askin'?" growled a bite-sized homeless man. He crawled out of the flap of the single-sleeper mountaineering tent and looked up. His scraggly face and exposed body parts were blackened with filth, a stark contrast to the obviously spanking-new tent of red and white stitched nylon.

Beemer took a step closer, his face lit by the failing flame of a coffee tin fire.

"Where do you get a tent like that?" asked Beemer, his body shivering.

"I know you?" asked Bite-Size in a rat-a-tat stuttering. "I know you?"

"Dunno," shrugged Beemer. "I'm cold. Dunno where I am."

"You h-h-h-high?" waved off Bite-Size. "Ggggggo way."

"Not high. Just cold 'n' hungry. Figure I should get me a tent like yours."

"You ddddddon't know this place? Then you dddddon't belong—do not belong—don't belong." Bite-Size put a spark of finality from behind the tent's flap.

Beemer wasn't lost. He knew to the meter precisely where he stood. And it hardly assuaged his discomfort. He'd sauntered up Lake Avenue until he reached the intersection at Alta Vista. Instead of venturing the short two blocks to Lucky's bungalow, he felt it wiser to lie in wait. Remain invisible while he spied, skulked, and plotted a revenge worthy of remembering. So, he chose to follow a pair of dumpster-diving vagrants who'd been pillaging restaurant leftovers behind one of the city's main drags. They led Beemer to a homeless encampment near the base of the mountains.

Fire country, thought Beemer. *Hell, I can smell the fresh dried fuel of sage and chaparral.*

The unregulated community of pup tents and cardboard hovels had flowered along the sandy track that circled behind a fifty-foot knoll that separated civilized sprawl from flat tiers of empty overgrown lots. The tracts, bulldozed a few decades ago for homes that had never been erected, allowed for each of the thirty or so vagrants to claim up to an entire quarter of an acre for his own use. It was the bright colors of Bite-Size's tent and still-burning fire that had drawn Beemer near.

"What's one of them cost?" persisted Beemer.

"If ya gotta ask—gotta ask—you can't afford."

"Buy it from ya?" asked Beemer.

Bite-Size's head appeared again, his dirty mane tucked under a ragged San Diego Chargers beanie, the gold embroidered lightning bolt the color of jaundice. Despite the grotesqueness of the cap, just looking at it warmed Beemer's ears.

"Cost me fifty at the Big 5. Fifty, fifty, fifty! After-Christmas sale," bragged Bite-Size. "That's, like, a half a day workin' a good off-ramp. Worth double that too!"

"All I got is this." Beemer snapped the $20 bill handed to him by the charitable lady on the train.

"Twenty? Sheeeeeeit."

"So, it won't buy me a tent?" asked Beemer, slurring his words in hope of sounding slow and dull. "What's twenty bucks get me up this way?"

"Blow job from Maggie," grunted Bite-Size before getting stuck in a stammer. "Getcha two—getcha two—two—two—two—two. But—but—but you don' know the way to the nnnnnnnnnest. I'll take half that twenty. Show you the way."

"Any good?"

"Mmmmmmmmmaggie?"

"Her hummer."

"Pipe took all her teeth—all her teeth," laughed Bite-Size. "Need I say more, nnnnnneed I say more?"

Beemer gave a "Show the way" gesture. Bite-Size scrambled out from his new tent. The vagrant wore soiled sweats, cut off at the calves like capri pants. His feet appeared to be freshly socked in thirdhand Velcro sandals.

"New socks?" asked Beemer, still pretending to be interested.

"Big 5, I sssssssaid." Bite-Size was already twisting toward a path through the shoulder-high brush directly behind his tent. "Wanna know what Bbbbbbig 5 stand for?"

"What?" gamed Beemer.

"Fffffffive fffffffinger discount!" guffawed Bite-Size.

When on his feet, the homeless man was smaller than Beemer had imagined, barely five-foot-two or -three—his age impossible to calculate. Beemer imagined the man's size had led to a lifetime of diminishment, an ugly bull's-eye for schoolyard bullies.

Hell, wondered Beemer. *He could be my age. Could have gone to my middle school. How many times might I have already kicked his skinny ass?*

The odds were remote. The idea of it had flashed across Beemer's mind in the seconds before he realized that the trek to Maggie's was turning into more of a hike. Uphill. Then came a gulch not quite as deep as the one that Cappy had ordered the strike team to cross before the fire had engulfed them. Beyond the gnarled thicket was a plateau, long ago flattened by earth-moving equipment and rimmed in smokeless starlight. Did Maggie live up there? Or perhaps it was staked out by Bite-Size's larger friends, ready to pluck Beemer of his $20.

It's time, called out his calmer self, the voice not fully connected to his inner idiot.

"Yo. Turn around," said Beemer once his feet felt the bottom of the gulch path.

"Almost there, almost there," assured Bite-Size.

"Need you to see this first," insisted Beemer.

"What now?" Bite-Size had stopped and spun a quick one-eighty to face Beemer.

Beemer's move was swift. He threw an armlock around Bite-Size's head and slipped the screwdriver underneath the man's rib cage, sinking it upward and into the heart. Despite the gush of blood over Beemer's hand, he hung on, momentarily suspending the little man's body weight until he began to twitch with oncoming death. He made sure to pinch the woolen cap as Bite-Size slipped away and slumped to the dirt.

Beemer's instinct was to smell the greasy skullcap. *No*, his wiser brain advised. *If you smell it, you won't wear it. And you'll be cold forever.* So, with little regard for anything but comforting his frozen ears, Beemer slipped on the headwear and went about the chore of hiding the homeless man's body.

Off the path, under the brush.

It would be a day or two before the smell of death would alert the neighborhood of homeless. Then again, maybe the vagrants' own pungent odor would mask the stench. By the time the body was discovered, Beemer would have moved on. Closed in on his prey. Quenched both his inner idiot and rational self with vengeance. He even imagined that when his task was done, he might walk into a local firehouse, pretending to be dazed and bereft from the horrific loss of his convict crew. How long before the state corrections authority and Cal Fire would return him to the Cuesta Camp to finish out his sentence?

In the moment, Beemer couldn't picture a more satisfying way to finish out his prison term. Fighting fires. That, and remembering how he finished his contest with Lucky Dey.

32

Downtown

How many shocks had Lucky received before he'd tripped into blissful unconsciousness? He stopped the mental tally at four. It had been a long series of Taser attacks and between each he'd felt himself briefly lose his vision and muscle function. When they returned, he'd find himself being dragged or carried by those two unrecognizable musclemen. Bodybuilders, he reckoned. Reeking of cologne. And when his nerves tingled enough to give him the confidence to fight back, he was dropped to the pavement for another bite from the stun gun's teeth-like electrodes.

When he woke he was cold and stripped of all his clothes. His limbs were immobilized. Was he paralyzed? His eyes were open, but there was no light for his optic nerve to gather. Had the shocks left him blind? Then feeling to his muscles began to return. He was upright. Seated. Arms trussed behind his back, legs secured to a chair, bound with who knows what. When he flexed to his tensile he heard the tiniest tearing sound. He guessed duct tape as the adhesive.

The room rocked left then right. Not an earthquake, he reasoned. The natural balance between his ears figured the movement to be that of shock absorbers.

I'm in a box truck.

If he concentrated he could smell the plywood paneling. When he wiggled his toes he felt the cold of the aluminum floor. The truck rocked again.

A man stepping on the bumper . . .

The sound of the latch being thrown was painfully loud, echoing and bouncing off the interior. Then came the rear door noisily lifting upward, the spring-loaded mechanics retracting until it slapped into place with a resounding *kuh-chang!* Framed in the opening were those same two musclemen, backlit by the lights of downtown's train yards and the faint art deco pillars of the 4th Street Bridge. He watched the shorter of the two men squat to receive a car battery, handed upward by the other. In the dimness, Lucky was able to spot the bulging brachii of the mens' oversized biceps. Bodybuilders. No doubt they were friends or employees of Bobby Bianchi.

The man standing on the bumper made for a bigger kick from the shock absorbers. He climbed inside the cargo space and pulled down the retracting door until it latched closed. Once again, Lucky was plunged into darkness.

A flashlight snapped into bloom, the beam briefly wobbling before finding Lucky's face, causing him to squint.

"Yeah, all right," croaked Lucky. "You got me. Now whaddayou want?"

"Shut up, thief!" boomed Dakota before showing his reach by slapping Lucky hard across the face. "We ask. Y'all talk. Simple. Understand?"

"Right," nodded Lucky, not giving a rat's ass about the pain to his face. If anything, it created some heat on his skin. He tried not to shudder from the cold creeping closer to his marrow.

"Where is it?" asked Buggie from behind the flashlight.

"Where's what?" returned Lucky with an obvious eye roll.

Smack! Dakota's fingers raked Lucky's face.

"So, that's it?" annoyed Lucky. "You gonna slap whatever you want outta me?"

The flashlight beam flicked from Lucky's face to the car battery on the floor. ACDelco. New and probably just off the shelf from a local AutoZone, Pep Boys, or Costco. If Lucky lived, those would be the first places he'd look for video of the muscleheads making their purchase, probably with a credit card. That was how so many criminals got nicked.

Coiled next to the ACDelco was a set of equally new jumper cables.

"See that?" directed Buggie. "We're gonna get it out of you, no matter what."

"Shocking," croaked Lucky.

"Shut the fuck up!" bit Dakota.

"Mind telling me what *it* is?" exhaled Lucky, as if he didn't know. "Ask me straight up. Maybe I'll tell you."

"Where's Bobby's Beatles collection?" tried Buggie.

"Straight up?" repeated Lucky. "I don't know. He's mistaken about—"

Smack! Dakota delivered another four-fingered slap, this time across Lucky's temple.

"Right," heaved Lucky. "You're gonna torture me. Before you start, can I ask a coupla easy questions? After that? Have at me. Torture away."

"What?" asked Buggie.

"You know how to work those jumper cables?" Lucky asked. "If you don't, I got a Triple A card in my wallet. Maybe they can help—"

Crack! Dakota pumped a short, sharply aimed fist into Lucky's nose. It crunched at impact, turning his already mangled snout into a red sieve.

"YouTube, dickhead," angered Dakota. "Nothin' you can't learn how to do. Including getting truth out of dirtbags like you."

"Right, right, right, right," relented Lucky, tasting the metal of his own blood. "I'm tired. Been a long three days. So, serious question. No joke. Okay?"

Lucky's eyes had been adjusting. Despite the flashlight beam focused on his face, he was able to make out the men's features. The tall blond and blue-eyed muscleman looked like feature casting out of a Nazi recruiting film. The smaller well-manicured of the two had been born with a set of unfortunate eyes, wide round orbs with very little in the way of lids.

"When you're done with your torture," continued Lucky. "And you determine that I don't know squat about Bobby's Beatles collection—"

"But you do!" spat Buggie.

"Sure, right," agreed Lucky. "But for argument sake, let's say I don't. What you gonna do after? Let me go? Yeah? No? Then what? I'm a cop—"

"Hobby cop," interrupted Dakota.

"Reserve," corrected Lucky. "Before that I had eighteen years in L.A. Sheriff's and Kern. Now, kidnapped while I'm on duty. You don't think I have friends?"

"We don't care that you have friends—"

"You say you don't, but you really do," corrected Lucky. "Either that or you're both as stupid as stupid gets." He kept his voice even and matter-of-fact despite the discomfort of the moment. "Kidnapping? Torture of a police officer? You know the weight that carries? Ever hear of compounding felonies?"

"You're a dirty cop!" argued Buggie.

"Or so Bobby has convinced you," replied Lucky. "But let's say I'm not dirty. After you hook me up to Mr. ACDelco there and get nothin' outta me because that's what I know. *Nothing.* Only way you guys walk is if you kill me. You ready for that?"

There was no instant retort from either of the muscleheads. Both pursed their lips into horizontal thin lines of creeping doubt.

"All right. So, bite down on this nugget. Either of you killed a man?" asked Lucky, upping the ante. "Not as hard as you think. But gettin' rid of the body, all the evidence, DNA? That's the actual bitch of it. But, hey. It doesn't have to come to that. At least not until you call up Bobby. Tell 'im the truth, which is I don't know shit. That's when he's gonna panic, realize the stupid that he's done. He's gonna order you to cut my throat and get rid of the evidence . . ."

Lucky heard the faint yet distinct sound of Dakota trying to dry swallow.

"Hey," added Lucky in what he hoped would be his verbal coup de grâce. "This cargo truck. Is it a rental? And did either of you use your own credit card?"

Despite the minimal spill from the flashlight, Lucky could still read the gleam of Dakota's teeth. Two perfect fixed rows of candy-white forming a shit-eating grin.

"You think we're stupid," declared Dakota.

"No," corrected Lucky. "I think you're a couple of almost-smart dudes who know the right thing from the wrong thing."

"Naw," drawled Dakota. "You talk at me like I'm all muscle and no brains. Bet you think I don't know the positive side from the negative side of an electric charge." With his huge sneaker, Dakota slid the heavy car battery closer to Lucky. He uncoiled the jumper cables, squatted, and attached the correct clamps to the battery posts.

"Dakota used to work as an electrician," bragged Buggie. "On movie sets."

"Shut your yap, Bugs," angered Dakota. "Now he knows my fuckin' name."

"And now he knows mine!" shot back Buggie.

"How about I promise to forget the both of you?" offered Lucky. "So far? All you've done is inconvenience me—"

"Nuh uh," interrupted Dakota. "You said assault on a police officer. Kidnapping."

"You did!" confirmed Buggie.

"Ya see?" agreed Dakota. "So, what's a little torture to the charge?"

Holding the free ends of the jumper cables, his hands protected by the rubberized clamp handles, he touched the copper alloy teeth together. *Pop! Crackle!* Sparks arced between poles.

"Bugs?" Dakota indicated with his chin.

Unfurling a beach towel, Buggie slid behind Lucky. He twisted the towel in the middle and lopped the thick part over Lucky's nose and mouth, applying pressure by pulling back on it like reins on a horse.

"Where is Bobby's stuff?" asked Dakota before jabbing the electrified clamps into Lucky's ribs.

It wasn't at all like the Taser, which had delivered a survivable jolt. The lower-powered car battery burned his skin while delivering a slow charge that rippled through ligament and bone.

Lucky tried like hell not to scream. He failed.

33

"License, registration, proof of insurance, please?" asked the bored-sounding highway patrolman, as if this were his millionth traffic stop in a single shift.

Though it was technically a request, Bobby knew it was an order.

"Can I first offer an apology for my speeding?" Bobby's hands were wisely at the ten and two o'clock positions on the Audi's steering wheel, his fingers unknowingly gesturing with obvious impatience.

"Sir? Driver's license, registration, and insurance. *Please*," underlined the patrolman, safely standing to the left and rear of the Audi's driver, hand resting on the butt of his holstered pistol. In his left hand was a small tactical flashlight.

"Yeah, yeah." Bobby stretched across to the glove box, popped it wide, and withdrew the leather-bound owner's manual. Inside the sleeve was his registration and proof of car insurance. But when he reached into his back pocket, he suddenly realized he had neither a pocket nor his wallet. "Shit."

For Bobby, the last few hours had been a three-ring circus. Barbara and the children had returned from their extended stint at the Four Seasons Hotel, carrying far more shopping bags than luggage, as well as enough Popeye's fried chicken to feed the entire cul-de-sac. A long-simmering marital argument erupted in shouts across their McMansion. Barbara eventually locked him out of the bedroom with only his mobile phone to keep him company. Bobby pounded and kicked at the door with such a volume that it left his two youngest girls weeping behind their own latched doors. Locked out and alone again, he angrily retired to the guesthouse—man cave/office—next to the backyard hole that was rebar-ready for the first of three concrete pours. Bobby's future sound bunker was roped in safety tape, the yellow ribbons shimmering whenever the moonlight would sneak through the streams of smoke. Bobby shut the doors and windows and stomped and yelled in a vein-popping steroid rage. When he was finished, he settled in for bottled beers and the vintage porno films his father used to finance.

At 2:19 a.m., his phone woke him.

"Better be good," Bobby answered, the chemical rage in him rising before his eyes could focus on the phone number.

"He's finally talking," chapped Dakota in a clipped and distant voice. "But says he'll only tell you the rest to your face."

"Tell me the rest of what?"

"Where your shit is," clarified the bodybuilder. His voice echoed in a telltale sign that he was on a mobile speakerphone.

"Fuck that," croaked Bobby. "Your job is to get it out of him. Call me back when you know—"

"THAT'S RRRRIGHT!" howled Lucky's pained voice—part mad as hell, part wounded. "YOU WOP, PUSSY, FUCK-TOOL—"

"Shut up!" shouted Buggie.

Bobby heard a sharp slap across Lucky's face.

"That the guy?" asked Bobby, snapped awake. "That the cop?"

"Seriously, dude," said a breathless Dakota. "You're gonna wanna get in on the fun. Especially after all the crap he said about you."

"WANNABE GANGSTER? HA HA FUCKING HA!" squealed Lucky. "TOO PUSSY TO DO THE DIRTY WORK?"

Bobby heard Lucky hocking up a mouthful of phlegm and spitting it.

"Where are you?" he asked, fueled on his own fury.

That had been nearly twenty minutes before the lone highway patrolman had lit him up for busting the speed limit on the southbound lanes of Interstate 5. While Bobby waited for the cop to run his car for wants and warrants, he kept his eyes on the sky-reaching lights of downtown. Somewhere underneath the high-rises, glowing signage, and twinkling Christmas lights of the still-decorated palm trees was the parking lot and rented box truck where Dakota and Buggie had stashed that name-calling bastard Lucky Dey. He couldn't imagine the sun coming up without getting his own licks in.

"Know the speed limit, sir?" asked the returning highway patrolman.

"I was exceeding—"

"Asked if you know it."

"Sixty-five . . ." exhaled Bobby.

"Clocked you over ninety-five. That's a thirty-mile-per-hour differential. Doing that without your driver's license? I have the option to put you in bracelets and have you spend the rest of the night in county jail."

Bobby burned at the patented monotone of authority. The voice of the highway patrolman might as well have been Lucky's breathing in his ear, raising every enraged hackle.

"But the system says your license is up to date," continued the highway patrolman. "So, here's what we're gonna do. In addition to ticketing you for breaking the speed limit by thirty, I'm citing you for driving without a license on your person. That's gonna require a trip to the DMV to—"

"Good to go," leaked Bobby, not meaning to interrupt. He painted on a fake smile. "Sorry. Yes, officer. I understand. You got a job to do."

"Sit tight. Be right back for your signature."

Bobby counted off the minutes until he reached the number six. Six excruciating minutes it took for the highway patrolman to complete his duty, in the end gifting Bobby with two citations and a final warning to keep his speed under the limit. Bobby thanked the officer, waving out the open window with his left hand while crumpling the pair of tickets in his right. After tossing the refuse into the passenger footwell, he dropped the Audi back into gear and checked the navigation on his phone. He was still nine minutes from his destination. As he pulled back onto the freeway, careful to set his speedometer on a flat sixty-five miles per hour, he wondered if those nine minutes would stretch to something like eleven or twelve.

Patience, he breathed.

The nearly empty parking lot—a flat and slightly elevated plateau above the railroad yard—was cloaked in darkness. Parked in a corner was the same U-Haul box truck that, hours earlier, had fronted his house. It was backed in the rearmost space. There were no lights visible.

Bobby parked two slots away, stepped from his Audi, and pricked his ears for the sound of voices. When he heard nothing at all, he wondered if the U-Haul was soundproofed. Or perhaps that damned hobby cop called Lucky Dey had passed out or expired from whatever flavor of anguish the muscleman minions had inflicted.

Bobby circled to the rear of the truck and gently rapped two knuckles on the retracting door. Almost instantly, the lock was released and the spring-loaded panels began to rise automatically in a tic-tic-tic until a louder clank. The retractable door stopped. Bobby stared up at the inside, unable to see beyond the blackness.

"Dako—" Bobby's larynx was cut by a sudden air-plugging constriction. He automatically grabbed at his neck, feeling a leather belt that tightened like a noose.

"Lemme help you," sounded Lucky, who pulled at the business end of the belt, dragging Bobby Bianchi up and over the bumper and into the cargo hold. While Bobby gagged and choked, Lucky cleared the man's legs out of the way and pulled down on the door. The sound of it relatching paired with an echo that was fast deadened by the plywood walls.

Bobby's gagging continued as Lucky led him by the belt end until he found the folding chair. As Bobby began to flail, Lucky withdrew the stun gun from his rear pocket—the very same one utilized by Dakota and Buggie at the beginning of his abduction. He drove the electrode teeth into Bobby's sweatshirt and pulled the trigger. Bobby convulsed, his entire body turning to jelly with a single charge.

"Only three more," hissed Lucky. "'Cause that's how many they hit me with."

True to his word, Lucky applied the stun gun three additional times, rendering Bobby to human blubber.

Lucky strapped Bobby to the chair with the leftover duct tape, then flicked on the flashlight. Bobby was just recovering when a close-up blast from the flashlight lens flooded his vision.

"Don't worry. Not gonna strip you naked like they did me. Don't need to see your shrunken junk to know you're a candy stacker," Lucky said, referring to Bobby's anabolic steroid abuse.

Lucky relooped his belt into his bloodstained pants, then trained the flashlight on his own torso and the dozen or so raised, beet-red welts from his jumper-cable torture session.

"You like?" aimed Lucky. "At least your boys did the torture part right."

He saw Bobby's eyes switch left and right, afraid and partly expecting Dakota or Buggie to step in to assist.

"Where are they?" wheezed Bobby.

"Hell if I know," shrugged Lucky. "After they'd convinced

themselves that I didn't know jack shit about your burglary, they figured that's as far as they were willing to go. I let 'em walk in exchange for putting on that little phone show. You know, the one that got you here. That, and . . ."

"And . . . ?" asked Bobby as if cued.

"Crime and punishment," Lucky directed the flashlight on the plywood walls of the truck's cargo bay. "Aggravated kidnapping? That's codes 207, 208, 209. Torture? That's a 206."

Bobby's eyes followed the beam. The walls were smeared with blood and spatter. So was the aluminum-alloy floor. Then Lucky regarded the scrapes and cuts on the knuckles of both his hands.

"The big one," said Lucky. "What's his name? Dakota? Yeah. He's your employee? Hope you pay good medical. 'Cause he's gonna need a redo on his dental work."

"Whaddayou want?" spat Bobby, summoning perhaps his last lick of indignation.

"Third and last time you and I gonna face off. First time, I let you off with a warning. Second time? I stood on your doorstep hoping to clean the slate with the understanding I had nothin' to do with your robbery. Follow so far? Nod if you do."

Bobby nodded, his chest filling up with hope that it all would end right there. His pupils would meet Lucky's, then dart away, focusing on one of those fresh welts from the torture he'd ordained.

"Third strike is right here and now," impressed Lucky. "Albeit only after your dumbfuck muscle boys played ACDelco on my innocent ass."

"I hear ya," agreed Bobby with a trio of overly enthusiastic head bobs. "Misunderstanding gone really, really wrong. I'm good. You good, right?"

"I'm good?" Lucky stood back, arms wide. "Lookit me. I'm a human braille map. This petty shit you did comes with years in a state lockup. But then you and me know what happens to guys like you. Money. Connected. Bet porn daddy's got lotsa City Hall pals. So, yeah. First things first. Junior needs to taste his own bad behavior."

"Whoa!" called out Bobby, his eyes following as Lucky bent over to collect the handles of the jumper cables.

Snap! The teeth of cable clamps sparked when Lucky touched them together.

"Like that?" asked Lucky. "Exactly how they started with me."

"No, no, no, no, no, no!"

"Hey. Look at me. I survived," salved Lucky. "So will you."

Snap, snap, snap!

Bobby's screams—high pitched and bordering on girlish—began before the copper teeth so much as touched his flesh. The man's howls were piercing, inflicting punishment to Lucky's ears.

Friday

34

Santa Anita Park. Arcadia. 11:00 a.m.

The storied racetrack had never once failed to provide Oren with veritable chills. That special clash of goose bumps were the best kind—a chemical mix of anticipation, excitement, and the fear of the floor collapsing beneath him. The opening of the new season had begun the day after Christmas. It was just two weeks, followed by a four-month break before the ponies returned mid-April for the duration of spring.

I've been busy, Oren had excused of himself. That, and he hadn't any actual cash for wagering, though that hadn't kept him from browsing the daily racing forms as a tune-up for his big return.

The dawn had felt crisp. Almost wet. Because the track was so far to the east, there was barely a whiff of detectable smoke, this despite the constant local news updates claiming the fires were barely contained and had already destroyed twenty-one homes. Oren couldn't help but wonder which homes? Had they been leveled because of the fires he started? Or were they the product of someone else's accident or a utility company's malfeasance? Oren found himself unable to divine the source of the sourness in his stomach. Was it pride? Or repulsion?

The racetrack appeared as he'd left it. In fact, it hadn't much changed since long before Oren was born. Per his habit, he arrived hours before the first race. The massive parking lots that surrounded the venue were practically empty. Only employees and hardcore racing addicts showed up so early. The latter seeking lucky parking spots before stumbling, hungover and in search of a caffeine fix, toward the grand teal-stuccoed buildings topped by white spires. The historic facility had been freshly accented with sweeping striped awnings.

Just the way I left it? As if...

Oren knew much of the story. Very little had been altered since Santa Anita Park had first opened its doors in 1934. In a region that seemed so quick to tear down and upgrade venues, Santa Anita Park was about as close as a person could get to stepping into a time machine. Once inside the labyrinth of halls, platforms, whiskey bars, and restaurants, all Oren needed was to squint away the TV screens and automated betting machines and he'd feel as if he were living some post–World War II fantasy. He'd even dress for the occasion in vintage loose twill slacks, saddle shoes, and a bowling shirt under a wool cardigan. His wardrobe was a collection of thrift store bargains, bought with his earliest winnings from a straight-up bet on the most spectacular piece of horseflesh he'd ever spied.

Hip Slick. Oh, Lord, what a beauty.

The cash to support his return was supposed to have been supplied by Peter Bianchi. Oren had plotted and assembled. He'd hiked the mountains, mapped the locales, and studied so much local meteorology that he wondered if he'd be considered employable by one of the local TV newscasts. And though the late summer, fall, and early weeks of winter had been the driest on record, the high-pressure desert conditions required for his fiery plan to rob Bobby Bianchi of his precious Beatles collection hadn't materialized until New Years Day, meaning Oren had already missed almost a week of first-class horse racing.

And I'm still goddamn penniless.

If he were to get flush by the full spring season, he was either going to have to list the house for a quick sale or fence pieces of the stolen collection without getting caught. He'd trolled the internet, pricing out random items from Bobby's collection, starting with the framed Andy Warhol lithograph of John, Paul, George, and Ringo. But the market was saturated with both real and fake versions. Bids on various auction sites barely topped $500. As for a pawnshop, he couldn't imagine getting half that much. There were the two gold records, one of them from 1964—the single "Something New." Oren learned it was the follow-up to "A Hard Day's Night" and valued at just shy of $20,000. A healthy number, but an actual gold record was a worry. His gut told him the item could be easily traced. And unless he knew the pawnshop was crooked, offering it for sale might set off alarms.

There were Beatles figurines, signed photographs, sheets upon sheets of Beatles postage stamps, a metal lunch box, an original *Yellow Submarine* movie poster, a quadruple-signed photo of the band's first performance at Dodger Stadium, never-played 45 RPM vinyl singles, pins and buttons, rare Japanese box sets, and hand-signed love letters between John and Yoko.

Then there were the vinyl albums. One of serious consideration was the banned "butcher cover" for the 1966 *Yesterday and Today* LP, depicting a gleeful Fab Four in white smocks, holding or shouldered with bloody doll parts and pieces of sliced raw meat. The value of the album was around $100,000. But instead of selling it outright, Oren thought he might be able to pawn it in exchange for a high-interest loan of, say, twenty grand. It was salivating. By pawning it, the record and jacket might not show up in any stolen police reports. The same was true of the limited-release 1980 double album called *The Headlines*. The value of the record had less to do with it being a rarity and more to do with the number of the edition—666—the rock 'n' roll sign of the devil. Oren was able look up what Bobby had paid for it at auction. His winning bid had been a clean $111,000.

Oren was impressed.

The final piece of collectible vinyl was all too familiar—John Lennon and Yoko Ono's *Double Fantasy*. At first glance, it was little more than a hurriedly signed record—Lennon's fast-moving black pen had quickly slashed across the gray tones of the black-and-white cardboard sleeve. Oren remembered the moment when he'd first held it. Bobby had been showing off his private collection to partygoers one by one. Upon being handed the plastic-sheathed album, Oren had remarked with a simple and polite, "Cool."

"So much more than cool," Bobby pimped. "See that right there?" With his index finger, Bobby indicated a hard-to-read stamp on the upper right-hand corner.

"What's that?" Oren had innocently asked. "Is that some kinda bargain bin marking?"

"That, my ignorant friend," replied Bobby, "is the evidence number."

"Evidence?"

"Yeah. That's the record. The one and only."

"Don't get it. Was it stolen from somewhere?"

"Kind of," Bobby had sniggered. "Ever hear of Mark David Chapman?"

"Not really," Oren had shrugged.

"Mark David Chapman was John Lennon's assassin," grinned Bobby, eyes popping with the excitement of telling a great tale. "Lennon signed this for Mark David Chapman on the day he died. Coming out of the Dakota Apartments. He signed it right there. Got in his limo with Yoko, spent the next few hours at the recording studio. When he returned, Chapman was still there. Shot Lennon dead on the sidewalk."

"And this was the . . ."

"The record Lennon signed for Chapman," relished Bobby. "Eventually, it goes missing from the NYPD evidence lockup. It's only passed hands through private buyers. No auction records. No paper trail. And now it's mine, mine, all mine. Forever, like."

"Holy crap."

"Wow, right? And when I finish my sound bunker, guess what's the first piece of wax I'm gonna play?"

Oren was repulsed. He'd handed back the plastic-covered album as if he were Superman after being handed a mug full of kryptonite. He'd felt gooseflesh all the way down to his ankles. His knees weakened. It had felt like death to him. Evil. And by association, that meant Bobby was evil. In the moment, Oren had felt the ugliest of fears and wanted distance. Not fifteen minutes later, Peter Bianchi had cornered him between a pair of queen palms behind Bobby's backyard bar. That's when he had floated the idea of the two of them cashing in on Bobby's collection. In haste, Oren had moralized that it would be righteous to steal from the likes of Bobby. That Bobby, in his unmitigated unctuousness, deserved what he got. And if that meant losing his collection? So be it.

"And every last precious figurine, gold record, all of it. Not insured," Peter had guffawed, as if placing a very appealing cherry on top.

Now Peter was dead.

Since his own murderous act, a cloak of denial had hung over Oren. He'd forgotten entirely about the nefarious John Lennon record until Thursday night, when he had pored over the stash searching for something to pawn. And then there it was—in Oren's hands, just as it had been that fateful night. He felt no vibrations. No evil curse. Only opportunity. Oren's web searches for the evidence-marked album proved almost fruitless. There was only one photo, published time and time again by different media sources. Oren examined and compared the online photo to the sealed vinyl record. After going over practically every last digital pixel, the album appeared genuine.

If it's for real, how much is it worth? Or better yet, worried Oren, *how much just to get the cursed disk out of my possession?*

Oren knew that pawning stolen goods was illegal as hell. Licensed pawnbrokers were required by law to vet every potential item against reported stolen goods databases. Plus, they needed to videotape and properly ID the items' sellers. But technically speaking, Bobby's John Lennon album had never been stolen. Not even once. Or insured. Oren sincerely doubted that Bobby could have—let alone would have—included the Lennon record on his laundry list of stolen collectibles.

So, Oren pawned the evil album and carried a flat stack of cash out of Glen Annie's Pawn and Coin's glass door. He secured an on-the-spot $5,000 loan with the signed *Double Fantasy* LP serving as collateral. The establishment was eight miles due east of Santa Anita Park. Oren had picked the shop because he'd been a longtime customer without a blemish on his record.

He drove the sixteen minutes west to Arcadia and the race-track. He even landed on his lucky parking space, a southernmost slot fronting Huntington Drive. From there it was a short walk to the ticket booth. Oren barely gave any attention to all the famil-iar faces, avoiding all eye contact to prevent any useless small-talk encounters. He paid $2 cash for a racing form, then swerved away from the escalators and whisked past Seabiscuit Court and the blooming arrays of winter flowers meticulously cared for by the park's groundskeepers. Those were decorations for the tourists and Sunday gamblers. Hardly for the hardcore. He let his nose lead him to the sweet scent of the paddocks. There a man could inhale the smell of fresh manure, horse sweat, alfalfa, muscle liniment, and saddle soap.

My paddocks, breathed Oren. Because for him, it was the pad-docks where the real magic happened.

The twelve-stall open-air port was a viewing area where fans could observe the trainers and groomers as the animals were prepped before each race. The jockeys in their colored silks would carefully oversee the saddling before mounting and heading off for a couple turns around the walking ring followed by the on-track warm-up. Each serious gambler had a system. Some were number crunchers with their noses stuck to racing forms or online databases on their mobile phones, factoring in track conditions, race length, jockeys, and the horses' personal records. All this to make their expert bets. Other gamblers were all about the warm-ups, judging a horse by its attitude and gait as it eased from the walking ring to the track. Was the horse excited and sheening, or pacing itself for the bell and race time?

Oren's method was all about the paddock. It was the closest the paying public was allowed to the animals prior to a race. Mere feet. His practice was about complete and total reliance on three of his senses. Smell, sight, sound. Oren trusted his nose to detect any odd scents, chemical or otherwise. Were they drugged up on Lasix or Butazolidine? A sweat-wetted horse was a bad bet. Was the horse calmly allowing a trainer to tie its tongue from interfering with the bit? That sometimes equaled a good bet. Oren liked a good flank-to-shoulder ratio, a streamlined front, a high motor in the rear. He preferred lean cheeks to muscled, knife-shaped necks to those that resembled a human thumb. With his ears he'd tune in to the sound of a horse's breathing. Was it calm and unhurried? Or rapid, the beast already burning calories in pre-race anticipation? He'd admit it was unscientific. Yet that was the fun of it—trusting his base instincts and perhaps even a connection to the animal. And if and when that particularly curated horse won?

"Better than sex," he'd once said to his wife toward the end of their marriage. "At least, sex with you."

"What you think of the bay?" asked a gin-blossomed track regular in a half whisper, leaning in close enough for Oren to guess the cheap brand of juniper-based liquor he'd been nipping.

"My eye's on the five horse," shared Oren with a practiced lie. He'd never reveal his personal pick. Never. Ever.

"The roan?" said the track regular, surprised. "She's a dog in hooves."

"Then why ask?" It was Oren's polite version of "Fuck off." The track regular took the hint and sidestepped his way until he was squared up with the next stall.

Oren's attraction was the chestnut—the number-three horse in the first race. According the racing form, the animal was called Rincon's Ghost and was going to be hauling a rookie jockey of no repute over four short furlongs. It was a bad bet by most accounts, including Oren's. The horse, though, was of a particular color— *that particular color*—a rum chestnut red with streaks of black in the mane and tail. Oren would never place a wager of any kind on the animal. Then again, he couldn't stop gazing as if it were a car wreck.

My car wreck, realized Oren.

It had been three and a half years and almost a month since he'd inspected a nearly identical horse. A filly. Two years old and leggy, despite her sub-thousand-pound weight. She'd been named Hip Slick by her owner. Why? Who knew why owners named an animal an odd combinations of words. Vanity? Whatever. Oren didn't put a micron of stock in a racehorse's name. It was all about his gut, his psychic connection with the beast.

And connect he had.

It was, in Oren's dark recollection, the moment *she* had looked at *him*. While Oren sized up the filly, he felt as if he were being pored over by her. There was, in his unmitigated estimation, no doubt whatsoever—not unlike the certain way a man and woman measured each other in a singles bar.

Just without the sexual ingredient, Oren had justified to himself.

But Miss Hip Slick seemed to have her own game of measuring the onlooker. Or gambler. With her head cocked forty-five degrees, her left eye, though shielded by racing blinders, had appeared fixed on Oren. She was not merely surveying, but looking into him. Messaging him. She connected in an eerie way, teasing and exciting Oren at his nerve endings. He wouldn't remember how long the stare lasted. Ten seconds? Twenty? A minute? Once the filly was saddled and the seismic moment broken, Oren beat his feet to the Turf Terrace, where he would watch the races from his reserved table. First, though, he would bet. That fated Sunday afternoon in May, at twenty-four minutes before the second-to-last race, Oren had placed a $58,000 bet on the chestnut number-ten horse, the lithe filly named Hip Slick. The money represented the lion's share of the week's paychecks due to his pest-control crews.

Oren was picking at a plate of cold onion rings when the bells sounded. At the far side of the track, the gates released and with them eleven horses surged, atop each animal a silk-clad jockey. The number-ten horse wore a white-on-purple number, easy to spot against the vertical brown and sage backdrop of the San Gabriel Mountains. In a matter of seconds, Hip Slick eased from the thundering cluster into a quick, gliding lead.

And he was feeling the rush, as if his psychic filly had already crossed the finish line. At twelve-to-one odds, her win was going to pay $696,000—more than ten times his biggest single-race score.

The sensation might have been called premature ecstasy.

Oren's eyes closed and he breathed in the smells of the moment and the sound of the announcer live-calling the race. Then he heard a cacophony of shrieks. Women, mostly. As if a curtain in the human fabric had been torn. A horse had stumbled. Not unusual. Sometimes when horses are bunched too close, calamity follows. An animal trips and jockeys and other horses go flying, not unlike the peloton clusters in competitive cycling. One bike goes down and it's like dominoes falling.

But not my girl, thought Oren in the micro breath before he reopened his eyes. Hip Slick had been out front. Leading. The rest of her run would be easy, a foregone conclusion.

Meant. To. Be.

When Oren refocused on the race, horses were scattered but still surging into the last turn before the final stretch. For a number of skipped heartbeats, he couldn't find the number-ten horse—the purple and white number. The sounds in his head were an underwater garble, his vision blurred from concern. As the horses blew across the finish line, Oren saw every color *but* purple.

His gaze suddenly reversed, tracking clockwise until he landed on the struggling filly, flat on her side, neck flexing, legs kicking at nothing but air. Circling her, frustrated hands gesticulating in the air, that matching silken jockey who'd been astride the two-year-old before she'd tragically crashed to the earth, her front leg snapping like a number-two pencil. In a matter of minutes, two veterinary trucks rushed to the field. A tent was quickly erected over the horse, under which every race enthusiast in attendance knew what was happening. The injured horse was being euthanized, most likely by a captive bolt gun. After that, the carcass would be winched onto a flatbed and shrouded by a black tarp before being driven out the nearest track egress, all in time for the day's next race to run on schedule.

Oren, horribly stung by the loss, renamed the magic filly.

Hip Slick and Dead.

He hadn't stayed for the twelfth race. By the time he'd returned to his parking spot, he'd told himself that he'd already shaken off the loss with a timeworn "Win some/lose some" shrug.

The big bet on Hip Slick had been what gamblers call a bad beat. Oren's worst to date. But he tried to keep some perspective. He still had a thriving business and a positive cash flow, that week's kitty earmarked for the paymaster notwithstanding. How he chose to spend his bug-killing profits was his business and his alone. And what his wife didn't know wouldn't hurt her.

Only Hip Slick turned out to be far more than just a bad beat. She'd been bad luck. The worst. From that day forward, it seemed to Oren that he couldn't win a solitary bet. From the complicated multi-race picks to combination bets—a.k.a. boxing—to the easiest gamble of all, betting the favorite horse to merely show. And the more he would lose, the more he would wager, all in hope of getting back near even one day.

And three years later, here he stood: a criminal—a murderer with a fresh stack of $5,000 in his fist from a high-interest pawnshop loan.

"Do you have a bet, sir?" asked the pari-mutuel clerk, a hefty African-American woman in a hot pink wig.

"Where's Betsy?" asked Oren.

"That the name of a horse?" asked the clerk.

"The clerk who used to work this window," replied Oren.

"Dunno, sir," smiled the woman. "Do you have wager to make?"

"I do. But I usually bet with Betsy."

"I hear ya. Can't tell you where your Betsy is," she flirted. "My name's Dazzleen. And my husband? He thinks my Friday color is his luckiest color."

Oren watched her amusingly, but still with a distinct air of suggestion, flick at those fake pink-streaked curls with matching lacquered fingernails that defied physics.

"Fine, then," Oren finally relented. "I wanna box a bet. Five-thousand dollars."

"'Kay. Horses and races. Beginning with . . ."

35

Altadena

Gonzo woke to the familiar sound of groaning pipes and a running shower. She rolled to her flank, rubbed her face, and dared to open her eyes. As she suspected, the other side of the bed was empty and unslept in. Yet there Lucky was, steaming up the bathroom. She could only hope he wasn't sucking out the final gallons in the water heater.

She accepted that the hours Lucky had been working were crushing. Her own schedule hadn't been that much more civil. If her job didn't come with the added danger of operating a low-flying aircraft, she was certain her bosses might have dumped double and triple shifts onto her too. Besides the distracting obstacle of constant smoke in the air, every time she needed to throttle the helo into an ascent, the pictures through the cockpit windshield gave her a panorama of goose bumps. The city and its never-ending topography appeared hemmed in by fires. At one point, she'd ticked off as many as nine, from Malibu's Tuna Canyon to as far southeast as Chino Hills in San Bernardino County. The fear that welled up was the same that hit any first responder who understood the risks involved in an emergency situation that encompassed thousands of square miles. With every added blaze, the numbers of those assigned to battle and regulate each fire would be sliced from thin to thinner. Danger levels elevated. And that constant cabal of criminal element would be sure to take advantage.

Fortunately, there weren't any fires near Altadena, but that could change at any point. Their antique house was close enough to the steep and fuel-ready slopes of the San Gabriel Mountains that they kept all their important documents and photographs in a go-bag in case they ever had to evacuate on short notice. Such was suburban living in much of Southern California.

Slowly waking, she maneuvered herself to a seated position at the edge of the bed. Already, worries about everything from the wedding to where Lucky might have spent the night crept into her consciousness. His back couldn't take another night on his office couch. And her psyche couldn't handle the thought of Lucky stealing one last premarital sexcapade. *What was that woman's name? The office tease? Angie? She was hardly Lucky's type. If he even has a type.* Lucky was a male and a cop—a subcategory of humanity that had a proclivity for infidelity. Truthfully, women cops weren't much better. Neither Gonzo nor Lucky were without regrettable indiscretions, be it drunken sex, partner sex, or even revenge sex.

Her palms sweat. She rubbed them dry on her cotton flannel pajama bottoms and forced herself to stand.

"Incoming," she called out, not needing to give him a warning. The word just came out of her mouth without much thought.

The door to the tiny master bath swung inward, releasing a plume of built-up steam.

"Jesus," she said. "How much hot water does it take?"

"Didn't mean to wake you up," toned Lucky from the other side of the shower door, the pebbled glass obscuring any clear view of his nakedness.

Gonzo wiped the mirror with a hand towel, hoping to get a close-up glimpse of her face before the surface fogged again. She bypassed her best features, those deep brown eyes, classic Mediterranean nose, and naturally red lips, and instead reviewed the creases—purchased with worry and age—etched deep in her golden-brown skin. She was forty-one, a year older than her betrothed.

But wiser?

Before she could answer her own silent query, the hot water knob squeaked to the off position and the shower door snapped outward. More steam released. As she wiped at the mirror again, she snuck a look at Lucky as he unfolded a fresh towel.

"What the hell?" shot Gonzo, spinning fast to get the full picture of her man.

"Yeahhhh . . ." was all Lucky could muster. Weak.

"Jesus. Are those burns?" she practically gasped.

Lucky lifted both arms, looking south at the reddened welts that covered his torso. Some looked as small as bugbites, others were elongated, the outline of the jumper cables' teeth welded into his skin.

"Technically, yeah," replied Lucky. "Hadn't thought about drying off. Think maybe I should air dry."

"Can you please explain what the fuck happened to you?"

"Coupla knuckleheads," began Lucky. "Decided to kidnap and torture me. Aside from that it was a slow night—"

"Torture?" Gonzo's mouth was agape. Nothing in her could imagine a circumstance that could have led to Lucky receiving such torment. "Are you screwing with me?"

"Wish I was—"

"Jesus, Lucky? What?"

"Just sit," he asked, lowering his voice. As far as he knew, teenage Travis might be just outside the bedroom door, ear stuck to the resonant panel. He reached back inside the shower and turned on the cold water to mask their voices.

While Lucky allowed the air molecules to wick his bare skin, he explained his past forty-eight hours, from the first Porter Ranch encounter with Bobby Bianchi to the punishment courtesy of Mr. ACDelco and those muscle-brained body builders, Dakota and Buggie. He conveniently left out the last element of the story—the part when he'd exacted similar suffering on Bobby Bianchi.

"And since then you've been what?" said Gonzo, exasperated by it all. "Downtown? Putting all this in a report? They took pictures of your body, right?"

"Let's just say I left the offenders in worse shape than me," summated Lucky.

"Seriously?"

"Shit's stretched enough. Think I wanna tie up a coupla detectives over some stupid misunderstanding?"

"Not a misunderstanding on your part! Christ, Luck. That's aggravated assault on a police officer. They coulda killed you. And it just rolls off your back like—"

"Nothing's rollin' off my back. It hurts like a mother," corrected Lucky, his voice sharpening. "And I don't need any more reminders. It was the kind of situational shit that ends up in the hands of lawyers and departmental paper pushers. That's more than I can summon right now. Believe me. Those dipshits don't want any part of me after how I left 'em."

"And what about this Bobby guy?"

"Bianchi. Yeah. Well, that's gonna take some massaging. His old man's a connected kind of somebody. So I'm gonna tread that lightly. Think they got the message, though. I had nothin' to do with his Beatles shit."

"Beetles?" The word hit Gonzo in a non-sequitur slap. "Bugs?"

"Beatles," corrected Lucky. "As in, 'She loves me, yeah, yeah, yeah.'"

"This?" Gonzo's splayed fingers gestured to Lucky's punished body. "Because of some asshole's record collection?"

"Look. I got, like, two hours of sleep on the tile." Lucky's reference was to the kitchen floor. The cool ceramic pavers under his body had been his second-phase analgesic, the first being 1,000 milligrams of Advil chased by an ice-cold beer. "I'm back at it in an hour."

"You're calling in sick."

"I'm not."

"Someone needs to tend those burns—"

"Can we please not?"

"Lucky—"

"How's this? Okay? I take a little detour, hit up my favorite doc for Band-Aids and a bag of IV fluid?" The favored physician ran a mid-Valley urgent care. Somewhere on the drive between Altadena and Sherman Oaks, Lucky would need to come up with an amusing lie to excuse the evidence of his torture.

"No opioids?" stiffened Gonzo, always carrying a strong concern about Lucky relapsing back into the arms of his painkilling addiction.

"If it hurts too much to do my duty?" answered Lucky. "I'm back home in an ice bath."

"Promise?" Gonzo faked a boo-boo lip. But with anger still swimming just beneath her skin it came off more like teenage sarcasm.

"How's this?" he teased. "I promise to marry you on Saturday."

She wanted to slap him and then hold him until he changed his mind. Only she knew he wouldn't. Lucky was stubborn that way. She was equally headstrong in her own detrimental way. But they loved each other. They'd made a family together. And sometimes the only way forward was to never look back. His pledge to marry her on Saturday was about the most romantic string of words he'd ever uttered. In reply she'd balanced on her tiptoes, careful not to touch his torso, placed her palms on his stubble, and kissed him fully before stripping off her sleep garb and disappearing into the shower.

Sure enough, there was only five minutes of hot water left. She scrubbed her body, dried off, and dressed. By the time she'd exhumed herself from the bedroom, she could feel that she was alone in the bungalow.

Alone if I don't count the newly unemployed Karrie.

Lucky's adopted daughter was a lot. At least she was for Gonzo. Theirs was a roller coaster of a relationship. Over the past few years, Gonzo had done her level best to mother the moody teen. Only Karrie didn't want to be mothered. And hers was a convincing argument. A former life of abuse had left her hard to reach in certain emotional places.

Gonzo had applied everything from kid-gloves treatment to some very tough love with a success rate less than stellar. Her latest trick of treating Karrie like an adult had proven to be a surprising tonic. The force in their conversations had all but defrosted, leaving a surprising warmth. Lucky had even joked that he didn't trust it. But the household as a whole felt more connected than just contiguous.

Karrie's bedroom door was shut. Gonzo thought maybe she should knock softly and tell Karrie through the door that she'd be alone in the house. Then Gonzo thought otherwise. Let the kid sleep. The job at the cupcake shop had come with lousy management and even worse hours. She resolved to text Karrie within the hour.

She peeked out the kitchen window to the driveway that ran up the side of the house to the detached garage. Lucky's and Travis's cars were gone. Left were Karrie's Prius and Gonzo's nearly mint Dodge Ram extended-cab pickup. Metallic black. The rear license plate rim was bejeweled in her singular effort to feminize the gas-sucking beast. Both windshields were dusted in ash, a sign of how many miles a brief shift in wind could spread the fires' snowflake-like cinders. While chasing a handful of vitamin supplements with a Red Bull, she attempted to mentally locate the remaining members of her family. She placed Lucky as westbound on the relatively short 134 freeway, oddly recalling that recently it had been renamed after President Barack Obama. She pictured Travis at his special-needs high school in Pasadena.

Tall as Gonzo was, she still needed to step up to get in her truck. The door closed with a heavy, satisfying thunk. Just as she pulled the seat belt across her torso, she glimpsed a vagrant in her rearview mirror—a homeless man in a San Diego Chargers beanie. Travis had already flagged the vagrant in a text to Gonzo nearly two hours earlier, complete with a snapshot and the caption:

there goes da hood

The man in question, a gangly six-feet, draped in ill-fitting jeans and a blue and red soccer jersey, shuffled slowly on the side-walk, arms awkwardly waving in slow motion to nothing and nobody in particular.

High as my helicopter, thought Gonzo.

Sorry as she felt for him, she could only pray he wasn't dangerous and that he wouldn't choose their bungalow for the kind of quick smash 'n' grab burglary some local itinerants performed to pay for their meth habits. She kept a sharp eye on him as she backed the Dodge Ram out of the skinny drive. At the rumble of her truck, she caught him twisting her way. His face appeared to have been practically erased in scabbing scratches. The same for his hands, which she'd initially clocked as being gloved. But no, the unfortunate transient had clearly been in some kind of bloody scrape.

Gonzo briefly wondered if she should alert the nearby sheriff's station. Then she argued otherwise, considering how stressed all units and personnel were by the fires. Like Lucky, every deputy was pulling crazy hours. Her last and lingering thought in regard to the strange man was that he was just another one of the tens of thousands of shelter-resistant homeless currently plaguing the entire Southland.

With no friggin' solution in sight.

Gonzo did choose caution over Karrie's slumber, speed-dialing her mobile number and then clicking the speaker button on her own smartphone. There was barely a half ring before her call was sent to voicemail.

"Heads up, sweetie," recorded Gonzo. "Neighborhood's got a creepy homeless dude. Stay safe. Love you."

As Gonzo clicked off, she accelerated, giving one last glance at the transient in her side-view mirror. She saw that he was walking west, almost dancing along the sidewalk, seemingly trying not to make an unlucky step on a crack in the concrete. It salved her to see he was walking away from the bungalow.

Keep walking, brother, prayed Gonzo. *Keep walking.*

36

Absolutely liberating, thought Greg Beem.

His homeless act felt as magical as Harry Potter's invisibility cloak, only the camouflage wasn't some see-through illusion. He was, in fact, an all-out eyeful. As long as he didn't use drugs in public, expose himself to children, threaten anyone, or trespass, his performance left him wholly ignored.

The day had begun with a rude awakening at first light. The hijacked tent where he'd slept through the night had come under attack from a switch of a tree branch.

"Tha's no' yer house!" screeched a woman.

Somehow, the idiot had woken first. Without thinking, Beemer ripped at the flap, rolling his body and nearly taking down the fiberglass tent rods—all in the scramble to confront his accuser.

Then a name crossed his subcortex, placing a wake-up call to his calmer self.

Mmmmmmmmm-aggie.

It was exactly as if he were hearing the stammer of his most recent victim. Only it was in his head. From that hard, deep slumber, Beemer had stirred to find a pixie of a woman with a bird's nest of gray-streaked black hair, threatening him with a supple twig the length of a rapier. She continued to gum her diatribe.

"I know'd tha's Craig's tent!" she accused. "He showed me yest'day after he set it up!"

"You must be Maggie?" defended Beemer, guessing the name based on her toothless maw.

"How you know me?"

"Fella told me," lied Beemer, burying his idiot behind an "Aw, shucks" pose. "He said guard his tent while he was away. Guess I fell asleep."

"That's his woolly!" Maggie pointed her stick at the dirty Chargers beanie.

"So? My head was cold!"

Beemer guessed she'd hadn't yet discovered the body. He checked his pulse, pleased he'd been able to dial it back to under seventy beats a minute. In the moment, he was in control. He was also hungry as hell.

"Breakfast?" Beemer invited, waving that $20 bill.

"Already ate!" she spat, stalking off.

Beemer trekked alone to a nearby McDonald's, gobbling back two Big Breakfasts with hotcakes, eggs, and sausage before doubling back in the direction of the Alta Vista street address.

Lucky's house.

The morning air was clean, moist, and without a trace of smoke. *A boon for firefighters*, he imagined. The sidewalks fronting a mix of pre- and post–World War II bungalows were sometimes wet from automated sprinklers systems feeding all the uniformly green lawns. In his head he played a game of step on a crack, break your mama's back while performing the mannerisms of an inmate he knew. The jailhouse junkie was famous for getting intoxicated by inhaling jenkem, the foulest of prison concoctions. The fermented fuel was distilled from a mix of urine and feces, and the high was described as psychedelic.

Beemer's chosen route through Lucky's neighborhood was a counterclockwise rectangle—go east one block, cross the street, then west, and repeat. The cyclic behavior was both part of the mask as well an excuse to keep covering the concrete directly in front of Lucky Dey's house, about once every eleven to twelve minutes.

On his initial pass, Beemer checked off four vehicles in the slender driveway, stacked grille to bumper. Then on his fourth or fifth loop, he spied his first of the four known residents, a skinny teen with two sets of car keys. The young man's smart, skater-style fashion was undermined by his awkward and hurried gait. He backed the old Crown Victoria out of the drive, carefully parking it on the street before returning to the house and then climbing into a maroon Kia Soul.

That would be the boy named Travis, marked Beemer. The teen appeared to be off for his day at school.

Six laps later, upon arriving at the end of the block and crossing the street, Beemer caught his first sight of Lucky. Not that he could positively identify the man. It was a simple conclusion. The man walking out the front door and down the path to the Crown Victoria was taller than average, fit, uniformed as a county deputy, and sported a buzz cut.

Lucky Dey, Beemer quite easily inferred.

The last person Beemer registered was a tall Amazon of a woman. He spied her climbing into a black Dodge Ram pickup, after which she'd made some very obvious eye contact. He was across the street when the truck eased backward from the home's driveway. He could feel her stare, even in his peripheral vision. At first it was through her rearview mirror, then a second time as an over-the-shoulder look-see once she was in the street and shifting gears. The last was via her side-view mirror as the big Ram slowly rumbled away.

Lydia Gonzalez. He was certain of that. It was catching her gaze that gave Beemer a chill to remember. This was because Greg Beem rarely suffered them. Chills. Gooseflesh. That subconscious, autonomic cold so familiar to others was practically alien to him. And the four previous times he could recall getting the feeling had been specific, memorable, and significant.

My first crush.

My first kiss.

My first kill.

My first bullet.

Beemer had assigned that last item to Lucky Dey. The surprise slug had entered through his back, right below his left shoulder blade, before exiting just below his clavicle. It had landed like a sledgehammer, but thankfully missed his heart by inches. He was equally surprised that he hadn't drowned right afterward. The river had carried him nearly a quarter of a mile before he'd caught hold of a jagged concrete boulder. After pulling himself clear of the water, Beemer had sat for a spell, cold and catching his wind. He recalled feeling wet to the bone, with the only warmth being his own blood spilling onto his fingers. That's when the chill had overcome him.

He'd named that chill Mister Mortality. And Mister Mortality had tapped him on the shoulder.

Beemer continued his high and homeless act for eight and a half more loops, during which he eyed the last car in the drive-way—a neon yellow Toyota Prius—parked deep near the detached garage. Yet the house continued to reveal zero signs of life.

It's now or never, inmate.

The bungalow wasn't just the home of a police officer. There were two cop names fixed to the mortgage papers. Therefore, Beemer assumed there'd be security of some sort. An alarm. Cameras. Maybe even a guard dog. The latter was his biggest concern.

The plan itself was dangerously simple. While breaking in,

he'd appear just as he had pretended, wildly intoxicated on some chemical—a vagrant on a mission to smash and grab anything that could earn him some quick cash. A laptop. Jewelry. And if he happened upon that fourth family member . . .

The adopted daughter . . . what was her name again? Oh, yeah. Karrie.

If he encountered her, Beemer had resolved to either crush her skull or choke her to death. The only question was if that would be revenge enough. Perhaps, with that one act alone, he might become overwhelmed with satisfaction. His vengefulness sated. Maybe from there he could plot his return as the lost and lucky convict firefighter who'd somehow become separated from his team.

Beemer's plan for the break-in was to cause maximum havoc, be it dealing death or merely releasing some unnerving form of chaos. He thought that dragging Lucky Dey's nerves closer to the edge before delivering a final deathblow would be the sweetest of deserves—a most satisfying recompense. Something his memory could dine on while finishing out his incarceration.

The crazed vagrant act continued all the way up the narrow driveway. He broke a back window by hoisting a lightweight patio chair and pushing it clean through the frame. He swept the sill of glass shards and thrust himself inside, tumbling awkwardly over a pair of electric guitars perched on gig stands. *The boy's room*, he quickly mustered. Gaming console, complete with a curved high-definition computer screen. Hanging from the ceiling was a child's mobile of model aircrafts, slowly twirling from the sudden change in atmosphere.

The home alarm was accosting: a shrill, vibrating trill emanating from elsewhere in the house. There was no dog barking. If the girl was home, she'd surely been alerted.

The boy's door had been propped open with a decorative doorstop in the shape of a flying pig. Either an antique or a reproduction, it was heavy and fit easily into Beemer's right palm.

Two minutes, asshole.

The timer in Beemer's head was already winding down to a

collision with zero. If by chance a police unit or private security patrol happened by, he'd be arrested in a big "So what?" He was a vagrant. He had no ID. By the time the authorities figured out who he was—assuming they would even attempt as much—he'd be bounced back onto the street to resume his ploy. He might even pee himself in the back seat of the cop car as part of the ruse. The thought tickled the idiot in him.

But that's only if you're not covered in the girl's blood.

With that ten-pound flying pig cocked over his head, ready to lower it and crush a skull crowned in strawberry-blonde hair, Beemer scrambled through two tight turns until he arrived at a closed bedroom door.

The girl's room.

With the squealing alarm on full assault, he waited for the door to fling wide. In his mind, he saw her face. The hair. Freckles. Blue eyes staring back just like the only photo he'd ever seen of her, which was the one on her California driver's license. Age eighteen. Not that innocent. Yet still the apple of her "father's" eye. He imagined that when the flying pig doorstop connected with the top of her head she would look stunned, eyes searching for meaning in the scratched face of the man who'd killed her as the first trickle of blood turned into a cascade over her forehead and button nose right before her knees gave way.

Only the door never opened. Beemer twisted the knob and pushed. The bedroom, brimful of morning daylight, was kempt, the bed neatly made. The only sign of life was the whiff of a recently lit scented candle.

Move, asshole.

Beemer snapped up a laptop and a tablet from Karrie's desk. In the master bedroom, he speedily rifled through the drawers of a tall oak dresser, tossing Gonzo's silky panties as if in search of gems or cash. All the while, his fingers felt around every corner as if he were digitally violating Lucky's wife.

Not his wife, dummy. They're not even married, he reminded himself.

In all those dark web searches, Beemer had discovered no record that Lucky and Lydia had ever married. He had to confess to himself that the knowledge alone lessened his thrill. Who was Lucky's woman? What was she to him? Just a girlfriend? A roommate of convenience? Was theirs a new-age, common-law marriage?

As his mental clock clicked he wadded a handful of stretch cotton panties into a ball before veering into the bathroom. He opened the tub's cold and hot water valves fully, briefly stalling at the sound of the pipe moaning, and then screwed the bunched panties into the drain to create a stopper. The tub began to fill.

Next he moved to the kitchen. He'd spotted the side door when he'd crept up the driveway. That's where he'd planned his exit.

He whisked past the alarm, a plug-in Wi-Fi device sold at big box stores. The ear-cursing noise forced Beemer to briefly muff his ears before heading towards the oven, a refurbished, double-door Wedgewood, its white enamel gleaming from tender loving care. He turned on each burner without triggering the ignitor. A rotten egg smell instantly filled the space. Beemer knew it was mercaptan, a chemical added as a safety feature to give odorless natural gas a woeful scent that tasted of sulfur.

At that side door leading to the steps and the driveway, Beemer found a light switch. He toggled it on and off, revealing a ceiling-mounted light fixture some six feet inside the threshold. Vintage glass. He returned the switch to the off position and quickly snatched up a broom leaning in the corner and used it as a bat. The fixture's aged, brittle glass shattered. A gentler hack cracked the incandescent bulb.

All he needed was something to stand on and a single sheet of toilet paper.

"The shit firemen know about starting fires," Cappy had once said during all those brutal hours of training. He'd seen in Beemer a spark of extra intelligence. "Play your cards right, son, and you might one day make an ace arson investigator."

Clearly, Cappy had never gotten a glimpse of Beemer's inner idiot, leaving the convict to wonder if his captain's faith was that blind or if Satan himself had gifted Beemer with the superpower to conceal.

Four, three, two, one. Time's up! yelled Beemer's alarm.

He'd run out of time. But as Beemer was twisting for the exit, his eyes caught a manifest of names—a computer printout on the kitchen counter. At the top of the page was written "RSVPs." Some twenty names in all, most with handwritten red check marks next to them. Stopping to look at it was little more than instinct—an inner curiosity. In hope of understanding what the names meant he scanned the surrounding notes and papers. There were directions to a church. Next to that, a yellow receipt from a florist. A contract with a Mexican restaurant named Ponchito's. That's when Beemer's eyes lifted. Pinned to a corkboard framed on a kitchen cabinet was a wedding license issued by the nearby city of San Gabriel.

Well, whaddayou know?

Lucky Dey was getting married. And so soon—the very next day.

"Well, Lucky Dey," said Beemer aloud. "This here's your wedding present. From me. To you."

37

The soon-to-be Mrs. Lucky Dey was a bundle of nerves. Worse was that she couldn't put her finger on precisely what was irritating her limbic system. The sight of Lucky naked and scarred from electric burns should have been enough to shake her. Or maybe it was the fact that while the city appeared to be burning all around her, she was planning a wedding.

My wedding.

Her wiser self wanted to believe that it was just plain old pre-wedding jitters. But her stubborn side didn't want to yield to such petty emotion.

"It's just a flippin' wedding," she admitted aloud as she looked for the swimsuit section in a Pasadena Marshalls.

In her one extra hour before reporting to the flight deck, Gonzo had made a quick stop at the discount mart in search of suitable honeymoon swimwear. She was briefly interrupted when her phone whistled.

Karrie: what creepy homeless dude?

Gonzo quickly tapped out a reply for Karrie to simply look out the front window. Karrie's reply came as a surprise.

Karrie: i would look if i was home.

Gonzo: Where r you?

Karrie: slept over at a friends. where u?

Gonzo: Shopping for honeymoon bikini.

Karrie: want my help?

Karrie was halfway home when she redirected her Lyft driver to Marshalls. Once there, the bride-to-be and her maid of honor stood at a rack of synthetic tops and bottoms, both their hands sorting through the colorful prints.

"It's not just *a* wedding," replied Karrie. "It's *your* wedding." She fished out a Lycra string bikini, holding it up for Gonzo's approval. "Hey. Whaddayou think of this one? It's cute."

"Tiger stripes?" Gonzo shook her head. "You can see me in that?"

"You could totally rock this," encouraged Karrie. "And seriously. It's really not 'just a wedding.' Not for any of us."

It is just a wedding.

Gonzo had been whispering the thought to herself for over two weeks. Small. Manageable. And after a three-night honeymoon in Cabo San Lucas, it would be one and done. Everything had already been organized. A quick Catholic ceremony at the historic San Gabriel Mission, followed by a Mexican feast at Ponchito's just across the street. With no father to give her away, she'd opted for her son, Travis, to walk her down the aisle. The idea morphed into a friendly argument between Gonzo and Lucky over who should be best man. Lucky had already asked Travis and the teen had answered with an excited yes. With Karrie acting as maid of honor, the ceremony promised to be a family affair, their made-up brood bracketing the bride and groom.

"I can do both!" Travis had enthused in an amusing tiebreaker.

"Problem solved," Lucky had agreed in a palms-up shrug.

Gonzo lifted a macramé swimsuit, its immodest patches of material the barest minimum of square inches.

"Now, who would wear this?" she joked.

"You?" kidded Karrie.

"I'm forty-one." Gonzo dropped the bikini and shifted gears. "So, tell me. What's his name?"

"What's whose name?"

"The guy?" prodded Gonzo. "Or girl? Not that it matters."

"Guy," confirmed Karrie. "And I'm bringing him to the wedding."

"Bringing who?"

"Him."

"You're not gonna give it up, are you?"

"Just a dude I like."

"Whatever," relented Gonzo, choosing to examine a more demure suit in green and gold. She asked, "Jamaica or Brazil?"

"Who cares? That's you, you, and you."

"That *is* me," she agreed.

"Modest. But still super fuckable."

"Really, Karrie?" annoyed Gonzo.

"Sorry," the teen apologized. "Carried away being maid of honor and all."

"You wanna do dirty talk with me? Fine. Start telling me who your new boyfriend is and—" Gonzo's phone whistled from her back pocket. "Trav?" she answered the moment she saw his picture on her screen.

"The creepy guy!" burst Travis over the phone. "He's in our house!"

"You mean the one on the sidewalk?" she asked, hoping she was wrong.

"The crazy dude in the Chargers beanie!" Travis shouted. "I'm looking at him right now!"

"You're at home?" she suddenly worried.

"I can see him on my cameras!"

Travis had been experimenting with security cameras—or spy cams, as Lucky liked to call them. Tiny. Cheap. Connected to their wireless system, Travis could monitor their home from school. To Lucky, it was slightly disconcerting. To Gonzo, it was Travis dabbling in what Travis liked. Tech, tech, and more tech.

"I can hear the alarm—" Travis stopped. "He's got Karrie's laptop under his arm. He's leaving now through the kitchen door."

"Hang up," she ordered. "I'm calling the sheriff's station right now."

"Should I call Lucky?"

"Hang up, Trav! And don't go home!"

Shit, Gonzo thought. Another damned break-in. From Travis's description, it hardly compared to the mayhem from two years before. *Crazy Armenians*. But in a matter of seconds, she already felt just as violated.

If one more thing goes sideways before the wedding . . .

"What's going on?" asked Karrie.

Gonzo held up a stalling finger as she redialed.

"This is LAPD officer Lydia Gonzalez," she said the moment a deputy answered the direct line to the Altadena sheriff's station. "My house on Alta Vista was just broken into by a vagrant. I have a description. Ready to write this down?"

38

Panorama City. 10:20 a.m.

The aging seat belt retractor whimpered as Lucky gently pulled it across his stinging torso. When he was a rookie deputy, Bledsoe had trained him to never wear the safety restraint as it seriously curtailed the speed with which a cop could dislodge himself from a radio car. Those two seconds might be the difference between a deputy's life and death.

That was before the FBI entered the discussion. And the stats were clear. More cops died in vehicle accidents than from facing down violent offenders. City and county insurers had followed with dire edicts: police officers caught not wearing seat belts would essentially be forfeiting all health benefits. Lucky's plan covered Karrie, and after her accident and brutal year of the best rehab, he couldn't imagine shouldering that kind of financial load.

So, Lucky clicked the seat belt tongue into the receptacle.

Anyway, I'm not a real cop anymore.

Bobby Bianchi's dismissal echoed between his ears.

I'm just a hobby cop.

Lucky ached for sleep the way a newborn ached for mother's milk. After seeing his favorite urgent care doctor and having his torso wrapped in rolls of dry hygienic gauze, he'd driven purposefully, in the most unhurried fashion, in the general direction of his destination.

Porter Ranch. Again.

Driving north on the 405 freeway, his vision blurred. Horizontal, rainbow-tinged striations of light made his windshield appear as if it were melting into refracted colors.

"Shit," he uttered, frustrated by his inability to stay awake.

He safely pulled off at Roscoe, opened the window, and sucked the scent of baking hops into his nostrils. The Budweiser brewery, the iconic eyesore that stood dead center in the San Fernando Valley, was known to cook its famous mash in the mornings. Some thought the smell was sour, others sweet. The neighborhood, Panorama City, was a mix of industry, tiny blue-collar homes on half-sized lots, and a constant tug-of-war between local Hispanic gangs. Lucky parked under the shade of Motel 6 on Haskell, closed his eyes, and tried to catch a few winks.

He'd pulled some crazy shifts in his career. Longer even than this last week. And he knew others who managed inhumane hours, surviving on catnaps and coffee. He once met a firefighter—a Ventura County battalion chief—who'd worked eleven straight twenty-four hour shifts.

So then, why do my eyes wanna slam shut?

Lucky had resolved to be late to his shift, hoping that thirty minutes of sleep would tide him over.

There'd been looting alerts in the parts of Porter Ranch that bordered Aliso Canyon. In 2015, an underground natural gas storage facility had developed a leak. Evacuations had followed. So had litigation and complaints from local residents with a laundry list of health problems. Southern California Gas Company, the owners of the site, drilled relief wells and reinforced all caps and valves. Despite that, some neighbors continued to claim illnesses, even the ability to smell the odorless gas from what many considered one of the worst environmental disasters in US history.

Despite that Oren's fire—now known as the Limekiln Fire— was no longer an immediate threat to some neighborhoods, an overabundance of prudence was employed in the tracts bordering Aliso Canyon. Though many of the nearby Tuscany Estates residents were legally allowed to return to their homes, the entire area remained under the flag of caution. Added to residents' concern about looting was a growing suspicion that an escaped prisoner was on the loose—a convict firefighter. While the crew captain and members of the inmate team had been discovered burned to death in a charred arroyo just north of the Santa Susana Pass, it was suspected that a twelfth firefighter might have survived. LAPD homicide detectives were equally concerned that there was a link between the missing firefighter and the dead sheriff's deputy beaten to death in nearby Chatsworth.

Lucky inadvertently peeked at his watch. It had already been ten minutes. He should have been snoring by then. If there was one thing Lucky was expert at, it was napping in a car. He'd drop the seat back, put up sunscreens when it was daylight, and leave a note on the windshield warning that he was an armed cop.

Disturb at your own risk.

Yet at a time when his body screamed for slumber, Lucky was somehow failing. His body could not submit. He wondered if it was his skin. The burns hurt like hell. Yet he could recall sleeping in far worse pain. Burns were just on the surface, but they stung like peroxide bubbling on a scraped knee. Perhaps that was it. Aching versus stinging. His torso felt like multiple tattoos were being administered at the same time. He tried to purge the pain from his brain, willing it to ignore the signals from his nerve endings.

If he couldn't succumb, simply resting his neck would have to do. He set a timer on his phone for fifty minutes and resolved to keep his eyes closed until the alarm sounded. If sleep wouldn't come, he'd put himself on pause and accept whatever kind of respite he could manage. He switched on the radio to a sports talk broadcast in hope that the voices would bore him to sleep.

Lucky's phone eventually sounded at 11:38 a.m. He couldn't recall if he'd slept at all or had just ignored himself into a fifty-minute coma. Though his eyes or body didn't feel the least bit fresh, the clock didn't lie. He'd rested himself. Fifty minutes. He reasoned that it should be enough to get him to through twelve more hours of duty.

Westbound on a North Valley artery called Devonshire Street, Lucky accelerated the rattling wreck of a radio car down the five-lane boulevard—two stripes west and two stripes east, the middle stripe reserved for safe turns when entering or leaving traffic. Lucky would later recall feeling something he used to refer to as winning the stoplight lottery. Capturing the prize required a certain population of vehicles, a speed that was without urgency, and the providence of timing. Lucky was greeted by green light after green light. At a distance of almost an eighth of a mile—or roughly seven hundred feet—the stoplight ahead of him would silently switch from red to green. The sensation never failed to please.

Ahead of him, to his west and north, were the hills of Chatsworth and the lower mountain slopes where the fires had done so much damage. What little natural material that hadn't been consumed by the flames appeared patchworked into a quilt of charred black acres interrupted by the occasionally cherry red stripes of spent chemical fire retardant. The environmentally friendly Phos-Chek, delivered in twelve-thousand-gallon dumps via dive-bombing air tankers, was a simple mix of phosphate and sulfate salts, artificially colored so pilots could read the accuracy of their attack. To Lucky, it made the mountains look as if they had been tagged by errant graffiti artists.

As every light turned electric green, Lucky found himself

overwhelmed with an odd sense of well-being. His skin no longer stung, nor did his muscles ache. Even the usual twinge of tightness in his rehabilitated back appeared to ease. For a split second, he felt rested enough to take on the rest of his shift without chemical assistance.

It's all gonna be okay.

But how much of Lucky's recollection of the green-lit drive down Devonshire was real versus how much was hallucination? He'd piece that together at a later date. Because when his lids unconsciously lowered over his eyes, finally serving up that much-required sleep, his rattling black-and-white crept left and crossed into the center turn lane. The eight-cylinder engine was humming. And Lucky's speed at the moment he lost complete control was fifty-two miles per hour and accelerating.

39

Encino

From the driveway, the mid-century modern home at the end of Encino's Laurilynn Lane looked like an architect's idea of a fashionable bunker. The concrete pillbox-like façade was as forbidding as its owner, Joey Bianchi. The only invitation of warmth was a Christmas remnant, a plastic wreath still hanging on the solid front door. But once past the entry, the single-story home stretched out across a gentle knoll in pleasing squared and triangulating horizontal lines. The floors, benches, and countertops were all hand-formed polished concrete.

And cold as fuck, thought Bobby.

In his bare feet, he stood like a slumped statue, naked but for his red Calvin Klein briefs. It was as humiliating as his father had meant it to be.

"You're saying that it was the hobby cop?" asked Joey. "He did all that to you?"

Joey was in shadow, seated on a worn leather couch, his wrinkled facial features barely readable. In opposition, Bobby's injuries were on full display as he was posed directly beneath a skylight.

"Yeah," was Bobby's single syllable answer. "Now, why you doin' this to me?"

Bobby's eyes gestured to the large sliding glass door that was partially opened to the swimming pool and immaculately tended gardens. Beyond was a multimillion-dollar view of the San Fernando Valley. Leaning against the jamb, arms crossed, and vaping plumes of scented nicotine, was a thick man in an expensive suit.

"You gonna act like a baby, I'm gonna treat you like one," answered Joey. "I mean, you are asking me to clean up your shit?"

Bobby didn't need to answer. It was purely rhetorical. Vintage Joey.

"Maybe you'd be better off if I fit you for some adult diapers," added the cruel father. "Hey, Meltz. What size you think Bobby would take?"

Meltz, a.k.a. attorney Bruce Meltzer, twirled his electronic cigarette like a pencil in his fingers before inhaling another lungful of vapor.

"I'd say he's a man-sized baby," offered Meltz. "But hell if I know. Me and Stacy could only make girls."

"Praise Jesus." Joey tossed up his arms in a mock hallelujah.

"Dad. Can I get dressed?"

"You want me to fix this?" snapped Joey. "Then you and your baby boo-boos can stand there while me and Meltz ponder a remedy."

"I'm cold—"

"Shut up."

"This is humiliating—"

"This is your old man being pissed the hell off!" barked Joey, his voice rocking off all the hardened surfaces. "I told you to leave that shit alone. I told you to get insurance. Your little brother told you to get goddamn insurance!"

"I know," begged Bobby.

"Speaking of Peter," swerved Joey. "He's not returning my calls. Be a good brother and find out what's got into him."

"Okay."

"Now get dressed and get outta my sight."

Bobby shot over to the concrete hearth and pulled on his gym shorts and T-shirt.

"Your fault, Meltz," said Joey, though the words were clearly directed at Bobby as he was stepping into his flip-flops. "Should never have been an irrevocable trust."

"You're blaming me?" laughed Meltz. "Ha."

"Hadn't been for you, I'd have revoked Bobby's money a long time ago," chastised Joey.

"At least I didn't squander mine like Pete," angered Bobby.

"Best thing that ever happened to your big brother," grinned Joey, despite looking anything but happy. "Least he knows the value of a dollar. Maybe the two of you can get together and learn the value of a father."

"Hey, Bob. Think you kids call that a mic drop," added Meltz.

The front door slammed, leaving Joey to sink deeper into the couch, dropping his chin into a slow, head-shaking lament.

"Whaddayou gonna do?" waxed Meltz. "You can divorce your wife but you can't divorce your kids."

"That supposed to be some kind of wisdom?" growled Joey.

"All I got for you."

"What about Bobby's playmates?"

"The bodybuilders?"

"They'll disappear. So all we got left to deal with is the cop."

"Hobby cop," corrected Joey.

"With a gun and badge," argued Meltzer. "So, a cop all the same."

40

Northridge

As soon as Lucky's eyes unconsciously shut, he transformed from driver into helpless passenger, quickly descending from stage one of the sleep cycle to stage two. All while his black-and-white careened headlong and without control. It cut at a slight but increasing angle across the broken yellow lines of the left-turn lane—no-man's-land, an asphalt DMZ—designed for low speeds and safe navigation. There was no curb, no defensive guardrail. All that existed to keep Lucky and the rattling Crown Vic from entering oncoming traffic was yellow thermoplastic road paint.

The car's tires, newish with relatively fresh tread, hungrily ate up the pavement. The steel grille guard added extra threat to defenseless eastbound cars.

Serendipity was the word that would later come to mind and

permanently etch itself into Lucky's hippocampus, the brain's long-term memory repository.

Lucky woke at the force of first impact. And the miracles at work were twofold. As the radio car roared into the two lanes of oncoming traffic, it narrowly missed the left rear fender of a white FedEx truck. The two tailing drivers, one in a blue Hyundai and the other cruising at fifty miles per hour in a late-model black Lincoln, were staggered within two hundred feet of the oncoming sheriff's black-and-white. Both drivers dropped heavy feet onto their respective brake pedals. One swerved left, the other right. Lucky's unit split between the two cars, missing each by millimeters before rushing headlong over a rise in the road.

The rattling Crown Victoria struck the angled concrete wall at a recorded sixty-one miles per hour. The car bucked and propelled up the concrete as if launching up a twelve-foot ramp. The car twisted and tore through a frame of heavily rusted, ivy-choked cyclone fence like a razor slicing a Christmas ribbon. That was when Lucky woke—airborne and disoriented, as if in a slow-motion dream. The eyeblink before the second impact, Lucky realized it wasn't a dream—and that it was going to be bad—perhaps his last gasp of life. The rest was a series of images accompanied by a constant sound of ruptured metal meeting plastic and earth. Lucky didn't feel the airbag deploy. His rebuilt low back yelled at the straining g-forces. He tried not to gag as he tasted dirt and turf at the back of his throat.

And then it was over—but for the ringing in his ears and the sounds of a dying black-and-white. Lucky was nearly upside down, strapped into his seat by the life-saving three-point harness. What was left of the radio car appeared to be leaning against a tree. He was afraid to twist his neck, worried about what bits of vertebrae might come loose. The only glass left in the vehicle was the front windshield, askew in the frame like a flattened piece of gum, cracked to the point of opaque whiteness. Swerving his eyes left and right, he saw only grass, untended and green, but tipped in brown from the week of hot winds.

Where the hell am I?

It was followed by a secondary thought. *What the hell happened?*

He pushed aside the deflated airbag and gently braced himself against the steering wheel before reaching across himself to unhitch the seat belt. The receptacle popped. The belt released. And gravity forced Lucky down to the crumpled roof. It hurt to breathe, so he slowed himself, gave a couple gentle heaves, eased to the passenger window, and rolled himself downhill until he was touching the grass. It was cool, moist.

And I'm alive. So far . . .

Lucky felt sore and hardly mobile. Yet he braved pushing up until he was on his knees. Ten or so seconds later, he was standing, fully erect, turning in place in a foggy effort to fully get his bearings. His vision wasn't quite tracking. Objects in the foreground lagged, a certain sign of concussion. When Lucky was able to gather a wider view of the radio car with its every surface deformed—chassis twisted, roofline flattened—he wondered how in God's green Earth he was still alive, let alone standing.

Speaking of God's green Earth . . .

He was in some kind of park. Centered atop a knoll was a two-story stone country house. English or Irish. Out of place. Down on Devonshire, cars had stopped and gathered. Where the black-and-white had cut through the cyclone fence, three people stood, and a fourth had already climbed the wall and was jogging in Lucky's direction.

"Are you okay?" called the jogger. "Jesus, is anybody else in the car?"

Lucky shook his head no. He thought he could feel his brain rattling inside his skull.

"What about you?" breathed the man, whipper-thin, fifty or sixty years of age, wearing khakis and a safari vest.

"I'm fine," waved off Lucky, his words more rote than truly reflective.

The man's head snapped at the sound of sirens. When Lucky

heard them, a memory triggered. He was at the Oakridge Estate, a historic North Valley site where he'd once attended a Sheriff's charity function. He vaguely recalled knocking back one too many beers then wandering outside for a rare cigarette, only to have been warned off by a security guard shouting at him for blazing up in a smoke-free zone.

Lucky regarded the destructive path of his black-and-white. Clearly, he'd fallen asleep—or passed out—behind the wheel and crossed four lanes of traffic without causing injury to anybody but himself. By either good fortune or pure providence, the crash site was populated by little more than a few tree squirrels. For miles and miles of Devonshire Street—the private park was the only swath that was neither a business nor somebody's residence. The realization of it stole his breath. It was miracle enough that he'd survived. That he'd done so without taking another life—*an innocent life*—was beyond comprehension.

Two LAPD uniforms hiked up the slope from the street, the lead officer waving his arm above his head in hope of getting Lucky's attention.

"Anybody hurt, deputy?" shouted the uniform.

"Just the black-and-white," joked Lucky.

"Hey. How about we find you a seat?" suggested the uniform.

"Really, I'm good," said Lucky.

"How many fingers am I holding up?"

"Two," cracked Lucky. "Both middle fingers 'cause I just took a shit in your pond."

"Deputy. I need you to sit and wait for EMS."

"I'm fucking fine!" snapped Lucky.

"Seriously. You look anything but fine. What's your name?"

"Lucky Dey."

"Deputy Dey. You've been in a serious accident. I'm ordering you to sit down and wait."

"I'm late for shift—"

"Sit! Down!"

Lucky must have thought there was a chair behind him,

because he dropped backward, finding only air before crashing into the weeds. He awkwardly rocked backward. He instantly thought of how foolish he must have looked.

"Deputy Dey," asked the uniform. "Have you been drinking?"

"No," shook Lucky. Again, he thought he could feel his brains swishing back and forth.

"Are you under the influence of drugs or prescription medications?"

"No."

"Do you remember what happened?"

"Benadryl," corrected Lucky. "Or, wait. Zyrtec? Have dog allergies. Seriously, guys. I'm late for shift."

"Where's your shift?"

As Lucky began to form his answer, his mouth poised to release the information, he found he could summon nothing. Not an address, a neighborhood, a zip code. His mind was blank. Lucky hadn't a clue where he was supposed to report—this despite the knowledge that he was late.

Oh, shit.

41

Altadena

"Out of the fucking way!" bitched Gonzo at the man in his all-electric car. He was traveling so slow he could be driving Miss Daisy, all the while clogging Lake Avenue's left lane, which was supposed to be the fastest one.

Karrie had never seen Gonzo so much as break the speed limit by more than five miles an hour, wrongly concluding that Gonzo clearly confined all her speed-seeking for those hours strapped into her LAPD Bell JetRanger. On the two-and-a-half-mile trip from Marshalls to their Alta Vista Street bungalow, Gonzo had kicked her truck's engine into the redline. And just after Karrie had snapped on her seat belt, she'd noticed Gonzo wasn't wearing hers.

"Gun's in the console," Gonzo gritted. "You mind handing it to me?"

"Seat belt's to your left," answered Karrie with a slight tremor in her voice. "Mind buckling up?"

By the time Gonzo clicked the seat belt, she was already turning up Alta Vista.

"We're looking for a man," urged Gonzo. "Six feet, gangly, face covered in scratches."

"The homeless guy?"

"Homeless doesn't mean harmless," warned Gonzo before complaining about what was missing in her windshield frame. "How the hell is it we're beating sheriffs?"

With a block and a half left to cover, neither woman could see a single L.A. Sheriff's black-and-white near or around the bungalow.

"Travis said he actually saw the dude leaving our house?" confirmed Karrie.

"I don't remember. But I don't see any . . ." Gonzo cut herself off, slowing the truck to concentrate on every neighborhood driveway left and right, hedges, shadowed porches, and porticos. "When I saw him, he was to your right, walking away from the house. Watched him through my side-view mirror."

Twisting the wheel at slow speed, she eased the truck in front of their home, stopping only when the front tires landed on the driveway ramp. Her eyes scoured the property, seeking any tiny thing that might be out of place. Karrie's Prius remained at the end of the driveway in front of the detached garage. At a distance, there appeared to be no sign of damage.

"He's probably gone. But who knows how many houses he smashed and grabbed?" reasoned Gonzo before touching the door release. "Stay in the truck. If sheriffs show, let 'em know I'm armed PD and in the process of clearing my own property."

Gonzo unskinned her pistol from a black nylon shoulder holster and was checking the chamber and safety when her phone began to rattle annoyingly in the cupholder. She was going to ignore the ring, but glanced anyway. Onscreen the caller was identified only as HOOPER.

Of course, she thought. *I'm late for preflight.*

In lieu of completely ignoring the call, she imagined that maybe she could briskly answer, explain her circumstance as a home emergency, and promise to be downtown as soon as humanly possible.

"Whoever this is, I'm sorry," answered Gonzo. "But I got a homeowner emergency—"

"Gonzo," interrupted her lieutenant, the heliport's assistant commanding officer. "Regina Parker over at Hooper."

"Listen. I'm really sorry about being late, but I'm parked in front of my—"

"It's Lucky," the officer forced. "So far, all I know is that he's okay. But he's been in a serious car accident."

"What?" Gonzo's face fell slack.

"Northridge Station caught the call. Hospital's on Roscoe. Need the address?"

"But you said he's okay?"

"All I heard is that he walked away. But they're gonna check him for internal injuries."

"If he walked away, why didn't he call me?" yelled Gonzo, her emotions bubbling over in an accidental spray of spittle.

"Was a really bad wreck. Forget about your shift. Just get yourself safely to Northridge."

"Yeah," was all Gonzo could muster. "Yeah, okay."

"Really hope this doesn't put a crimp in your big day," the lieutenant tried to ease. "But better you're all healthy for the wedding."

"What wedding?" exhaled Gonzo. "At today's rate, ain't never gonna be a wedding!"

Gonzo hadn't meant to hang up on her lieutenant—or sound so hopelessly negative—yet for accidental emphasis her thumb had acted as frustrated punctuation.

"What about Lucky?" worried Karrie.

"Car accident," muttered Gonzo, caught between the danger to her home and the sudden news. "He's okay. Least that's what they said. Okay. Walked away. But hospital . . ."

"Hospital?"

"Look," shifted Gonzo. "You stay here. Wait. And I mean *here. Outside the house.* Wait for the sheriffs to come. Let *them* clear the house. Are we straight?"

"But I wanna go see Lucky!" pleaded Karrie.

"Then follow me after the sheriffs are here," insisted Gonzo, shoving the 9mm back into its holster and then the center console.

"My car keys," lamented Karrie. "They're in the house."

"All the better reason to wait for a black-and-white. If they're not here in five minutes, call them again. Watch commander is Sergeant Conklin. We good?"

Karrie nodded, pushing open the passenger door with her foot and sliding out.

"Do not—"

"Go in the house," finished Karrie with a semi-snotty thumbs-up. "I won't."

"Sorry hon," altered Gonzo. "And considering how you're feeling, I'd totally understand if you gave me your middle finger," apologized Gonzo. "Love you."

The tires kicked up a spray of pebbles as Gonzo backed the truck into the street. As it surged back in the direction from where they'd just come, Karrie lifted her middle digit mockingly in the air for Gonzo to catch in the rearview mirror.

"Love you too," Karrie softly sang. She insecurely wrapped her arms about herself and checked the sidewalk in each direction before she mocked, "And so far, no crazy people."

Karrie stood on the very same crack on the driveway's ramp for something shy of five minutes. Bored and with no sheriffs on her immediate radar, Karrie behaved in her most teenage fashion. She withdrew her smartphone, checked her texts and social media, and decided to dial Frosty.

"Workin', baby," he answered. "What ups?"

"Like, everything," whined Karrie, involuntarily hugging her-self, her arms disappearing inside her navy blue Pasadena City

College hoodie while she cradled the phone between her shoulder and ear. "I don't even know where to start—"

A triple electronic beep played in her ear. She stuck a single arm back through her sleeve and grasped her phone. The screen staring back at her was black, reflecting nothing more than her fevered freckles. The battery was dead.

"Really?" she complained to nobody but the immediate atmosphere.

Karrie pivoted twice, first east, then west. Her field of view was unfortunately clear of deputies coming to the rescue and, fortunately, the crazed homeless vagrant Gonzo had described. Another quarter turn and Karrie was face-to-face with the bungalow again. She saw no movement, no signs whatsoever of anybody lying in wait.

And if there is somebody? I will shove my foot so far up their dirty ass . . .

She gazed at her dead smartphone and assessed the house. Her house.

My. Home.

Armed with only her house key and three years of Brazilian Muay Thai martial arts training, she resolved to enter the house to get a charging cable. In and out. Simple.

Across the street and two doors east was the Alta Vista Street lookie-loo. Known more as a shut-in rather than a friendly neighbor, she would later report to the Los Angeles Sheriff's investigators that she'd watched the strawberry-blonde known as Karrie Dey stand for some time at the foot of 4387's driveway. She'd witnessed that after fifteen or so minutes, Karrie had walked up the driveway with that distinct, not-yet-rehabilitated hitch in her step. In the woman's recollection, not moments before the bomb went off, Karrie appeared to enter the bungalow through the side kitchen door.

42

Lake Balboa

"Yo, *Peter Pecker Eater!*" shouted out the younger brother, tongue as glib as could be. "You better not be naked or dead in there. That's some shit I won't be able to unsee."

Bobby had just passed the threshold of Peter's condo. He'd found the key under a potted succulent, a chorus line of which appeared to be hanging on for dear life on the dining room window ledge. In a rare moment of brotherly affection—as well the promise to look out for each other's property—Peter had revealed the location of his spare key in exchange for a key and the alarm code to Bobby's house.

"Hey, big man!" called Bobby, louder as he continued into the tight foyer. Dead ahead was a framed 2 Sheet—a larger than usual movie poster—for Martin Scorsese's *Taxi Driver*. It pictured Robert De Niro, hands in his jacket pockets, gazing downward as he ambled along a Times Square sidewalk. "Yo, Pete! I know you own guns. So better not shoot me for checkin' up on you! Haven't been answering your phone, bro."

Bobby's voice felt as if swallowed by a vacuum of stale air. That, and the condo was icy, as if the heat hadn't been turned on for days.

You asshole. You better not be dead.

The younger sibling was girding himself, often having been afraid Peter would die early from a stroke or heart attack or the onset of debilitating diabetes. It wasn't that Bobby really cared that much about his only brother. He was more worried about being left behind as Joey's only son. Peter, being older and fatter and having pissed away his trust, gave Bobby a sufficiency of superiority in both his own and—he hoped—his father's perspective. In a "dead Peter" scenario, Bobby feared his father would lay upon him a crown of blame.

"C'mon, dude. Wake the hell up!"

After peeking into a kitchen so small that one could wonder how Peter could even maneuver in it, Bobby slid down a slight corridor to the master bedroom. Though unmade, the bed was empty. The accompanying bathroom was a mess, towels left on the floor, the toilet seat in the upright position, and the tub covered in Peter's gray and black hairs.

His pace unconsciously quickening, Bobby checked the guest room only to find it messily stacked with cardboard boxes floor to ceiling—leftovers from Peter's pre-bankrupcy life. Bobby searched the living room, windows darkened with black-out drapes. This was Peter's gaming cave. Mounted on a wall were three high-definition screens, cables connected to controllers, snaking across the carpet to a dark sectional leather sofa. Through a pair of sliding doors was a den that served as Peter's office. It was habitually unkempt. File cabinets were partially open, folders sticking out of drawers like triangular shark teeth in metallic jaws.

Peter's desk was little more than a folding buffet table and a lower lumbar–supporting chair. Amidst the papers and printouts was a large monitor attached by an HDMI cable to a notebook computer. When Bobby touched the mouse, a box for a password appeared on the screen.

Certain Peter wasn't anywhere to be found, at least inside the condo, Bobby lowered himself into the desk chair and swam backward through his own thoughts. *Password? What kind of password would Peter use?* What little Bobby knew of computers was to ask Barbara for tech support. His own passwords for his phone and iPad were an easy-to-remember four-digit number. And his personal MacBook was easily unlocked with a favorite movie catchphrase. In *Dirty Harry*, Clint Eastwood's Harry Callahan utters, "You gotta ask yourself one question. Do I feel lucky?" The follow-up dialogue, "Well, do ya, punk?", was Bobby's go-to celebrity impression as well his password.

welldoyapunk?

Peter had even admired Bobby's password choice. Over some beers, the brothers had traded famous catchphrases. Barely a minute into the game, Bobby realized he was outmatched. Peter's reservoir of film dialogue was bottomless. He would reel off classic lines from *Psycho* to *The Shining* to *Marathon Man*.

"Is it safe?" recalled Bobby.

So, that is exactly what he keyed into the password prompt.

Isitsafe?

The phrase was instantly rejected. Bobby proved smart enough to attempt different variations of the same line—changing capitalization, punctuation, and inserting numbers instead of letters. And that was just from one catchphrase out of lord knows how many Peter would've been able to summon at the snap of his hammy fingers.

Bobby banged the buffet table out of the sheer frustration of it, mentally cursing his father for tasking him with finding his older brother.

My fucking adult big brother, who could be anywhere!

Resentment bubbled up inside him in a bitter stomach gas.

Bobby regarded the sting on his skin from the torture he'd earned at the hands of that evil hobby cop, Lucky Dey. The Vicodin tabs he'd chased with an energy drink were wearing off. In front of his eyes flashed images from that morning of standing nearly naked in front of his father and Bruce Meltzer. It was so emasculating. He felt as if he had been stripped of his manhood. And his father had appeared to enjoy every second of it.

The asshole sadist.

Bobby quit then and there, and headed for the front door. He resolved to google a private detective to track down his missing brother. But between strides to the door, he'd suddenly changed his tack. Cruising Yelp would be a smarter choice. He'd find some five-star-reviewed agency, give them a credit card, and Peter's whereabouts would most likely be gleaned with little more than a PI's mouse click. The idea appeared so obvious, so simple and effortless. He chastised himself for not thinking of it on the drive from Encino to his brother's Lake Balboa doorstep. *Even better*, he mused. *If the private investigator succeeded in finding Peter, why the hell not engage the agency to run down my Beatles collection?*

As Bobby turned the last hard right before Peter's front door, again he glimpsed the huge plexiglass-framed *Taxi Driver* poster.

"You talkin' to me?" pinged in Bobby's brain.

Good pull, he complimented himself for recalling the snippet of classic movie dialogue. *Take that, Peter Pecker Eater.*

His fingers gripped the doorknob, but it was as if Bobby's muscles refused him, stalling his exit from the condo just moments enough for him to wrench his neck some ninety degrees. He faced the *Taxi Driver* 2 Sheet.

"Can't be," Bobby openly uttered to nobody but the picture of Robert De Niro as the murderous Travis Bickle.

Bobby backtracked to the den and Peter's sloppy desk space, re-lowered himself into the modern mesh chair, and keyed one final Hail Mary of a password.

youtalkingtome?

The computer's gaming speakers electronically pinged the program's rejection. Still emboldened, Bobby attempted more iterations of the catchphrase, changing case and punctuation.

You Talking To Me?

YOU TALKING TO ME?

Youtalkin'tome?

Suddenly, instead of that annoying noise of the computer vetoing another failed attempt, a digital wheel appeared in the middle of the screen. The machine was waking. Bobby's patience returned as he relaxed backwards into the support of the chair. Finally, the monitor filled with a desktop display as cluttered as Peter's buffet table desk.

Bobby directed the digital cursor until Peter's calendar revealed itself, conveniently opening to the present day. The boxes representing the days of the week were empty back to the previous Sunday, days before the fires and the forced evacuations. He'd seen Peter since, the last time being the day after the robbery. Peter's next appointment was to see a chiropractor the following Monday morning.

Nothin' here, decided Bobby. Then, as if on automatic, he opened Peter's browser to check his search history.

"Seriously, Pete," said Bobby to the computer. "If I find nothin' here but porn searches, I'm gonna puke."

Only instead of seeing time stamps, dates, and pornography URLs, Bobby was surprisingly quick to notice a familiar-looking manifest.

www.beatles4me.com

www.collectorsweekly.com/music-memorabilia/beatles

www.ultimatebeatlescollection.com

www.yokono.co.uk/collection/beatles

Peter's Beatles searches went on and on for pages. The searches covered days. Odd hours. Working hours. The queries appeared as obsessive as Bobby's had been during his early Beatles days. Yet Bobby felt so out of body—alien and curtained by a film of unreality—that he still hadn't put the puzzle pieces together. Then he decided to open his older brother's email folder. There he discovered a mixed bag of correspondence, the majority of which was business related, all addressed to Peter's Gmail account.

Yet there were other emails, a few of which were from familiar senders. Fellow collectors who had been trading missives with Peter to a secondary email handle, one that looked specifically designed to mask the sender's identity.

Q4pFFFpwo&^$@gmail.com

The content of those emails were like punches to his gut. Bobby broke out in a flop sweat, as if every pore in him had opened, wetting all those electrical burns inflicted by Lucky Dey. It sent him to his feet, stripping off his T-shirt while struggling to fling open the glass sliding door behind Peter's desk. Bobby needed cooler air. In an exasperating struggle, he kept muscling the slider left, over and over again, cursing loudly, his eyes boiling over with tears, until he at last figured out the door wouldn't budge past the wood dowel in the slider's channel.

Bobby removed the dowel and stumbled onto the thin slice of balcony, a second-floor overhang that faced the building's center drive. To the left was a stackable plastic chair with a matching side table. Atop that was a rusted peanut can Peter used for an ashtray. Next to the can was an eighteen-inch plastic water pipe—a bong for smoking weed.

So, this was my lil' brother's favorite space to blaze away on bowlfuls of medical marijuana. Was it out here that he plotted to rob me?

Bobby felt as if in a nuclear meltdown.

How am I gonna tell my pop?

Where the fuckin' hell is Peter?

Will my father ever forgive me when I kidnap Peter and peel his skin until he tells me who the hell put him up to this?

43

Altadena

Pyrotechnic experts measure explosions—whether accidental or full of mayhem's purpose—in size and speed. Bombs and their exponential damage were often equated with the number of sticks of dynamite a particular blast would have required. Newspaper and TV news editors were quick to use the scale, not so much knowing themselves, nor did their public, the destruction a single stick of TNT could inflict, let alone any number thereafter.

Demolition experts were quick to look at the speed of the bomb—how quickly the explosive material went from inert to reach its full destructive potential. There were additional factors to consider, such as the density of the surrounding materials, pressure and containment of the charge, plus atmospheric levels of oxygen and humidity. Most elements in the equation were fractional, but in regard to an explosion's ability to cause harm to property and, more importantly, living, breathing people, the numbers could add up to a shock wave that landed somewhere between a slap in the face and instantaneous death.

The natural gas bomb so quickly engineered from the darker recesses of Beemer's brain had the advantage of favorable conditions when it came to pressure and containment. The little Craftsman bungalow, despite its age, was relatively airtight as hundred-year-old houses go. The small volume of square feet and lack of a basement, along with the recently resealed and shingled roof, allowed the gas burners on the old stove to reach into every possible corner and crevice with an ever-increasing density. Thus, the millisecond after the spark from the shattered light bulb met the square of toilet paper Beemer had fixed to it, the atoms of energy-producing carbon and hydrogen didn't so much as ignite, but combust instantaneously, each charged molecule running from the other at nearly light speed.

The neighbors would remember the blast as a sound both sharp and low, as if a lightning bolt had landed dead in the middle of their suburban street. Walls shook. Windows cracked and spilled from their frames. Neighborhood dogs panicked, spun in place, and sought their owners or the cover of coffee tables.

One eyewitness to the event was a homeowner—an out-of-work voice-over actress—who'd been on her hands and knees in her front yard attending her forest of white roses. Between snips of her pruning shears, she couldn't help but involuntarily peek at the goings-on in front of the Dey/Gonzalez home. Like so many witnesses to unexpected explosions, she couldn't remember the actual sound. The event replayed in her head as a silent visual. The Craftsman bungalow was there—its neatly manicured front lawn, bricked path, and bay laurel hedge. And then it was not.

The detonation itself was recorded from multiple perspectives by neighbors' wide-angle, high-definition doorbell video cameras. Disappointing to some, there was no discernible fireball like the ubiquitous eruptions in movies and on TV. Those effects were achieved using slow accelerants like gasoline that would bloom into spectacular yellow and red camera-happy eruptions. The nearly invisible disarticulation of the bungalow was closer to something between a birthday balloon popping and instant vaporization. The less molested particles of rock, wood, and glass were carried distances of up to a quarter mile.

Gonzo's, Travis's, and Lucky's phones began blowing up in a high-speed conveyor of calls. Word spread quickly within the LAPD and Sheriff's Department. Anybody who had Gonzo's or Lucky's number began texting or calling with hopeful "Are you okay?" messages.

Then came the family group texts, a private digital thread reserved for just Lucky, Gonzo, Karrie, and Travis.

Travis was at his desk in AP Calculus. Gonzo was stopped at an off-ramp in Sylmar. Lucky was reluctantly parked at the end of an emergency-room bed in the hospital's MRI queue awaiting his turn. An LAPD uniformed officer had only just returned his cell phone, having discovered it cracked and impaled in the soft turf near his wrecked radio car.

After a quick collage of "I'm safe" texts there became an abundantly clear absence. Karrie wasn't joining in. There were no words tapped out by the eighteen-year-old who was, like so many of her peers, permanently attached to her mobile phone.

> **Gonzo:** dropped her at the house 15 minutes
> ago
>
> **Travis:** k's phone shows she not receiving
> texts
>
> **Lucky:** calm ur jets. lotta reasons why Karrie
> mght not be with phone
>
> **Travis:** jimmy twiz sez our house is gone.
> maybe her phone blew up

Gonzo: stop it Trav, getting ahead of ourselves

Lucky: fuck this. on my way to u

Gonzo: ten minutes from you. be out front

Lucky: copy

Then, in fat, mother-bear capital letters, Gonzo texted:

Trav, STAY EXACTLY WHERE U ARE!

Gonzo unconsciously added some lead to her right foot, gassing the Dodge Ram until she found herself topping eighty miles per hour, expertly cutting in and out of impeding traffic.

And that's when she caught herself.

Threading between cars . . . the pickup truck, top-heavy due to the lift kit . . . her fear-induced acceleration . . . made for a seriously unsafe cocktail that could only add to the day's tragedy.

Jesus, Gonzo. Slow your ass down!

Lucky had just been in some kind of near-death car wreck. If she were to crash, have any form of accident, what might that do to Travis?

And Karrie? she whispered to herself.

Gonzo filled with guilt. It was she who had demanded Karrie stay in front of the Altadena bungalow.

With a warning, she attempted to excuse. *Do not go in the house.*

But it was a warning Gonzo should have known Karrie would never heed. The headstrong teen had faced so much horror in her young life—abuse, the loss of her parents, kidnapping, and a body-altering hit and run. Gonzo was proud that instead of cowering from life, Karrie had chosen to face it full-on—fists up and clenched and ready to roundhouse kick the world in the face.

No, feared Gonzo. Karrie would never have waited for the sheriffs to arrive. Karrie would have damned the torpedoes and cleared the bungalow herself.

The tears came in a flood, clouding Gonzo's vision and forcing her into the slowest-moving lane. She kept picturing the two of them, barely an hour earlier, picking through bargain bikinis in the quest for some sexy honeymoon swimwear.

What honeymoon?

A darkness grabbed her. It was overwhelming. She felt cloaked in a sudden grim sadness, as if all that she knew and loved was about to be snuffed out. With her cuff, she wiped at her eyes and tried to settle herself, leveling her gaze on the horizon.

Ahead was smoke, black and pushing west again. Yet another round of Santa Ana winds. That would mean flare-ups and the possibility of new fires. The city she loved and its spectacular surrounding mountains appeared to be burning all around her.

The tears, only briefly interrupted, cascaded again.

"Fuck!" she screeched.

She hated crying and the sound of her own sniffling sobs. She hated feeling sorry for herself, as if weeping were a form of emotional weakness.

Pictures of Karrie kept appearing to her like snippets of home video. Strawberry-blonde and, oh, those green eyes and damned gorgeous freckles.

Gonzo pulled off the freeway and wheeled the truck south, unable to stem her awful anguish. She navigated, wet-eyed but careful, certain to triple-check stoplights and crosswalks, afraid she'd compound her pain by causing an innocent death. With a mixture of relief and dread, she saw the red sign directing her to the hospital's emergency entry and guided the pickup into the ambulance drop-off lane.

The emergency room's automated sliding doors slid left and right, making a wide-mouth opening for stretchers and personnel. Cutting up the middle was Lucky, hardly himself, his body awkwardly crooked. He reached for the passenger-side door, pulled himself up and in, and breathed two quick words.

"She's okay," exhaled Lucky.

"What . . . ?"

"Karrie." Lucky winced as he shut the door. "She's all right. She wasn't in the house when it happened."

"You know that for real, or are you just saying it as some kind of affirmation to the universe?"

"I talked to her. She's safe and unhurt."

Karrie's safe, breathed Gonzo to herself, checking the receptors in her brain. He'd said it. Repeated it. She'd heard it. Yet somehow, before sweet relief was able to salve Gonzo's self-inflicted mental wounds, a secondary concern surfaced in the form of a clarifying question.

"What happened?" she asked. "I mean, seriously. Do we have a cunt hair of a clue as to what the hell really happened?"

44

Karrie had strolled down the bungalow's driveway to the side kitchen door. Standing on the first step, she'd inserted her house key into the passage lock. As she was twisting the knob, a booming voice called out over a loudspeaker.

"MISS! DO YOU LIVE IN THAT HOUSE?" The sheriff's radio car's speaker squelched as the deputy behind the wheel released the key to the microphone.

Seeing the black-and-white SUV, front tires gripping the driveway ramp, Karrie stepped away from the kitchen door. With palms open and wide, she answered with a strong nod of her head. Unfolding from the car was a hefty deputy, well over six feet and with flawless black skin, probably sixty pounds over his academy graduation weight, his bulletproof vest adding a jovial thickness.

Protectively positioned behind his car door, he gestured for Karrie to walk toward him.

"My mom called for you guys, like, fifteen minutes ago!" rang Karrie.

"What's your name?"

"Karrie Dey. My mom is Lydia Gonzalez."

"Got any ID?"

Karrie produced her driver's license. Upon inspection, the deputy pushed his car door shut while keying his shoulder mic and reporting to dispatch that he was 10-7, meaning he was out of the car.

"Sorry it took so long," apologized the deputy. "We're spread a bit thin."

"The fires," agreed Karrie. "My dad's with Sheriff's."

"Yeah? Outta where?"

"Lennox. But that was way back. He's reserve now. He was just in a car accident. That's why Gonzo dropped me—"

"Gonzo?"

"My mom," said Karrie. "Stepmom, I mean."

"So did you see this vagrant?" segued the deputy.

"My mom did. And my brother. He's got security video of it."

"And we do not know whether or not he's still inside your house, yeah?"

Karrie nodded in the affirmative.

"And you were gonna go inside anyway?" The deputy's inflated face, full of fatherly judgment, rested on Karrie's.

"I'm pretty okay at taking care of myself." Karrie let him see the set of her jaw. For contrast, she followed with a girlish smile.

"No idea what a vagrant can do, what he or she is on," he straightened. "I'm not keen on a face-to-face with one and look at me. I'm big, fat, and got me both a Taser and a pistol."

"Guess you wanna wait for backup?" joked Karrie, instantly regretting her tone. "Didn't mean to say—"

"I'll do a walkaround," intoned the deputy, his voice deep as a whiskey barrel. "Those your keys in the door?"

"Yessir," said Karrie.

"Mind sitting in my back seat?"

"Of the black-and-white? I do something wrong?"

"For your safety," he eased. "Either that or set yourself up across the street. Sidewalk."

"You got a phone charger?"

"Man oh man," grinned the cop. "I got a little girl. She four years old already. This what I got to look forward to?"

The deputy opened the rear door of the radio car. When Karrie climbed in, he fed the cable of his mobile phone charger through the safety screen so the teen could take advantage of the V8-generated juice. As she waited for her depleted phone to wake, she observed the deputy amble toward the front of the house, readjusting his duty belt until it found a more comfortable hitch on a pair of hips more slender than his belly. First he checked both the sidelight windows flanking the front door, cupping his hands on the glass to block the sun's reflection. Then, stepping in front of the fat queen palm that grew between the dining room window and the lawn, the deputy peered inside yet again, patient. Karrie guessed he was checking for strange shadows or movement.

"ANY PETS?" he called back to Karrie.

"NOPE," she countered. "NOT ANYMORE."

Karrie briefly remembered the old mutt, Oprah, the rescue pup Lucky had to re-rescue while working six months in Compton—this despite his awful allergies. The sweet animal had fought to her dying breath when she had her own chance to defend their bungalow.

The deputy continued by rounding the southeast corner of the house at the driveway and, with his right hand resting on his holstered weapon, gave a quick look into the window over the kitchen sink before stepping up to the side door. He touched the doorknob and tickled Karrie's key chain. Dangling from the clasp was a small canister of hot pink pepper spray. The deputy gave a brief chuckle.

Karrie's phone was threatening to come alive, the battery icon appearing onscreen in animated red. Focusing her eyes past the screen safety mesh that divided the radio car's front and rear seats, she could barely see through a front windshield turned practically opaque due to the angle of the sun. With the front wheels of the vehicle parked on the driveway ramp, there was an upward tilt. Karrie was barely able make out the top of the big deputy's high and tight haircut when he reached the rear of the property, first inspecting the locked doors to the detached garage. Then he briefly disappeared into the backyard before returning to the driveway, checking the windows of Karrie's Prius before returning to the kitchen side door. He stopped at the step and gave a wave and a brief thumbs-up in Karrie's direction. At first, she thought the thumbs-up was for her benefit. But then she wondered if he was gesturing to the radio car's dashboard camera, dutifully recording his actions for posterity and insurable liability claims. She even wondered if there was a mounted camera recording her in the back seat, phone cradled in her right hand while she nibbled at the fingernails of her left.

That's when her phone came alive. The device began to vibrate and ding with texts and social media notifications. Karrie checked the screen, bending her neck and looking down.

She never saw the blast. The shock wave, though, was not to be missed—as if an invisible sledgehammer had crushed her entire body. It rippled through the car while all the side windows dissolved in imploding pebbles of glass. Still, something within her responded—a survival gene—sending her diving into the footwell, arms up and covering her head.

Her ears rang. Through the pitch of squealing frequencies, it sounded like hail pelting the black-and-white's deformed rooftop. And in the stillness that followed, a dissonant concerto of house and car alarms rang in full revolt. Karrie couldn't calculate how long she'd lain there. Her body felt as if it were vibrating, every cellular inch shaking.

Jesus, Karrie, she urged herself. *Get it together.*

She grabbed the door handle with both hands and pulled to release the latch. Nothing engaged. The door was locked. Remembering she'd left the opposite door open, she lunged across the back seat, only to discover that gravity and the shock wave had combined forces to shut the door. The latch gave just like the other. Nothing. Angrily, she slapped a hard palm heel to the protective window screen. And even though all the side window safety glass had shattered from the concussion, there remained matte black window guard devised to keep prisoners from kicking out the casement.

Karrie found herself caged—almost hyperventilating. Panic overcame her until she had the presence of mind to sweep and feel the back seat for her phone. Her fingers grazed it under her right thigh. She pulled the screen to her face, thumbs already operating the device.

The phone was dead . . .

Again?

And despite that the black-and-white's engine was still rumbling, the power cable had somehow been sucked back into the front seat. Out of reach.

Karrie sat there and shuddered uncontrollably for minutes on end. Her teeth chattered. Her only measure of control was stifling the scream she wanted to bellow, a harrowing yearn to howl for help. Any aid whatsoever. Somehow she knew, surveying what she could of the damaged landscape, that an awful event had occurred—a horrible happening when she'd been a millisecond from being erased from planet Earth. It was like being in that metal box again, surrounded by nothing but blackness.

Help is coming was the mantra she repeated in her head. *Help is coming. Help is coming. Please, Jesus. Help is coming.*

45

After being looked over by paramedics, Karrie was assisted into another black-and-white, where she refused the rear seat in lieu of being seated as the front passenger. After a three-minute drive to the Altadena sheriff's station, Karrie allowed herself to be interviewed by a pair of uniformed women deputies. That was until Lucky and Gonzo arrived. There followed some long, chill-killing hugs. Then Lucky took Karrie by the hand while asking the deputies to please excuse them for a few minutes. Lucky and Gonzo walked Karrie outside, helped her into the back seat of Gonzo's pickup, and drove out of the parking lot without so much as a thanks and so long.

Karrie never asked why. The moment had been all about trust. Minutes later, Gonzo had the truck parked in the drop-off lane of Travis's school. While Gonzo rushed in to sign Travis out for the day, Karrie chose to move the spotlight from herself and back to Lucky.

"Enough about me," she lamely joked. "Like, what happened to you?"

"Docs think it was a cocktail of too little sleep and combining over-the-counter meds," he replied dully. "Turns out Zyrtec and Benadryl taken at the same time are a really bad marriage."

"You fell asleep at the wheel?"

"Shortest nap ever."

"And what did the MRI say?"

"Didn't stick around to get it done." The inference was obvious. Karrie was his paramount concern.

"So you could be bleeding to death," she said. "Right now. On the inside. And we wouldn't know it."

"So far, my urine is the correct color," he calmed. "So we have a reason to be optimistic."

The conversation ended there. Karrie knew not to probe too far with Lucky. Or pretend to play mother. Soon Travis joined her in the back seat. Karrie hugged a boy who felt limp, already spent from hours of worry. Difficult-to-wrestle feelings tended to suck Travis back inside his skin. He told Karrie he loved her and was glad she was okay. After buckling his seat belt, he opened a game on his mobile phone.

Karrie could have asked where they were going. But if Lucky and Gonzo had wanted to say, they would have told her. And in the moment, it didn't really matter. The four of them were back together. Alive. Like a wolf pack.

But where's Frosty?

She fired off an update to her boyfriend. Her thumbs madly tapped out a soul-shaking recitation of her morning and early afternoon. After hitting send, she switched to her phone's location settings, making certain it was on.

The destination Lucky had in mind was Fontana, a desert-edged drainage flat at the base of Mount Baldy, nearly fifty miles due east of downtown Los Angeles. The incorporated hamlet was a collection of scrub and asphalt strips inside the boundaries of Southern California's Inland Empire, the westernmost edges of San Bernardino and Riverside Counties.

"Inland," Lucky had long ago surmised, because the landscape appeared hopelessly landlocked despite the barely one-hour commute to Huntington Beach. "Empire," he later read, because some turn-of-the-century newspaper gonad decided the name would ring of riches to potential land investors and citrus farmers.

Ground zero for Lucky Dey and his clan was a no-tell one-story strip of rooms called the Sleepy Winks Motel. Lucky chose the joint less for its comfort and more because he more knew the layout. It was known as a cheap flop as far back as when he was a teen. The motel's blinking neon sign was conveniently halfway between a selection of Orange County surf spots and the snowboarding-happy slopes of Snow Summit and Mountain High. The owner had been glad to rent to rowdy underage teens with cash, weed, and cases of malt liquor whose idea of a perfect three-day weekend was carving icy turns in the morning and riding sunset waves the very same afternoon.

"Board, rinse, drink, repeat," Lucky had once coined. He'd even dropped a little coin on some dirt-cheap custom T-shirts silk-screened with his words.

Twenty-six years later, the motel was still in business, the blinking neon shut-eye on its last sputtering legs. The surrounding fields, once used to grow sweet onions, were ripe with flowing thigh-high wild grass.

"Wait a minute. You're not Edhatu?" Lucky semi-asked once he was greeted at the check-in desk. Appearing from a hole of an office behind an equally small counter was a bespectacled man of Indian extraction. Fatted cheeks. Tired eyes.

"I mostly go by Edgar," replied the man, curious eyebrows arched over Lucky's recognition. "Easier for people to say. Nobody's called me by my Hindu name for a long time—"

"Yeah, yeah, Edgar," smiled Lucky. "And you should remember me."

"But I don't," said the desk clerk. "But maybe you know I've been here so long. Been many, many guests."

"Damn. I thought you lost your job cuzza me," Lucky smiled.

It took a few more reminders for Edgar's brain to recollect—until Lucky had added enough detail about *the incident*. It had involved Edgar's old boss, the original motel owner Lucky's crew used to call the Swede. He was a predator of an immigrant who'd sometimes work the check-in counter wearing only a bath towel and a slick coating of baby oil. When seventeen-year-old Lucky discovered the Swede's perverted game of secretly videotaping motel guests, he'd made an anonymous pay-phone call to the San Bernardino Sheriff's. Within days, the proprietor was busted and the motel was shuttered.

"I'm the owner now!" informed Edgar with a smile and a flash of life to his eyes. "Took many years to pay my family for the loan. But the Sleepy Winks is all mine."

Promising to catch up later, Lucky paid cash in advance for three nights in a pair of adjoining rooms.

"And the reason for your visit?" Edgar had asked.

"Family retreat," Lucky had waved backward as he exited the office.

Retreat. As in we're running the hell away from home, career, et al.

"Who's hungry?" called Lucky after opening both motel room doors. "Pizza place close by, assuming it's still in business."

Karrie was hit by the stale air and must. The room she was to share with Travis was neatly made with thin sheets and bedcovers and an early generation flat-screen TV perched top of a mid-century bureau.

"You know what we like," shrugged Gonzo, realizing she didn't even have a backpack to toss onto her and Lucky's queen bed. "Need the car? Thought Karrie and I could hit up the local Walmart for lady provisions. Could pick you up some dude items. Like clean underwear?"

"Cash only," advised Lucky. From his money clip, he peeled off three $100 bills.

"Whoo-hoo. Spending spree." Gonzo forced a smile, waving the Benjamins at Karrie.

Gonzo dropped Lucky and Travis off at the nearly empty pizza parlor. The pair waited inside for their to-go order while sipping on fountain root beers.

"Show me," said Lucky in reply to Travis asking if he wanted to watch the security video of the bungalow's intruder.

The video, stored on some distant cloud server and delivered via cellular data, played back over the teen's oversized phone screen. Travis's two interior cameras—one high outside his bedroom, the other angled from the corner above the front door—captured an impossible-to-recognize man some thirty years old. His clothes appeared ill fitting and relatively worn, but clean for a vagrant, except for the smudged and worn woolen Chargers cap. Gone was the hallucinating and gesticulating demeanor demonstrated on the street, replaced by a bizarre and fevered dash for what appeared more like inflicting mayhem than searching for valuables to steal.

"Stop it right there," said Lucky, curious and clipped.

Travis froze the video on his phone. The intruder had just wiped past the foyer camera. In the move, it was almost as if the man knew there was a camera three feet up and to his right. When swinging left toward the kitchen, he had raised his right lacerated palm as his fingers splayed in an unconscious attempt to block the lens from capturing his scratched face.

"How do I back it up and zoom in?" rushed Lucky.

"Just slide your finger along the action line," pointed Travis. "Then thumb and index finger like this to make it bigger."

Following Travis's instructions, Lucky reversed the images a second or so, then enlarged the picture, centering it on that badly scabbed palm.

"What's on his hands?" asked Travis.

"Looks like road rash. But that's not what I'm seeing."

Enlarging the picture even more, Lucky pored over the perverting pixels that depicted the mark inside of the man's left wrist. Blurry yet distinct enough to see what appeared to be a tattoo.

"What's that?" asked Travis.

"Tat," whispered Lucky.

"Like a distinguishing mark, right?"

"Exactly what it is."

"So cops might have that in a database?"

"Maybe."

"Maybe yes?" said the teen, hopeful for some recompense.

Maybe yes. Maybe no.

That tattoo wasn't just any old ink. Lucky had seen that symbol twice before; days earlier when a dying deputy had drawn the tattoo in blood on his own left wrist. And six years before, when Lucky had shaken the hand of the man who'd approved the permanent mark. Greg Beem.

Captain Chaos.

46

Woodland Hills. 12:01 p.m.

The backdrop was nothing less than spectacular. A blue sky with distant streams of smoke, over blackened hills dotted with signs of life—little patches of stucco, tile rooftops, and greenery surrounded by nothing but scorched earth. It was visual testimony to the competence of firefighters at saving valued property amid the chaos of wind-driven blazes.

At the westernmost reach of his City of Angeles, Mayor Ramon Avila stood at a portable rostrum—loosened tie, rolled-up shirtsleeves—a tangle of microphones and cables curling away from him like snakes escaping the coming flood of political bromides. The mayor was six feet of perfect posture, broad shoulders, and golden brown skin. Handsome to a fault. His gleaming smile was always camera ready, be it for a fan-friendly selfie or the current phalanx of news cameras aimed to capture his every charismatic tic.

Handsome is as handsome does, recalled Bruce Meltzer.

The line was from one of his favorite movies, Robert Redford's *The Candidate*. Though it was made and released in 1972, it foretold a time when a politician's ability to charm a lens was as, if not more, important than his or her policy points.

Meltzer had found a few square feet away from the throng, clinging to the one spot that wasn't as dusty as a horse corral. Only an hour before, his Salvatore Ferragamo loafers had been buffed to a deep chocolate luster. Now they were tinted beige by the sandy Valley soil that had grown those fast-burning wild grasses. He stood, feet together, atop what appeared to be a couple of buried cinderblocks, listening to Mayor Ram preach to the midday masses tuning to local channels 5, 9, 11, and 13 about his brave first responders and what he, as politician in chief, was doing to assist.

And maybe take a little credit.

Before taking the stage, Ram had acknowledged Meltzer with a wink, promising a private chin-wag after the press conference on the way back to his three-Suburban convoy of staff and security. And sure enough, after Ram said his final thank-yous, he gestured with a nod in the direction he was walking. Meltzer abandoned his spot and traipsed on a downhill angle across ankle-deep drifts of dry silt left in the wake of the recently bulldozed firebreaks.

"Guess you didn't get the memo," joked Ram, his long strides forcing shorter-stemmed players to quicken their steps.

"What memo?" played Meltzer.

"Footwear," smirked Ram. "Your Ferragamos look pretty fucked."

"Mayor's got a foot fetish?"

"Just a fan of fine shoe leather." The mayor stopped at the open rear door of his armored Chevy Suburban. He leaned and slipped off a hiking shoe, replacing it with his own polished loafer.

"Louboutins," appreciated Meltzer, pricing the pair of red-soled loafers at just south of $1,000. "You pay for those on your salary?"

"My allowance is my allowance," brushed Ram. "So, hit me with whatever brought you and your low-class loafers to my press conference."

"Our ears only," warned Meltzer.

"Gimme twenty feet," ordered the mayor.

As ordered, his security detail and driver vacated their positions, setting up a simple but wider perimeter.

Impressive. His own personal cone of silence, thought Meltzer.

"I have a client with a stone in his shoe," said Meltzer with some gangster-style crypto.

"That mob-speak for *a problem*?" chuckled Ram.

"No laughing matter. Mr. B has an issue with someone who works for you."

"City Hall?"

"Personnel."

"Do I know this person?"

"I dunno. Ex-sheriff. Name's Lucas Dey."

"Lucky Dey," corrected Ram. "Yeah. I'm aware of him."

"Interesting."

"I put him in that job so I could keep an eye on him," explained the mayor.

"Has trouble staying in his lane? Or doesn't play well with others?" suggested Meltzer.

"Both. And let's leave it at that."

"Can't imagine what it takes for one ex-cop to rise to your level of attention."

"I'm assuming he's the rock in your client's shoe?"

"Stone."

"And?"

"Considering what we do for you?" broached Meltzer. "Could be an uncomfortable stone for all of us."

Considering what we do for you, continued Meltzer in his head, *you should be willing to pull the damned trigger*.

As usual, Mayor Ram played it cool, poker-perfect, giving away nothing in the way of body language or facial expression. It was as if he suspected there was a camera hooked to an artificial intelligence algorithm 24/7, focused on his face, ready to read his every nefarious thought. Mayor Ram knew very well what guys like Bruce Meltzer and Joey Bianchi did for him and for most members of the city council. Their game was funneling ill-gotten monies to various coffers, mostly in exchange for the fast permitting of large real estate projects. It's how big business was done in Los Angeles, how the rich got richer and the powerful remained in current and future positions of power.

"Hey. You guys do what you gotta do," shrugged Ram. "Your business is your business. Mine is good governance. That's it."

"So you don't have a problem—"

"Said it was your business. All you need to hear from me."

"Lucky Dey technically works for you."

"You asking me if I'm gonna miss him?" straightened Ram. "No. I won't miss that shit magnet. Nobody will."

47

Inland Empire

*F*on-tucky, recalled Frosty.

That's what many of his former gang brethren called Fontana. Not just because it was semi-rural and long considered cracker country by the Pimp Player Hustlers, a Crip set in nearby San Bernardino. Fontana was also the home of the Auto Club Speedway, a two-mile oval on the NASCAR tour. Once a year, the Dixie-based circus of stock-car racing would roar into the Inland Empire, burning hundreds of thousands of gallons of gasoline and Budweiser beer.

Frosty had even gone to a race eight years before. The noise was a mash-up of obnoxious and awe. The sound of unchecked horsepower had caromed off the mountains and traveled even deeper into the earth. Just before endeavoring east in the muscle car he'd been restoring with every fourth paycheck, he'd geo-mapped that redneck racetrack just to see how close it was to the Sleepy Winks Motel.

Because he'd been stuck in the flow of outbound commuters, the drive was as drawn as the driver. He'd kept his ears tuned to KNX1070, the only twenty-four-hour news channel left on local radio. Every fifteen minutes or so, the story would be updated. "An Altadena house was destroyed in a gas explosion, killing one Los Angeles sheriff's deputy and causing neighborhood damage. Investigators are investigating. More later."

"I'm gonna pray for that family," Frosty's mother had called after him. "All the way there and back. Okay. And you lemme know when you arrive. Out wheres again?"

"Fontucky," Frosty had answered.

"Where's that?"

In lieu of explaining, Frosty turned, kissed her rosy cheek, and then departed.

At a distance, the motel looked untenable, a low, single-story strip of rooms between former patches of farmland. Frosty wondered how it could sustain itself in a world full of Holiday Inn Expresses and Quality Inns. Convinced the answer rested in the convenience of the racetrack only a quarter mile away, he parked between imaginary gravel lines next to Gonzo's pickup, turned off the engine, and set the brake. He was barely half out of the seat when a motel door swung inward, revealing Karrie—wrung out, mascara-smeared, and emotionally tapped in a singular visage.

"Hurry the hell up," forced Karrie. "Lucky is about to explain why he's still the king of shit magnets."

Frosty eased into the doorway, his eyes taking a few seconds to adjust to the darkness. Travis was on the closer of the two beds while Lucky leaned against the bathroom doorjamb. Gonzo was in a straight-back chair near the bureau, her stare furious and fixed on Frosty.

"What's he doing here?" she asked, surprised and not yet knowing whom to accuse.

"I invited him," said Karrie without a hint of apology.

"He's not family—"

"He is too family!" shot Karrie. "At least as far as I'm concerned."

"Gonz—" began Lucky, his voice low and full of warning.

"You," Gonzo pointed at Frosty, unforgiving and strained, "stood in our driveway with a gun muzzle aimed at the back of his head." Gonzo's accusing finger tracked to Lucky.

Frosty, hands in his pockets, gazed down at the floor, defenseless and deflated.

"Mom . . ." began Karrie.

"Nope, huh uh." Gonzo wagged that finger.

"She's right," shrugged Frosty, his voice cracking with remorse. "You got all the rights to bring it. Am guilty as charged."

In the intervening years since the night when Frosty's life had flipped from wrong side to right, forgiveness had come from every quarter but Gonzo's. If anybody understood her animus, it was Frosty. He could barely forgive himself, despite having handed his life over to Jesus Christ and the good deeds the Good Lord might have in mind for him.

"Give him a break, Mom," added Travis in a sharp plea. "He's Karrie's boyfriend."

It was a pin-drop moment. While Gonzo was processing Travis's assertion, Frosty held up both his hands in surrender.

"Ya know," relented Frosty. "Y'all might really need to talk it out as a family. So I'll be right outside here—"

"Shut the door, will ya?" charged Lucky, motioning with four fingers for Frosty to remain. "If he's with Karrie, he's family. End of argument."

"Says you!" elevated Gonzo. "It's not like there's gonna be a vote on this either! I'm pissed off enough! Now you ask me to get blindsided and be okay with it?"

"You want him to step outside?" shot Lucky. "Then you tell him and see who follows. You might not like what happens. And then what?"

Gonzo stewed in a long, bitter stare, arms tightly squeezing herself, barefoot and burning holes in the dingy cut pile carpet. Lucky furtively gestured for patience from Karrie and Travis. The silence felt endless. Eventually, Gonzo pinched the bridge of her nose, an early sign of an oncoming migraine. Her eyes closed and she exhaled slowly.

Karrie quietly stood, locked the door, then returned to her corner of the bed. As she sat, she gestured for Frosty to park next to her.

"Been sittin' for hours already," whispered Frosty. "I'm good on my feet—"

"Sit, Frosty!" snapped Gonzo, relenting in a show of slow-motion jazz hands. "You were saying?"

"I was just gonna suggest—" said Karrie before Gonzo interrupted.

"*Lucky* was saying . . ." cued Gonzo, "that he's a shit magnet."

"Right . . ." picked up Lucky, centering himself before reaching deeper than he ever had at an Alcoholics Anonymous meeting. "Yeah. Thought with the new job I could stay out of it."

"The shit?" emphasized Gonzo.

"My shit," continued Lucky, owning it. "Lotta baggage in my trunk. And I guess it's how I do what I do. Kick up a fair amount of dust."

"Ya think?" dripped Gonzo, overemphasizing the sarcasm while not bothering to return recriminating looks from Karrie and Travis.

"But this time I don't have to do what I used to do," defended Lucky. "I'm not fixing this. That just kicks up more dust that turns into more shitty cargo. We're here. We're a family. We're safe. What happened at our house—*to* our house—whatever that was. Sheriff's can figure that. In the meantime, we sit tight. We're off the grid. I say we stay off it until stuff blows over or gets resolved."

"To think we were gonna get married tomorrow," shot Gonzo.

Lucky knew better than to engage her straight up in an argument. Her verbal acuity wasn't worth the tangle. She was angry with every right to be angrier.

"So, Frost," edged Lucky. "Second thoughts about steppin' in it?"

"Family shit?" clarified Frosty. "Who don't have family shit?"

"Did you know?" asked Karrie, eyes searching Lucky. "About him and me."

"Suspected," admitted Lucky. "Makes sense."

"So that's it?" asked Gonzo, urging Lucky to get back to the subject at hand.

"Almost," said Lucky.

"There's more?"

"How about we take a walk?"

"And if I don't feel like a walk?" Gonzo's eyeballs swerved with Lucky as he crossed to the door. He pulled it open, gave her a brief but hopeful gaze, and stepped out onto the gravel. His footsteps slowly receded until the room was once again in silence.

Gonzo heard Karrie whispering, followed by Frosty's not-so-hushed reply.

"She pissed off," defended Frosty. "Go easy. She got a right."

As if refusing Lucky's invitation was tantamount to agreeing with Frosty, Gonzo pushed out of the chair, slipped into her unlaced trainers, then stalked off after Lucky.

The sun was in its final forty minutes. Walking side by side along the road's shoulder, Lucky conveyed to Gonzo his suspicions regarding Greg Beem. He told her of the murdered deputy and the drawing in blood. And what he had seen on the home security video.

"What are the chances?" she queried.

"That he's alive?" confirmed Lucky.

"Hard to imagine that Looney Tune homeless dude on our street was him," she argued.

"That 'homeless dude' set up the gas bomb. Weren't for that poor deputy? That woulda been Karrie."

"Fucking ghost." Gonzo rubbed her face, hoping the friction would make sense of it all. "After all the nightmares."

"Ghost no more."

"He found us in Altadena. He can find us here."

48

Altadena

The kind of sonic concussion that followed an explosion, whether from military ordnance or plain accident, never failed to give Beemer's inner idiot a tickle. It wasn't the noise. The sonic nature of detonations varied based on so many variables. Air density. Atmospherics. Barometric pressure. No, for him it was the sensation of the shock wave passing through his bones. There was an intimacy to it. Close enough to feel, but far enough away to survive and relish the moment.

After placing that thin slice of toilet paper gently pinched between his fingers against the broken bulb's filament, Beemer had retreated back to the homeless encampment, hoping to fit right in. Only his wake of death had already turned into chaos. While starting the climb on the dirt road from Lucky's neighborhood to the abandoned subdivision, he assumed the voice was none other than toothless Maggie's. She was howling at anybody who could hear that her friend Craig had been murdered.

The body had obviously been found.

Before he could switch to plan B—if there ever had been a plan B—Beemer cut ninety degrees left, dropping off the dirt track and fast-slipping downhill to a coyote trail that traced the boundary of the suburban tract. At the very first easement, a rocky Water Company drainage ditch that creased between a pair of quarter-acre home sites, he ducked low in a hunched attempt to hide behind the cinderblock barriers.

That's when the sweet concussion hit him. The sound of the blast washed over him, passing by like a bullet that missed wide. But the shock rattled up the ditch like an ocean swell and popped him in the chest and face. The wave was short. Effective, yet oh so satisfying in the way it resonated deep in his flesh. He paused, his mental cat tongue lapping at it, breathing in the moment before getting back on the move.

Between Maggie's screeching and the soul quenching he received from the blast, Beemer was feeling his internal timer running down to zero. In a matter of moments, police and fire would be certain to flood the area, not to mention news crews and social media hounds descending with their ubiquitous camera phones.

By the time he reached the first suburban street, Beemer was plotting his journey back to the fire zone. Once there, he could drop the homeless act—perhaps even recover his orange inmate togs—and reappear as Dave Bustamante, the lost and bedraggled convict firefighter.

There was a drainage culvert beneath the street. As Beemer crouched, considering the wisest route—a simple but efficient stroll across a suburb's blacktop or a military crawl through the three-foot-diameter pipe—a parked car in the nearest driveway called to him. Just the night before he'd been on the prowl for a late-nineties Honda Civic. He touched his pocket, if only to make sure that deadly screwdriver hadn't jogged loose.

The rest was about speed and boldness.

One strike with the screwdriver and the safety glass of the driver's-side window collapsed in a curtain of harmless fragments. Beemer next dove behind the wheel, his right knee cracking against the column.

Damn, he cursed. *Seat's set for a midget.*

After releasing the catch, the bucket seat railed backward. Meanwhile, he pounded with the butt end of the tool on the column housing. It came apart with little effort, exposing the ignition housing. Beemer jammed the heavy screwdriver shaft into the ignition cylinder until he felt the protective pin snap, then cranked it clockwise until the battery kicked. The car choked, revved, then eased into a classic Japanese purr.

Here we go, exclaimed his cogent self. *Reverse gear, swing west, and get back to the firefight.*

There was, however, Beemer's second self—the inner idiot.

Captain fucking Chaos.

The alter ego was begging for the most minimal of detours—a block east, then a drop south two streets to Alta Vista. There hadn't yet been a fire siren. How much time would it take for Beemer to wheel the Civic by the house—or what was left of it? Just putting eyes on it would perhaps mollify the inner idiot back into his cage. Maybe he'd even stay shuttered in the dark until his extended—*and yeah, it's sure as hell to be extended*—incarceration as Dave Bustamante was in the bag.

His slow-motion turn down Alta Vista reminded him of his days in the Special Forces fighting in Fallujah. Sometimes following the wake-up call of an IED explosion—usually packed in the trunk of a car—as his unit rounded a street corner, the first thing that struck Beemer was the stunned residents, shocked out of their hovels, gobsmacked at the destruction. Peering through the Honda's dirty windshield, Beemer witnessed a neighborhood gathering on every third front lawn or sidewalk—the very same sidewalk where, barely hours earlier, he'd been engaged in those loops playing the part of a crazy vagrant. A few stragglers had stepped onto the street, unthinkingly staring, wondering if their eyes were deceiving them. Where there had been a bungalow, there was no more, the parts beyond the foundation, stonework, and plumbing scattered like rubble.

"Shit." The word escaped Beemer's lips when he noticed the sheriff's SUV parked with its front wheels on the driveway ramp. He snatched the wool cap from his own scalp and sunk low in the seat. His first instinct was to stare dead ahead. But that was before his inner idiot nudged.

Frickin' house blew up. Nobody lookin' at you. And anybody who's anybody would be lookin' too.

So, Beemer allowed his head to twist right, taking in the ecstatic beauty of his handiwork. The cop car was merely an unexpected ornament to his effort. Easing past, Beemer was able to read the figure in the vehicle's rear. Female. Blonde. Was it the adopted daughter? And why the hell hadn't he heard a siren? On the other side of the radio unit was his result. The bungalow had been vanished, leaving little but leftover debris and broken windows in the homes next door. Beemer imagined the molecules in the detonation moving fast, like a soap bubble popping. It was there. And then it wasn't. The missing bungalow left the neat neighborly street appearing as if it had earned an ugly gap-toothed grin.

After a slight acceleration, Beemer made his first left turn, swinging the Civic south and with the full expectation of returning to the fires. There, his left eye caught something odd. A man in a windbreaker, middle-aged, solid, balding under stringy hair . . .

And strolling?

The man had a to-go drink in his hand with a big red 7-Eleven logo on the side.

This Mr. Big Gulp is strolling and just sippin' on his super soda? After what I did a bare half block away?

Once again, he was back in Iraq. After an IED explosion, the key to finding the bomber was to look for the most nonchalant character among the shocked and awed—someone who had been expecting a concussive crack in the local fabric.

Only I'm the bomber this time.

Beemer felt both insulted and curious about Mr. Big Gulp's seeming lack of urgency or concern. It irked him enough that he slowed the car a notch, kept his eyes tracking, and observed Mr. Big Gulp climbing into the rear seat of a navy blue GMC Yukon. Beemer quickly clocked a few other passengers, each appearing equally indifferent, African-American, splashed with bits of bright red accents—hat bills, hoodies, T-shirts.

Bloods . . . Gangbangers . . .

None of it fit. No way. No how. The Yukon's grille was nearly all the way to the street corner, giving every passenger a clean view of the vanquished bungalow. Beemer wondered just how long they'd been there. Had he missed them entirely? Had they all been there to watch or record his homeless act? Had they been fooled? Amused? More importantly, had they watched him enter and exit the property?

Who the hell are those guys?

49

Porter Ranch

"Yo! O-man!" sounded Bobby, the bass in his voice resonating in a muffled echo that dripped from Oren's basement ceiling. "Obi-Wan!"

At the first note, Bobby's voice sent a jolt of worry through Oren. The ponies were already calling him back to Santa Anita. He'd been poring through Bobby's Beatles collection, appraising his next pawn. He'd been deciding between more vinyl—both unopened, the cellophane wrappings shading the records in amber. It was between a Russian pressing of *Rubber Soul* and the *Yesterday and Today* album complete with the original "butcher" cover. Then came Bobby's hollering. For the briefest moment, Oren thought he'd been caught. Red-handed. Reason soon returned.

Bobby can't see through walls . . . or into my dark heart.

"Obi-Wan!" shouted Bobby again. "Know you're home, buddy. Need your professional help!"

Surely, Bobby had first tried the doorbell and Oren hadn't heard. But he could feel the man's friendly thumping against the walls of his house. The footsteps and sound rotated counterclockwise until Bobby's shadow fell across the cracks under the storm door. Bobby banged his foot against the jamb.

"O-meister! You down there?"

In his stocking feet, Oren raced up the steps, making certain to lock the basement door shut, slipping the key into his zippered sweatpants pocket. He slipped into a pair of rubber Crocs he'd left by the rear kitchen door and stepped out into the waning daylight. Bobby had just turned around the corner while continuing to bang his fist against the stucco.

"What, what, what?!" returned Oren, remaining near the door, not in the mood to chase him.

"O-man," appeared Bobby after reversing directions. "Why you no answer the bell?"

"Was in the bathroom," excused Oren. "What's your thing?"

"Pinching off the ol' loaf?" beamed Bobby, his broad smile not quite reading as fake as it truly was. In their last encounter, Bobby had inquired about his older brother's whereabouts with a strong spicing of concern. Oren for sure knew Bobby hadn't found Peter. So, why the big grin?

"You found your brother?" defended Oren, despite knowing the actual truth of it.

"Pete's off the map," shrugged Bobby. "He'll pop his head up. Probably after a week binge-eating the buffets of Vegas."

"Thought I heard 'expert advice.' You got a pest problem?"

"Construction thing with the rebar. They're pouring concrete tomorrow morning. Just thought you'd give my sound bunker a looksee. Wanna know if anything strikes you as weird. 'Cause once they pour, it's that way or the jackhammers."

"Yeah, yeah. Can't put it back on the truck if it's wrong."

"While there's some light left?" pointed Bobby to the sky.

Oren pulled the kitchen door shut, trailing Bobby around the side of his own house, both of them crossing the cul-de-sac in semi-tandem instead of side by side.

"How's Barbara and the kids?" asked Oren, hoping some small talk would ease his own inner tension.

"Who knows?" sounded Bobby, slightly annoyed. "Gave me a serious ration of shit for not going to this school thing tonight. So they're all at the thing, and I'm here again. Me and my Beatles bunker."

And nothin' to stick in it, thought Oren.

In those few paces along the west side of Bobby's house, near where Oren had cut the alarm wires, he felt a tiny bit sorry for his neighbor. Sure, he saw Bobby as an obnoxious, entitled, lucky-sperm-club blowhard. But though Bobby appeared to have a life and love from family, he was so lonely—looking forward to spending his relaxation hours inside a custom sonic bunker, listening to fifty-year-old records by four sixties-era mop-tops.

Sorry? Not as sorry an asshole as me.

Rounding the rear of the property, instead of approaching the hole in the ground to where the steps would be, Bobby led Oren to the steepest edge.

"From this angle, it looks like a swimming pool," forced Oren. Off Bobby's quizzed look, Oren explained, "Deep end here, shallow end there. I mean, it's not a pool shape. But you can see the rebar cage is similar to when pool builders are about to pour the gunite."

"You know pools?" asked Bobby.

"I know a guy who knows pools. Was an old client of mine. Rey Palomino over in Granada Hills?"

"Never heard of him."

"Does beautiful work. If you're ever thinking of redoing your pool, he's the—"

Bobby shoved Oren. In a surprise move, he'd pinched Oren's neck from behind and muscled the former wrestler until he lost his balance. Oren tumbled over the edge of the hole, his body battering against the twisted cage of rebar. Had Oren seen it coming, he might have had the muscle memory to thwart Bobby's shocking play. Instead, he came to rest almost fifteen feet down, cut and bleeding from the painful places where the high-carbon steel had sliced his body.

"I know!" accused Bobby. "You were in on it!"

"Whaaaa?" groaned Oren. He touched the top of his scalp and felt the ooze of his own blood, yet still held out his fingers as if to confirm the red in the fading light. His fingers looked as if dipped in black oil.

"You! My fuckin' brother! And that fucking hobby cop!"

"What are you talking—"

"Don't play dumb!" Bobby punched at the air, his feet pawing the edge of the hole like a pacing panther. "I saw all my brother's emails! You were in on it with him!"

"You're high!" coughed Oren, trying to right himself only to become more tangled in the rebar. His leg poked through a gap, touching the soft dirt underneath with his toes, both his rubber Crocs having been dislodged from his feet as he'd tumbled end over end.

"Stop lyin'! I know!" screamed Bobby.

"Yeah? Whaddayou know?"

"I know Pete gave you my alarm code! I know that cop stood guard while I'm guessin' my good neighbor, buddy, Obi-Wan, asshole, fuck Oren hauled my collection to who knows where."

"Prove it."

"Said I saw the emails."

"Just 'cause he shared your code with me—"

"Stop fuckin' lying!"

Oren grabbed a handful of rebar, sticking his feet into the gaps like the rungs of a ladder.

"You're not gettin' out of there until I know where Peter is and what he did with my shit."

"Suppose I could stay down here. Wait for you to bury me in concrete."

"You see this shit?" Bobby stripped off his T-shirt, his rippled, steroid-assisted torso cast in blue twilight, rimmed in the white incandescent of his house. "Your hobby cop friend did that to me!"

"Right. Like I give a tinker's damn."

"Maybe I should put a car battery to your tiny ass," spat Bobby. "See what you really know."

"You should talk to your brother," suggested Oren, channeling his inner spite while attempting to misdirect. "Keep the dirty laundry in the family."

"Where'd Pete take my stuff?"

"Like I know?"

"And he better not be selling to that butt-plug collector. Felix fuckin' Consadine! Yeah. I saw that email too. Felix gets my stuff? He's gonna bleed me until I get all my shit back."

"Look at me," pissed Oren, arms wide. "You're mistaking me for someone who gives a shit."

"You wanna ever get out of that hole, you better start giving a good goddamn."

"Really? Me? You seen how I live?"

"And it fits. Why you and Pete would wanna steal from me."

"Know what I want?" expressed Oren, his voice suddenly plaintive.

"I don't care what you want."

"One last good day at the track," continued Oren. "Then I say, let hell come."

"Why don't I jus' bury you right here?"

"Why don't you just ask me what it would take?"

"A shovel. How's that for a start, you shriveled Polack prick?"

"You want your stuff back?"

"Finally, you're getting my point."

"Finder's fee."

"What?"

"I get your stuff back from Peter," slowed Oren. "What are you willing to pay?"

"How about I let you live?"

Oren, having found a balance point, continued to eyeball the half-naked Bobby. He played out their stupid argument in his head, attempting to gauge where and when it might reach a compromise. The dialogue ping-ponged between his ears without end.

"You're a lousy negotiator."

"Who's in the hole, dumbass?"

"You want to get back at your brother?"

"I hate my brother."

"He hates you. Get over it and come up with a number or just kill me here."

Back and forth, it was ceaseless and without an obvious exit, a verbal wrestling match certain only to end in a draw.

"Think I'll just cut to the chase," decided Oren.

"Cut the what?" missed Bobby.

Oren lowered himself into a crouch, feeling with his fingers for a smooth spot on the rebar, and then sat with his legs crossed.

"What're you doing?" Bobby's voice hardened. He unconsciously felt control slipping away. "Seriously, O-man. I'm gonna get the shovel and get this over with here and now."

Oren's reply was a slight wriggle, seeking a more comfortable resting position for his butt muscles. He stared dead ahead into the dirt.

"So, that's it?" asked Bobby, so frustrated, his voice rose almost an entire octave. "You wanna die today? Or you wanna walk away with somethin'?"

Night had almost overcome day, leaving the hole in Bobby's backyard almost black, devoid of light. He could barely see the top of Oren's hair-challenged scalp.

"Ten thousand," offered Bobby. "That's ten Gs for my stuff, my brother, and proof about the hobby cop's part in it. Because I want that prick's badge."

Oren remained silent, Zen-like, listening to Bobby's feet squishing back and forth in the mix of wet sod and dirt.

"Think my offer deserves a reply," spat Bobby into the hole.

"In a negotiation, silence can be deemed as a reply," returned Oren out from the relative darkness.

"I'm not negotiating!" defended Bobby.

"But that's precisely what we're doing," calmed Oren, his mind skipping ahead again. Ramifications. Odds-making. Weighing outcomes. "And it's looking good for you in regards to getting your stuff back."

50

Boyle Heights. 6:29 p.m.

It was as nondescript as one might expect a government building to be. Beige. Concrete. Two stories when viewed at ground level. The parking lot was cracked asphalt, qualifying as just another city surface in desperate need of repair. The Los Angeles County Department of Medical Examiner-Coroner's office was pound for pound—or cadaver for cadaver—the busiest coroner's office in the entire United States. Eleven thousand–plus deceased bodies deemed a suspicious death were processed in that one building per calendar year. That was an average of thirty dead people a day, carted countywide by blue- and white-striped vans. Upon each dubious arrival, every lifeless body—man, woman, or child—was weighed, fingerprinted, triaged, bagged, tagged, then shelved in a five-hundred-body-capacity, forty-degree-Fahrenheit, refrigerated crypt until one of the round-the-clock staff of pathologists could slot the cadaver for an autopsy.

Though significant as it was in regard to the actual numbers the unit could absorb, the crypt didn't come close to resembling what most might imagine—a mausoleum-like space, tall-ceilinged with refrigerator doors that opened to individual trays on greased rails. It was more like an industrial warehouse with stainless-steel shelves from floor to ceiling containing naked bodies in various states of plastic-sheeted dress or undress. The bodies were moved from rack to rolling table and back again via a natural gas–powered forklift.

Not unlike his Reaper pal Lucky, Abel was enjoying a second career on the county dime. He'd seamlessly transitioned from coordinating the intake of prisoners at the men's central jail to doing pretty much the same job at the downtown mega morgue.

Only my guests here ain't near the same hassle as them knuckleheads I'd check in at the high-rise hoosegow.

The job could have easily been all desk jockey all the time. A real seat-spreader with Abel passing the hours behind a computer screen. From there, he could administer his authority electronically—save for contractual meal, snack, and bathroom breaks—without ever relieving his chair. Only Abel liked to get out of his assigned perch, assisting incoming transportation crews, supervising the initial divining of just how long the decedent was dead, obvious causes of death, and most importantly, putting a name to the body.

"Abel got himself a two-fer," cried out the transport driver, backing through the automated swing door into a triage room so sterile it might have been mistaken for a hospital.

"All you got?" Abel swung from his desk, already fastening the one button on his lab coat that could barely contain his ex-cop's belly carved from a longtime affection for exotic beer. His ruddy, pock-marked nose was the other giveaway to his after-hours boozy predilections. Abel grabbed a pair of disposable rubber gloves.

"I know I'm not the ME," followed the transport tech, a roundish woman with a bob cut, at the rear of the first cart. "But my money's on a love spat gone cattywampus."

"Cattywampus?" repeated the driver. "Exactly what year were you born?"

"I have colorful parents," she defended before continuing. "My bet it's a murder-suicide."

"I didn't see no gun on the scene, no markers for shell casings," countered the driver.

"Revolver. Bagged and tagged before we showed."

"Ten bucks it's a drug murder."

"Where?" injected Abel, unzipping the body bag to discover a red-stained male corpse, blood-blackened eyes still open wide to reveal an eight-ball hemorrhage.

"Northridge," answered the driver.

From Abel's immediate once-over, the cadaver was at least six-foot-two or -three, male, well-muscled, the torso as well as the face badly bruised. Death had most likely come from a single bullet one inch above and forward of his right ear.

"This one would be the suicide?" guessed Abel.

"Should see the smaller one," said the roundish tech. "Just as ass-kicked. One in the head, two in the chest."

"I wannna die at the YMCA," sang the driver to the tune of the Village People hit.

"Murder-suicide at the Y?" asked Abel.

"Naw. Some gym parking lot," explained the driver. "Crunch Fitness. It was the gay part that I thought was funny."

"If I was gay, that'd be considered workplace harassment," joked Abel.

"But you're not gay," insisted the driver with a slight air of uncertainty.

"DBs come with any ID?" switched Abel. "Just to make my life easier."

"There no baggie in there?"

"Oh, wait. Found it." Pinched underneath the corpse's arm

was a clear plastic evidence bag containing a neoprene wallet with all contents removed so they could be loosely examined without leaving fingerprints or DNA. Among the credit cards was a medical marijuana ID, a membership card to Gold's Gym, and a California driver's license. Holding the bag to take better advantage of the light, Abel looked at the driver's license photo—a shaggy, surfer-looking lad with blue Germanic eyes and a wide grin bearing perfect teeth. At a glance, the data appeared to match the dead guy. Then Abel read the name aloud.

"Dakota James Jones," read Abel before something in the back of his brain clicked with an "oh" and a "shit."

The transport driver and tech reversed through the automated door to retrieve the second cadaver. During the seconds-long hiatus, Abel hurried back into his closet of an office and began flipping through a stack of handwritten notes. He didn't get far before arriving at the correct slip of paper. On it was scrawled just two names and a telephone number: Marcus Buchwald and Dakota Jones.

Shitballs, thought Abel. Lucky Dey was like the Nostradamus of Lennox. He predicts and shit happens.

51

Fontana

Lucky stood in that former onion field, grown over in weeds and recurring vines, the sky above replete with a blanket of stars. The atmosphere was clean and without the usual gray iridescence that left the night without any true blacks.

"You gotta come back," begged Jorge Lopes, his Reaper pal and the official Sheriff's representative charged with reaching out to the suddenly AWOL reserve deputy. Lucky held the phone gently against his bruised ear. "You didn't even wait around for the MRI. C'mon, Luck. Be reasonable."

"When have I ever *not* been reasonable?" asked Lucky.

"You want chapter and verse?" argued Lopes. "Too many questions need answers."

"I'll answer every one when I know my family is safe."

"Safe from what?"

"You seen my house? Oh. Wait. It's gone. You can't see my house." Lucky's sarcasm was as thick as sour mash.

"Think about it. If Fire and PD knew what you knew, they might be able to help."

"I give answers, all it does is open another can of worms."

"Funny how that happens. Only to you."

"Need a few days, Jorge. Please."

"Powerless, dude. I'm just the messenger. And, seriously, if it weren't for the fucking fires, you'd have a half dozen investigators sending bloodhounds after your white ass."

Lucky had done the easy math. And it added up to an investigative cluster. From the murdered deputy he had been the first to see, to the complaint against him by Bobby Bianchi, to the fatigue and drug-aided accident that could have killed God knows how many, to the mysterious explosion that demolished his house, the constant point of inflection was Lucky and Lucky and Lucky again. He was the ultimate person of interest.

The world's biggest shit magnet. Again.

"Shit's gonna land where it lands," defended Lucky, not a fan of letting fate make the call. "My job's my family. Until I'm sure they're safe . . ."

"Do whatcha gotta do," conceded Lopes in semi-agreement. "Don't wanna see you lose that sexy new job of yours before you've done a year."

"Cart before the horse," warned Lucky.

"So, no wedding tomorrow?"

A beep sounded in Lucky's ear. He looked briefly at his screen and saw a name next to the alert for an incoming call: Abel Lee.

Shit, thought Lucky. *This is gonna be some seriously bad news.*

"I'll be in touch," Lucky said to Lopes before switching to the other call. "Yeah, Abel?"

"You said to call if . . ." began Lucky's Reaper friend at the coroner's office.

I said to call if one of two names showed up on Abel's intake docket.

The concern had been nagging at Lucky ever since he had sent those two muscled henchmen home with no information—only bruised bodies and egos to show for their torturous efforts. He'd tagged the duo as little more than a pair of hired clowns in the service of wannabe mobster Bobby Bianchi. Lucky had hoped the spanking he'd meted out on Bobby and his bozo posse would be enough to put a cork in whatever the misunderstanding was in regard to the Porter Ranch robbery. Though he did have a fractional worry that one or both of the musclemen would end up dead for having failed their insipid assignment. Were that to occur, Lucky would instantly know that he was playing with an enemy more dangerous than some silly trust-funder who'd just lost his precious Beatles collection.

Bobby's daddy, Joey B.

Lucky pocketed the phone and crouched to his haunches, as if the weight of his dilemma were pinning him to the earth.

Jesus, Lucky. What the hell did you do now?

"Shit magnet!" he said aloud, cursing himself.

When he finally stood, he inhaled some of the night air, expelling it in a nerve-easing count of one, two, three, four. He pivoted, shoulders squared, and regarded that eighteen-room motel. The words *No wedding tomorrow* rang in his ears with a decided sting.

No damned wedding, indeed.

His eyes settled on the lone motel and the near-bucolic surroundings—endless suburbia and industry west, mountains north, desert east. He worked to push aside his physical pain, acutely resigning it to his mental back burners in lieu of a few cogent minutes of planning for the immediate future.

The motel appeared empty but for his family's two rented rooms. The building looked as it always had to him—overlong, more like a farm shed with curtained windows or a beached canoe parked on a gravel strip. The low peak of the simple gabled roof had been restriped recently with galvanized weather stripping. But for the sparse exterior lighting, the flickering neon sign, and the dim office lamp, the only signs of life were those curtained windows of rooms six and eight, the illumination emanating as if from the beating hearts of those he loved most.

Ideas began to form, and with them the liabilities of each potential action or inaction.

"Just gimme twelve hours," he asked of the distant deity called God.

It was less of a prayer and more of a request to an ultimate power whom he didn't really know. Or was scared to know. But it would have to do. And he would have to plan for the worst. People were coming—men with guns and plans to do harm to him and whomever.

Screw Greg Beem, he decided. Lucky Dey was about to go to war with the mob.

Saturday

52

Fontana

The dream had been disturbing. Worse, it was nonsensical as hell without turning into a full-fledged nightmare. At least not until the moment she awoke. As Gonzo briefly recalled, she was in hotel. Luxury. Mexican decor. Only it wasn't Cabo San Lucas or anywhere else she knew. She could tell that it was her honeymoon. And in the adjoining room were Travis, Karrie, and Frosty.

And I'm not even mad at him?

What caused her heart to race was that Lucky was nowhere to be seen. There'd been a resort-wide search. Night had come with the flick of a light switch. And Gonzo's pulse had begun to race at dangerous speeds. A medical team had been called. The plan was to use a defibrillator to shock her heart back into the proper rhythm.

A Mexican medical tech stood bent over her, electric paddles at the ready, while a nurse used scissors to tear open her nightgown, exposing her bare torso. Her breasts were swollen, just like they had been when she was nursing Travis. Yet her immediate concern was about scarring. Would the electric connection against her skin burn and give her permanent welts like she'd seen on Lucky?

Where, oh where, is Lucky?

"Ssshhh. It's okay," Lucky whispered.

"Not okay!" she screamed in the dream. "It's gonna burn!"

"It's okay," said Lucky again. "Time to wake up, honey."

"What . . . what . . ." mumbled Gonzo, her eyes fluttering open to a warm, fabric-filtered light.

She was awake and out from under the nightmare, rescued by her no-longer-missing man.

"Hey," he said sweetly.

"What's going on? What time is it?"

"Like, five minutes to sunrise."

"Is everything okay?"

"Everything's good," he whispered. "Need you to get up."

"Why?" she asked, feeling as if she might succumb to her grogginess. "Wait. You need sleep more than me."

"I'm good. Let's get up."

"You didn't answer me."

"Maybe because it's a surprise," he pulled. "So, here we go."

She allowed him to help her upright. She slid her legs over the edge of the bed, let her socks sweep against the rug.

"Is it cold?" she asked.

Lucky passed Gonzo a pair of white jeans and the fleece sweater she'd purchased at Walmart. He kneeled on the floor to assist in lacing up her flight shoes.

"Coffee?" she asked.

"Waiting for us," hurried Lucky, tying a double knot.

"What's with the service?" Gonzo's eyebrows sharpened as she gazed across her nose at him.

"Time-sensitive situation."

"Why's it always have to be a 'situation'?"

"Cross you gotta deal with." He rose and stepped back a few steps. "Ready?"

"Ready for what? Every cell in my body wants to go back to sleep."

Lucky swung the motel room door open. The slightest streak of sunlight creased the room like a slash of molten honey.

"Ouch," she said. "Sunrise?"

"Beautiful, isn't it?" he grinned.

"Might be better with sunglasses," she said, guarding her eyes with split fingers. "You said there's coffee?"

"And it's getting cold. So move your sweet ass."

"Yes, sir," she mocked with a sleepy salute.

Lucky offered a hand. She gripped his calloused mitt and followed him out into the morning. As Gonzo's eyes began to adjust, she saw a trio of figures standing in the middle of that old onion field, swathed in golden light. Forcing her pupils to constrict and focus, she recognized Travis standing opposite Karrie, both bearing the widest of smiles. Between them and two steps back stood Frosty, hands folded over what looked like the same kind of Bible she'd spotted in the motel room's nightstand.

"What's in Karrie's hair?" squinted Gonzo.

"Same thing that's in your coffee?" nudged Lucky.

He handed her a small bouquet of purple and yellow wildflowers stuck into a venti-sized paper coffee cup from Starbucks.

"Promised you I was going to marry you on Saturday," said Lucky, so soft his voice rattled with emotion. "Today's the day."

"No way," she laughed.

"It's happening right now," he insisted. "Or. If it doesn't fit the picture you'd planned in your head, we can wait on it. You can go back to bed—"

"Hell no, I'm not going back to bed." Gonzo threw a short, sharp elbow. "This is so sweet."

"Then shall we?" He offered his arm.

"And *soooo* not you," she added, slipping her arm into his.

"Even a neolith can evolve."

Arm in arm, they began the fifty-yard stroll up nature's aisle. Karrie and Travis began to make the musical sounds of "Here Comes the Bride," setting Gonzo off in fireworks of girlish giggles.

"I can't believe this," she confessed.

"Believe it, Mom," jibed Travis. "It's happening."

"In an onion field," joined Karrie.

"Is this even legal?" wondered Gonzo aloud.

"I'd picked up rings just before I wrecked that black-and-white." Lucky revealed his pinky finger. Circling above and below his knuckle were his and hers wedding bands. Platinum. The unfiltered sun magically gleamed off the polished metal.

"And you?" Gonzo asked of Frosty.

"Ordained a couple hours ago," shrugged Frosty. "Turns out there's an app for that."

"Seriously?" laughed Gonzo, not quite herself yet.

"Are we ready?" asked Frosty.

Lucky squeezed Gonzo's hand, then turned her to him.

"Yeah?" asked Lucky, his eyes searching hers.

"Yeah," smiled Gonzo. "Let's light this candle."

"Here we go, then." Frosty opened his Bible to the first of the verses he'd chosen for the occasion. "'Set me as a seal upon your heart, as a seal upon your arm, for true love is as powerful as death . . .'"

Short as the ceremony in the overgrown onion field was, Lucky lingered on the last syllable of every spoken word. His. Hers. Frosty's. There were the vows spoken and repeated, unchecked laughter, amusing stutters, stammers, hysterical asides from the best man and maid of honor, along with lemon yellow licks that danced in Gonzo's brown eyes. It was, in that ten to fifteen minutes of beginning day, a slice of perfection. Of true happiness.

This is what happy looks like, grinned Lucky, if only saying it to himself.

The thought itself felt as close to aspirational as any he'd ever heard or summoned. Ever since his little brother Tony had been murdered by Greg Beem, Lucky hadn't seen a true future for himself. A true and happy future. Now, he did. And it was good.

53

West Hollywood

"Your tits are in the way," the old golf pro had complained. "Simple as sauerkraut."

The thought was insulting. *And intriguing*, Angie's sub-self kept repeating. It seemed that upon the stroke of every hour, her brain would nudge her psyche as a reminder that she was in the middle of a moral wrestling match.

That, and my big tits are in the way.

The comment had come the night before, slipping past the smoke-stained teeth of her seventy-odd-year-old golf pro. She'd started her journey on the links in an attempt to meet a better class of men. After getting a reputation as an easy lay while in the Navy, she'd joined Sheriff's, going from military mattress to station house slut.

Flatfoot floozy, she'd sometimes joke with one of the many deputy dogs she'd happily bedded. Sure as a hellion, Angie had her fun while a sheriff's deputy. But at a steep cost. Being a sexually liberated woman had left her childless, lonely, and living in the same rent-controlled WeHo apartment she'd first occupied when she'd been originally assigned to the West Hollywood Station. She'd spent everything she'd earned on plastic surgery, luxury singles cruises, and sessions with a published sex therapist who had suggested that she take up golf.

Why? she'd asked.

"Because," the shrink had suggested, "you might meet a better class of man who's interested in something other than using you as a sperm receptacle."

Some six months later, after Angie had geared herself up with golf equipment and a closet full of matching sportswear, she'd dedicated herself to learning the awful game. But mastering the sport had turned from a frustration to an obsession. She wanted desperately to make that little white ball soar like the Korean women she watched on TV. Gene, the lanky, chain-smoking ex–major league pitcher turned teaching pro, was her newest instruction acquisition. He was towering, favored panama hats and Hawaiian shirts instead of billed caps and polo shirts, and couldn't give a devil's rip what anybody thought of him.

Comfortable in his own skin, Angie had quickly surmised.

"How much you pay for them zeppelins?" the pro had croaked.

"You do know that kinda talk can get a man in serious trouble." Angie had straightened, golf ball teed, her eyes trained on Gene. His freckled complexion tinted in the green glow of the overhead lighting. The driving range was city-owned, a quarter-moon curve of fake, cushioned turf divided into individual stalls.

"What?" asked the pro, lacking any concern. "This my Me Too moment?"

"You heard of it?" she volleyed. "Then you should know better."

"You see any Koreans with big racks on the women's tour?"

Angie had to ponder the question for a moment.

"So, how much you pay?" he continued his big-breasted harangue.

"What's it to you?"

"'Cause it's like this," he gestured. "You spend somethin' like two thousand on them sticks, bag, all that. You wear designer clothes. And that ain't cheap, knowwhatImean?"

"Not yet."

"What I'm sayin' is, this golf thing is an investment. Your investment. You payin' me sixty-five an hour. Yet you got these really fake—yet eye-catching, I might add—pair of sweater melons that prevent your arms and shoulders from making a simple rotation through the golf ball."

"Oh," she meekly replied.

"It's like teachin' a milk cow to do a hundred-yard sprint—"

"I got it," Angie interrupted.

Insulting as the exchange was, on the short post-lesson walk back to the parking lot, she'd been seriously weighing whether she'd erred in any of her three separate breast augmentations. And if she'd had her fun, why not reinvest in breast reduction surgery? All for the sake of her golf swing.

But neither that question nor the pro's verbal coarseness was the true reason why Angie awakened every hour on the hour. It was her conscience.

After her lesson, Angie had shouldered her golf bag and headed for the parking lot, a mostly empty stretch of asphalt but for those few driving range rats striking the last of their bucket of little white balls. She'd left her red and white Mini Cooper locked and under a streetlamp. When she'd swerved around the chain-link gate with only twenty yards left to her car, she'd stopped at the sight of a man of average height, weight, and general description, leaning against her car, arms across his chest, his face obscured by the downward shadow from an Angels baseball cap.

"Get off my car!" Angie barked, letting her golf bag slip off her shoulder. She withdrew the first metal blade her fingers touched. A shiny eight iron.

"Just wanna talk," returned the man.

"Don't know you." Angie made certain her words fell with punctuation. "Don't want to know you. So, scram."

"You're Angie from personnel," said the man, sounding unflattering and unimpressed.

"Whadda you want?"

"Mayor needs your help."

Dragging her bag, Angie closed the gap in order to lower her voice.

"When he wants to talk to me, *he* talks to *me*," she insisted.

"Not for this one."

"I don't like this," she warned, suddenly checking the space around her for anybody else who might be listening, watching.

"Just a request," relayed the man. "Time sensitive."

It was after ten at night. Angie had stood there in her neon golf attire, eight iron gripped like an ax, measuring the man and whether or not to listen to what he had to say.

That had been last night.

After that unknown man leaning on her car had impressed on her enough bona fides in regard to her relationship with Mayor Ram, he had expressed an urgent need to locate former deputy Lucky Dey.

The mayor's men, as far as she knew, were all cops. LAPD—square-jawed, jar-headed bodyguards or consultants. The man in the parking lot didn't present like a police officer, former or otherwise. His appearance and demeanor seemed bloodless. Lawyerly, even, with a distinct air of threat. Though he hadn't spelled it out, Angie guessed the man wanted Lucky harmed. Or dead. Yes, she'd argued with herself, she'd agreed to spy on the fellow former deputy.

What's wrong a little office skullduggery? she'd reasoned.

The fight within caused her stomach to be angry. All night long, she'd squelched the acid with fistfuls of flavored Tums. The angst would have caused far less inner inflammation had she an answer for the man.

If only I didn't know.

Days before, on that morning when she'd crept Lucky's office and searched his work computer, she'd installed a bit of digital spy software onto his phone. It was called Spysy and cost Angie only $9.99 in the app store. The software was specifically designed for paranoid spouses concerned about cheating mates. Once embedded in the electronics, it secretly tracked a cell phone by using the device's ever-constant GPS.

I mean, why the hell not? she'd easily excused herself. Maybe it would be fun to log into her phone and see just what the enigmatic former deputy was up to when nobody was looking.

The night before, when she was supposed to be warming up for her golf lesson, she'd opened the app and zoomed in on the map. *Fontana?* she'd quizzed. *What the hell is Lucky doing in Fontana?*

And that had been that. Well, until her lesson had concluded and she'd met that unremarkable man in the Angels cap. He'd left Angie with a phone number to text when—and if—she got ahold of information about where Lucky Dey could be located.

She sat at her kitchenette table, a Formica antique she'd inherited from her mother. Angie regarded the phone number while listening to her single-serving Keurig hiss out the final ounce of her morning coffee.

Call the number and Lucky dies.

Though she couldn't be certain of the thought, it weighed as if it were a true and binary decision.

Don't call and what happens to me if they find out I knew?

It was a devil of a dilemma. She was loyal to a fault—loyal to Mayor Ram. But there was that other fealty. To cops. Fellow deputies. Politics was one thing. Even a little gaslighting now and again felt within acceptable boundaries. But signing another officer's death warrant? *Above my pay grade*, she excused. She shouldn't be the one to decide.

And I'm not deciding, she reasoned. *I'm only giving up coordinates. I'm not pulling an actual trigger.*

"Screw it," she said, grabbing her phone, resolving to call the number before tanking up on coffee and croissants. Then she'd do some research on the best SoCal plastic surgeons known for breast restoration.

54

Fontana

For the reception, Gonzo chose the nearest IHOP. The wedding party crowded into a corner booth, each ordering a different pancake combo. The bride ordered the Mexican tres leches stack. The groom, the double-blueberry stack. Half a dozen flavored syrups along with forkfuls of cooked, sweet dough were passed like traded Pokemon cards. The coffee was weak, but the laughs and love were strong.

With the bride and groom retired to an afternoon honeymoon in their stale room at the motel, Frosty, Karrie, and Travis caught a late matinee before returning to the motel around 5:00 p.m. When Lucky heard the trio clamoring into the adjoining room, he climbed out of bed and began to dress.

"So, that's it?" copped Gonzo, her voice light with easy air. "All it takes to make an honest woman of me?"

"Not holding my breath," jibed Lucky. "C'mon. Time you get moving."

"Me?" she cooed, sitting up in bed with only the sheet for warmth. "Where do I have to go?"

"I fucked up," he flatly admitted, back straightened after pulling on a long-sleeved T-shirt. "That game of electroshock therapy? You know, the gangster wannabe?"

"The one you promised me was under control?" Gonzo stiffened.

"Halfwits who did the deed turned up at the coroner. Abel said murder-suicide, but I can't afford to buy that."

"And you found this out—"

"Last night," he cut her off. "Only a matter of time before they figure out where I am."

"So that explains today."

"Yeah."

"Doesn't explain why the hell you wouldn't tell me about it last night!"

"You gonna make this our first fight as a married couple?"

"So, your big plan was to marry me and send me packing?"

"You, Travis, Karrie. Frosty's gonna take you someplace I can't ever know about."

"And Lucky the shit magnet does what? Sticks around motel hell to face down unknown bad guys?"

"Got a call in to some Reapers. Promise you. It's all gonna get handled."

Gonzo's hands went to her face, covering her eyes and cheeks in exasperation. She exhaled. "Jesus," she pissed. "When is it gonna stop with you?"

"It stopped this morning. When I said 'I will.' Meant it then, mean it now. Just have to get to this mob spawn's dad."

"Yeah, right!"

"It was a misunderstanding," he snapped. "It still is. I have to believe there's a leverage point and a resolution—"

She shot out of bed, grabbed a handful of clothes, and

vanished into the bathroom. The door slammed shut. Lucky heard the shower angrily switch to full blast, causing the plumbing to moan as if they were in their bungalow.

Our nonexistent bungalow, he thought in silent lament.

A knock softly landed on the door to the adjoining room. Lucky sidestepped and opened it, his eyes still in the direction of the bathroom.

"Everything oh-kay?" asked Frosty, politely lingering just inside the threshold.

Lucky peeked around the doorjamb, seeing both Travis and Karrie parked on the beds, then eased the door shut behind Frosty.

"Thin walls," suggested Lucky.

"Think we got a problem," switched Frosty, his voice hollow and low. He gestured outside. "Intersection. 'Bout two hundred yards southeast and across the field. Yukon or Caddy. Then a second car—red rental job—doing to-and-fros about every couple minutes."

Before Lucky could pinch the curtain to take his own look, Gonzo appeared from the bathroom, zipping on her Walmart skinny jeans.

"What kind of problem?" she inserted.

"Could be nothin'," said Lucky.

"Yeah. Could be," said Frosty. "But if it was me pullin' a layin'-in-wait kinda game? Those the same spots I woulda posted up for a looksee."

Gonzo fired a quick glower in Frosty's direction, as if to say "Of course an assassin knows how other assassins might operate."

"What you packing?" snapped Lucky.

"My nine and the clip that's in it," she said, saltier by the second. "That's it. You?"

"Impounded."

"You're shitting me!"

"Travis," barked Lucky, circling back to the adjoining door. He opened it to find Travis already on his feet. "Earthquake kit. Is it still in your mom's truck?"

"Yeah." Travis appeared half scared, but equally thrilled. Lucky tossed him the keys.

"Get both canvas bags out of the toolbox," instructed Lucky. "Eyes only on the task. No lookin' around like you know something."

"I'll do it!" insisted Gonzo.

"Don't wanna risk spookin' 'em." Lucky twisted for the room phone. "Just like I said, Trav. No peeking. Just the truck and back."

"Lucky—" started Gonzo.

"He's gonna be fine!" Lucky picked up the room phone, squinting to read the DIAL FRONT DESK option. He pressed the button and barely waited two rings. "Edgar? It's Lucky. I'm thinking of throwing a party. You got rooms for me?"

"Currently?" answered Edgar. "You and your family are my only guests."

With his hand resting on the doorknob, Travis took a deep breath, pulled the lid of his snapback low, and tried to look cool and relaxed as he sauntered into the early evening. His mother's Ram pickup was parked with its rear end to the railing. In a few strides the skinny teen had crawled up into the truck's bed and unlocked the aluminum saddle box fastened between the rails. He removed two navy blue canvas bags. Then, as he allowed the spring-defended lid to lower, Travis couldn't help himself. His eyes, guarded only by the flat brim of his cap, caught the distant silhouette of a large SUV.

"Shit," he chastised himself.

I looked.

Speeding up his movements, Travis dragged the canvas bags out of the truck bed, banged the gate shut, then returned to the motel room, swinging the door behind him and latching the bolt.

"What are we doing with tools?" asked Travis, trying to shake off the shivers.

"Whatever we can," answered his mom, as if already in sync with the fast-evolving plan.

55

Behind the Yukon's deep-tinted windows were three rows of assassins. Five men in all, seated two by two by one. As kill crews go, it was tight and young.

"Gotta drain it," announced the stringy-haired man sucking on a Big Gulp, the one middle-aged white man in the group.

"No shit," jibed the beefcake driver. "All that soda you swill?"

The man in the black hoodie with a jaw as square as Superman's had been keeping his eyes between the motel and his rearview mirror. Mr. Big Gulp, who'd claimed to have commuted to the gig all the way from Vista, a northern San Diego hamlet, had by Beefcake's count already peed six times in three counties.

"Don't knock a man with a prostate," teased Lil Rod, the teacup-sized killer occupying the rearmost row. He'd automatically taken the back bench, claiming to have been relegated to third-row occupancy since grade school. "That prostate shit's gonna hit us all. Got two uncles already with the gonad problem."

"You know there's drugs 'n' shit to stem that flow," offered Mr. Big Gulp's seatmate, a barrel-toned man who'd introduced himself as Dough Boy. His head was topped with a red Cardinals fleece cap.

"Doctor wanted to write me a prescription," replied Mr. Big Gulp. "But said the side effect is a limp dick. So guess my decision, assholes? Who's got the hat?"

Dough Boy removed the fleece cap from his head and palmed it over the car's dome light. Mr. Big Gulp popped the door handle and slipped out into the dark.

"Got the kid in the truck bed," narrated the black man with retro Ron O'Neal sideburns copped straight out of the original *Super Fly*. He kept his one open eye to the night vision scope braced against the SUV's front right pillar. "Looks like more luggage."

"Maybe they're in for the night?" asked Beefcake.

"Like there's a shit ton to do out here?" said Lil Rod. "Spent near a year in Berdoo-doo. 'N' they call it Berdoo-doo because there's shit to do out here but get weed boners and chase Skanksquatch."

"Skanksquatch!" repeated Dough Boy, his laughter unchecked.

"Ssshhh!" Beefcake lifted a walkie-talkie to his mouth and keyed the mic. "Time for you guys to get a room," he relayed.

"Copy on the room," replied a soft voice, feline, practically cooing.

"Yo," complained Lil Rod. "Did that Lamps guy offer to work cheap just to get next to that?"

"That," answered Dough Boy, "is the dude's missus."

"No way!" insisted Lil Rod. "Seriously. *Mr. and Mrs. Smith* kinda married?"

"Yo. Car's not soundproof! Keep it the fuck low." On the right edge of Sideburns's lens appeared the headlights of a red rental sedan. "Awright. There they are. Game on. We snappy."

Behind the steering wheel of the red rental car was the

husband, otherwise known as Lamps, his hipster beard glowing blue from the shine of the motel's neon.

"Oh, Honeybritches?" sung Lamps. "What you think about we havin' some on-the-clock bumpin'?"

The wife—Honeybritches—barely considered whether her husband's invitation deserved a reply.

"I'll get the room," she volunteered. "Should give you just enough time to sit there 'n' hump your hand."

"Tha's not sexy. Not at alls," he volleyed.

"Close as you gonna get tonight." Honeybritches swung the door shut, her short blonde wig bouncing as she high-heeled her way across the gravel to the office door.

Edgar was already at his post behind the check-in desk, having been alerted by the wash of headlights.

"Good evening, ma'am," he greeted.

"Need one room, one night," replied Honeybritches.

"Room rate is eighty-six dollars."

"You're kidding me," she said, arms akimbo and looking about the shabby space as if to say, "Eighty-six dollars for this shithole?"

"Plus the usual state and county taxes," smiled Edgar.

"Take cash?"

"Of course. But I'll need a driver's license or passport."

From her purse, she extracted a wallet and a single, crisp from-the-ATM $100 bill. As Edgar held it up to the light, examining it for authenticity . . .

"You checkin' that 'cause I'm black?" accused Honeybritches, her delivery soft enough not to be rude but with still enough verve to push most men onto their heels.

"I don't judge," defended Edgar. "I don't even care what you charge by the hour."

"Man in the car is my husband."

"Could be a woman in the car. I said I don't judge."

"Want a room facing the street, somewhere in the middle," requested Honeybritches.

"Back corners are all I have," said Edgar.

"Now, that's not real," she argued, gesturing an open palm to the door. "I count two parked cars."

"Most of my rooms are reserved for a private party," confessed Edgar. "Seriously. Best chance at a quiet night is a corner room."

Quiet is not at all the kinda shit we have planned.

"Whatever," she said. "We'll take the corner."

"Your pimp and you?"

"My husband, you Bollywood reject!"

"Never could dance," winked Edgar. "I will need his ID as well."

"Already ahead of you." Honeybritches placed a pair of California driver's licenses on the counter, clicking each like they were playing cards. Both IDs were spotless and, unlike that $100 bill, faked to perfection.

"Missus Lampley," read Edgar, keying the fraudulent details into his computer. "I'm putting you in twelve. That's on the other side, right behind the office. Checkout is noon. Just park in front of the room. There's ice and vending machines between rooms five and seven. I'll be here at the desk in case you require anything else."

"You're here all night, yeah?"

"Pretty much 24/7," said Edgar. "My motel. My life."

"You're dedicated. Respect."

Her smirk took on more of a squint than obvious condescension. The proprietor had just added himself to her kill list. She smoothly allowed her eyes to perform a second sweep of the room for security cameras, confirming one hard-wired unit, most likely connected to a hard drive. She wisely guessed the proprietor hadn't yet made the upgrade to a wireless, cloud-based system. Honeybritches made a mental note to make certain that they wouldn't leave the motel without the hard drive in hand.

But the idea of there being a party brewing? That gave her pause. She signed for the room and accepted two card keys, one for her and one for her husband, then bid Edgar a cheery goodnight before returning to the rental sedan. She landed in the passenger seat with a sound far heavier than her weight gave away.

"All good?" asked Lamps.

"Lucky to get a room," she answered before picking up the walkie-talkie and keying the mic. "Yeah. We be in room twelve. Not what I wanted."

"And why not closer to the target?" voiced Beefcake in reply.

"Shithole practically sold out," keyed Honeybritches. "Somebody havin' a party."

"Get into your room. Will get back to you when it's time to make a move."

"All good," she replied before directing her husband. "Behind the office. Back her up and around to the right."

"Who's throwin' the party?" asked Lamps.

"Far as I know? Lindsay frickin' Lohan and her posse of crack hos."

"Aren't you in a frame," he judged.

"No matter how hard you try me . . ." she slapped at both her leather-clad thighs, "You are so not gettin' any of this while we are on the job."

"Keep workin' the tease," he played as he shifted the car into reverse. "And the better it'll be when you break ass down and beg me for it."

56

The ax blade cut into the bathroom ceiling, causing a hailstorm of chipped paint and plaster. With every upward swing, Lucky's body rippled with pain. His right foot slipped and he nearly tumbled from his stance on the toilet seat.

"C'mon. Let somebody else do it," suggested Gonzo.

"Almost done. Hand me the pry bar." Lucky kept his eyes upward and into the football-sized hole he'd made.

Laying across the bathroom threshold was one of those two earthquake prep bags, unzipped to reveal a collection of tools. As Gonzo fished inside for the pry bar, she snuck a look at Frosty, manning a post at the edge of the window shade.

"Where's Travis and Karrie?" she asked.

"Started already in the other room," said Frosty. "Tell Lucky that it looks like the couple in the red Malibu took a room in the back."

"Pry bar!" demanded Lucky.

"What's up there?" asked Gonzo for the third time, as if withholding the heavy pry bar was a quid pro quo.

"Gotta see it to believe it," was all Lucky would answer, his hand still outstretched for the tool. "And chance it's still up here is pretty slim."

"I would really appreciate it if you don't use the word 'chance.'" With that, Gonzo relinquished the pry bar.

With the claw end of the tool, Lucky hooked it inside the hole and, like an experienced firefighter, began pulling down large chunks of Sheetrock until the opening was wide enough to handle his broad-shouldered frame.

"Right," said Lucky, as if preparing to face something unpleasant. "You're in charge down here. Go help the kids and hope to hell I don't fall through the ceiling."

"And if the shit hits the fan while you're up there?"

"Call 911 and don't spare the ammo."

"Ha, ha, and ha." Despite her continued sarcasm, Gonzo positioned herself below, elbows wide with her hands resting on her overtaxed head, and watched Lucky struggle to pull himself up through the framing two-by-fours. Out of instinct, she stepped forward, offering locked elbows and cupped hands as a stirrup for him.

"Thanks," he wheezed before finding a secure handhold and pulling his body through the hole he had made in the ceiling.

Call 911, Gonzo's brain kept screaming in reply.

There had been a brief but heated discussion that eventually involved the entire familial four plus Frosty. Gonzo argued that they should use an emergency call as a ruse to both roust the assassins as well as add cover for an escape. Lucky battled back that it would be an escape to nowhere. In a matter of hours, they'd been tracked *and* trapped. The better defense was to be patient, own the real estate on which they stood, and wait for the Reapers.

If they survived, Lucky planned to take his case directly to Joey Bianchi and negotiate terms. It was, as he kept reminding himself, a misunderstanding.

And if agreement wasn't at all possible? Gonzo had queried.

The best Lucky could offer was to cross that bridge when they came to it. In the end, Karrie and Frosty sided with Lucky. Travis abstained, the fear in him causing another retreat inside his skin. The awkward teen didn't want to vote, upset the applecart, or go against anybody—especially his mom—let alone die.

It was everything Lucky could do not to just walk out the front door, arms over his head in surrender, even if to his own execution, all in service of saving his family. But he pretty much knew how that would go, especially after their magical morning. His family would never accept his human sacrifice. The selfishness of it would be tantamount to an unforgivable suicide.

The attic space above the old motel was nearly the precise dimensions and built as Lucky had remembered. All the interior beams and roofing substructure were meticulously spray-painted a matte black. The catwalk, a two-foot-wide piece of planking, cushioned with anti-squeak rubber flooring, ran the entire length of the motel. The tiniest slices of light leaked up from the three occupied rooms, revealing fishnets of cobwebs and collected dust from stem to stern.

Pushing away the threads, Lucky edged toward the northern end of the motel, careful his footfalls left little noise. The Swede, he imagined, would have been pleased that his construction, some thirty-plus years later, remained as soundproof as when he'd finished it. The video mounts remained, as if poised and ready for the Swede to return with his camcorder. The exhaust fans the oily creep had fitted in the ceiling of each room would intermittently malfunction whenever he chose to record his peeping sessions.

Emanating from corner room twelve, shafts of light penetrated the blackness in streaks. Uniform. The ceiling fan was unengaged. Lucky crept forward. He peeled the layers of cobwebs from his face while bracing against one cross strut at a time, arriving above the room with near-breathless concern. As he looked for a spot to kneel, he wondered how the hell the Swede, with his unwieldy bulk, had managed to remain balanced while peeping and doing whatnot. With each arm braced against a ceiling joist, Lucky lowered himself push-up style until his eyeballs met with the light from below.

Squeeeeeaaaak.

Lucky froze, biceps fully engaged, his low back in a rage of pain and near spasm. Beneath, he could see that murderous couple. The TV in the room sounded as if tuned to ESPN's *SportsCenter*, the volume having swallowed what little noise Lucky had rendered. The husband sat dressed, relaxed on the bed nearest the window, his attention fixed between his mobile phone screen and the television.

On the opposite bed was the hardware.

Lucky tallied a sawed-off shotgun with a bandolier stacked with red twelve-gauge ammo. Next to it was a compact Heckler & Koch submachine gun with fifty-round clips. Neither weapon was close to California legal.

On the white pillow, gleaming back at Lucky, was a nickel-plated Model 1911 .45-caliber pistol, his personal favorite flavor of handgun. He'd carried that very same model for years, preferring the weight of both the frame and the slug. As a general rule of ballistics, whoever or whatever was struck by a .45-caliber bullet usually went down and stayed down. The weapon looking back at Lucky was a slick gangsterized version. Flashy. Meant to impress.

Is there a bullet in that pipe meant for me?

A toilet flushed. Lucky eased breath into his lungs and adjusted his view. The wife appeared, buttoning her skintight leather pants. He could see the seams of her faux blonde wig. The couple were wordless in their little communication. And neither looked the least bit distracted from their ultimate intent.

Satisfied with the sortie, Lucky carefully doubled back to the hole he'd punched in the bathroom ceiling.

"I need Frosty," he called.

"What'd you see?" worried Gonzo.

"Two hired hitters," whispered Lucky. "Look like a pair of flat-liners waiting on the green light."

"And you wouldn't have a clue when that might be?" Gonzo's query was rhetorical.

Before Lucky could reply to her verbal sting, she'd cut out to change posts with Frosty. Lucky hung at the jagged hole, eyes shut, attempting to rest during those few seconds lying prone.

"Whatcha need?" returned Frosty, neck craned up at Lucky's anguished face.

"A plan," said Lucky. "I need a fucking plan."

57

"**A**nybody feelin' left out?" zinged Lil Rod from that third-row seat. "I mean, come on. Supposed to be a party, right?"

Mr. Big Gulp let the mockery slide, wisely choosing to keep his lips tight. This wasn't his team. He was merely the contractor—a middleman between the kill crew and the money. His only duty was to make sure the deadly deed got done. He'd conscripted soldiers before, preferring to hire out through either black or Hispanic gangs. It was Sideburns's big play to garb up as Bloods. As a North Long Beach Crip, he was a sworn enemy with nearly all Blood sets. But for the Fontana exercise, why not put a Blood-red cherry on top of the bloody sundae? After being pitched the grand idea, Mr. Big Gulp had simply rubber-stamped it with, "Sounds great. Knock yerselves out."

When the murder was to actually go down, Mr. Big Gulp

planned to retreat to a distant perimeter and get paid without having to take his weapon off safety.

"If they throwin' a party?" added Dough Boy. "It's for ghosts or ain't nobody's phones be workin'."

While keeping his right eye stuck to the scope's diopter, Sideburns glanced at the dashboard clock with his left. 9:53 p.m. He could feel the perspiration gathering at the back of his neck.

Heavy weighs the shotcaller's crown, thought Sideburns.

"Your call," reminded Beefcake.

"No shit it's my call," answered Sideburns.

The current plot was to wait for the party and observe how it unfolded. During the noise and debauchery, the crew would wade in like they were uninvited guests, faces hidden behind balaclavas while flashes of Blood red were imprinted on the retinas of the witnesses. It was to appear less like an execution and more like a splashy gang murder. Yet, as time wore on, there appeared to be no imminent shindig to serve as camouflage. It was on Sideburns to choose his next particular poison.

Wait longer?

Or move now—fast and furious?

Or abort and stalk until the next fat time?

That's what Sideburns called the moment of opportunity—a fat time—when the target was sated and without expectation.

Ripe as a hot peach.

"Yeahhh," growled Sideburns. "Think we gettin' ourselves gamed by this grab-ass dep-u-teee." He twisted in the seat, snatching a gander at Mr. Big Gulp to see if his Caucasian guest had an opinion to offer.

"Your crew, your call," relinquished Mr. Big Gulp, hands open, palms displayed in mock surrender.

"Kinda hungry," said Sideburns. "Know this chicken-and-waffle joint in the S.B. Grits like butter. We get it done now, you bring the green?"

"Happy to pay for a job well done," agreed Mr. Big Gulp.

"I could go for grits," chimed Lil Rod.

"Then, here we go," decided Sideburns, flipping open a pay-as-you-go burner phone and nodding to Beefcake, who pushed an unmarked compact disc into the Yukon's player.

Mr. Big Gulp's nerves jumped as the speaker system popped with the sound of recorded gunfire and people screaming.

"Sounds real, yeah?" grinned Sideburns before dialing 911. "Watch this shit."

"Emergency," answered the operator.

"IT'S HAPPENIN' NOW!" cried Sideburns into the phone. "EVERYBODY'S GETTIN' SHOT AT!"

"Do you have a location?"

"THERE'S A SHOOTER AT THE BASKETBALL GAME."

"What basketball game?"

"SUMMIT HIGH SCHOOL! PEOPLE DYIN' IN HERE!"

Then Sideburns cut the call, clicking off and snapping the battery from the phone.

Smoooooth, thought Mr. Big Gulp. Fontana's small-town police department, only eight radio cars strong, would no doubt be scrambling every ounce of its limited resources to the emergency call.

"Summit High School?" asked Mr. Big Gulp.

"Top end of town. 'Bout three miles away."

Almost as if cued, the whine of a siren broke through the Yukon's soundproofing. Heads twisted. Out the rear window appeared a distant lighting array, blue and red, spinning atop a speeding northbound radio car. The lights and siren scraped across the flattened horizon, unimpeded, in a rush to stop a school shooting.

Like that, thought Sideburns. The O.G.—or Original Gangster—of the group, he played the role of wise man. Since age twelve, when he'd begun slinging dope as a Crips Rollin' 20s wannabe, he'd sponged up every bit of gangland tradecraft he could. Thus, he'd brag, his longevity and the gray tinge by his temples. He was upper management. Yet when the call went out for a hit job on a sheriff's deputy . . .

Not jus' any deputy. A Reaper deputy called Lucky fuckin' Dey, the O.G. reminded himself.

Sideburns didn't have to think twice about throwing his hat in.

"Helluva trick," levied Mr. Big Gulp, impressed with the efficiency of Sideburns's ploy to suck all possible police units from the vicinity.

"Saw it in an old movie," monotoned Sideburns. "Imagine my happy face when I found out the shit really works. Like, every time."

"We going in or what?" pressed Beefcake.

"This where whitey takes a hike," pointed Sideburns.

"Meet you at the waffle joint." Mr. Big Gulp gave a noisy suck on his straw before shouldering open the door. "Hat?"

Once again, Dough Boy jammed his fleece beanie over the dome light. Mr. Big Gulp popped the door lock and slid out feet first. He shut the door behind him with a delicious General Motors *whump*.

"Headlights on dark and we rollin'," ordered Sideburns before pressing the mic button on the walkie-talkie. "Comin' in now from the front. Mr. and Mrs. Smith? You take the corners."

"We gotcha," squawked Honeybritches.

Beefcake turned the engine over and dropped the Yukon into gear, easing it back onto the blacktop. The fingers of his left hand hit the automatic window switches, lowering each pane of glass to let in the night. Road noise was the only sound, the rubber from the tires meeting asphalt getting faster and louder with every gained foot.

The windshield acted like a movie screen, slowly filling with the motel's horizontal outline. Then Beefcake jerked the wheel to the right, gunned the engine, and kicked rocks as the eight-cylinder beast swung into the motel's gravel lot.

"Dough Boy go to room right!" barked Sideburns. "Lil Rod goes left!"

Beefcake hit the brakes, sending the Yukon into a short four-wheel slide to a dusty stop.

"Kill 'em all!" Sideburns snapped the release lever, using the last foot pounds of gravity to assist the door in swinging wide enough for him to clear the barrel of his scattergun, a been-around, police-issued pump-action. He'd bought the shotgun because the bluing on the metal was faded and practically matched his skin.

Me and this piece here, he'd said to the gun seller, *we belongs together.*

And up until that murderous moment, Sideburns had proudly notched five bodies onto the wooden pistol grip.

58

Lamps looped the strap of the submachine gun over his head and under his right arm, then checked to see if Honeybritches was at his rear before reaching for the door latch. His wife pulled down her balaclava as if to answer his silent question, the sawed-off shotgun comfortably dangling from her shoulder like she was carrying a designer handbag. Lamps nodded, pulled down his mask, and opened the motel room door.

From the bags of earthquake supplies, Frosty had chosen the bolt cutter. Forty inches in length, the tool had bright yellow rubber-coated handles and smelled of packing lubricant. Frosty silently slid into position, three feet to the right of room twelve's doorjamb. And he was as prepared to die as he was good with God. He'd been praying; the only guilt he felt was that his heart rate remained shy of eighty beats per minute.

Still a killer, Frosty concluded. *And Jesus knows it.*

Once in position, he braced himself against the wall and allowed his eyes to close briefly. All his nostrils could detect was the lube on the bolt cutter's heavy blades. His ears picked up the rush of a car engine, tires chewing at gravel, then a fast braking followed by a slide.

"It's on" were all the words his brain could process. The yellowed bug lights over each rear motel room door appeared to streak across his pupils.

Frosty heard the latch thrown. He cocked the bolt cutters over his elbow, loaded his weight onto his right foot as if waiting to swing at a high fastball, then began his act at his first visual registration of movement. The closed blade assembly of the bolt cutters struck the masked outline between the first person's nose and left eye. The man's head snapped backward, his feet kicked at air.

"LUCKY!" shouted Frosty.

Above and balancing on a pair of ceiling joists, Lucky stood only feet from the pervert-built catwalk, a thin half-inch sheet of drywall between himself and the motel room below. He'd been braced there, legs shaking, sweaty hands gripped around that ax handle. At Frosty's verbal signal, he hopped upward, brought his feet together, and allowed gravity to have its way. His nearly two hundred pounds snapped a hole in the motel room's ceiling, barely breaking the speed of his fall.

"How'm I gonna do it?" Lucky had whispered back at Gonzo only minutes before. "How many times you called me a blunt instrument?"

"Think my exact wording was a 'human wrecking ball,'" she'd clapped back at him.

Lucky plummeted in an eight-foot, ceiling-to-floor free fall. He had only a glimmer of hope of executing a soft tuck and roll. His left shoe caught the edge of the twin bed nearest the bathroom. His foot twisted sideways before impacting with the floor, briefly dislocating at the ankle. His body followed, his fall only slightly retarded when he bounced off the opposite mattress before folding entirely on the cheap, stained carpet. For a microsecond, Lucky couldn't tell up from down.

Still, he felt for the ax handle.

Honeybritches's first thought was that her man had slipped on something, an obstacle obscured by his clumsily worn balaclava. Then came the shout. Somebody calling "LUCKY!" She was already swinging the sawed-off shotgun when the ceiling caved in behind her, shifting the room's air pressure. It was instinct that made her pivot. She was already pulling the trigger to the semi-auto action. *BOOM! BOOM!*

Lucky felt the shock of the gun's muzzle, spitting volleys of double-aught buckshot. The air in the motel room was instantly filled with shredded mattress foam and polyester pillow fill. He spun against the bedframe and turned his head away, his face touching the cold ax blade.

BOOM!

The third blast hit the lamp and nightstand, wood and glass and plastic splinters stippling the top of Lucky's buzzed scalp. He knew the next trigger pull was going to be a kill shot, as the woman would have sidestepped to her right for a clean shot.

Only Lucky didn't hear a fourth shot. He heard the woman screech, "OW!"

After stepping over Honeybritches's earth-flattened husband, Frosty had dropped the heavy bolt cutters across the woman's arms. The blade smashed across her thumb, which was folded around the barrel support. As the shotgun dropped, she spun at Frosty with a claw of red acrylic nails. His flesh came loose with the first strike before both her arms and legs wrapped around him in a death grip. It was when Frosty felt her teeth digging into his cheek that her body went rigid and a gush of warm blood spilled across his chest. Honeybritches's grasp eased and she fell away to his feet.

Lucky stood opposite Frosty, ax in hand, slickened with blood. Between them lay the killer wife, body quivering, gash in her neck where the ax blade had severed her spinal cord.

"Step aside," wheezed Lucky.

Frosty swiveled as Lucky raised the ax again, took one step forward, and struck downward. The husband, barely finding equilibrium and having rolled into a half crawl, was already fumbling for the submachine gun when Lucky sunk the blade into his skull.

The quiet was followed by four wall-shaking gunshots. Equally spaced. *BOOM! BOOM! BOOM! BOOM!*

"Gimme the shotgun!" urged Lucky, limping badly on his twisted ankle and sticking out his open hand in hurried expectation.

Then Lucky saw it—that nickel-plated Model 1911—the pistol's rosewood grip sticking out from the killer's jacket pocket. He snatched the weapon, cracked the slide back to see if a cartridge had been properly chambered, checked the safety, and stuffed the piece into his waistband.

59

The frontal attack was frighteningly efficient. As the Yukon braked directly behind Gonzo's pickup, three doors opened and out popped three armed, masked killers. Sideburns took the lead, calmly stepping up to the pair of motel room doors, aiming the shotgun's muzzle at the doorframes opposite the latches. He unleashed four concussive volleys at the hinges. Dough Boy took the left door, kicking it to the floor, the lights from inside blasting at his eyeballs.

Lil Rod hadn't the body mass to knock down the door on the right. So, Sideburns gave it a shove and slid aside as Lil Rod entered, AR-15 ready to stitch anything that moved. Like the room next door, it was fully lit through the bathroom, the adjoining door linking the rooms slung wide open. From the corner of his left eye, Lil Rod caught Dough Boy framed in the shared doorway. Dough

Boy gave the slightest headshake to Lil Rod before easing ahead. Both motel rooms appeared lived in, yet utterly uninhabited.

Dough Boy reached the bathroom, a pistol in each fist, the barrels of his twin .40-cals in the lead. He saw the floor—covered in plaster and pieces of Sheetrock—and lifted his gaze and both gun muzzles upward until he was locked on that gaping hole in the ceiling.

"THEY UP IN THE RAFTERS!" shouted Dough Boy.

It was as if Lil Rod's ears were directly attached to his nerve endings. His muscles responded by turning the AR-15 upwards and letting loose a clip-clearing series of gunshots—one after the other—high-pitched, ear-piercing cracks. As the room instantly filled with drywall dust, spilling from hole after gaping hole, Lil Rod heard a second, faster barrage coming from the room next door. Lil Rod's reaction to Dough Boy's shout—an utter non-idea to sizzle the ceiling with bullet holes—had acted as a contagion. Barely a second after he began punishing the ceiling, Dough Boy had begun punching his own holes in a double-fisted shelling of the attic space directly overhead.

There followed an eerie silence interrupted by soft metal-meets-plastic clicks as both Dough Boy and Lil Rod ejected their empty magazines and reloaded.

Sideburns felt his nerves pulsing like heartbeats in his finger-tips. No less than five paces from those demolished motel room doors, his pump-action shotgun was braced against his right hip. Considering the fusillade of gunshots he'd just heard, his expectation should have been that the massacre had been successful. Only something was missing. Screams. Wails. In group executions nobody goes down as if they were bound and gagged. Sideburns had heard no telltale bleats of human misery.

"What it be in there?" queried Sideburns. "We done with it yet?"

Sideburns never heard a reply. Nor did he anticipate the concussion that came from his right. His body was penetrated from ear to ankle by a phalanx of double-aught pellets. He went down as if blown over in a sudden gust of wind.

Then there was Beefcake. His left hand had already been applying pressure to the Yukon's car horn when he realized he'd left his own pistol resting on the dashboard. He was fumbling for it when the last image his retinas recorded was his brains and skull matter painting the SUV's interior. Rushing up to the open window was Frosty, that submachine gun in hand, muzzle spitting even more bullets into the door for extra measure.

Displaying more than a just a limp, Lucky had doddered outside on that recently dislocated foot with nothing less than resolute intent. He turned the shotgun sideways, barrel aimed at the first motel window, and discharged three successive shots, covering the room with thirty-six nearly symmetrical punctures. He kept moving left and offered the same treatment to the adjoining room.

BOOM! BOOM! BOOM!

Just as Lucky's gunfire had erupted, Dough Boy had been climbing atop the toilet seat in hope of hoisting himself up to get a peek through that ceiling hole. For a split moment he thought maybe he'd abandon the climb and just dive for cover inside the bathtub. Thus, as the shotgun salvos continued, the big man found himself caught between decisive actions. The rush of peanut-sized buckshot penetrated the wall, cutting holes in his gut, hips, and knees. The weight of his upper body overtook his lower, collapsing him in a heap on the tile floor.

By chance, or luck—anything but grace—Lil Rod caught only one of Lucky's pellets. He'd been in a squat, lifting the bed ruffle with the muzzle of his assault rife, prepared to unleash unholy hell on anybody who might be hiding underneath, when the windows exploded inward. A low projectile creased the top of his head, burrowing a tiny row into the bone of his skullcap. Deadly, it wasn't. But it did feel as if a hammer had dropped on his head. He rolled away, defending against the trailing hail of glass, and crawled past the foot of the bed, seeking shelter in the mirrored closet. The carpet was bathed in shards, slicing his palms. Blood clouded his eyes. He removed his balaclava. And when he straightened slightly, wiping the red from his eyes, he saw it—right through the demolished closet slider.

A fresh hole in the wall.

It was crudely cut. Sized for a human. Lil Rod read the hole as serving two immediate needs. A way out. And where he'd most likely find a trio of possible hostages.

60

It had been five years since that consequential day when Gonzo had been paired with Lucky. Yet despite the couple's obvious ups and downs, Travis had taken to it all as a boyhood adventure. The boy's obvious geekitude, physical awkwardness, and somewhat delayed adolescence allowed him to keep the inherent dangers of living with Lucky at mental arm's length. From that early moment when the boy had been fascinated by the scalloped bullet scar in the back of Lucky's head, to being actual inches from Lucky the moment he was about to be assassinated, to the murder of their dog, to a deadly wreck in his mother's old truck, and now the evisceration of their comfy home—*his home*—and their hasty retreat to Fontana, somehow he'd been able to emotionally file it away in a repository he might have named Fun'n'Games with Lucky Dey.

But that was before the first gunshots.

Travis had been living on adrenaline since the joy of the sunrise wedding. And receiving the assignment to actually ax and hammer-claw an escape hole through the motel room wall had come with a further jolt of teen adrenaline. Lucky had directed Karrie and Travis to hack through to the unoccupied room next door from the inside of the closet, a shallow space guarded by a mirrored sliding door. It was quick work. The twenty-four-inch space between the wall studs had no insulation. The Sheetrock was easily kicked through and peeled away, leaving enough room for the teen to slip through and into the pitch-blackness of the closet next door. He'd slid the identical closet door aside, revealing a dimmed room with a single queen bed. Karrie had followed closely. Gonzo took up the rear, guiding the mirrored slider shut behind her.

"Under the bed," Lucky had ordered. "Do not get out from under the bed until someone in authority gets you! Whatever you do, stay on the floor!"

The space between the bedframe and floor smelled as if it hadn't been vacuumed in decades. That, and there was barely room to squeeze under, let alone breathe. The feeling of claustrophobia was instantaneous and Travis had begun to unconsciously whimper. To calm him, Karrie crawled next to him, her lips at the back of his neck so she could whisper her assistance. Sandwiching Travis in from the other side was his mother, all six feet of her defending him, her pistol poised in the direction from which they had come.

"Slow inhale, one, two, and three," Karrie had whispered. "Exhale, one, two, and three."

Travis nodded, tuned into his sister's soft sounds, and followed her lead. His heart was racing and he'd just begun to feel his nerves ease when the sound of the first shotgun blasts shook the room.

"No, no, no, no, no, no, no," he whined.

"Shhh, shhh, shhh, shhh," Karrie tried to soothe.

"Don't wanna die, Mommy," Travis whimpered.

"I love you, Travis," said Gonzo, "but I really need you to shut the fuck up!"

Karrie wriggled, slipped an arm between Travis's shoulder and neck, and clamped his mouth shut with her hand.

They heard voices. Men. Muffled. Followed by a cacophony of gunshots. Travis screamed, his shout caught by Karrie's cupped palm sealed against his face.

"Shhhh, shhhh, shhh, shhh," she urged.

"Lucky's dead!" Travis yelped in wide-eyed fright, his words leaking through Karrie's fingers.

Then came those six successive shotgun blasts as those mirrored closet doors turned into sheets of falling glass. Pellets had penetrated the cheap doors, the ancient cardboard backing hanging like a weak Band-Aid.

Somehow, the shock wave had quieted Travis to a quiver from scalp to toenails, his poor amygdala causing his nervous system to freeze.

Another silence befell them, leaving only the hiss of a burst water pipe somewhere nearby.

"Motherfucker!" wheezed a voice he didn't recognize. He could feel Karrie's body tense and his mother's breathing quicken. There was a thump and more breaking glass, followed by the closet door sliding open and the crunch of shoes grinding the broken mirror shards into the carpet. It was a man's breath. Fast. Forced.

"GONNA KILL ALL Y'ALL!" screeched Lil Rod.

Gonzo pressed her pistol forward, sideways against the floor, the muzzle poking out from the hanging edge of the bedspread. In the mix of gray and slits of electric light seeping from the hole to the other room, she was able to make out a pair of shoes—black sneakers—edging nearer. She waited for a bead, a site picture over the topline of her 9mm that would allow her to fire a pair of shots. If she could knock out his ankles, his legs would give out. When he fell to the floor, she could finish him.

If he doesn't finish us in a burst.

Considering the number of shots fired in the earlier volleys, Gonzo figured he carried an assault weapon—a semi-automatic rifle with a high-capacity magazine. If the man started pulling the trigger as he fell to the floor, there was no guarantee the bullets wouldn't be through the bed and into her son.

Or Karrie.

She tried to slow her breath, steady her hands.

One step closer, she said to herself. *Just one step . . .*

"Y'all under the bed, are ya?" croaked the voice.

That's it, thought Gonzo. *Now or not at all.*

She was squeezing the trigger when a familiar vocal entered the equation with a simple, sharp, single-syllable notice.

"Hey!" snapped Lucky.

There was the briefest of pauses. Then the room flashed white and echoed with an ear-shattering *BOOOOOM!*

Maybe it was Travis's uncorked screaming that masked the rest of what Gonzo saw. The body landed right in front of her, dropped like a marionette's puppet after its strings were cut. Only it was a soundless, slow-motion kind of movement that came with a wet finale. As the body slapped the carpet, the whipping motion finished with a spray of warm blood, leaving a spatter of red across Gonzo's frozen face.

61

Lucky had to assume Frosty had succeeded in neutralizing the Yukon's driver. He'd only heard the double crackling of the submachine gun behind him and to the left when he was charging through one of the room doors. His halting stagger was like a hurried shuffle. His eyes swept the space, keying instantly on the open closet and that cavity he'd trusted Travis to carve. As he rushed ahead, his left foot gave out. He bounced hard off the carpet, turned his shoulders, found a quick knee, and pushed up again without a single care if his next step would fail again. He hopped ahead, right foot mostly, until he was falling into the closet, the barrel of the shotgun thrust ahead. He leaned into the exposed drywall, twisting the sawed-off through the blackened hole.

His site picture came into frame. It was near dark but for the light filtering in from behind him. He saw a slight figure, back to him, shoulders hunched, the outline of an assault rifle swinging low towards the bed skirt.

"Hey!" Lucky huffed, low and guttural.

The killer's head swiveled, his torso following suit. Next would come the muzzle of his rifle.

Wait, thought Lucky's lizard-brain synapses firing in a peculiar recognition. The face turning to him was bloody. But the eyes . . . *I know these eyes.*

Lucky pulled the trigger, the muzzle flash turning the assassin's pupils white. The killer dropped. If the assassin's eyes and face had been anything close to recognizable just seconds before, all had been obliterated by the torrent of shotgun lead.

"Everybody good?" Lucky asked.

"We're good!" Gonzo shot back, her voice sounding surprisingly close.

"Hold in place. Need to sweep for secondary suspects."

"Lucky!" cried Travis.

"All good, Trav," sounded Lucky. "Stay where you're at. Doin' great."

The miserable angst in the teen's voice rattled Lucky. He'd never heard such fear from the boy—so much overwhelming emotion. While plodding around—part stumbling, part hopping—as Lucky checked the room next door and the surrounding panorama, he imagined the boy's future.

My family's future . . .

Lucky saw an endless queue of psychiatrists and psychotherapists, a particular genus of humanity about whom he held certain prejudices. Some therapists had true value. Most were a waste of education and money. He promised himself he'd find Travis the best shrink they could afford because his stoic teen boy had most likely been grievously cracked by this latest episode.

Lucky found Frosty out front, facing away from the motel, legs locked in a guarding stance, both hands on the submachine gun, still ready to fight. But once Lucky had cleared into Frosty's periphery, he saw the tears. Frosty's eyes were wet with regret.

"Said I wouldn't ever again," cried Frosty. "But what if this is what God made? A killer man who's good for nothin' but death?"

"We're all gonna be fucked over by this one," agreed Lucky, joining Frosty on guard. "But we'll get through it, okay? You're family now. We're family. Hear me?"

Frosty could barely offer a nod.

"Gotta perimeter-sweep the property." Lucky placed a gentle hand on Frosty's shoulder. "Let's finish this up."

Frosty chose to retrace the motel property in a clockwise turn. Lucky circled in the opposite direction, relieved to discover Edgar was safe and uninjured. At the first barrage of gunfire, the proprietor had folded up under his back office desk, dialed 911, and prayed to Allah.

"That was not the kind of party I expected," confessed Edgar.

"Other than the one couple," clarified Lucky, "did anybody else check in?"

Edgar's answer was negative. By Lucky's math, the body count was six. Was that all there were? Was anybody else coming for his head?

The answer, in Lucky's immediate estimation, was yes. One more.

62

For Greg Beem, watching the show unfold was like witnessing a living painting—or an ever-evolving canvas of motion and mystery. To think he'd planned to have already been back fighting fires . . . or at least in the custody of Cal Fire Corrections officers. He had hoped his excuses for getting knocked unconscious, separated from his team, and subsequently lost would land on receptive ears. But that hadn't happened. His inner idiot's unquenchable curiosity had hooked him by the nose, convincing him to follow that GMC Yukon loaded with Bloods plus that one Big Gulp–swilling white dude. The tail had led him all over the map, eventually bringing him some forty minutes due east to where the Los Angeles area's suburbia petered out in a contrasting mix of farm green and high-desert death.

He'd drawn the conclusion that there was a second vehicle, a sister rental sedan, red, making for a total head count of seven in a two-car caravan. The two cars came together in the parking lot of an Applebee's restaurant and stopped side by side, pointed in opposite directions. He'd observed a brief conversation before the Yukon and red car split. After that, Beemer tailed the Yukon five more minutes until it landed near a drowsy, low-slung flophouse called the Sleepy Winks Motel.

And there lies Lucky Dey, Beemer bet.

He had no evidence. Only intuition. Beemer somehow *knew* the motel was ground zero for Lucky Dey and whoever else might be in the deputy's orbit. He'd ditched the Honda Civic down a dirt road and doubled back on foot. He kept to the weeds and surrounding untilled acres, ultimately choosing an inconspicuous sniper-like hide in a particular fertile section of brush with views of both the motel and the SUV.

The idiot was, for the moment, happy to be at arm's length— or at least entertained into silence. Not bad, considering how long Beemer had been without proper food or hydration. On the floor of the stolen Civic he'd discovered a trove of discarded Taco Bell bags and wrappers in the passenger- and rear-seat footwells. In each bag were leftover, mostly unused salsa packets, hot and mild, dumped in by the handful from generous drive-thru cashiers. Hours on end, after the dashboard clock's minute hand had completed an hourly sweep, he'd tear open and suck back two salsa packets. Barely a nibble, yet a treat. Sustaining enough.

He'd trained as a sniper, proving his ability to secrete himself for days on end in an uncomfortable hide. Only his marksmanship skills had never developed to military satisfaction. His ultimate skill proved to be killing in close combat.

The sunset was the most strange. Five days of western wildfires had so clouded the atmosphere that the sun was little more than a thumbhole painted the color of a Bloody Mary. But Beemer hardly noticed, as he was focused on the slowly unfolding drama. He was able to spy the entire family coming and going from their motel rooms. In addition, he'd added that fifth wheel, a lithe young black man whose body language with the strawberry-blonde daughter spelled some kind of romance. Did mom and dad know? Did they approve?

And which one of you would Lucky miss the most?

Darkness fell under a starlit sky. Through the long hours, Beemer noted the almost consistent sojourns of Mr. Big Gulp into the nearby weeds to relieve himself. He'd spied the teenage boy collect some heavy duffel bags from the rear of pickup truck, followed by the black couple in the red sedan checking in and apparently taking a room somewhere on the back side of the motel.

Beemer assured himself, *It's happening soon.*

It was almost as if he could smell the silicone lubricant worked into to the weaponry about to be unleashed.

Some other assholes are going to get their just recompense before me. Who? It didn't really matter. At this point, all he could do was try to take pleasure in the suspense before the show. Front row and center. He was about to see some significant fireworks long before the opening day of Major League Baseball or the Fourth of July. Yet as the minutes continued to tick, there came an overwhelming feeling.

FOMO is what one lifer of an inmate had framed it.

"FOMO. It's that shit that makes all the kiddies worry. The fear of missin' out."

As many times as he'd frontally assaulted urban strongholds in Iraq, twice as often he'd been in a backup unit, eyeballing the perimeter. Beemer would often bet with himself how the mission would go down. Body count. Them versus us. Would there or would there not be a counter-ambush? He'd watch each planned blitzkrieg unfold and be impressed with his own ability to second-guess the outcome. For the motel assault, he'd predicted that the man and woman who'd checked into the rear room would set up at the far corners, flanking any escapees, cutting runners down in crossfire. The men in the SUV would provide the metal and muscle for a frontal bushwhack. He reckoned Lucky and his family hadn't a chance. He was just about to make his own mental wager of five dead bodies in the two motel rooms plus maybe one nonfatal injury to the crash team when he heard the GMC Yukon surge. Even with the headlights off, he could make out the SUV's fat shadow cutting across about eighty yards in front of him, entering the parking lot on a beeline to the those two occupied motel rooms.

"Just like I called it," Beemer breathed to himself.

He'd never been more wrong.

Just after the frontal assault had been initiated in textbook fashion, the two motel room doors taken down at the hinges, shadows had entered into his periphery, right and left. His first assumption was that they were that man and woman who'd moved into the room in the back. Next came a riot of gunshots from inside the motel, capped off by both shadowy figures pinching in from their own oblique angles. The shadow with the submachine gun took out the Yukon's driver. The other figure, showing a decided hitch in his step, shotgunned the team's rear point man.

Hoooooolllly shit, mouthed Beemer.

Next he watched the limping man blast out the motel windows before charging in on his own. The drama of Beemer's panoramic play was capped off by a single blast that, unlike the rest, was more muffled. From somewhere deeper inside the building. Eventually, the killer with the bad limp reappeared, siding with his partner before they began what appeared to be a boundary sweep.

Had to be him, figured Beemer. *Had to be Lucky Dey.*

Soon the night filled with the wail of sirens. First arrivals were the local cops. Fontana PD. Then arrived local firefighters and EMTs. More first responders joined the party. By forty minutes, Beemer estimated no less than a dozen San Bernardino County Sheriff's vehicles, five ambulances, three fire trucks, four Sheriff's coroner vans and trucks, and even an array of unmarked police units from the almighty LAPD and L.A. Sheriff's Department.

Awe.

The word tickled Beemer's tongue. As in, *I'm in awe*. Just the number of spinning emergency lights stuffed into and around the motel's parking lot was astonishing. Helicopters circled, the news choppers hovering and holding at an altitude thousands of feet above the PD's local air support. It was a miracle of a sight.

Every so often, Beemer would glimpse Lucky or Lydia Gonzalez, as well the teenage boy, the blonde daughter, and her black boyfriend.

Around midnight, Beemer's hiding spot was nearly trampled by a crew of news stringers, fighting for positions that offered the sexiest camera angles for local and national news outlets. *Time to bug out*, he reasoned, retreating deeper into the dark without a single witness to so much as make a note of his presence.

It was as if Beemer had never been there.

Sunday

63

Fontana

"Whatever they ask, however many times they ask, however many different police officers ask you the question," instructed Lucky, his words of encouragement bordering on a fatherly demand, "tell the truth as you know it. As your remember it. Every little detail."

At the first note from a distant siren, Lucky had gathered his family of five outside the motel office on the parking lot gravel. Despite their collective and individual shock, he admonished them to listen and both buckle up and buckle down, as they were about to be accosted by a barrage of police agencies.

"All anybody needs to know is that what happened today started yesterday in Chatsworth with my accident," trusted Lucky. "Then Altadena, then here. Everybody with a spare detective team is gonna want a piece of this. And it's gonna be a marathon. They're gonna separate us to see if our stories don't line up, give us time together, then repeat. Just keep it real. Leave nothing out. And we'll be good."

"How can we ever be okay after this?" shook Travis.

"'Cause we're alive," breathed Gonzo. "And we still have each other."

"And why do we always tell the truth?" asked Lucky, seeking a very particular reply.

"Because it's easier to remember," finished Karrie.

"Tell the truth to everybody in authority," reminded Lucky. "But never ever talk to the media. Period. End of subject."

As predicted, the multi-agency descent onto the Sleepy Winks Motel grew like a fast-metastasizing fungus. Fontana PD had been first, roping off the entire motel property as a crime scene. San Bernardino Sheriff's followed with more than triple the manpower, setting up an evidence-processing camp across the nearest boulevard at a competing flophouse. They requisitioned the available motel rooms to use as interview suites, divvying up keys amongst the coroner and visiting Los Angeles Sheriff's detectives and LAPD investigators.

And the night wore on.

Separately and together, Lucky et al. were questioned ad infinitum. Local deputies were dispatched to retrieve caffeinated beverages and easy-to-digest snacks in an effort to play host and keep the family comfortable and awake. Because of his age, Travis was interviewed with the aid of a social worker who had introduced herself as a certified psychologist. Just as it had all been foretold by Lucky, the hours leading up to dawn unpacked nearly precisely as he'd described. It was grueling, yet also a great consolation to be surrounded by so many kind men and women carrying guns.

The sky turned gray and the sun threatened to bust open the horizon with a great and cleansing light. And though there'd be more interviews to come, the collective authorities thought the Dey family deserved forty-eight hours or so of rest. The San Bernardino Sheriff's divided the duty of driving the family to a

Pasadena hotel in a pair of their gold-emblemed white patrol units. Gonzo and Travis in the first car. Lucky, Karrie, and Frosty to follow soon after.

"Hey, Travis," Gonzo said. "Why don't you ride up front? Not a lot of opportunities to see what it's like from the front seat of a patrol car."

Travis shook his head, his eyes practically concealed by his sweatshirt's hood. The boy wanted nothing more than to melt into his mother. If that meant riding in the less-than-comfy rear seat of the radio car, so be it. As he crawled into the car, Gonzo lingered with Lucky.

"We still haven't talked, you know," said Gonzo with a sobering hush. "All this. What it means for the future."

"Hopefully," replied Lucky, "that ring on your finger means we'll have plenty of time to work out whatever needs to be worked out."

Gonzo kissed him, short but hopeful, pulling on his index finger before letting go and following Travis into the rear of the sheriff's unit. Lucky pushed the door shut, rapped on the roof, and they were off.

After five westbound minutes on Foothill Boulevard—a.k.a. Historic Route 66—the sun peeked over the horizon in a retina-searing blast. As the cabin began to heat up, Gonzo felt her armpits moisten, and the twisting hairs at her temples wet in a sudden sweat.

Post-traumatic sweat disorder, she laughed to herself.

The silly saying was something she'd pulled from somewhere in her deep recesses. Rookie year. Her training officer claimed to have coined the phrase to explain the certain comedown that followed stressful events. Cops were known to break out in unsummoned fits of perspiration after they'd removed themselves from a fire.

"Mind rolling down the windows back here?" asked Gonzo before turning to Travis. "Little air might be good for us, yeah?"

The deputy behind the steering wheel waved a hand, then toggled the rear windows to half-mast.

"Far as they go," said the deputy.

"It's fine, thanks." Her arm around her only son, Gonzo pulled him close and whispered. "I love you, buddy. We're gonna be okay."

Travis, his ear to her chest, could only shake his head no.

"Yeah, yeah," breathed Gonzo. "Feels that way right now. And that's okay. But, in time, the heebie-jeebies go away. Promise."

Gonzo rested her chin on the hoodie covering her son's head. She felt another waggle. Back and forth, back and forth. If she'd felt it once, she'd felt it a million times, ever since Travis was a troubled toddler. She'd try to reassure him and his only reply would be to swivel his little head in small, negative twitches.

"You say I'm wrong, but I know I'm right," she automatically singsonged.

The teen slid his head down closer to her lap, pulling his knees up in something almost fetal. This is when he revealed his smartphone screen. Framed was a video still from the security camera footage he had downloaded moments before their Altadena bungalow had been demolished. The image was of the homeless intruder, zoomed in on his anarchy tattoo in grainy relief.

Travis put an index finger next to the tattoo on the screen, then transferred his fingertip to touch the back of the seat in front of her. Message sent.

Gonzo received the message like she had just stuck her toe into an electrified light socket.

Lucky had expressed concern about Beemer being a present threat. Only the threat had been conflated and then sunk with the motel attack. She exhaled, then flicked a quick glance ahead. The deputy in the rearview mirror, complete with aviator sunglasses affixed, was unfortunately grinning back at her, some of the scratches on his face disguised by two-day stubble.

"Yeahhhh," was all the fake deputy said with a vocal fry.

Gonzo's face slackened. She broke her gaze, turning her chin to the right as if that moment might be her last to fill her eyes with something of beauty. Her arms stiffened as if to pin her son to her lap.

"You had to come back."

"No *had to* about it," returned Beemer. "Mother Nature had her say. Was she who brought me back. Seriously. Was just fine where I was."

She didn't attempt to interpret his meaning or intent. She'd only just finished her situational assessment. Seat-belted in the back of a police vehicle. Doors locked. She and her son in a veritable human cage with a certified mass murderer gripping the steering wheel.

"Now what?" she asked, sounding resigned, but hardly so.

"Like the wind knows why it blows a fire one way or the other?" Beemer took a moment for her to lock eyes with him again. "I've generally been pretty good with taking what comes."

"Like I came to you?"

"Like ten minutes ago," he continued. "I took out the cop. Took his uniform. His car. But did I know it was you who was gonna get in? No. But, hey. I'm okay with that."

"You'd rather it have been Lucky?"

"You? Him? I dunno which of you started it. But he's the one who put a bullet in my back. Whether I hurt him in reply, or somebody he cares about? That's the wind saying. Not me."

As hard as Gonzo pushed to keep her nerves in check, Travis was vibrating, his entire being a series of unstoppable shivers. She stroked his back in slow, loving flourishes, her left eventually reaching for and grabbing hold of the seat belt's latch. She eased the belt across her son, quietly coaxing him to buckle up.

"My house," said Gonzo, allowing a little grind in her voice. "That was the wind?"

"Called a metaphor."

"Yeah?"

"Look ahead," said Beemer. "See the horizon? All that smoke and destruction?"

"The fires," she agreed, playing along.

"Fire," corrected Beemer. "Fire behaves according to the environment in which it is burning. It's a lot like us. Alive. Oxygen-dependent. But hardly responsible for what crosses its path. It just is. It eats, it breathes."

"So, you're like fire?" she nearly joked.

"We are. All of us. Every last human being. We are all fire. The only difference is how hot we burn."

"Maybe a nurse should take your temperature."

"You're funny."

"I'm here all week."

"You're the one who flies helicopters, yeah?"

"Maybe. What else you know about us?"

"I know you're getting married."

"Past tense," corrected Gonzo, holding up her wedding band for Beemer to catch in the rearview mirror. When she saw his eyes swerve, she reduced her number of viewable fingers to one. Her middle digit. Fully extended.

"Message received," said Beemer. "You're a real pistol, huh?"

"Here's something you don't know," she continued.

"What's that?"

"Way back when? That hot shit you took in the back?"

"Yeah?"

"Wasn't Lucky on the trigger," she said, enjoying what she could of the moment. "That was me."

Beemer's pupils snapped back to the rearview mirror.

"Believe it," punctuated Gonzo.

"Mom!" complained Travis.

"All good, Trav," she replied. "Remember Lucky sayin' we should tell the truth. 'Member why?"

"'Cause it's easier to remember?" trembled Travis.

"Mom's right, ya know?" added Beemer.

"Where you takin' us?" barked Travis.

"To where the wind blows," replied Beemer, his voice almost serene. He heard a seat belt tensioner unwinding. In the mirror, he saw Gonzo snapping her restraint into the buckle assembly.

"Buckling up," she said before showing him her smirk. "For safety."

"You expecting a rough ride?" queried Beemer.

"I am," she said, her face morphing to concrete. "Are you?"

There was a threat to her voice. A knowing. She snuck her hand across to Travis and gripped his vibrating hand.

Beemer flashed at her face again. His focal plane forgetting to adjust to what little he could see through the glare of the rear windshield, he picked up a brief metallic flash. Dangerously close.

Before he could so much as think to react, the impact came.

64

The San Bernardino sheriff himself had a few final questions for Lucky Dey. Cop to cop. He'd been at home in a peaceful slumber when his phone had rung at 3:15 a.m. It had been his colleague and skeet-shooting pal, L.A. Sheriff Paul McGill, who had already been informed of "another Lucky Dey shit show" in Fontana. He'd dressed and driven in his personal car to supervise the crime scene.

The sheriff had been ready to return to his hearth and home when he spied Lucky lingering with deputies outside the requisitioned motel. He'd braked, geared his black Cadillac STS into park, stepped out of the car, and summoned Lucky with the kind of "Come here now" gesture only true commanders of men had mastered.

"How ya doin'?" asked the sheriff, not sounding the least bit concerned about Lucky's well-being.

"Good enough," lied Lucky, before realizing the glibness in his tone. He exhaled and decided it might be prudent to kiss the sheriff's figurative ring. "Listen, sir. Very grateful for your department's response and understanding—"

"Not about understanding," interrupted the sheriff. "'Bout professionalism. Why I'm here. Also why your former boss woke me at about a quarter past my usual dream time. Wanna know what your sheriff told me?"

"As quizzes go?" defended Lucky. "I kinda prefer multiple choice."

"Said you're an asshole and first-class shit magnet."

"Has a familiar ring—"

"So, don't thank me for handling your traveling shit show," spat the sheriff. "And speaking for all other elected sheriffs, keep your fucking crap load to your own area code, will ya?"

Lucky had no reply. In fact, he hadn't even heard the insulting rhetorical request. This was because he'd stolen a peek at his phone in response to a text alert. Gonzo had written in the family's group thread. It was brief. And clearly urgent.

> kidnapped
> greg beem
> stolen radio car

Without a goodbye or even glancing up from his phone, Lucky turned a quick shoulder and slipped past the self-righteous sheriff. And that fast, he'd dropped into the man's new Caddy and put it in drive, the sudden acceleration forcing the driver's door to shut. The spinning rubber left the sheriff with a face full of gravel.

> westbound foothill blv

Lucky knew exactly what he was doing. By carjacking the sheriff's car, he'd just rallied the entirety of the San Bernardino Sheriff's Department to the chase. He could only hope Karrie would share Gonzo's text with the other deputies.

The Cadillac handled as advertised in those ubiquitous television ads aired during the entirety of football season. He was already topping one hundred miles per hour, looking out for stop signs, cross traffic, red lights, and that one stolen white radio car. When it came into his view on a mostly rural straightaway, Lucky backed off the gas a quarter mile to its rear and began the kind of closing creep one might expect from an impatient Sunday-morning driver.

You're late to church, Lucky pretended. *Unworried about a stupid traffic citation.*

Lucky was picturing a pit maneuver, the grille-to-bumper trick oft utilized by cops to temporarily disable a fleeing vehicle during a car chase. The maximum safe speed for a pit maneuver was thirty-five miles an hour, though Lucky had once performed a successful pit at fifty-two. And though it had been a rousing success, he'd received a formal reprimand.

The stolen radio car was traveling at a steady sixty-five.

Steering with one hand, Lucky texted Gonzo with an inaccurate, thick right thumb.

> seatbels
> gonna pit
> mak sur u hit flor

Green fields of winter beets spread to the left and right. At worst, Lucky guessed, the radio car would spin clockwise to the right before flipping in the dirt. Only days before, he and his bad back had survived a quadruple gainer with the aid of a safety belt and airbag. He was betting on Gonzo and Travis to get the message before he sent his final missive.

> countdwn from 10

Nine . . . eight . . . seven . . . six . . .

As the seconds ticked off and Lucky timed the accelerator, he prayed.

Please, please, please, Jesus.

Impact would come with the Caddy moving seventy miles per hour, the initial nudge creating a net sum akin to a five-miles-per-hour collision. It was the aftereffect that employed much greater forces with a potentially far more dangerous outcome.

The move required Lucky to ride nearly grille to tail on the radio car. Then, with a punch to the gas, he turned the wheel and kissed the radio car's left rear bumper. The trick was to kick the target's rear wheels into a sideways slide. The spinning tires, losing traction against the asphalt, would throw the car into a clockwise rotation. When traveling at such an increased speed, it was like a whirling top at the end of its gravity-defying revolutions. It would wobble dangerously into a violent kick.

Gonzo and Travis were prepared for the nudge. Beemer wasn't. Less than a heartbeat after he'd seen that metallic flash in his rear windshield, it was as if the car had hit a sheet of ice. The spin was radical. Dizzying. At just past 180 degrees, the rear axle assembly bucked across the road's shoulder, snapping the strands of barbed-wire defense like worn guitar strings. Then it was greens and dirt and dust tossed in an upside-down cyclone as the radio car spun and spun until the friction against the ground snapped it onto two wheels. Instead of flipping, though, the centrifugal forces waned, returning the airborne tires to earth with a spine-compressing crunch.

In the seconds before he noticed that glint in his rearview mirror, Beemer had been experiencing a strange and compelling balance between his calmer self and his psychotic inner idiot. The two ids had somehow found a profound collaboration—the idiot enjoying the gratification that would come with his sweet revenge, and his wiser devil appreciating the slowing of his heart rate and the sense of control over his passengers and the vehicle itself, as well as the colorful serenity of that beautiful Sunday morning.

Then had come the nudge. And from the first spin until the radio car had finally come to rest, all previous equanimity had vanished. The idiot had taken the helm. As the dust settled, clearing the windshield frame, Beemer could see all the twirling emergency lights. Cop cars were lining up on the blacktop, sixty yards beyond the wrecked radio car's grille. Doors were popped open like defensive wings, armed deputies taking cover with weapons switched off safety. A helicopter arced from behind the phalanx, setting up a circling perimeter, the thumping of the rotor blades upsetting the momentary calm.

Beemer unbuckled, sliding down in his seat while fumbling for a switch marked loudspeaker. He pulled the car's microphone to his face, keying the button and causing the external speaker to squelch with feedback.

"I HAVE HOSTAGES!" boomed his voice across the beet fields. "KEEP CLEAR OF MY CAR! REPEAT. KEEP THE FUCK AWAY!"

Beemer struggled with the safety release on the retention holster clipped to the duty belt, finally retrieving the Smith & Wesson pistol he'd stolen from the deputy he'd stabbed with the heavy-gauge screwdriver. He'd left the poor man bleeding to death in a ditch. He rapped the screen separator with the muzzle and copped a quick glance over his shoulder as if he wanted to make certain that he indeed still had hostages. The most he could glimpse was their backs as both Gonzo and Travis had unhooked their belts and dived into the footwell.

"Sit the hell up!" Beemer barked at them. "They need to see I'm not lyin'—"

Tap, tap, tap.

At the sound near his ear, Beemer suddenly twisted. The tapping was gentle and against the driver's window. As Beemer recoiled, his close-contact battle experiences told him to lead with the muzzle of his gun. Whatever or whoever was there would see his pistol speak before they even saw his eyes.

The safety glass exploded inward, shattered by the first shot.

Three more gunshots followed in quick succession—loud, bucking eruptions that filled the cabin with noise and spent gunpowder. Beemer's muzzle had never made it past the steering column as four .45-jacketed hollow-points punched holes through his ear, skull, cheek, then neck.

Greg Beem was dead before his body slumped across the console.

Confined to the empty window frame was Lucky, that nickel-plated Model 1911 poking through the open space. With his left arm, he reached through and removed the pistol from Beemer's twitching fingers, then placed both pistols on the radio car's roof. He stuck his open palms high into the air in an act of surrender.

"It's over," exhaled Lucky. "Stay in the car. Let the deputies do the rest."

65

Porter Ranch

The Homeowners Association for Tuscany Estates had strict rules regarding noise levels, the most sacrosanct being a moratorium on Sunday construction projects. When it came to his sound bunker, Bobby Bianchi had more than once run afoul of the committee. Then there had been the time setbacks due to the fires. Add to that the catastrophic toll to his ego from the fallout of events following his robbery, and Bobby felt entitled to have something go his way.

So he phoned his cement guy.

The contractor was a full-time employee at one of the Valley's largest concrete mix and delivery operations. The contractor's secret side gig was on Sundays, when the business was shuttered, he'd borrow a truck or two from his boss, mix up some of that precious gray mud, and make deliveries at an almost 50 percent discount off the market price.

At 7:01 a.m. that quiet Sunday morning, two concrete mixing trucks and a pump truck made the right turn onto the cul-de-sac, Via Medici, setting up in front of the Bianchi home. The peace of the early hour was disturbed as those three diesel engines set 1,000 RPMs over their normal idle and powered the massive, tumbling concrete agitators as well as the pump truck, its erector set–like pump arm craning across the property's eight-foot trimmed hedges.

Into the backyard streamed the largely undocumented crew, eight strong, armed with shovels and troweling tools, ever ready to carve the acoustic curves along the guidelines set by all that bent rebar.

Bobby appeared, setting up a lawn chair atop the yard's highest point. In celebration, he lit an aged Cuban cigar and sipped from a $100 bottle of Reserva de la Familia tequila. He settled in for the consecration, perched like a petty king as if he deserved all future pleasures that were to come his way.

The rat-a-tat sounds of the Spanish-speaking workers mashed with the revving pump engine, adding annoyance to the neighborhood. Bobby imagined his house phone ringing and ringing with complaints, the most shrill from Dean Garfinkle, the association's street representative who lived three doors down.

Fuck him, Bobby said to himself with a gleeful glimmer. *Asshole's why I disconnected the phones.*

Manuel, the concrete crew chief, was a middle-aged and mustached man with a prodigious beer gut. He reached upward, gripped the handles at the end of the pump arm, and used his weight to manipulate the nozzle.

"Aquí vamos, aquí vamos!" warned Manuel.

The crew climbed down into the cavity, shovels poised. The wet concrete shot from the nozzle like a dusky milkshake, splattering across the rebar cage. Like expert pottery makers, the men poked at the coagulating goo, making certain there were no pockets of air while smoothing the cement with the backsides of their blades.

King Bobby was comparing the contrasting grays of his cigar smoke with the deeper hue of the wet concrete when he heard the first shout. It was high-pitched and as blood-curdling as a horror vixen's. It drove him to his feet. He waved away the exhaust from his cigar to see the crew separate, instinctively widening in a circle. There were more screams, plus excited Spanish riffs far beyond Bobby's ability to comprehend.

Manuel called to stop the pump and pushed the swing arm to the side. He crouched at the edge of the hole, trying to focus on just what in *el infierno* his crack team of masons were freaking out over.

In the chasm's deepest point was a dropped shovel, spattered in fresh concrete. Hooked over the neck of the shovel was what looked like a broken tree root. Thinking it was just that, one of the masons had reached down to remove it from the muck. At first touch, though, a shock had run through the man's arm straight to his heart. What he had thought to be a missed piece of debris was both soft and hairy with an all too familiar feel.

A severed human calf with a large foot still attached.

Thus endeth the Sunday workday, grinned Oren.

He'd been so pleased with himself ever since Bobby had him precariously trapped in that ready-to-be-cemented hole. While Bobby thought he was negotiating with Oren for the intact return of his collection, Oren had finally figured out how to dispose of Peter's frozen parts. The plot had come to him like a lightning bolt from heaven.

In the dead of that night, four hours after Bobby had released his temporary prisoner with his new marching orders, Oren had hauled those frozen pieces of Peter Bianchi and shallowly buried them under the latticed rebar in Bobby's hole. After he showered off all the mud, he stretched out under a street-facing window in one of the empty bedrooms upstairs. He'd grabbed a dingy folding gym mat—a come-across he'd long used for a bed in the back of the Baby-Raper—set it under the sill, cracked the window, and waited for dawn. His simple scheme could go one of two ways. The first and most obvious being the construction crew's discovery of Peter's detached parts as they poured the concrete. If they failed to find the body and successfully cemented over the foul evidence, the backup plan was to make an anonymous phone tip to the LAPD. Oren, the helpful neighbor, would claim to have witnessed Bobby burying human body parts in his backyard. Sunday's construction would elevate any suspicions.

Oren hadn't felt such sure-thing tingles in eons. It was like placing a $10,000 bet on a pony guaranteed to finish no worse than second place.

He'd been flat on his back underneath the window when those sounds of terror broke through the throaty drone of diesel engines. He could feel the gooseflesh popping across every inch of his skin. It was a thrill unlike any other, coupled with the weight of Peter's murder being magically transferred from his shoulders to Bobby's.

He wondered if, after his asshole neighbor's subsequent arrest, his old man would consider putting up a bond for his son's release.

Monday

66

The success of Joey Bianchi's Crohn's disease diet depended on the old man handpicking every bite of food that entered his delicate digestive system. Three days a week, after those hour-long sessions of pool therapy, he'd make three market stops. First was the butcher shop at Jim's Fallbrook Market, where he'd purchase either fresh fish or grass-fed beef. The last stop, at least during the eight-month growing season, was Tapia Brothers farm stand. The middle stop was nearly always Whole Foods in Tarzana. He appreciated the cool underground parking and the liberal number of handicapped spots so conveniently close to the escalator.

At Whole Foods Joey would visit the grinding station, where customers could squeeze out their own nut butter. Joey's happy concoction was one part almonds, another part peanuts, a third part unsalted macadamias. The tasty goo would ooze into a pint-sized paper container that conveniently fit into his Range Rover's cupholder. On the drive back to his Encino home, he'd often leave the lid ajar so he could dip his right index finger in and suck off the tasty sludge.

And I'm cravin' that goo today.

Joey needed a salve. Despite the risk of inflaming his Crohn's, he'd hit the bottle the night before. Bourbon. Maker's Mark. He'd polished off nearly an entire fifth in an attempt to numb his thoughts and nerves after a horrid, no-good, very bad day. Not only had his eldest son been discovered dead and dismembered, but his parts had been found at the bottom of the backyard hole his other son had been attempting to cover in concrete. Joey's youngest boy had been arrested for murder. The subsequent indictment and bail hearing was scheduled for first thing Wednesday morning.

My goddamn sons are gone.

In that awful moment, all he could look forward to was his nut butter ritual. Salt. Oil. Flavor. It wasn't a cure for the night before, but it might begin to calm his rioting bowels.

Joey stepped onto the down escalator. Despite the cool temperature, Joey was still leaking after the hour of hydrotherapy, perspiration wicking through his blue-striped sweatpants and zip-up. As the escalator dropped from daylight into the greenish glow of the underground fluorescents, Joey made out two men positioned at the bottom. Neither looked familiar. One was as tall and bulky as the other was short, graying, and spindly.

Cops, guessed Joey. If they'd been killers, both would have already cleared their weapons, their fingers pumping out bullets with every squeeze.

"Mr. Bianchi?" said the fat man on the right. "Need a minute of your time, if you wouldn't mind."

"And if I did mind?" croaked Joey.

"Painless," said the smaller man, outstretching a hand. "My

name's Lopes. His is Bledsoe. And to make it easier, we're parked right next to your Range Rover."

"This might be the part where I request my attorney," defended Joey.

"Yeah, we getcha," said Lopes. "Your lawyer's gonna thank you later for not including him on this one."

Lopes gestured toward the handicapped parking area as Bledsoe opened the passenger door of a deep blue Chrysler 300. The invitation already reeked of a mobster cliché—when the target is in the front passenger seat with his back to the killer who's holding a garrote or a small-caliber pistol at his head.

"Nobody gonna hurt you," promised Bledsoe. "Scout's honor."

"You were a Boy Scout?" asked Lopes, slipping into the rear. "You're a freakin' fountain of secrets."

As Joey eased his old-man bones into the car, he felt a presence behind him. A third man was already in the rear leather seat behind the driver. Bledsoe opened his door and dropped in, the car practically bouncing on its shocks. The cabin pressure sealed as the last door closed.

"My condolences," began Lucky from the back seat.

"Who's sending?" snapped Joey.

"My name's Lucky Dey. You might've heard of me."

Joey's hand arrogantly reached for the rearview mirror, adjusting it so he might look Lucky in the eye.

"You had a bad day yesterday," continued Lucky. "Mine wasn't much better. But I promise you this isn't about getting even. It's about getting right."

The interior of the car was dim. Joey could barely make out more than the features on Lucky's right side, the one visible eye appearing puffy and tired.

"First things first," continued Lucky. "I had absolutely nothing to do with Bobby's robbery. Now, whether you believe me or not is irrelevant. You still came at me Saturday night. Far as I know, somebody's still got orders to hurt me, my family. Now, in a minute here, I'm gonna ask you to give me something *I* need in exchange for something *you* need. Fair trade or not, it's gonna happen. You still with me?"

"I'm still in the car," replied Joey.

"If, after this conversation, you still wanna take me out?" growled Lucky. "Suppose I can't stop that. But here's your problem. I got this tattoo on my calf. Sheriff's thing. Grim reaper with a gun. Mine is numbered. My two guys here? Same ink. Same club. Different numbers. Here's what it is. On the day you take me out? You can't count the hours before one of us takes you out. How many Reapers are we?"

"Last count?" replied Bledsoe. "Eighty-one inked."

"Sure as shit enough of us for you or your mob connects to never ever get to," added Lopes.

"But see? Nobody but nobody will have to get to you," argued Lucky. "That's because your need for payback was misguided. All I did that night was my job. And that was to keep your mouthy kid from reentering his property during a mandatory evacuation."

"You don't know that I ordered anything," defended Joey.

"No. I don't," relayed Lucky. "But what Bobby sent at me was junior varsity. What came after—what went down in Fontana— that was all pro."

"Yet here you are," grit Joey.

"Here we both are," agreed Lucky. "Now, here comes what you are going to give me."

February

67

Downtown. 5:17 p.m.

"They got you burning lotsa diesel today," said the old-timer in overalls.

"Last load," returned Lucky. "After this, I'm gettin' a cold one."

"What's yer poison?" The old-timer, his head a nappy rug of silver, rubbed his ear in curiosity as if the idea of cold beer would cure the scratchiness in his throat.

"Whatever's in the fridge when I get home," answered Lucky. "My hope is there'll be a Dos Equis with my name on it."

The old-timer cast his eyes upward above the loading dock to the downtown towers stretching up into another amber sky.

"That Mexican dark stuff's same color as the sky lately."

Lucky followed the old-timer's eyes. Once again, the city was choked in smoke. The Santa Anas had kicked back into gear. It had barely been two weeks since the January fires had reached containment. And now a new set of wildfires were burning from Ventura to Orange County, spreading firefighters and first responders paper-thin across three counties. Depending on the winds, the sky could be snowing with flakes of ash.

But this time, Lucky hadn't been called up. He'd resigned as a reserve deputy. Because of the injuries sustained—physical and emotional—Lucky had also been granted a temporary reprieve from his job in the city's personnel department.

None of that meant that Lucky wasn't busy being Lucky.

The three-story brick shithouse of a building in front of Lucky—only blocks from the personnel department—had been of interest to him ever since Angie, his snoopy colleague, had pointed it out. As both the city and county were at last moving to a digital record-keeping system, every physical piece of investigative paper was marked for the shredder. Thinking about the destruction of all those files, perhaps along with the secrets they held should data bytes on some invisible cloud ever get hacked, lost, or deleted . . . Lucky just couldn't abide the idea.

So, on that Friday morning in late February, he had borrowed an unmarked moving truck, temporarily changed the license plates, then backed up to the records building's loading dock and informed the lanky, overall-wearing caretaker that he was there to remove all the digitally copied records that were marked for destruction.

"About time somebody picked this mess up," the old-timer had said.

To pull off his paper heist, Lucky had a dummied driver's license, a Transportation Division ID badge, and point A to B orders to deliver the records to a secure depot in nearby Pico Rivera. Then, to relieve concern about facial and body recognition systems capturing his crime, he'd grown a three-week beard, applied temporary military tattoos to his bare forearms, and donned a dirty Dodgers baseball cap and amber-tinted glasses.

As it worked out, the old caretaker hadn't required Lucky to show him a thing. Rather, he showed the former deputy the easiest route from the loading dock to the records repository and how to operate the natural gas–powered forklift. From 9:00 a.m. until the drowning sun, Lucky was able to move five truckloads of paper secrets. Pallet after pallet.

Where Lucky was going to store them, he would never to tell a soul. Not even his new wife.

"Shame about all the fires we been havin'," said the caretaker. "Least it keeps the city employees in lotsa overtime."

"What about you?" asked Lucky. "After all the paper is gone?"

"Hell, I dunno. Another building. Some other such city bullshit will need lookin' after. Jus' please don't ask me to retire. My missus would go banana bat loony bins if I was spendin' my workdays home with her."

"I'm with ya," chimed Lucky.

"Have a Mexican beer for me. I gives you the old man's permission."

The pair shook hands. Lucky lowered the truck's roll-up door, locked it in place, swung off the dock, and added a grateful wave.

It was Friday rush hour. Along with Lucky, the last load of stolen records wouldn't make its destination for better than an hour and a half. That was fine with Lucky. As he waited in the queue of cars creeping a few yards at a time along Spring Street, his hands were free to check off another task. He pulled up a local number he'd stored on his phone. He'd squeezed the ten digits out of Angie after he had confronted her about that bit of office skullduggery that had nearly gotten him and his family murdered.

"You're mine now," he'd informed Angie. "Your side hustle is now what I tell you to do and nobody else. Are we clear?"

Angie had swallowed hard before answering in the affirmative.

Lucky regarded the phone number, thinking about what he was going to say as he recalled how the détente had come about: Joey Bianchi in the passenger seat of Bledsoe's Chrysler 300, Lucky in the left rear. The deal struck had begun with Joey informing Lucky just how his family had been so efficiently tracked to the Sleepy Winks Motel. That information had eventually led Lucky to both Angie and the politician whose number he was preparing to dial.

In exchange, Joey received information that had landed in Lucky's inbox. During that torrid week the month before, after hearing about Bobby Bianchi's accusation toward him, Lucky had put out feelers for anybody trying to hock any of the Beatles memorabilia listed on the manifest of stolen goods. He received a lead from a friend in the Sheriff's robbery division and emailed Joey security photos plus the name and identification of a small but powerfully built bald man pawning a rare Beatles album to Glen Annie's Pawn and Coin in Glendora.

The seller's name was Oren Elek Mankowski. And he lived directly across the cul-de-sac from Bobby Bianchi.

Before Lucky could punch up the number on his phone, a message popped up on his screen. It was from Karrie.

u heard anything about F?

F was code for Frosty. And though the communication was only in text, Lucky was able to imagine the hurt coming from her, as if the single query had been tapped out by the awful lump in her throat. Worse even, Lucky's answer was going to be flat no. The most likely reason was because of another F.

Fontana.

Since that ugly Saturday, Frosty had apparently fallen off the face of Mother Earth. Neither his mother nor his Gra'nana had seen hide nor hair of him. On the drive back to Los Angeles, Frosty had shown wit and grace, even publicly cuddling with Karrie in the back seat of a San Bernardino Sheriff's van. He'd accepted their love and appeared to be returning the affection in kind. But neither Gonzo nor Karrie nor Travis had witnessed Frosty's broken side the way Lucky had in those shallow minutes following the shoot-out.

The young man who'd promised God and the world that he'd

never take another life had been broken in two. There'd been a fissure in him and Lucky had seen it up close. They'd all prayed that Frosty would resurface, perhaps wounded, but at least safe. They'd all been through a wringer, each mending at different rates in their own time.

Lucky decided he wouldn't reply to Karrie until after he rechecked his sources down Compton way. In the meantime, he had a phone call to make. Lucky pulled up the number and dialed.

"This is Ram," answered the voice on the third ring.

"Mr. Mayor," said Lucky, neither questioning nor charming nor even pretending to be respectful.

"Yes?" the mayor asked after a beat.

"This is Lucky Dey. And now that you know that I have your private cell number? I strongly suggest you do not hang up."

"What do you want?" he asked following the most pregnant of pauses.

"A few words."

"I'm listening."

"I want you to worry," said Lucky. "I want you to hope to hell nothing bad happens to me. Otherwise . . ."

"Otherwise what?"

"That's for me to know and you to lose sleep over."

"Dear Lucky," replied the mayor as if dictating a memo. "I haven't a clue what you're implying. But here's a quick reminder. You are a precious one in over four million. That's the number of citizens I represent as mayor of this vast and diverse city. I'd like to think I treat every single one of my constituents with equal love and respect. The same goes for my unrivaled interest in their personal safety. And that, believe it or not, includes yourself."

Perhaps the mayor was worried that Lucky was secretly recording the call, for despite his carefully chosen words, his tone wasn't nearly ambiguous. There was a distinct threat to Ram's voice, all while he pretended to sound unconcerned.

"Really appreciate the thought," feigned Lucky. "That said, I would seriously keep my safety in mind when you contemplate the actions I've taken today."

"Actions?"

"Just like you. I'm all about those who matter to me and keeping them safe from harm."

"I have no idea what you are talking about. But how about this? I sometimes like to sit down with a constituent and talk things over. Privately. Face to face. Hear out their grievances. So let me offer this. Lucky? Do you drink beer?"

Lucky let the mayor's question linger, then gamely chose to end the call.

Join Doug's mailing list
for sneak previews, exclusive content, and
news on the release of the next Lucky Dey Thriller.

Visit www.eepurl.com/b93Bfr

About the Author

Doug cut his teeth writing movies like *Die Hard 2, Bad Boys,* and *Hostage* until sharp enough to pen the Lucky Dey crime thriller series. He lives in Southern California with his wife.

You can learn more about Doug at www.dougrichardson.com and drop him a line at bydougrich@dougrichardson.com. You can also follow him at www.facebook.com/bydougrichardson, on Twitter @byDougRich, and on Instagram @bydougrich.